Bead Bai

Sultan Somjee

CreateSpace

7290 B. Investment Drive

Charleston, SC 29418

USA

This is a work of fiction. All resemblances to people and
events are either coincidental or used fictitiously as products
of imagination.

To the memories of those Bead Bais of East Africa who lived their old age in Canada and somewhere else in the West when they were compelled to migrate once again some forty years ago.

To
Shelina,
Asian African stories,
some we tell, some we hide

Authar Bomjee
February, 2015

Stories are how we explain, how we teach, how we entertain ourselves, and how we often do all three at once. They are the juncture where facts and feelings meet. And for those reasons, they are central to civilization — in fact, civilization takes form in our minds as a series of narratives.

Robert Fulford, Canadian journalist and author in 'The Triumph of Narrative: Storytelling in the Age of Mass Culture', 2001.

Introduction

The Satpanth faith, meaning the True Faith, which originated in Saurashtra in India (Saurashtra here denotes parts of present-day Gujarat, Kutch, Sindh, and adjacent border areas of Rajasthan) belongs to a cluster of many other such minority religions of India. Exact data on how many there are across India are not easily accessible, but we know there are communities practising a spectrum of worship styles that cannot be specified as absolutely mainstream Islamic or Hindu. There are also those who may be living secreted lives due to persecution or the pervading social stigma in a society framed by religious and caste distinctions. Evidence of such diversity of worship emerges at the numerous shrines of pirs across India where one would find celebrations of cross religious venerations.

For centuries following the 13th, in the wake of the Mughal invasion and influence, there grew amorphous pockets of worshippers in India that honoured certain Islamic beliefs within the greater Vedanta liturgy. Communities called panths (or paths) developed that weighed teachings of Hindu gurus and Moslem pirs or guru-pirs (gurpirs), as the Satpanth Ismailis call them today, honouring the two wisdoms. Ethnographer JJ Roy Burman *(Gujarat Unknown: Hindu-Muslim Syncretism and Humanistic Forays, 2005)*, documents five known such Islamic pir

i

influenced groups including the Satpanth Ismailis in Gujarat. Certain Islamic beliefs that imams, sheiks and ayatollahs, representing the Prophet's progeny, embody a human-divine if not a profoundly religious-secular duality resonate with India's own ancient Vedic beliefs in generational incarnations of the celestial being as human. While researching a certain pir's community in India, anthropologist Dominique-Sila Khan writes that, she realized she was 'investigating the fascinating issue of plural religious identities.' *(Preface, Crossing the Threshold: Understanding Religious Identities in South Asia, 2004).*

Satpanth Ismailis (also called Satpanth Khoja), however, are one among the larger ethnically and regionally scattered communities of Ismailis whose homelands stretch from the Middle East to China. In the East, Ismailis of varied racial backgrounds live as minorities among majority Sunni or Shia Moslems, Hindus, Christians, and secular communists. Sometimes, they live in simulation showing copied outer identities to avoid portraying difference. Though their worship traditions differ, all Ismailis profess being one people in their allegiance to their 49th Imam whom they acknowledge as the descendant of Prophet Mohamed, known to the non-Ismaili world as the Aga Khan. In general, the Satpanth Ismailis refer to the Aga Khan as Saheb, which is changing to calling him Hazar Imam or Living (Present, Visible) Imam.

From mid-19th century onwards, there was a steady migration of Satpanth Ismailis from India to East Africa increasing to greater numbers in the late 19th to early 20th centuries. Already by the early 20th century, some Satpanth Ismaili merchants had developed trade networks running from the East Coast of Africa towards the Congo. Their foot caravans included beads among other goods such as blankets, cloth, foodstuff, and building material. The bead trade developed through trial and error as the merchants tested preferences in colours, lustre, sizes and shapes, among the ethnic people. A story is told of how one Mohamed Jivan, a merchant of Nairobi in early 1900s, invested in a stock of beads that he could not then sell. He had to move out of Nairobi and leave Kenya, before his failed investment ruined him. When he was finally able to sell all his beads in Arusha, about 200 km away from Nairobi, in Tanganyika, he decided to settle there. Then he called his family to Arusha, and continued the bead business. Thus, over time the bead merchants of East Africa learned how different and particular were the over hundred ethnic groups when it came to their art. Prominent among the Satpanth Ismaili merchants were names like Allidina Visram, who was a twelve-year-old boy when he landed in East Africa in 1863. Allidina Visram later owned over a hundred shops and employed young men disembarking from the dhow from India, alone and penniless as he had been when he arrived. Stories handed down in families tell of how these young men learned to trade in the interior of East Africa, and how they then went on to start their own small businesses selling beads among other things in remote areas - wherever they saw opportunities. There are also other stories. Stories like how, sometimes, when a girl from a wealthy family married a poor man, capital to invest in a store was bargained or offered as part of her dowry. Other family stories mention how the woman's jewellery from her maiden home not only provided security for borrowing the initial capital, but also gave protection for businesses from collapsing. Thus, in time, Satpanth Ismaili family stores spanned the African geography - the forests, grasslands, highlands, the Great Rift Valley, plateaux, and deserts. A room built behind the store was the home, and often the home-store had another room furnished as a jamat khana or the prayer house. Often their home-store was on the only street and they were the only Asian African family in the area. Later, when more families arrived, they built a communal jamat khana that would be the fulcrum of their social life.

Soon, after the completion of the Uganda Railway (1902), a good number of Satpanth Ismailis all over the greater British East African Empire, started their businesses selling beads among other things. As early as 1905, Rajan Lalji, a Satpanth Ismaili, ran a flourishing bead business in Nairobi supplying the stock to the rural bead merchants along the old caravan routes and the new railroad into the interior. So large was the trade in ethnic beads that one entire street in commercial Nairobi was known as Moti Bazaar or Bead Bazaar. Moti is the Gujarati word for bead. Moti Bazaar was also called Khoja Bazaar, because many of the bead merchants were Satpanth Ismailis, who are also known as Khoja.

When their children reached puberty, the parents sought matchmakers, usually from among the concerned relatives, to arrange honourable marriages. Satpanth tradition required that at marriage, the bride be dressed in the *bandhani*, a silk tie and dye shawl with a heavy silver embroidered border. Then, at death, the other rite of passage, her marriage *bandhani* would cover her as if she were a bride again. A woman's death was spoken of metaphorically as marriage to Saheb, and that she would go to him shining as she was on her wedding day. The *bandhani* was so much valued by the women called Bais in the community, that they guarded it over generations of changing dress and marriage norms in Africa. Later, when they emigrated out of East Africa, the Bais carried the family *bandhani*, some of which would be over a hundred years old, to Canada and wherever else they settled in the Western Diaspora.

While in East Africa, the merchant's wife, mother, and daughter at the family store, handled beads among other household and shop tasks. The Bais put the beads on view on door panels and racks on the shop veranda where they came in close contact with indigenous men and women. Between 1920 and 1950, two of the well-known Khoja Bead Bais of Nairobi were Chak Bai and Puri Bai, while in the rural areas, two of their contemporises were Santok Bai at Ngong Town in Kenya, and Jethi Bai in Arusha, Tanganyika. Often the Bais came as child brides, raised many children, and made the family home in urban and pastoral Africa around the equator. Among them were those who worked with beads until they passed away as grandmothers.

From the early days of the 20th Century, the availability of wide varieties of beads from the entrepreneurial Indian bead merchant, reaching out to the distant ethnic people in British East Africa, heightened diverse vernacular expressions of body décor in patterns and colours. One such body décor is the *emankeeki* of the Maasai. The emankeeki is circular. It's a beaded neck to chest decoration resting on the shoulders that married women wear. It displays meticulously worked out patterns according to Maasai aesthetic schemes that relate to shapes in nature, such as of clouds, animal coats, trees, rocks, and mountains. The vast Maasai geography is itself known by colours, as are their stories, personalities of God, and their much loved cattle.

While visibly, the Satpanth Ismaili bead merchant's family on the savannah lived apart from the prevailing presence of the Maasai around them, they were to an extent, dependent on the pastoralists for the sale of beads. If the rains failed, the pastoralists' livestock weakened and their cycle of rites was interrupted. No beads were sold. As a result, the bead merchant often fell into debt and looked for alternative means to survive. On the other hand, the highly visual people like the Maasai, valued rich tactile displays of beads in Indian shops that spoke to their collective art memory and codes of personal adornment for both men and women.

Hence, throughout East Africa, the Bead Bais like the men, were inadvertently bringing into their homes ethnic African words and expressions, foods, stories, geography, and both utility material culture and artefacts of beauty. Many became fluent speakers of ethnic languages, and like the region's populace around them, they spoke little or no English or Swahili. There were also families that came to believe in indigenous herbal medicine and spirit mediums for physical and mental cures. Some consulted ethnic spiritual practitioners called *waganga* for both aversion and infliction of evil. Such practices were not wholly alien to the Satpanth Ismailis' own beliefs in spirits and traditional knowledge. Thus, with time, though inter-racial marriage was rare, a community culture evolved that was Asian and African or Asian African.

Though inspired by real events and the Bead Bais whom I had met, this work is fiction that began with observations, listening, and pondering over photo albums. Albeit, I did readings to expand on stories from the exhibitions I curated and characters fashioned by my memory. The verses and art imagery are creations from my ethnography and their interpretations are prompted by the rhythm of Satpanth Ismaili and Maasai folklore. The book, however, has been greatly extended by my imagination and tinted by my impressions, perceptions and understanding of what I remember, and how the events and characters took shape, and were re-shaped during the course of writing. Thus, needless to say, the introduction, historical rundowns, glossary, and readings of cultural symbolism, including the verses, are entirely from my point of view.

Sultan Somjee

December, 2012

Note:

Minorities that practise worship drawing from vernacular spiritualities, yet observing certain affective Abrahamic sources, exist around the world. Their histories vary. Today, within the Moslem communities residing in the Western world are the Yarsan, Alawi, Druze and Yazidi (immigrants from the Middle East). These religious minorities within a minority share with the Satpanth Ismailis a history of secretive worship, migrations, and elements of pre-Islamic and salient Islamic beliefs. Others like the Mandaeans, refugees from religious persecutions in Iraq and Iran, follow alternative (i.e. non-mainstream or state prescribed) Abrahamic interpretations affable with their ancestral beliefs. The Kabaa itself, to which most Moslems turn when praying, was a house of worship belonging to the old religion, where an annual pilgrimage took place. When the Moslems conquered the tribes, both the shrine and the ritual of Hajj were adopted by Islam. In Africa, certain groups preferred to re-interpret Christian scripts brought by European missionaries in a way that spoke to their ancient traditions. These groups came to be called African Independent Churches.

Then there are those whose devotional literature is inspired by unison of Islam and native religions of pre-partitioned India. Among these are the Sikhs, Kabirpanthis, Dadupanthis, Pranamis (the group that Gandhi's mother, Putli Bai, belonged to and the temple that Gandhi went to in his childhood), and the Ahmedi Moslems who honour Krishna's divinity among others in their post Mohamed Abrahamic scripture. There are also those known as the followers of Swaminarayan and Sai Bapas, who believe in the latter day Das Avatar (the tenth incarnation of Lord Vishnu) foretold in the ancient Vedic teachings and retold in Indian folk tales and cinema today.

Part One

Stories from Shantytown

Shri Amritlal Raishi, a well-known pioneer businessman and a respected elder of the Oshwal merchant community in East Africa, writes about the beginning of the Indian shantytown bazaar in Nairobi at the turn of the 20th Century:

Jevanjee started building shops on his plots on both sides of (what is today called) Biashara Street with building material left over from the railway construction job. The front portion had two shops and living quarters behind the shops. The structures were simple. The floor was spread with stones stuck on mud. Walls and roof were of corrugated iron sheets of 24 gauge. At the far end, lavatories were erected with a small platform and buckets laid, with an opening in sanitary lane. The buckets were emptied every night in a tank mounted on Municipal carts driven by oxen.

As soon as the shops were erected, they were occupied by merchants of all castes of Hindu and Muslim communities: Ismailis, Bohras, Memons, Lohanas, Brahmins, Jains, etc. Tailors, shoemakers, barbers, carpenters, blacksmiths, of both Hindu and Muslim communities were there.

1

They started selling merchandise of every kind in those days. The customers were mainly the artisans employed by the Railway. The Punjabi merchants, apart from foodstuff also sold tobacco needed in hookahs, Indian herbs and spices.

The commercial area was called "Indian Bazaar," and was famous throughout East Africa. The street was named as "Bazaar Street" later on and was renamed "Biashara Street" after independence.

OLD TIMES AT BIASHARA STREET AS REMEMBERED BY MR AMRITLAL RAISHI. (UNDATED PAPER IN THE COLLECTION OF RAMZAN BHAI RAJAN WHOSE FAMILY STARTED A BEAD SHOP IN THE INDIAN BAZAAR IN 1905).

The same Indian Bazaar about the same time is described in THE NAIROBI MASTER PLAN FOR A COLONIAL CAPITAL (HIS MAJESTY'S STATIONERY OFFICE, 1948 LONDON):

Three streets and one cross street made up the Indian Commercial Area composed of one-storeyed buildings – in the front they contained shops, at the back there were living quarters not only to the traders but also to the host of sub-lessees and lodgers. Outside, lay the immense expanse of the Continent, but the majority of the Indian Community was pushed into a small space of 6 acres.

Contemporary accounts speak of dreadful overcrowding and that in a town of not more than 3,000 Indians. A meat and vegetable market adjoined the bazaar.' The report lists other non-commercial Indian areas of Nairobi, namely the Railway Quarters and The Dhobi (washermen) Quarters. It mentions the Indian worker area as the 'huge evil smelling swamp' along the Nairobi River where 'each house is practically a lodging house with, in some cases, as many as forty people in them.

The report also refers to Military Barracks outside the town. Military historian, S.D.Pradhan (INDIAN ARMY IN EAST AFRICA 1914 -1918, NEW DELHI 1991), writes that between 1914 and 1918, India sent 17,525 soldiers to East Africa to fight the Germans. Of these 2,865 were killed and 2002 wounded. Not included in this number would be

2

the cleaners, clerks, cooks, sappers, miners, technical, medical and other military support and service staff. Indian soldiers, writes Pradhan, played a vital role in the defeat of Germans in East Africa fighting numerous battles and ultimately capturing Kilimanjaro to the south of Nairobi. Hence, there would have been a presence of a large population of Indian forces in Nairobi, the major strategic, commercial, military hospital, military supply and railway town of British East Africa.

1

Jugu Bazaar

15th March 1922 Nairobi, Kenya Colony, British East Africa.

I was born in Nairobi on the day when the colonial soldiers opened fire on the crowd protesting against the imprisonment of Harry Thuku. Harry Thuku, a soldier in the Kings African Rifles, the star battalion at the legendary parades of the British army in Nairobi, had just returned home to Kenya from the war in Burma. He now defied the governor's order on the wearing of the hated *kipande*. The kipande itself was just a numbered metal identity pass, which all native casuals in the Indian business streets and plantation labourers in the White Highlands had to wear with a chain around the neck. However, it was because of the memories of chained slaves that were not so distant from the workers' minds that they could not but see their new metal ID as a symbol of slavery. Thus, it did not surprise anyone when the bazaar folk talked cagily about the growing numbers of disgruntled workers around the country who objected to the wearing of the pass. "But," they would argue, "it's the law of Kenya Colony that all native subjects of the king must be seen with the metal ID at work." What they did not know was what I learned much later in my adulthood, and that was if the law were not peacefully obeyed, it would be brutally enforced. The Empire needed to recover from the first war by developing its colonies as quickly as possible, so it would be ready for another war. For that, a disciplined African labour force like Indian commerce and skilled builders was essential.

The street where I was born is called Jugu Bazaar. Here the merchants of the Indian Ocean spread out cloth, spices, and beads in voluminous displays of variety. Here would sit Indian women in circles grinding rice, mung, millet and sorghum on stone hand mills. All through the day, the stones made crushing, breaking, grinding noises gr...gr...gr. The sights, smells, and sounds around the rotating mills filled the air, some within private households behind the stores, and some more public at the doorsteps where the housewives prattled and ranted while they watched over grain pulverized for a charge. In time, this boisterous street came to be called Jugu Bazaar. Njugu is a Swahili word for peanuts.

The street is still there in Nairobi today if you walk along the Indian Bazaar and go through the alley behind the Jamia Mosque towards Rani Bagh. It's also called Victoria Gardens. It has a statue of Queen Victoria, stout and veiled in her golden years. Indians who come to the garden on Sunday afternoons – men play cards while women watch over children on swings, would say with no less pride that the garden honours Queen Victoria, a student of Hindustani and lover of Sufi poetry, majestic pageants, and paintings of the land. The garden, they would reminisce, is a namesake of a grander one in Bombay of their grandfathers' days. It also has the queen's statue but it was when she was young and did not wear a veil. They would say how their grandparents mused over the queen's raj, splendid in displays of the might of conquest and splendour of submission of ten thousand turbaned soldiers on horses, camels and elephants at parades. This Empire was now cultivating Africa with seeds from the harvest in India: the railway, the military, the post office, the roads, the civil service, modern commerce, and most importantly, the people trained to be loyal and to serve.

It was my work to serve tea and fetch water for men playing cards, and often I got to hear what they talked about. When the Uganda railway, also called the Lunatic Express, was finally completed and Nairobi became the principal town of British East Africa, the English and Boer settlers arrived at the railway camp town in large numbers, and pushed back the Kenya-Uganda border from the Great Rift Valley to Mount Elgon, fearing Uganda would become a Jewish state one day. They said for every mile of railroad laid, four coolies died. By the time the Lunatic Express was completed, hundreds more were physically incapacitated or mentally debilitated. Of the latter, many were those of weak minds who could not endure the hardships of building the Lunatic Express and ran away. They were said to suffer from the illness of the mind, a new discovery in medicine that Dr Patel in the Rani Bagh card group, explained as being called drapetomania, which caused the coolies to flee indentured work. Thus, those stricken by the disease of the railroad makers languished with local criminals in the dungeons of Fort Jesus in the simmering heat of Mombasa, where Indian suicide was not uncommon.

Dadabapa, who would be upset if not only he, but anyone else in the card circle missed the Sunday afternoon game, would say how the railway fired the scramble for Africa. Indian merchants, clerks and artisan families settled in corrugated sheet-iron shacks built from scavenged railroad construction material, creating a crowded shantytown. In the valley of Enkare Nai-robi, which is the Cold Water River in Maasai, sprawling Indian worker slums sprung up. The Cold Water River flowed under the acacia groves that put beauty in the hearts of the Maasai. They called it Nakuso Intelon, 'the waters that are adorned'. In the splendour of the rising sun, the acacia tops at Enkare Nai-robi glowed like beads adorning the body. At that time of prayers, some would say, "The trees taught us to wear beads."

Above the cold river on the flat ridge streets, were wooden houses on stone stilts of wealthy Indian traders, landlords, clerks and service staff in the colonial offices.

Within the sounds gr…gr…grinding of stone mills, bazaar-business bustle, family blusters in tin roofed store-homes, temple bells and muezzins calls, is a story that has as many shapes as the sounds and smells of oriental Nairobi. Sometimes my story looks like a square, sometimes a triangle, and sometimes it's a circle. Hear me and feel my story when you see how the lines of all shapes meet, some earlier, and some later, as the story is told. I am the steward of my feelings inside and my words outside. They are one in my story.

2

Birth Stories

Naaras Dai Bai, the traditional Khoja midwife of the Indian bazaar, was the one who told me about the day I was born. I was perhaps, six or seven years old when she told me about my birth. This was at the ritual Repast of Seven Little Virgins that she prepared once a month on Thursdays at her house. The wooden house where Naaras Dai Bai lived was in Moti Bazaar above the slums along the swampland at Nairobi River that flowed under a shaky wooden bridge. Naaras Dai Bai's home stood on stone stilts and had a red tin roof. Moti Bazaar, which ran behind the jamat khana, was a busy business lane, so named, because of the lively commerce in ethnic beads called moti in Gujarati. The sacramental meal of seven virgins was a manta, a vow that Khoja women took to feed seven chaste girls in order to fulfil a secret wish in their hearts, or to ward off evil, like a disease, or just to show shukhar in gratitude of the daily meal.

Naaras Dai Bai would begin with a prayer and the singing of the Song of Sati, exalting self-sacrifice that was a woman's virtue. Then, while she served kheer and puris to each one of us little girls, individually and lovingly, Naaras Dai Bai told us stories of the day when we were born and how we were delivered from the other world into her hands. We lapped up kheer and puris, chaap chaap, and listened wide-eyed. Naaras Dai Bai dropped an extra spoonful of sweet kheer into my bowl as she began to say, "Each of you girls slipped into these hands from your last karma in your own individual way. Ah, the feel of your birth in my open palms! Your birth smell in my nostrils! Your birth cry in my ears! Your first look in my eyes!" She used to say with a smile, which had a message. Having a nativity story of our own made us, the girls of the Nairobi Khoja jamat, feel unique. Naaras Dai Bai would tell us that we came into this world with a destiny that was written at the time of our birth. She used to say, we must walk along the path of our destiny with shukhar, meaning thankfulness for the contentment of what we have been given by fate, because we cannot change that.

Looking at me, she would say, "Can we, Saki?" She called me Saki; my name was Sakina. Dadabapa said Sakina meant the Spirit of Peace and it could be Peace itself. When I asked who gave me the name, Dadabapa would reply, "The day of your birth named you." Of the seven little virgin girls, I was the one most favoured by Naaras Dai Bai. I chewed papadam at the side of my mouth, kaar kaar karak like a crow cawing in my throat until its crust dissolved over my tongue. Naaras Dai Bai filled me with love as she continued:

"You cannot change the kismet that you come with, clenched tightly in your tiny blue-white fists at the hour of birth. I opened your hands, gently massaging your palm as big as my thumb, praying pirshah…pirshah… pirshah… so the evil in your kismet would leave and the good would stay with you while your future is written. I prayed for you to be free of mothaj. Free of the humiliation of dependence for your daily bread."

Naaras Dai Bai speaks now breaking into soft throat laughter but her voice is firm:

"It was not the usual quiet morning in Jugu Bazaar when you were born. Just as you showed your hairy head, we heard growling shouts, assertive and angry, coming from somewhere at the bridge over the Nairobi River behind the new jamat khana. After cutting the umbilical cord with a prayer of pirshah, I patted you several times on the back, Saki. When you cried, I was relieved. But Saki, you had me worried because you did not cry after the sixth pat and were turning blue. Sweat broke on my forehead. Babies who turn blue at birth will have obstinate characters. They come with anger from their previous karma. When you finally cried, you were so exhausted that when I laid you by your mother's side, you were too tired to take the breast. 'Rai Bai, now you have a daughter to help with house chores,' I whispered to your mother, 'she is beautiful, just like you. She has the likeness of a goddess, the devi she-deity Lakhsmi. She will bring energies of abundance into your home.' Then I placed my hand on your mother's forehead comforting her, pirshah …pirshah…pirshah. 'Next time, you will have a boy. Trust in Sarkar Saheb, the Lord of the Seven Skies.' I combed your mother's hair and laid her head down on the pillow, under which, she kept her Naklank Gita. Your mother could read, you know.

"Your grandfather was disappointed, but he took the umbilical cord and buried it at the neem tree that he had brought with him from his village of Haripur in India. You were his first grandchild born in Africa, his new land, his hope and home where he planted the neem tree.

"Your mother was tired and sad, but she took you into the crook of her arm. Over the three tattoo dots on her chin, her teeth gleamed in a wide smile. 'I see two women comforting each other,' I said to myself as I watched you both. Coiled around your mother's wrist over a red and green thread, was an old wooden Satpanth tasbih with chipped beads and a two-faced silver medallion, where the string was knotted into three miniature silver gunguru bells. I remember it well, because your mother did not allow me to remove the thread and the tasbih when I washed her. 'These do not separate from my body,' she said. 'When I am so exhausted that I cannot slip the beads through my fingers, my pulse counts the caplets in the rhythm of the heart at the wrist. This my grandmother said to me during her dying moments. This is her tasbih that was once around her wrist.' Your mother believed the tasbih would keep away the after-birth spirit, envious of the baby, that would lure new mothers into dark forests. I also remember your mother did not take her eyes off you while I cleaned you. The smile stayed on her lips when she fell asleep looking at you.

"Then I covered you both with a clean merikani cotton sheet and tried to relax in the armchair, but it was not for long. I heard a clamour coming from afar that made me uneasy. 'It seems like some sort of a commotion. A riot perhaps?' I ask myself. Pirshah! The commotion approached Jugu Bazaar, soaring like an incoming gale from the tropical thunderstorm that sweeps the silence of the savannah before

11

breaking into a roaring storm. Your Kaki Bai auntie and the neighbour from the bead store, who had come to assist me in delivering you, talked uneasily in whispers. They were preparing Dettol water and keeping the samavat hot, frequently filling it with live coal. They looked at each other and then at me, questioning, 'What's happening?' Then we heard a stampede at the Central Police Station on Kingsway. An unnatural quietness followed. All of a sudden, a hail of gunshots and a resonance grazed over the tin roofs of Jugu Bazaar like a charge of hysteric snorting buffaloes in the distance. We looked at each other again bewildered and questioning, 'What's happening?' A silence followed haunting the bazaar like graveyard dogs. The land fell into mourning when you were born."

Of all the birth stories I listened to, mine was unusual. That made me feel loved, and I loved myself because my story was different from those of all the other girls in the bazaar. Nothing so unusual happened when they were born. I would control my spirited girl-child giggles by sucking in my cheeks. Pressed to the teeth, cheeks stretched, hollowed, it hurt inside.

During my childhood, I heard Dadabapa, my grandfather telling many times over the story of the happenings on the day I was born. I think he told it so often, because he found it unbelievable that it was a woman who incited the men to defy 'the mighty English raj' as he would say. Like the other Indians in awe if not in admiration. Also, that I, a girl, was born not only on the same day, but also at the same hour. That was something of which he tried to make the meaning. When he consulted the bazaar astrologer, he said, "You named her wisely. The name would deflect misfortune of the birth day falling on your grandchild." In a way, the coincidence of my birth with the kipande occurrence consoled him, because a girl and not a boy, was born in his house. A girl is said to be paarki meaning 'loaned' because she will have to wed and leave for a home destined for her. However, his first grandchild will always be a girl, a native-born British colonial subject who would learn to speak late. He, like many of our neighbours in the bazaar, believed the massacre had shocked me at birth. An infant first senses the world at the threshold of the womb. That's when destiny is given before she takes the first gasp of air. I remained dumbfounded for almost four years.

In time, the telling of the kipande story also became another attribute we associated with Dadabapa, his odd habits and the fear in his predictions. His awe of the Empire. His morning meditation rituals. His standing long hours behind the shop counter. The kipande story, however, changed with his mood each time he repeated the events of March 15th. Nevertheless, the story was always moving. What remained constant was the tone of his voice hinting deep down at his own apprehension for the future of the English raj and Kenya Colony. He was a man who predicted the future, picking up forewarnings like when Ma accidently spilled milk in the courtyard and he declared a tragedy would strike the family. What made the ill-omened kipande story my story was that Dadabapa spoke of my birth in the same breath as if I were a reference point in the narration of the massacre.

Hence, I grew up listening to the story of the Kipande Massacre on the day I was born - that is how people remembered my age and whose daughter I was. These were turbulent times of mass meetings and protests of Indian workers against the Head Tax. When the leaders were arrested and thrown into prison, it caused a great furore in the bazaar. Then the unrest spread like grass fire to the Indian worker

13

settlements along the railroad stations from the Indian Ocean to the Great Lake at the equator.

My father once told me that the native workers who pulled rickshaws carrying English memsahebs in platter hats and who also brought merchandise in pushcarts from the railway station to River Road, Jugu Bazaar and Moti Bazaar instantaneously gave a name to me. That was custom. In Nairobi, a child at birth is given a name after the time of the day or after an ancestor, or she may be named after an event or even after the hero of an event as I was. Naming varies among the indigenous worker cultures of Nairobi depending on what part of the country they come from. They called me Muthoni, the woman who demonstrated in defiance of the raj and changed the course of history. However, my family hushed down this name whenever it was spoken lest it would stay with me.

Until the jamat khana ceremony of the sprinkling of water on my face that brings a newly born baby into the Satpanth Ismaili faith, they called me Bebli at home and never Muthoni.

Muthoni had awakened the land of Mumbi, the ancestral mother of the Northern Ridges that roll into the heights of Mt Kenya, and of Naiterukop, the she-beginner of Earth at the Southern Plains that flow into the infinity of Kilimanjaro, the Big White Mountain. Those who cultivate the slopes, call the Big White Mountain, Kibo, meaning the Awe of Divinity. My story sways between the two snow mountains of this verdant land they call 'White Man's Country' at the centre of the Earth in Africa where I was born. A woman's story is the story of land and divinity told in the feelings of her heart.

3

Speaking by mis-speaking

Though I did not talk, it was a wonder that the mute child in me could memorize embroidery on pachedi borders and draw the patterns on concrete floors with charcoal from the kitchen stove. Each stroke made a line that stood and ran before my eyes like girls making hop-skip-jump patterns on the jamat khana courtyard stones. My eyes would chase the girls, ribbon them in circles, curves, and zigzag lines. Then designs would emerge from their movements, transforming the lines into sound patterns like those that Dadabapa made when he sang the sacred songs of our Satpanth faith. I thought he made the picture-sounds just for me. I learned to hum in consonance with rhythmic vibrations swelling on his neck. Sometimes, he took my hand into his and made me touch the veins bulging over his splinter neck-bones that trapped the timbre in their cage as if in it was a songbird. When I felt the raga shudder in his throat, my eyes would light up and he would smile and hum again and again and again so I could hear the raga on my fingers. Do you hear the sounds? Do you feel them? He would ask. Then I began to throat sing

15

with him as he trained my hand to feel how neck bones and muscles moved with sounds. Then I finally talked.

My Dadabapa told me that the first comprehensible word that came out of me was 'Dadabapa'. It gave him immense pleasure to hear me say 'Dadabapa' and he would ask me to repeat it over and over again, patting his chest. He said that from that day, I was his favourite grandchild in the household. Four more grandchildren were born after me in the Nagji Padamsi family of Jugu Bazaar, but I was the last one to talk. I remember how Dadabapa carried me around in the house. In the store, he would sit me down on the glass counter and play animal games on my fingers – the thumb would be a roaring lion, the index finger a galloping zebra, the middle finger a giraffe looking over all the other fingers, and the little finger the trotting dik dik deer. The game would end with a tickle in the stomach. In the jamat khana, he kept me by his side on the men's side of the prayer hall, and, I think, I must have tapped into his heart when he sang the sacred songs of guru-pir. The guru-pir is the parent-mabap of the Satpanth faith. He is the mystery that we try to reach in the sacred ragas when we sing.

Soon after that, I learned to say 'Bapa' to my father. That's what my father said. One day, he told me that I said 'Mola--pa-pa' to the picture on the wall to the delight of all at home, and he immediately pushed a penda into my mouth. He let me eat the whole penda that only my younger brother, Shamshu, was allowed to do. It was as if I had said my first prayer. From that day, Dadabapa would train my eyes to look deep into Saheb's picture face. "Mowla-bapa," he would say. "Mola--pa-pa," I would repeat. Dadabapa chuckled whenever he told me the story of how I learned to speak mis-speaking Saheb's holy name. Everyone loved to hear me mis-speak Saheb's holy

16

name with such sweetness that can only come from an innocent child just learning to speak.

"*Mowla-bapa dawo kaaro*, Mowla-bapa make me good. *Ya Ali-bapa dawo kaaro*, Ya Ali-bapa make me good." He would touch the portrait of our Saheb and then me, covering my face with his open palm. My eyes closed and opened before Saheb's image on the wall. Dadabapa did this every morning with such love-passion in his voice that the picture's presence became as vibrant as it was vivid, and as close as Dadabapa's own self. Saheb was someone beautiful and loveable who lived in colours on the sober walls of our home. Growing up, I knew that the picture face bestowed blessed feelings to the home, and in my imagination, he flourished wonder and magical awe. The turbaned Saheb was one in the mandala of other nine god avatars to whom Dadabapa sang every morning and circled smoking incense sticks around the visage. He was someone who throbbed the ragas in Dadabapa's veins and tensed his neck's girth when he sang the sacred. So big, so loving, and so alive was he of the picture that everyone revered him.

Dadabapa himself was a small man, short and slim with a bushy beard, who held strong opinions about the right and wrong things to do, and the God-given roles of men and women in the family. He wore loose-fitting light cotton clothes and a red fez cap with a black tassel that swung and made his 'Nah!' sound a more emphatic 'No!' than it actually was.

In July and August, when it was still cold in Nairobi, Dadabapa put on his brown buscot waist jacket, hand sewn by my grandmother, Sohn Bai. It was also made of cotton. His beard was turning white, but it never became fully white.

17

Dadabapa's opinions were certain like his walk, straight like his red-lacquered walking stick with a rosebud knob. We took turns playing horse with his walking stick, holding it at an angle between the legs just above the knees. We sang the song of how Dadabapa's horse galloped to Mombasa. His walking stick, his beard turning white and the disciplined reading and re-reading of *Satpanth Prakash*, a Bombay monthly, contributed oddly to his show of austerity as the head of the family. Sometimes he would 'simplify' the stories in *Satpanth Prakash* for us. As he narrated, he would complain, "Mukhi Lalji Bhai, the editor, does not know his Gujarati is far above the folk in Africa." However, he himself had no problem, he would add quickly, "Because I was born in India."

4

Stories that angered the land

Stories were told just before dinner when we were back after the second prayer of the evening at the jamat khana. It would be a while waiting for the meal to be served. It would be when the children were hungry and quiet. "No food, no lala," Ma would say like her motto. Then she would begin a story and keep speaking and singing as long as it took to complete the cooking. We would listen, sitting silently, one leg over another, eyes shifting from the charcoal stove glowing warmth on our faces to the moves of her hand over the pot.

"Give me, a woman, your trousers, shouted Mary Muthoni Nyanjiru," says Ma pushing open the pot's lid and doing a few quick stirs through the curried steam. Then she pushed the cover closed to let the sauce bubble to a thickness that she measured by tasting it with a quick lick on the wooden spoon. I could not imagine a woman wearing trousers when in those days, Khoja women would not let the pachedi slip off the head in front of men. 'Give me, a woman, your trousers' was so fascinating a phrase that I quickly memorized and repeated

19

it, imitating Ma when I retold the story to my younger siblings. However, deep in my heart, I knew that this was a serious story. "Mary Muthoni Nyanjiru shouts and hurls a rock at the armed guards assembled at the Central Police Station on Kingsway, pirshah!" Ma Gor Bai continues gesturing as if she were throwing a rock clenched in her fisted hand. We watch her, thinking she is the protester at Kingsway Police Station. "What followed happened so quickly. A torrent of stones descends on the askaris and then the demonstrator's storm towards the police station, pirshah!" At this point, Ma Gor Bai would place both her hands over her head to show something tragic happened. "The white men in khaki shorts at the Norfolk Hotel panic. A roar from the mob bellows like a thousand buffaloes in chorus. Colonel Grogan takes one shot at the demonstrators; his askaris open a battery of fire; the white men in khaki shorts at the Norfolk Hotel shoot. In minutes, you see a bloodbath ... pirshah!"

"Pirshah!" I repeat speaking to the bloody picture in my head.

"A bullet hits Mary Muthoni," continues Ma Gor Bai speaking without a pause as if carried away by her own words into the picture of the story she makes for us, "she lies there tied to the red earth with her child strapped to her back, miraculously still alive. The child had finely shaven sticks, size of matchsticks, in each ear lobe. One day, her mother hoped to adorn her daughter with haangi-beaded rings when she would be a bride. It was not until the evening that the families come to identify the dead and take the infant home to her grandmother. They called her Njoki, meaning the one who is born again. Bodies are trucked to native reserves where the protesters were born, their umbilical cords buried under the shade of a peace tree where their ancestors resided, and where they were named, circumcised, married and had children. This is the verdant land of their birth at the foothills of Mt Kenya where the legend is told of one called Mumbi, the ancestor mother who had nine girl children. Kenya is a country of a thousand sights and sounds, a country not contained by one geography or told in one legend."

I shuffle closer to the charcoal stove, while still sitting with folded legs, where the cement is warm and the fading heat from the stove door warms my legs.

"A woman wanting to wear a man's trousers? Throwing stones at the English? What did she want? Can a woman do that?" Ma Gor Bai would exclaim in questions, as was her manner of speech. However, such questions had no answers, leaving only thoughts in my head.

If we tried, we could listen to Kaki Bai auntie humming in the shop while she swept the floor and dusted the glass counters. Finally, she came to layers of bead strings displayed during the day on the folding doors. We would wait to hear her sneeze and then we would giggle. It would be when she began counting the salt packages that she would stop humming. Then she started humming again when she made more paper cones, pouring three spoonfuls of salt in each one. Dadabapa needed to see exactly twenty salt packages when he opened the store in the morning. Meanwhile, the routine mirth of hyenas at the garbage behind the latrines would go on unnoticed filtering through the stillness of the night sky over Nairobi's Indian bazaar.

When the curry's simmer subsides, we become alert to the hunger moving our stomachs as if awakened from the legend of Mary Muthoni and Mumbi and the land. I remove a serving bowl from the shelf beside Saheb's photo, where Ma Gor Bai kept a handful of mung, the evergreen seed, for the baraka blessings of roji, the daily meal.

Men folk are talking at the dinner table as they usually do, catching up and telling each other what they had heard at the jamat khana that evening. Men's talk. Important talk. Jamat khana is where people congregate to pray and then they exchange news about travel, and about what they heard from Nairobi. Politics. Words come to the bazaar faster than the newspaper and even the morning news on the radio. Men would discuss new business risks and opportunities. However, mostly they talk about new government policies affecting Indian immigration, then taxes. Ma Gor Bai brings the steaming bowl of curry to the table, followed by Hawa carrying chapattis on a clay platter.

"The curry is cooked by an expert," my father compliments Ma Gor Bai.

"Oh! I was in such a hurry today and I didn't even taste how it is," replies Ma Gor Bai avoiding attention to herself. "Shall I bring some more? Hot, hengh?"

The three men, Dadabapa and his two sons, Husein and Noordin, talk about one Saurashtran lawyer who lived in South Africa. They called him Gandhi. They said he used to wear English clothes in South Africa. That he was a complete gentleman, pakka brown gentleman, with a tie, buscot and bowler hat. They said he too defied the raj and burnt his kipande ID.

"Imagine a Gujarati man wearing an English suit and then defying the English king!" I hear my Noordin Kaka uncle remark.

"They say his children also wore English clothes; ties, coats, boots, and even socks," says my father chuckling.

"Even socks?" asks Dadabapa. He smiles, amused.

"He defied the raj. He even burnt his kipande ID while wearing an English suit! And because of that," adds my father, "they broke his fingers with a baton and threw him in jail in Johannesburg. The London lawyer's suit did not help him! He was still a wog; a pakka wog in an English three-piece suit."

"Gandhi says Harry Thuku is a victim of English lust for power. He wants Harry Thuku's story to be read in India like his own. He worries the English when he makes such comments," says Noordin Kaka uncle.

"The Church in Kikuyuland is in a panic. The White Fathers warn the English about Harry Thuku trying to become the Gandhi of Kenya." My father's comment surprises everyone. He is not the political one in the family.

"Now such a missionary story would have interested India and it would have been told and discussed among the Liberals and the working classes of England," says Noordin Kaka uncle, the political one, the one with a side smile under his moustache. He also wears a goatee beard.

"But here in Nairobi they killed a woman, a child still feeding at her breast, and so many others," says Dadabapa. "The child is Sakina's age group, a few months older but she is of her age group." Dadabapa looks down, shaking his head as he continues to say as if the incident had just happened, "The land does not forget the anger we cause her. Spilling human blood angers the land. The government does not understand that. The land's mamta motherhood is offended when her children are orphaned. The government does not

23

understand that. It angers Ambe Ma. Here in Nairobi, Draupadi was declothed and Krishna could not save her. The land is a woman married to man. The mother, Tharti Mata. We are her children."

"The Nairobi massacre happened just three years after the one in the Punjab that angered Gandhi. They say killing of women in Amritsar awakened India to the path of freedom," says my Noordin Kaka uncle. He knows because he reads the secrets from the forbidden paper that he says is printed in faraway places that no one has even heard about. Some say these places are in Japan and others think they would be in Germany or Italy because only those countries would allow such news and messages against the great raj to be printed. At other times as I was growing up and understanding more, I heard my Noordin Kaka uncle talk about a Sykalwala Pundit, the Bicycle Priest, who moved like a fox along the railway line hiding in guards' cabin. The picture of the Bicycle Priest stayed in my mind, his white dhoti flying in the air as he pedalled the bicycle. Noordin Kaka uncle said the Hindu priest belonged to the group that carried the clandestine paper in their turbans and distributed it to the workers along the railway line. Many others believed that the man called Bishen Singh hanged in Mombasa had something to do with the night paper too. Nevertheless, I remember how his hanging shocked the people. Some began to live in fear and avoided the secret newspaper as if it had a disease. However, some galvanized their hearts for a long fight to come against the Empire.

Looking down, Dadabapa speaks again, more emphatically this time, ignoring Noordin Kaka uncle, as if his son's words, shaped by the fire of freedom politics were not as important as his own that came from the quiet wisdom of the legends of the land. Unlike his son, Dadabapa replies in parables. "When the people of the North Ridges descend to the savannah to acquire land and settle, they say, 'We have come to marry the land-bride.' The ceremony of tying man to the land begins like a marriage ceremony with a sip of honey beer dribbling from the calabash to the ground calling upon the ancestors to witness the union. Then, honey beer is poured into a cow horn, size of half a buffalo horn, and shared while the elders haggle over bride prize. It is the marriage of the land and people – the man's family, his clan and community. A relationship is made between the land, people and ancestors. That is peace. When you anger one you anger all and break the peace."

I grew up listening to such stories about Africa and India, and Indians in Africa and how they blended their African lives with Indian myths. Little did I know how these stories would grow into larger stories and change the world I knew when I was little and curious.

5

Stories arriving with the monsoons

In late November when the monsoons blow from India, families gather on the coral cliffs of Mombasa training their eyes over the blue horizon to spot dhows coming home. Young men would compete to be the first to sight the tip of the sail bobbing over the Indian Ocean like a sea gull. Then they would rush to the merchants to tell them their goods have arrived safely and collect a tip from each one. When the dhows dock in the old slave port of Mombasa, they would have a cargo of cloth, building material, household wares, blankets and beads. They would have fresh spices, seedlings of fruit trees and grain. With the dhows also came the returning residents and new immigrants and with them came family stories from the villages of Saurashtra. Some brought newspapers from the streets of Bombay and others were there who carried clandestine papers in their turbans.

After the evening prayers in the Nairobi jamat khana, men and women would gather separately, sitting in circles to listen to the recent travellers from India arriving each day by the new railroad from the port of Mombasa. They enquired about the well-being of their aged parents and younger brothers and sisters left behind in the old country they still called Desh, the motherland. Villages in India were connected with families in Nairobi and Mombasa and all along the Uganda railroad to Kisumu and even as far away as Uganda and beyond to the Belgium Congo. They interpreted the stories they heard mingling with other family stories, mingling joy and pain the way painters interpret pictures they make in layers from other pictures mingling light and shadow. They listened to how their relatives in the Khoja communities of Bombay, Rajkot, Karachi and across India, continued to be divided into Sunni, Shia Ithna Asheri and Satpanth Ismaili families and how the divisions in India were affecting the separation of the families in Zanzibar and remote villages of East Africa. How the jamat khana buildings were physically divided into bigger and smaller jamats of the ethnic Khoja of one heritage but now differing in beliefs. For some, it was the Satpanth song called the Das Avatar, which held them together in turbulent times. Their faith in Saheb, the Sarkar, the manifest imam, grew deeper in the mysteries of God's reincarnations, secrecy and chanting while they guarded the sacredness of daily prayers said in vernacular Gujarati, Kutchi and Sindhi. Others were pulled towards a new awakening about creation and public proclamation of their belief plainly thus, There is no God but God. Imam is not manifest, and with that, they now prayed in memorized Arabic.

Every year, fresh dhow stories coming with the monsoons fed the antagonism brewing among the descendants of forefathers who lived as brothers of one ancestry, one history, one language and one tradition. Inflammatory tales from the

27

old country fed like firewood into a furnace already blazing in Zanzibar and rapidly spreading inland.

Family politics that broke and bonded communities in Hindu-Moslem-British India and Hindu-Moslem-British East Africa echoed in the larger politics of the shanty bazaars of Nairobi. Local stories about the wars of ethnic people against the raj were retold mixing past and present, from the days of protests of railway coolies to the present anti-head-tax marches. Then we heard the first news of public executions of political prisoners in Kenya Colony. "The present walks with the past hand in hand and sometimes, when history repeats, it embraces the feelings of the storyteller," Dadabapa used to tell me as if I were an adult and would understand. I listened though, and what I learned from Dadabapa was that every story was like a stitch in the feelings of the time. "Life is like emotion's patches held together by stitches of time," I would hear him repeat, and I would try to understand what he meant. This was his favourite sentence. The sentence that I did not understand but I would say it anyway to my pupils at the religion school. Often he said this sentence to conclude a story that he did not conclude. "But," he would add, "such a story would tell itself to the end in its own time and in its own words."

After the prayers of the first quarter of darkness when the night is born and spirits walk about the graveyards, old men like my Dadabapa would gather around the bench in the jamat khana yard to talk. Sometimes their talk was charged with inside words that made terrifying pictures in my head. So vivid were the pictures to me that while standing between my grandfather's legs among a clump of legs of his peers, I would hear the tortured cries of demented railway coolies imprisoned in the dungeons of Fort Jesus. I would see fear in the eyes of escaped coolies lost in the arid scorpion and viper infested scrubland. I would hear Bishen Singh chant the freedom song from the dreaded black hole of Mombasa. Sometimes their words carried hate and alarm that frightened me. When we returned home, I let my eyes take the fear deep into Saheb's holy picture on the wall.

When news reached Nairobi about the destruction of the Khoja Naklank Ashram, there was uproar in the community. Dadabapa was deeply affected by what Meeshnari Shivji Bhagat told him. "There was ruin in the aftermath of assassinations among the Khojas. I saw Naklank Ashram burn to ashes before my eyes," said Meeshnari Shivji Bhagat who witnessed the religious violence. Naklank Ashram, the Khoja orphanage, was dear to Dadabapa and like Meeshnari Shivji Bhagat, my teacher at the religion school, Dadabapa had hoped to retire to the ashram and give his sewa service in his remaining days to Saheb. There was something in the musical voice of my teacher that kept me listening to him. Perhaps it was his deep faith – his love for Saheb or knowledge of history that I yearned for. Or was it because I admired how he read so swiftly? Or was it the books he displayed on his office bookshelf, his own private library? Or could it be because of something else happening to me? I don't know but I would stand at the doorway and listen when he came to Dadabapa's shop.

"Now where shall I go? Meeshnari says the ashram is burnt to ashes and the orphans are left homeless in the streets," Dadabapa would grumble, half as a complaint, half sadly, while munching his after meal paan as was his habit. He would stand in the store with his head in his hands and elbows digging into the clear glass counter top. For a long time, especially during the moments of sadness that seized him

29

more often now when he was aging, he had been planning and dreaming to retire to the ashram and leave the running of the business to his two sons. He would say to me in private that he wanted to rest under the neem tree where his umbilical cord was buried in the peanut fields of Haripur. However, we knew, if leaving home in the old country was difficult for Dadabapa, the return, even for a visit, would be impossible. We also knew that in his aging years, his mind lived in Haripur and he must keep dreaming of the journey to the neem tree in the peanut fields.

I listened to Dadabapa and I understood stories were listened to in the body. I knew that because sometimes my skin turned cold eavesdropping on Noordin Kaka uncle. He talked with deep passion about the native resistances that went hand in hand with the freedom movement in India and Indian worker protests in Kenya. Sometimes that was all he talked about evening after evening, the whole evening into the honeyed beginning of the third quarter of the night that would be after mid-night when the distant roaring echoes of the Embakasi lions died down. "They have hunted, eaten and are contented," one of them would comment on the lions.

Dadabapa and Noordin Kaka uncle had constant arguments about the subversive papers that Kaka brought into the house. "The English will hunt you down the way lions hunt the zebra on the plains. One day they will hang you like Bishen Singh," Dadabapa would warn Kaka uncle but my Kaka uncle would not listen to his father's fears. Instead, he would respond with pride, "If there is another war, I will fight for the Germans."

Dadabapa would not speak of his inside fears for his eldest son to anyone, not even to Meeshnari Shivji Bhagat, his peer and best friend with whom he played and talked politics on Sunday afternoons in Rani Bagh. Sometimes they also went for a walk together after dinner. However, in private, he would quarrel, curse and try to convince Noordin Kaka uncle to revert to Satpanth. What worried Dadabapa the most was that Kaka uncle kept what he called the Ghadar Party newsletter folded four times over, behind Ma Gor Bai's English teakops displayed in neat rows on the shelf. The newspaper came with freedom stories on the dhow from India according to the southerly monsoons that blew to Mombasa from Bombay.

However, later, when the bazaar slept, and you heard an occasional burst of hyena's laughter crunching into the stillness of the hour, Dadabapa listened attentively to Noordin Kaka uncle. As I lay down in my bed, my eyes wide open, I would strain my ear to hear their whispered comments. Noordin Kaka uncle would be reading from the secret newspaper. He would be reading stories about shipment of Indian plantation labour to the Caribbean, Fiji, Mauritius and Natal. How the British sub-contracted their colonial subjects to the French and Dutch. How there were protest marches and hangings of Indian dissidents in the colonies as there were in Kenya.

One day, Noordin Kaka uncle talked about another continent. He called it North America that was big like Africa. He said it was covered with snow and the people there lived in snow houses. It was a story that was so different that it made me wonder how the people lived there and what they ate, and if they wore beads. He told the tale of how a boat carrying British Indians to British Canada was forced to return to India from the port in Canada. Then the three of them would talk excitedly in murmurs about what they had heard in the bazaar

31

that day. They would slurp through clenched teeth and stretched lips talking about Indian worker suicides and deaths in the dungeons of Fort Jesus. They would raise voices in excitement when debating whether it was proper to form Indian workers strike committees and an Indian chamber of commerce. They did not particularly like the workers, but then they needed them to fight the colour bar so the English would not look down on them. They would employ the young Indian lawyer just arrived in town, English speaking, London exam-pass, London law-pass, like Gandhi, to be their spokesman with the government about new taxes and war levies. Noordin Kaka uncle would talk about the loss of more ancestral lands and the subsequent native resistances. He would curse the colonials under his breath when speaking about the flogging of black plantation workers by Kaburu, the South African Boer settlers, in the White Highlands. He would also curse the colonials under his breath when speaking about the butchery of the Kikuyu by the military colonels. "It's all about the land," he would insist. He connected the local wars back and forth, and then there was the mass exodus of the nomadic Maasai from fertile pastures to make room for White settlement. All these stories played simultaneously in my mind, one over the other, each one a patch in an ugly worldwide mosaic that Noordin Kaka uncle called the Empire.

It was also at night that they would discuss how to evade the new scourge of the head tax, how to cheat on tax papers; how to write the shop accounts in Gujarati so the profit would show only half the actual amount. They would discuss how much capital they needed to invest by categories of goods – in beads, blankets, tools, cigarettes, merikani sheets, and how much bribe money they should offer the Gujarati man from the government tax department when he came to audit. When it came to money, all three had to agree on the amounts for different purposes.

In the gigantic pattern of the Empire that repeated across the seas and continents, the stories of India and Africa were entwined like my own. Such were the stories that they held my emotions together like patches stitched by events. I did not know where these stories would go from here. They had their own way of finding the path. "Let the story tell itself," as Dadabapa would say, "twisting and turning it makes itself to the end."

6

Stories departing with the monsoons

In the month of April when the monsoons turn, becoming northerly winds, word goes around the jamat khana that the sails have been mounted at the lintels and dhows are preparing to cruise back to India. Those elders of the jamat, who are in good health and have been able to save some money, now pack their bags and prepare for the overnight journey by the new rail to Mombasa. In our hearts, we know that some will not be able to endure the voyage to India and see their old families, and others would not be able to endure the voyage back to Africa. Many would be buried at sea, but they would still want to fulfil promises made when they were young and left for Africa with a vow to return. They said India was their country, their motherland, their Desh. How can one not return to be live the old age and be buried where one was born? Such is the pull of hope.

One day, my teacher at the jamat khana school, Meeshnari Shivji Bhagat, strides into Dadabapa's shop with the dignity of a maharaja. My heart throbs faster as I walk into the shop behind him with a broom in my hand, wanting to be close to him, to listen to the music in his voice more than to sweep the floor. He is returning to India to volunteer at the school for orphans and has come to bid farewell.

"Give this to Major Lakhpati," says Dadabapa as he unwraps layers of white merikani cloth and removes my grandmother's dowry piece, the gold bangle with a leaf clasp. It was one of the two bangles crafted in the red gold of Saurashtra. Initially, there were four such bangles that he had kept from my grandmother's gold, but two had to be sold to pay debt incurred by my father's second marriage. My grandmother, Sohn Bai, was known as 'the lady who wore four gold bangles with leaf clasps.' That was her other name in the bazaar though they say Dadabapa more often called her his Radha for she was fair and nimble, and had a round face. Most of all, she was faithful to him. In Dadabapa's sunken eyes that are losing their light, tears well. Over the retina in each eye was a fine film, white and a little gluey. Meeshnari Shivji Bhagat understood the longing in Dadabapa's heart to fulfil his religious sewa-obligation in his old age. He takes the bangle with respect almost in an act of reverence with both his hands, one cupped under the other and touches it to his right eye and then to his left eye. I watch from a distance with my eyes full of envy as he bit the gold at the side of his mouth with his canines to appraise its purity.

All these years, the two bangles, the last security for the family against business failure, had lain wrapped in layers of merikani cloth tucked under Dadabapa's mattress. There was the uncertainty of yet another war between the English and Germans over African resources, taxes and labour among other age-old issues of Europe. We know businesses shut

35

down during wars, and men like my father and Noordin Kaka uncle would be recruited to manage war supplies and accounts, if not put at the frontline.

"Your grandmother's bangles give me great comfort. Should there be war and should there be no money in the store's cashbox, we would not have to stand before the Five Brothers Welfare Society looking at the floor. And I would not have to bear the shame in the jamat khana of being the recipient once again of their reluctant charity," Ma Gor Bai used to say. The Five Brothers Welfare Society was a Satpanth 'serve the poor' confraternity from times ancient.

Malek, Monghi, and I, did not talk about the bangles but our hearts were in that cloth wrap. Often I would wonder who would be the lucky two of the three of us to inherit a bangle. Sometimes on dreamy afternoons behind the stack of blankets in Dadabapa's shop, I would coil copper wire around my wrists, stretch my arms and imagine the bangles glittering on me.

The bangles were also the memory of my grandmother Sohn Bai, the marriage of my grandparents and the family gold that Dadabapa had saved so it could be inherited, an heirloom for his granddaughters when they came of age. That was custom. However, Grandmother Sohn Bai's bangle was all that Dadabapa could think of to send to the orphan's rescue fund. Major Lakhpati had made an East Africa wide appeal for assistance to help the Khoja orphans and families who were victims of inter-sect upheaval. Dadabapa admired Major Lakhpati, the Khoja artist and poet of Bombay, who was widely known as 'abd' or a slave in service of Saheb, the appellation he chose to signature his poetry. Major Lakhpati's reputation for organizing Khoja volunteers in India with iron

36

discipline comparable to that of an English war captain, spread side by side with news of communal violence. It was said that Major Lakhpati inspired elders like Varas Jamal of Kisumu to start volunteers groups in their hometowns and villages across East Africa, the tradition that lives on to this day. Dadabapa cut out every one of Major Lakhpati's verses from the community periodicals and slipped them between the pages of his accounts journal that he kept on top of the bead boxes. When his heart was heavy, he would read the poems silently standing at the counter. Sometimes he would read to me poems celebrating Saheb, the Lord of the Seven Skies and I would float in the seven heavens that he ruled among the jug mug glitter of starry diamonds of the galaxies.

I noticed how nowadays Dadabapa read the Naklank Gita more often and for longer hours than ever before. Sometimes he read from the early hours when he opened the shop to lunchtime. The red cloth bound book stayed in the corner of the shop tucked into the stacked pile of blankets at about the height of Dadabapa's waist. In between reading, he would serve the customers and then go back to the holy book. Sometimes he would read aloud to himself and I would listen to him as I swept the grey cement floor of the shop. Often the verses would touch my heart and well my eyes.

One afternoon, when I took a cup of tea to Dadabapa, as was my routine, I saw that he was not reading. He had his elbows pressed to the counter and his head in his open palms. Then as Dadabapa poured the tea from the kop to the saucer, he said something that took me aback, "Not many days are left for me now beta, my child. I wish to return to the neem tree at our family field in Haripur. There I will offer prayers at the graves of my parents, and ask for their forgiveness because I did not return as I had vowed to. I did not hear the story they would have told me of their childhood as the elders do in their old age when their bodies have no life but their minds are full of life in the past. When the old die with unspoken words because we were not with them, our stories too die with them. Every day of the week, I will make a prayer plate of their favourite foods for the jamat khana where they sat to meditate and sing the Satpanth song. I will ask the ancestral earth to bless me so I can do my sewa and serve the orphans side by side with Major Lakhpati. I will pick a pebble from my mother's grave and throw it in the well at the orphanage. I will dedicate my service to the peace of forgiveness that I seek."

Sometimes old people would tell children a secret wish in their hearts that they would not say to adults. I was not yet twelve but the child in me knew there was pain in Dadabapa's heart. Later when I was bigger and thinking about Dadabapa, I wondered if the pain of leaving India was what stopped him now from returning. That pain stays in you, becoming fear of being hurt again. It would be the fear of returning. The fear of seeing the farmhouse again without his parents who were long dead. Or would it be the fear of the pain of what he would say to his younger siblings who were grandparents now like he was? Then there was also the fear of what he would tell the land and the peanut trees.

Dadabapa drinks chai with the wind and then opens the Khoja Gita. That's how some neighbours refer to our holy book though Dadabapa always calls it Naklank Gita and sometimes Satpanth Gita. He did not have a bookmark but knew the exact verse he stopped at and where he should continue reading the next day.

On another day when I came to sweep the shop floor as was my routine, Dadabapa talked to me about his friend who he had met on the dhow coming to Africa. My father and Noordin Kaka uncle were listening while they laboriously carried on with stocktaking and did not say a word. It was a quiet, rainy afternoon in Jugu Bazaar.

"Your father, Husein, was born in Mombasa," says Dadabapa. "I arranged his marriage with your mother, Rai Bai. Marriages are arranged between children of Khoja villagers of Saurashtra who know each other. We keep our kinships, faith and lineages in Africa as we did in India."

There was a reason why Dadabapa wanted me to know what was in his heart. It was his way of talking in parables what cannot be said directly. I felt he had kept these words for me until I was old enough to listen and remember.

"I have a friend in Zanzibar and he has a grandson two years older than you are. We travelled together from India on that perilous voyage and we survived together. Like brothers, children of one mother, we shared meals. When we landed in Mombasa, he gave me shelter and food when I had nothing. At the sunken causeway from the island to the mainland, together we planted the mango seeding he had carried with him from his ancestral village. He persuaded me to work with Allidina Visram and I learned to trade in beads. One day you will go as a bride to honour the promise I made to him. It's a pious family. You will be happy with them."

The departing monsoons leave behind empty sitting places on the straw mat along the walls of the jamat khana. In the vacuum of each space is a carved figure invisible to the eye, of a Mawji Bhai, Chagan Bhai, Amershi Bhai and so on, who from their adulthood to the day of their departure for India, occupied that seat twice a day, every day at sunrise and sunset when the Satpanthis assemble for communal prayers in the jamat khana. Their peers like my Dadabapa, are aware of shapes in vacant spaces. Their hearts are filled with sadness not because they miss the travellers, but because they know in their hearts they may not live to see the next monsoon season that would take them to India. Mawji Bhai, Chagan Bhai and Amershi Bhai left for Desh with the monsoons this year. Desh is the country over the ocean whose images charged with feelings now return to haunt them in old age like how parents' memories haunt orphans in dreams.

.

7

Blending Stories Asian African

Noordin Kaka uncle liked an audience no matter who and whatever the ages, as long as they listened. When he was not talking or eating, he was reading and when he was not reading, he sat in a corner chair tapping his two fingers on his forehead, thinking. I never saw him pray or meditate, as was the custom of the Satpanthis. Although he was conceited and looked down on his listeners as illiterates, as he called them under his breath, people of all religions and castes listened to him and wanted to be on his side. Many in the bazaar were offended by his arrogance but kept quiet because of fear of losing an argument with him. His name, Noordin, means Light of Religion. However, he was better known as Dhururu, which means five cents. He was a stout, short man, under five feet in height, and I think people were happy, though they did not say it, calling him Dhururu, the short one, if only because he behaved like he was above everyone else. "But he is not," they would joke.

They called my father Husein Tongolo. He was a regular five feet eight and I think they called him Tongolo, ten cents, because he was the taller brother of Dhururu, five cents, the uncle I loved to listen to. Of course, I could never mention these other names of my Noordin Kaka uncle and my father to anyone when I was little.

However, I admired my uncle even though he rarely talked to children and women. His narrations of incidences that pointed to the injustices of the raj and the white-brown-black colour bar in Kenya captivated me.

Once Noordin Kaka uncle, talked about someone called Subash Chandra Bose who had started a freedom movement in India. "He is a communist," he said with pride. "He will lead us to a revolution."

"Gandhi led the burning of the kipande of the Indian mine workers in South Africa. For this he was imprisoned and yet another peace movement was born," Dadabapa was quick to reply. Immediately, Noordin Kaka uncle's countenance changed, showing mixed disdain and admiration. When his views were not accepted, he looked mystified. His eyes shifted.

"Gandhi returned to India from Africa preaching dignity of man, truth and freedom. He learned this in Africa. Didn't he? He organized civil disobedience and marched with a staff in his hand, naked to the waist and in his native slippers like an African elder," said Dadabapa. "Africa is a teacher of many things. Isn't she?"

"I heard in the bazaar today that he is burning English clothes and wears only Saurashtran dress now," added my father.

"Saurashtran dress?" exclaimed Noordin Kaka uncle partly questioning as if it could not be true.

"Yes, a dhoti," answered my father immediately.

"No shart, no bushart! Bare-chested like a peasant Momna in sandals," Noordin Kaka uncle's chuckle annoyed Dadabapa. "Now his wife, Kasturba, wears a simple Gujarati cotton sari. Only hand-woven cloth, you know," continued Noordin Kaka uncle in a singsong tone moving his head from side to side, dole dole, as they said was the Gandhi way. My Kaka uncle made word pictures of the man and his wife. I see them even today as they walk the march that defied the mighty raj.

"Can a bare-chested peasant in sandals bring freedom?" asked Noordin Kaka uncle in the same tone edging on mockery.

"Gandhi already has a large following and it's growing. He is more popular than those England-educated, suited and booted pakka gentlemen politician communist friends of yours in India," frowned Dadabapa.

Fairy tale like accounts of Thuku and Gandhi, animals and spirits, and the anti-raj movements in India and Kenya blend into a montage of sounds of freedom songs, heroes and traitors, cowardice and courage in my child's imagination. Noordin Kaka uncle often talked about African resistances against the raj and about the imminent World War with pride if not joy in his glinting eyes. "Another war would strike us from Europe," he would say, as if it were promised prophesy, "and that will weaken the England."

In my imagination, these stories churned with anecdotes of ancestral spirits and nocturnal beings, leopards and cheetahs that came prowling into Nairobi. Roadwork campsites were haunted by animal spirits of shetani the demons; rail workers came face to face with rhinos at Mtito Andei and buffaloes on the Athi Plains. The man-eaters of Tsavo were demons in lions' clothing that prowled the night. Shetani! They had no manes. African maneaters were male lions in female bodies like Indian witches. Animal spirit witches. Men-witches in female bodies who walked backwards in Africa as they did in India! Did they too come with us like the crows? Did they follow us as spirits do? Tales of African lions flowed into tales of saffron beasts of the jungles of Gir in Saurashtra. How they would spirit into villages or wait to ambush a farmer returning home! How they would selectively pick a coolie at the rail camp or the farmer's young wife returning from the river! How they would vanish into the thin night air to devour the human prey! How like the tigers they behaved!

Wild animals of the forests and savannah had personalities in the legends that they walked. I walked with them into African bush and Indian jungles. Elephant stories were about their long memories and buffalo stories about their unpredictable temperament. The memory of the elephant was such that she never forgot a wrong done to her, especially by humans. She would hunt you all your life and get you in the end; the raging buffalo sprayed her acid urine on you by spinning her tail when you climbed up the tree; the regal lion did not harm you unless he was hungry. But the vengeful cheetah would pounce on you whether she was hungry or not. Trickery of baboons, misty tree ghosts, unidentifiable poisonous reptiles, bad-luck and good-luck creatures populated the African nights outside my house in Nairobi, as they did in Dadabapa's Indian Haripur of his mind. There were also endless stories about scorpions and thread thin snakes that nestled in shoes for the night, or in the bed, and sometimes in the washbasins.

Indian animal stories blended into African animal stories. Indian spirit stories blended into African spirit stories. Indian politics – tales of heroes and traitors, blended into African politics - tales of heroes and traitors. Therefore, the magic of Africa became larger in mysteries conjured up in my mind by stories from the old country and Kenya, where I was born.

Then there was a story of one Iqbal Khan, who unknowingly carried his bistro bedding from Voi rail station to Nairobi with a cobra in it that horrified his wife, whose searing shrieks sent a panic through the railway quarters. On hearing the commotion, the town folk spilled out into the streets. They were armed with sticks, spades, machetes and rungu clubs, beating metal pots, and carrying lanterns and fire torches prepared to chase what they imagined to be a lion. Some were heard yelling, "Drive him back to the bushes beyond Ol-ng'arua swamps where he belongs!" It would not have been the first time that the men would have had to push the Embakasi lion back to the plains.

Here in the valley of Ol-ng'arua, at sunrise you would see Punjabis tending vegetables of all sorts – cabbage, eggplant, tomatoes, okra, and a variety of leafy edibles. Here you would hear washermen's families – men, women and children - slapping cloth on the flat river rocks. Early in the morning, before sunrise, they would descend from the sprawling dhobi quarters at the ridge across the Ol-ng'arua swamp that they called Nagara, and the town planners mapped it as Ngara, the Indian area.

Then there were other stories, merchant stories I listened to when I was a girl. These were told like legends of the jamat of East Africa. Dadabapa told me about a man called Sewa Haji Paroo known as the Merchant King of the Coast, whose heart was as large as his trade. He talked about the beads and goods caravans of Allidina Visram that he had seen camp at the Nairobi River. Here the carriers of the foot safaris watered their donkeys and lay their heads down to rest. Allidina Visram apprenticed young dhow stowaways and runaways who came penniless, escaping fate or simply compelled by adventure that seizes the heads of youth. He fed them, gave them shelter and taught them how to trade in the interior. In time, the boys matured and became shrewd bush businessmen. They ventured towards the jungles of the Mountains of the Moon and the northern frontier, to the deserts of Somaliland and towards mysterious Abyssinia, the land of the Queen of Sheba. They went to the southern frontiers beyond the depth of the Ngorongoro crater. Many carried beads to start a business as they were taught, to find a path into the depth of the interior and make a living. Then there were also those who perished without a trace of who they were and where they came from.

Dadabapa was one such boy who learned to trade working with Allidina Visram, the man who they called the Merchant King of the Interior. You would often hear him say that the greatest of all community sewa service in the memory of the Satpanth Ismailis, were of these men called the Merchant Kings of East Africa. "Was it not men like these and their wives who often managed the beads, who brought in the British Empire into the networks of their ancient trade connecting Asia and Africa? Then the Empire absorbed them.

Were they not the ones who taught the Khojas to trade?" he would ask.

The boyhood apprenticeship in trade also laid the footing of the itinerant bead merchant of East Africa. Eventually, this paved the way towards the emergence of the Khoja rural stores in faraway scattered places from the Indian Ocean towards the Atlantic. Thus, came about the Satpanth trading community, the bead merchant and his wife, the Bead Bai, who lived at the equator in Africa and raised a family.

In Dadabapa's narratives told to children, there were no tales of natives killing or wounding any of thousands of the Indian indentured workers and craftsmen along the railroad. No tales were of natives killing dukawalas who traded in remote villages between Mombasa and the Mountains of the Moon where the British Empire bordered Belgium's African kingdom. There were no such a story told to us sitting by the kitchen stove because there was none to tell.

Between stories of Africa, Dadabapa also spoke about Saurashtra, the Saurashtra of the mind that he lived in that we imagined. Often at mealtimes, he would remind us about the covenant of dharma. Every month on the evening of the new moon called chandraat, he would offer prayer of shukhar over milk and wheat chapattis in gratefulness of the month's roji, meaning nourishment. In addition, he would ask for unity of the broken community, peace of the founding fathers buried in Africa and shukhar to the land for its bounty.

Part Two

Indian Nairobi

As regards the Indian Bazaar ... Damp, dark, unventilated, overcrowded dwellings on the filth-soaked and rubbish-strewn ground housed hundreds of people of most uncleanly habits who loved to have things so, and were so let. Here was the soil, the "good soil" for the reception and free propagation of the plague once introduced. (Report by Dr Spurrier, Medical Officer, Nairobi 1902).

Later, it was again noted in the Nairobi Health and Sanitary Report about the appalling conditions in the Indian working class areas.

The houses, or better tin sheds for they lacked windows, were used indiscriminately as dwellings houses, shops, stores, laundries, wash-houses, opium dens, bakeries, brothels, butchers shops etc., etc. The amounts of goods stored varied from 800-1,000 tons, rats abounded, and the general conditions of life of the 1,500-2,000 inhabitants were miserable and filthy in the extreme. (Report by Dr W J Radford, the Chief Sanitary Commissioner, Nairobi 1904).

NAIROBI, MASTER PLAN FOR A COLONIAL CAPITAL. REPORT BY
PROFESSOR L.W. THORNTON WHITE ET AL, LONDON 1948.

8

Story of Sohn Bai

When the clock strikes the last quarter of the night, I am awake to the shuffles of Dadabapa getting ready for the rituals of dawn worship. I hear hyenas crunching into the rubbish heap in the alley behind Jugu Bazaar. My sister, Monghi and brother, Shamshu, sleep on my bed in Dadabapa's room. Hawa, our Swahili maid, sleeps on a gunnysack in the all sheet iron kitchen at the back of the stone house. Noordin Kaka uncle, his wife and two children, all sleep together in another room attached to our stone built room at the side. Its three other walls are made of sheet iron painted green.

Dadabapa lights the kerosene lamp hanging on a hooked wire from the ceiling before he begins to chant the morning raga. My father and Ma are asleep on a mattress in the shop next to our one-room home. Every night my Ma drags the cotton mattress into the shop and spreads the merikani sheets over it. In the morning, she drags the mattress back into the room and pushes it behind grandfather's bed until nightfall.

Dadabapa lights two sandalwood incense sticks and pokes them into the corners of the framed photograph of boy Saheb. In the picture, Saheb is sitting on takht, a spacious wooden divan, wearing a black cap and a silk robe with a high collar and intricately embroidered gold border. The photograph is hanging from a wood moulding that runs round the four stonewalls. Dadabapa engrosses in divine seeing while bringing his hands together whispering prayers for strength of that day, peace and contentment of shukhar for yesterday. In this holy picture, a jamat of barefoot Satpanth murids in robes and turbans, stand around the square divan, their hands folded in homage.

He lights one more stick that is also sandalwood and pokes it at a corner of my grandmother's photograph in a glass frame where two sides meet. Her photograph hangs besides Saheb's own picture. Gradually, the incense wafts over the stench from the alley that had rolled into the room when Dadabapa opened the door to go to the toilet in the courtyard. He speaks to his wife, my grandmother Sohn Bai in the picture. Each day, he would name her favourite fruit, a mango or passion fruit and a few of her favourite vegetables of which there were many - spinach, eggplant, okra, methi, bitter karela, cabbage, cauliflower, that he would take to the jamat khana that evening for the prayer offering on her behalf. "You will like what I will bring for you today," he would say to the photograph. The two pictures have brownish gold stains on the glass where the glows of the incense sticks twirl up dense wood smoke before they die.

After his salutations to the Saheb and my grandmother, Dadabapa would usually drink a glass of water, blow out the kerosene lamp and sit still on his bed, legs crossed, inside the fold of his blanket composing himself for an hour of stillness in meditation. Dadabapa's Swahili bed with tiled headboard is the highest piece of furniture in the house. It is also the most elegant piece of furniture. Occasionally he groans, shuffles, coughs, belches, and farts when he changes positions from his left leg over the right to his right leg over the left.

I hear my father snoring in the shop. Shamshu throws his arms around and cries in his dream. He is fighting with someone he curses. Unclean words at this hour of God. My sister Monghi turns in her sleep and breathes out a groggy lullaby, lala - lala … mm … mm … several times putting herself to sleep in her dream. A little later, she too snores, slightly and irregularly. I keep my eyes closed and listen to the sounds of the dying night. Puppies, early risers too, yelping, swirling in chase of their ribbon tails in the adjacent courtyard of the Pir Bhai family; hyenas grumping, grunting and wading in the open sewage outside the walled courtyard on their way back to the scrubland between the Indian River Road and African Kariokor area. There is an uneasy cackling of chicken in the wire mesh box, which Ma had Tara Singh make for her. Now it stands in the corner of the courtyard by the zambarua tree. In the evenings, I watch our calm and colourful fowl return home led by the proud cockerel of burnt sienna and red chilli hot colour plumage. I secure the latch on the little door before I run to the evening classes. That was the routine and my work.

When Dadabapa ends his meditation, he lights a cigarette. It will be his only cigarette of the day. By then, it's six in the morning and I hear Ma cracking charcoal pieces to fit into the stove. Strong crispy whiffs of Indian bidi streak through the dry sandalwood scent that has filled the room. Now grandfather sits cross-legged in his blanket, thinking, as he smokes waiting for his sons and grandchildren to join him for the morning singing.

Whenever we hear the sound of a clearing throat, in a series, we know his thoughts are sad. However, Dadabapa's throat clearing is not always a disturbing sound from inside. More often, he fakes khokharo to announce his presence like when he approaches Ma to give her time to draw her pachedi over her head in laaj, or when he is in the toilet, and hears footsteps coming in his direction.

"He sniffs in his tears like an English memsaheb crying," comments Ma as I enter the kitchen. True, he sniffs and sighs in rhythms regulated by his inhales and exhales; sometimes it is a cough with a wheeze in-between. Then he grates his throat as if to clear the irritation of tears dripping on his tonsils. "He makes those sounds whenever he is emotional … pirshah, pirshah, pirshah," Ma comments again. Then as if smarted by a sudden thought, Ma says a tasbih of pirshah for peace for Dadabapa. The three silver gunguru bells on the two-faced medallion tinkle soft clink clink in the rhythm of Om shanti, shanti … pirshah … pirshah … Om Ali.

Perhaps Dadabapa is thinking about my grandmother. Her name was Sohn Bai of the village of Amreli. Gor Bai, my stepmother, would tell me the story of my grandmother when we are alone in the kitchen dicing mangoes, lime, chilies, sticky green gundah and carrots for making pickles. Pickles take a long time to prepare, are made in large amounts meant to be preserved and eaten in small amounts over three to six months. Ma had heard some of Sohn Bai's long story from my Kaki Bai auntie, wife of my Noordin Kaka uncle and mother of my cousin-sister, Malek, and cousin-brother Bahdur. Meethi Bai, her friend, told her some of Sohn Bai's tale too,

53

and the rest she had gathered from the women in the bazaar and the jamat khana. Ma Gor Bai herself had not seen my grandmother but she spoke about her as if she had always known her. When ancestral stories are told, especially the way Ma tells them, they fill my life making my own story complete:

Grandmother Sohn Bai looked after the neighbour's family in Jugu Bazaar when the epidemic struck. The parents and their three children all had high fever that was first thought to be malaria, but when Dr. Ribeiro did the tests, he found it was plague. Your Dadabapa remembers Dr Ribeiro, the beloved doctor of Nairobi, who made his rounds on a zebra, checking on families in their homes, giving pills and taking notes. They say he was the one who first diagnosed some Somalis infected with bubonic plague and raised the alarm.

One day, something astonishing happened when Dadabapa came home after the evening prayers at the jamat khana. He found grandmother in her bed, covered with ash, looking black as charcoal and dead. He did not know if she had died of plague or if she had taken poison. She was a woman who never complained, so he never learned if she had a headache or fever. It is for this reason that Dadabapa called her Devi and sometimes Sati. In those days, all bodies had to be buried or burnt as quickly as possible by the order of the District Health Officer. There were rumours that the District Health Officer secretly urged those who were in close contact with the plague victims to take poison that killed them quickly and painlessly, so the disease would not kill their loved ones. However, no one knew for sure if this was true, because those who died suddenly before the fever killed them did not tell anyone. Dadabapa consulted a Kikuyu spirit woman who lived in Muthaiga's herb forest to find out about the death of your grandmother.

The Kikuyu spirit woman and Dadabapa were seen sitting, facing each other, under the acacia tree that people said was possessed and avoided it, especially in the evenings. The spirit woman read the intestines of a black goat while mumbling ritual words and shaking her calabash that talked. Three of them talked in deep whispers for a long time as if they were blowing wind into each other's words - the calabash, the spirit woman and Dadabapa. However, Dadabapa did not tell anyone about their conversation.

That was the year of the great plague of Nairobi when Jugu Bazaar was burnt down by the order of serekali the government, and Dadabapa lost most of his goods. Since the great plague, Dadabapa has been struggling to recover from the loss of his property and life's companion, your grandmother. They had been together since their marriage in Kuze jamat khana, in the old stone town Mombasa.

Part Three

Saga of the First Crossing

'Words from the ocean which our forefathers crossed as the first step to build our mosaic selves hoping more signs, more waves will reach our imagination, linked by one desire to reach man.'

Letter from Lyon dated 31st December, 1999 written by Khal Torabully, a poet descendant of coolie parents on the sugar plantations in Mauritius. Khal Torabully is the founder of Coolitude, a genre of literature that studies creative writings about the journeys and lives of Indian indentured labourers and making of the Empires in the Atlantic, Indian and Pacific Oceans from around 1856 after the first batch of Indian slaves arrived in South Africa to around 1920 when Indian indentured labour officially ended.

9

Losing the land

Whenever Ma Gor Bai hears Dadabapa's soft snorts and empty coughs, she would say he is thinking of his parents, small-scale peanut farmers of Haripur. Or could it be that he is thinking of his little brothers and sisters? I search the meaning behind his odd behaviour that fills me with uneasy sadness. Chap-panyo Dukar, the great famine of Saurashtra called the Famine of Fifty Six, twice impoverished his family. And repeated colonial taxes. It was not before my fourteenth birthday that I heard Dadabapa's inside story, the secret in him that he would not have told had he not fallen ill and wandered to the Saurashtra of his childhood in the concealed part of his mind. That was during the ten days when he was down with malaria, the bad type that seizes the mind. Dr Ribeiro said Dadabapa had to stay in bed and that someone should keep a watch over him all the time. I looked after him when he was hot and when he was cold. I looked after him when he had no sleep in his head and used to laze and loll on his back talking to the ghosts at the ceiling. Often, his hands would gesture stories unsaid that had stayed hidden inside him. When he spoke, it was as if he was reading pictures in the air:

When the drought of Chap-panyo prolonged, the earth turned hot everywhere, as far as you can see, so hot that it hardened into a rock and then it cracked in sharp edged pieces like a clay water pot. My father's last two cows died of thirst. Peanut plants turned brittle, nuts shrivelled and withered before the locusts came. Pests – I see black locust clouds over my head. Ma! Ma! She does not hear me. Then more pests - white grub infestation spreading like an epidemic scarab at the roots. Working all together, my father and me, all my brothers and sisters, working hard, we try to salvage the frugal crop and put it into sacks. However, the colonial agents carry away the gunnysacks of our dwindled harvest in payment of taxes my father cannot pay in rupees. We are forced to sell our wooden plough and tools to buy food, and even water.

Khojas, Jains, Patels, Bohoras and Lohanas from our village and the surrounding villages are leaving for Africa. Then a second famine scourges the fields in the middle of the great emigration. Banias close the shops and move out of villages. Then peasant farmers, potters, masons, tinsmiths, goldsmiths, dhobis, cobblers, barbers and carpenters begin to leave in large numbers. Even the low caste cleaners, the churas, the untouchables of Saurashtra, who lived at the fringe of Haripur, are now leaving for Africa with their families. I see them walking away in the heat from the cloudless sky, and then I hear the frenzied Brahmin pleading,

"Who will remove the dog's carcass, four days old, rotting, stinking at the temple's steps?" The ayurvedic doctor left yesterday with a bag full of pounded leaves and roots, and then the priests carefully wrapped their scriptures and temple deities in padded cloth packages, lifted them onto their shoulders, and went. They did not so much as glance at the three dogs, mere rib cases, eating the rotting entrails of the dog at the temple steps. The dogs took turns to turn around to show their greatly exaggerated canines and snarl at the crowd of vultures and crows daring to pick into the carcass. The midwife Ramba Bai left with her potlo bundle balanced on her head. We saw the thief Magan jump onto the priests' cart and then we did not see him again in Haripur. The revolutionaries took their raging hearts to Africa, and fiery verses tucked in their turbans. With them left the village poet and scholar with his ink, paper, holders and nibs in three sizes. Only the weavers and dyers remained behind. Some moved towards Jamnagar, Bhuj and Surat. And the Siddis remained too. Every morning I saw Siddis passing by our village walking in groups towards Junagadh, carrying cloth bundle potlas on their heads, wares on shoulders and babies at the hips.

Dadabapa's eyes do not move. What was it that he was saying? Was it a dream? Or was it real? Or was it a fantasy that wishes tend to create when you are weak in the head? Or was it a mirage conjured in adult mind out of suppressed childhood guilt? I get worried because I have never seen him act like this. Sometimes, I can hear clearly, what he says, and sometimes it sounds as garble to my ears. Whatever he says, when he speaks, he does not even blink to hold in the tear coming down his unshaven cheeks as he speaks in croaky whispers:

My mother and sisters went to the weavers' colony behind the jamat khana and spun cotton, dyed and dried the yarn for export. Their wages barely provided rice enough to feed the family. Should the rains come, we would not have seed for the next season because the rats had eaten into father's storage. Thirsty rats then died in the village wells while making desperate stabs to reach the water drops oozing out at the walls. Their cadavers polluted our little remaining drinking sources. Those young men who had left during the previous drought arrived with the desiccated monsoons. Some came to collect their families, some to get married, and some to pay back loans that helped them to reach Africa. Now before they return, they would recover their family jewellery from the village pawnbroker and carry it with them. They said sweet water, milk and honey flowed in Africa like rivers from the Himalayas, and that one could eat one good meal a day. At the women's satsang meetings, they discussed the famine and the great emigration of families out of Kutch and Gujarat. Elders sat in separate panchayat councils according to their castes. They sat around their own chosen village peepal tree the whole day long, discussing what they heard and what wisdom they knew from the teachings in the scriptures and what the astrologers told them. My grandfather, once the mukhi of Haripur, reminded the Khoja panchayat council once again, how much Saheb desired for us to leave Kutch and Gujarat for Africa. No sooner had he spoken than a multitude of questions assails him like

61

bullets from a barrel, "How can we abandon the land of our ancestors? How can we break the bond with the earth that is sacred? Here the pirs sought ginan in the song of the gurus of Hindustan under the peepal tree and hill temples. Who will tend the fields when the rains come? Who will clean the wells? How can we cross Kala Pani that protects our motherland?" Some put their fears into questions. Others show their reluctance to abandon their fields through their questions. And there were those who hoped the famine will pass. After all, famines have always come and gone, but their forefathers never deserted the land. "How can we leave the land where our prayers rest at the pir's shrine? How can we desert the sacred trees where our umbilical cords are buried? Who will pay our debts? How do we abandon the jamat khana? How can we…?" How can we this and how can we that? Their questions are endless and though there were no answers, they continue to ask why this and why that, as if their questions would delay the inevitable emigration. The elders' shifting eyes expressed doubts such as those that come from the fright of loss of direction of one gone astray in a jungle. Then someone asked a different question that made the panchayat assembly think again, "Why is it that every caste around Haripur is going to Africa but the African Siddis are not?" More doubts were now expressed in questions about the Siddis, "Why are the Siddis staying behind? What will they eat? Where will they get the water from?" These questions silenced all for a while before they began asking again, "Do they know something we don't? Do they eat people in

Africa? Will the English enslave us to work in mines and on plantations?" The elders shook their heads from side to side dole dole in agreement, "Yes there must be a reason why they are not leaving." Finally, the panchayat council sent Mota Bhai to enquire from the Siddis why they do not leave Saurashtra for Africa yet they had no food in their granaries.

When Mota Bhai returned, his hands were trembling; his voice shook when he told the panchayat what the Siddis said to him. "Our forefathers worked this land and fought for dignity. Here they served, ruled, cleared the jungle and built forts so we may live with pride," they said. "Our ancestors protect us now. If we leave, who will bring the unshaven coconuts and incense smoke to their altars? Who will dance the goma? Whom shall we consult when our children are born and their destinies made? Whom shall we consult at marriages? Whom shall we consult at funerals? Yes, we are hungry, and yes, there is no food in our granaries, but our ancestors reside here. This land is ours and we are free."

The Siddis then put questions to Mota Bhai that he said he not only had no replies to but also had never before even thought about. They asked, "How could the panchayats of Saurashtra, who had never been enslaved or dispossessed of their country, know what was in the hearts of the Siddis? How could they understand the African custom that revere the land where their ancestors are buried not cremated? Did the Indians have slave memories like those of the Siddis? Did their ancestors walk in coffles under the blazing sun? Ancestors, exhausted, beaten, starved and

63

sleeping in coffles? Ancestors, in coffles made to copulate to replenish the slave stock for their masters." Then a Siddi elder who was so thin and weak that he could not stand without shaking even when holding a stick, asked, "How could they? Their heads are full of what the English did to the Indians, not what the Indians did to the Africans."

Sometimes, in his awake dreams, Dadabapa's talk was just questions. Sometimes, the questions answered themselves and sometimes they created doubts because the answers were never said:

How could the elders of the Khoja panchayat have imagined an exodus of this scale when there was no mention of losing the land in oral histories so carefully handed down by the learned keepers of stories, genealogies and songs of Saurashtra? Even the Ramayana and Mahabharata did not predict a migration such as the one we were witnessing. Even the sages who cautioned about Kal Yoog, the Age of Blackness, that many believed was close at hand, were lost for words. It is true that the astrologers, reading the changing web of stars, warned about the coming calamities, something that was destined to happen in the age of Kal Yoog. But did they know about losing the land?

Over the next days, Dadabapa would speak to the pictures that people sick with malaria see. He would speak in between the heat and cold of his body, and like his fluctuating fever, his thoughts would come and go, connect and not connect. When he felt hot, I would paste cool henna on his soles. When he was cold, his teeth chattered, and he made himself small, pressing his knees to his chest as if he was hiding from the demons of illness. I would throw one more quilt on him, bring the charcoal stove from the kitchen and place it near his bed. There seemed to be no day or night in his dreams. I got used to waking up when he was restless, and sleeping when he was at peace in his mind, whether it was during the day or middle of the night. Once, around midnight Dadabapa spoke again, having not spoken the whole day. I thought he had no more to say but he spoke while everyone was asleep. This story kept me awake imagining the India of his childhood:

That evening my mother removes her siri – a small cent-size diamond studded nose button, and her two silver anklets, the last three pieces of adornment on her that was our farm's security should the tax collectors seize the land because of unpaid head and land taxes as they did to Nagji Bhai's and then Kanji Bhai's farms. Both our neighbours.

"Take these, son," she says to me, "they will pay your passage to Africa."

"And with this, son, buy your paper," says my father handing me some loose silver King Emperor coins and Kutch koris in a cloth pouch. He cries more than my mother does. He is letting his first-born son go. The one destined to care for the family field, to care for him in old age, to keep the forefather's name honouring the lineage. That's how it had always been. That's how our family history was told as father to son inheritance of one hundred peanut plants. He cries because he has no money to see me married so I could have at least left my seed behind as Mukhi Nanji Bhai's and Jeraj Samji Bhai's sons had done to continue their lineages before they went to Africa. That was custom. Then it would not have been so hurting to my father. He would have played horse with my son riding on his back. Carried him to the field on his shoulders like how he carried me when I was little. That would have assuaged the pain of his loneliness that stuns aged parents when their children as migrants leave and do not return when adults. Such was the loss of a son for my father."

Dadabapa talks while looking straight at the vacant ceiling as if he were in the past. Sometimes, he stares at me without a blink in his wide opened eyes. Malaria conjures such hallucinations in the eyes that they watch you like a vulture and do not see you. Sometimes Dadabapa's talk made no sense and it frightened me, and I tried to hush him, but Ma Gor Bai thought it was better for his mind to speak out what he had held within for so long. So I let him speak into the first light of dawn that fell like dimmed lantern flame through the grilled window frame:

> When the time comes to leave, I hold my parents' feet as I make a promise that I am going to Africa to look for work, and will return with riches. I weep as I take the earth at the base of the family neem tree where my ancestors had toiled with their bare hands, and earned a living that sustained both the lineage and honour. We worked the land, generation after generation, and seeded it; we harvested, and offered prayers of santosh invoking names of ten avatars over the harvest. Our offering was wheat and milk, a portion of the fruit of the labour of the farmer's toil, a prayer on a clay plate for the peace of our forefathers, as they had offered the fruit of labour of their toil at

the same village jamat khana. As peasant farmers do at shrines in India. We, who work the land with our hands, revere customs that keep us close to the land. This was bequeathed to us to uphold. The Earth is the keeper of our faith and customs. "We have never begged a morsel from the jamat," my father tells me. "You too will uphold the family honour. That is our custom and trust in Saheb the Sarkar." I hold the earth in my fisted hand, press it to my left and right eye, and then between the eyes on the forehead asking the land permission to leave, asking its forgiveness for leaving, and then its blessings on the unknown journey over the Black Waters. In that gesture, I pay my homage to the land and say shukhar to creation the sacred with my head below my heart like the village Sufi. I make a silent oath to our ancestral field that I will return to restore its health, beauty and prosperity as it was before the drought wrenched it all out of her like how the butcher drains out the blood of the slaughtered animal. My parents, sister and brothers weep when they see me, the eldest male child, the provider of bread, keeper of family stories and honour, their elder brother and their mentor, climbing onto Karsan Bhai's bullock cart. My thirteen-year-old sister who was given away in marriage to a widower, a textile merchant three times her age, because of our poverty, arrives to bid me farewell just when the wooden wheels creak to turn. We called her Dholki for she talked too much like a drum. We weep because we know in our hearts that I am losing the land, I am breaking the bond of lineage nurtured by the ancestral field. In all these, I am losing the family – my parents and all my brothers and sisters. My heart cries for it knows I am overlooking the promise of my birth not because I want to but because I have to.

Dadabapa cries profusely. I hold up his head to give him water. He shakes, though he has no fever and that scares me. I hear Ma Gor Bai at the stove and call her to come quickly. "Forgive me, forgive me," he says repeatedly and weeps calling me his mother. Ma Gor Bai standing by me, with a chaikop in her hand, tells me to let him weep. However, I tell her I do not have her heart in me to let my grandfather cry. How could I? I had never been a migrant.

"Sometimes, it is necessary to cry out the secrets held unspoken for so long," she tells me. Then, sitting on the edge of his bed, we wait for Dadabapa to continue which he does after a while having regained his strength:

Karsan Bhai cracks the whip and yells to the bulls to move. My family holds on to the cart while they walk with it to the stone that marks the end of our field. I feel something in me break as I leave the ground where my relations are buried and where I would have been buried at the roots of the neem tree. My mother's wails sear the honeyed quietness of the coming dawn. I feel weak at this hour of peace when the jamat in my village wakes to meditate and greet the new day. I press my ears in my palms to keep away the metrical turns of the wooden wheels, creaking melancholically out of Haripur. I sob and bury my face into the bundle of clothes my mother had packed so neatly in a clean bed sheet that releases a fresh smell to the warmth of my tears. 'Do not weep, son,' says Karsan Bhai.

I knew Karsan Bhai almost as well as I knew my own father and he always called me 'beta, son'. My friends used to joke about how Karsan Bhai ate with his whiskers that stretched over his cheeks from ear to ear. 'Where are his lips?' we used to ask each other because no one had ever seen his lips. He looks at my saddened face and his eyes well. He speaks to comfort me, "With heavy heart, I have taken boys like you to the railway station at dawn. All boys who leave for Africa know they will not see their mother again; she too knows she will not see her son again. I tell them to open their eyes when they feel the pain and fill them with this land of their ancestors not with tears, and keep her there. The land is a mother too." The cart trundles around the curves; the oxen lumber along the stony roads, snorting to the cold in the breeze pushing the darkness away like smoke. Karsan Bhai clicks his tongue, bellows out 'Chalo rey chalo!' and cracks his whip to the oxen's ears over their gaily painted horns. 'All emigrants leave their mothers behind, shanti, shanti, shanti.' He mumbles to the breeze to take his pain away with the night so he must do what he has come to do. "O my Mowla, why have you given me this charge of severing umbilical codes?" he says and immediately begins the prayer for peace, "Pirshah, pirshah, pirshah ..."

I do not want to hear Karsan Bhai. I do not want to see the withered peanut bushes I had planted with my father; the mango tree I loved to climb; the rocks on which I had lain and watched the sky for the monsoon clouds laden black against the golden sun sailing in over our fields before the famine came. I would be the first to run home and sing to my mother:

Mother, mother come and see
Gir's saffron beast has given birth in the sky
I see his black mane in a gold ring

I hear the hoofs of the oxen breaking into the caked mud pools and know they are flanking along the bank of River Una that irrigates our field. I know every stone along the bank and every tree where we hung our clothes when we went swimming. I know the spot where Rajan, the best swimmer among us, drowned in the monsoon floods that had swept weeds and uprooted plants from upcountry. Rajan got entangled in the undercurrents and we could not save him. We wept beyond the forty days of mourning and food offerings at the jamat khana. We were of the same age born thirteen years ago in midst of decades of great famines and wars of soldiers with fellow soldiers in the British army. The decades when millions perished and millions more left their homelands to slave on plantations and in mines of the Empire across the globe.

"Kemcho Sunderji Bhai?" Karsan Bhai yells out a greeting over his shoulder at a figure on the other side of the river. The man is wearing white Gujarati peasant clothes and turban standing alone in the cold haze that sits on the river before the break of dawn. The man yells back through the mist stretching out his arms but we cannot hear him against the wind whistling over Una's rocks and crevices. I hesitate to bid him farewell. He yells again with a gesture indicating he wants to embrace me goodbye.

70

Turning around, Karsan Bhai questions me with a puzzled look on his face. I stand up throwing my arms forward indicating I want to embrace him goodbye too. Then I see him squat on his haunches thumping his palms on his forehead the way Gujarati men cry the pain in their heart. I begin to sob again.

Sometimes Dadabapa varied the order of incidents in his life. Sometimes the details were repeated in mixed anecdotes gleaned during the trials of survival on the dhow to Africa, and then in Africa. Sometimes his stories were in songs like how the Satpanth missionaries tell the stories of guru-pirs to the night gatherings of the pious. Sometimes they came like nightmares that frightened me and sometimes they were like beautiful dreams. Dadabapa gazed into the past that made me invisible to him standing by his side. Sometimes he spoke of his past as if it was today and now. I did not feel I belonged to his India of 1903 the way he did. I did not know the peanut trees, his Haripur, his neem tree or the motherland of his childhood that he called Desh. The land of the Satpanth Khoja, the land he loved:

This was my land of the Satpanth Khoja, villagers of a common founding father, the Satguru Noor, the true guru and pir, the Light and Vishnu avatar above all. We made a faith knot of villages across Saurashtra, sang the song of creation, how life evolved from the fish to the amphibian turtle, animals and then came the human avatars who fought evil for sovereignty of the good. We danced Krishna's courtship dance, the garba, like it were a karmic circle- dha dhi na, dha tu na, and offered devotion in food, incense and flowers with shukhar on our lips. Once a year, neighbouring villages partook in a communal meal prepared by

71

women with veneration in their hearts and love in their hands, to serve the community and Saheb. Feeding the community called the jamat, is sewa and sharing a meal brings baraka of blessings to all givers and receivers of roji the morsel for sustenance of life.

Here is where I played gulidanda, jumped the river stones and bruised my knees. I snubbed and frowned when my mother scolded me because of my daring carelessness as she fixed turmeric paste over the cuts. Now I yearn to listen to her gentle reproach, words of anger so sweet to my ears today. Will I hear her caring reproaches again?

I know my family will be straining their ears to listen to the cheerless clinks of bells of the two bullocks fading into the sounds of twilight towards the British India Railway Station. Karsan Bhai removes his turban and puts it by his side like it were a hat built up in plastered layers, bands of cloth like a clay pot on a potter's wheel. The train will whistle at the station where the villagers are waiting under the banyan tree older than the station and it will take me to the vessel anchored at the port of Bombay waiting to sail to Africa. I know my brothers will be lying down. Their ears will be pressed to the ground, listening to the turn of the wheels groaning to the earth as I used to when my grandfather, the mukhi-elder of Haripur, went to Bombay on the same bullock cart of Karsan Bhai. He went to consult on conflicts over marriages broken by changing faith allegiances and new ownerships of community properties. This was when the Khoja jamat fractured and that hurt many because the faults ran through families and among those who loved each other the most and lived on the ancestral field.

Every evening, my father and Noordin Kaka uncle would come to sit by Dadabapa's bed. He was getting better and could look at you as if he sees you, but he still found it difficult to sit up on his bed with legs folded to say his dua prayer. He was becoming more conscious of his surrounding and calling me by my name and often in whispers blessing Ma Gor Bai and me. But his voice was weak and his hands shook bringing chai to his lips.

On one such evening, I heard Noordin Kaka uncle say in his usual style of the all-knowing preacher who should not be interrupted, "Was it not between those chaotic years of courtroom fights in Bombay that the Khoja, one people, one community, one family, all children of one Satguru-pir began first to argue among themselves and then fight, and then fragment? One group proclaimed to be Sunni Khoja, another Twelver Khoja and the third Satpanth Khoja." I look at Ma Gor Bai to say I do not understand what Noordin Kaka uncle is saying. I see her nodding her head drawing Kaka uncle's attention to her. Did she agree with him? Or was she just nodding to show she agreed to avoid an argument in the home the way mothers do? Sometimes mothers lie to keep peace and you don't know where they stand. I found myself following Ma Gor Bai's quietness of the inside and began nodding with her. "The dissidence brewing in India crystallized in Zanzibar and spread from family to family across East Africa. Families turned against each other. Cousins against cousins. Brothers would not talk to brothers. Fathers would not give their daughters in marriage to their village kinsmen of the 'other faith' of the Khoja. They said even drinking water from the home of a dissident relative was haram." I was curious to know more about the conflicts. However, the frequent 'mind how you speak' reminders from the adults in the family had me tongue-tied. Even Meethi Bai would occasionally throw a reminder when I wanted to say something. The reminders came simultaneously with other unexplained restrictions put on me - so many, so quickly. Like what I should wear to 'cover up', where I should not be seen going to, even to Rani Bagh with my girlfriends, like whom should I not be seen talking with. At times, my mind of a girl turning thirteen was in turmoil. My freedom was suddenly limited. My body was changing rapidly and I had no control over it.

Noordin Kaka uncle mistakes the quietness on the faces of the family audience to be our interest in his speech not shock. "Was Satguru-pir not the one who was declared variously a Sunni Moslem, a Shia Moslem, a Sufi and a Hindu of Bhagti practice or all these in one?" he asks. Was it to confuse us that he asks such a question? Or was it to put doubt in us about Satpanth that we knew to be the true faith?

"Who knows the truth but God himself?" replies Ma with a question to Noordin Kaka uncle. "But then who even knows the true imam? The living one or the disappeared one yet to come to save the world?"

Noordin Kaka uncle says nothing and walks away to his room. Was it that he does not know the answer or more likely, that he does not like to be confronted, especially by a woman to whom he does not even speak in the house?

I had many questions, but I dared not ask, though I listened carefully and quietly. My father listened carefully and quietly too, as that was his habit, but I am not sure if he understood or agreed with all that was said, and if he cared to know about conflicts among the Khojas. I am not sure if Dadabapa was listening either, or if he just let his son's words go because he had neither the energy nor the concentration he needed to listen. Had he been listening and had he had the strength, he would have been the only one who would have drawn Noordin Kaka uncle into an argument, man to man. If not, shut him up. He could do that because of parental respect that children must show. Anyway, Noordin Kaka uncle looked particularly red in the face that evening. From his clean black cotton pyjamas and knee long black shirt over it, I could tell he had been to the Ithna Asheri Khoja prayers at their mosque.

"It is this month when the Ithna Asheri Khoja moan the violent death of the Prophet's grandson Husein," Ma said to me when we were in the kitchen once again. We went to the kitchen not only to cook but also for privacy that women needed from men in the house. When I am quiet and listening to adult talk, Ma sees the questions in my eyes and tells me later in the kitchen what I want to know. "The decisive battle after the Prophet's death when Husein was killed affirmed not diminished Shia Islam. This month, the Shias moan Husein and celebrate the faith he left behind," she says.

During the month, much to Kaki Bai auntie's annoyance, Noordin Kaka uncle eats at the mosque where all Khojas, no matter what beliefs they hold, are invited to share a meal as one family people as was our tradition in the old country. Having feasted, they then listen to sermons from *Chiragh e Hidayat* about a new religion from Persia. Late at night, when the doors are locked and the churas have made their rounds and you know the hyenas are roving in the back alley, I hear hate words against Saheb coming from Noordin Kaka uncle's room. I cannot sleep thinking about Kaki Bai auntie and the pain in my beloved auntie's heart. Then a sudden thought comes to me. Jumping out of the bed, I come to check on Dadabapa. He is asleep. "Shukhar!" I say to him, "Your son will not upset you tonight." Dadabapa had slipped into his dreams of the old country or the journey across the Black Waters or something else I am yet to hear about. Perhaps he dreams about Sohn Bai, his wife who was my grandmother.

10

Crows on Board the Dhow

I give quinine to Dadabapa three times a day. In between, I hold him while he sits with his brown military blanket over his head, sniffing the steam of water boiled with the bark of the neem tree. Then after five days, Dadabapa breaks out in sweat every few hours. "He is on the path to recovery. Shukhar Mowla!" says Ma Gor Bai. I sigh and in it whisper a prayer of shukhar followed by pirshah, pirshah, pirshah for peace in the house. Dadabapa's voice is clear and much stronger now. I am not sure whether he speaks in a dream or not, because he keeps his eyes closed:

> When I arrive at the quay in Bombay, I am holding a paper bag close to my heart. In it is a seedling of a neem tree from our field that my father had carefully uprooted, moistened the roots and wrapped it in a brown paper bag with a handful of soil. "Water the tree every three days at the roots, just one cupped hand." His words rumble in my ears. "The tree, like all trees, is the source to regain strength. When you are

weak from sweating in the heat of the fiery sun of Africa, imagine sitting under the tree's shade to sip a little water and recover the moisture in your body. Then you know the tree that shades you comes from where you come from. To know that is strength."

At the visa office, I pay for the paper to leave India.

"How old are you?" asks the man at the desk.

"Thirteen."

"Say you are sixteen," he says pointing to the floor near his legs where there is a cloth bag with coins in it. I drop a Kutch kori in it.

"Where were you born?"

"Haripur."

"Have you a letter from office saheb?" I keep quiet. "Say Bombay when you are asked." He says and points to the bag again. I drop another Kutch kori in it.

The man shows me where to press my thumb on the document. He stamps the paper. Another man grabs my arm, unfurls the sleeve and injects a needle. "Cholera," he says pushing me to move on. I walk on half dazed.

Arab crafts are docked in an array. There are Arab, Persian and Bhadala sailors loading the vessels with textiles, grain, spices, rice, flour, metal containers and construction material. There are jute sacks filled to the brim with onions, rice, cabbages and potatoes. Bird catchers in hitched up, curled-over-waist dhotis and

78

oversized turbans are haggling over prices of crows in cages hanging from their shoulder poles. I know the black crows of Saurashtra are sacred because they carry ancestral spirits. Was it not the crow that offered to disguise Yama, the God of Death, in his sleek feathers and escape the demon king Ravana? Since then, in my village, the crow is venerated in the hope of deceiving death. From the coolie's back, a raucous murder of crows heaving in a basket cage, fluttering black silk feathers, cawing kaa-kaa-kagrow, foreboding death and bringing hope, is loaded up onto the deck and left there in the raging sun. I feel comforted. My ancestral spirits will sail with me and protect me.

I was surprised to see Siddis of Saurashtra leaving India for the first time now after their arrival as slave soldiers in the rajas' armies. But listen, they speak a language I have not heard before! Who are these dark people? The question stays in my mind.

Dadabapa's speech deepens into memories that flirt in the fresh alertness of his mind that recovering from sickness brings to the head. His voice fluctuates with every sentence depending on the feelings it carries like how the intonations of Gujarati syllables change with every serif, side curve, under loop or a stroke with an eye. His face expressions and the feelings he gives to the words alter each time, even when it is the same story that he is repeating. He reads the pictures in his mind that he has kept like treasures hidden within the labyrinth of a mountain cave:

In the chaotic bustle are families who have travelled from far distant Punjab, Baluchistan and Afghanistan, now patiently squatting by the crafts. I hear sailors standing by the vessels shouting Muscat, Bandar Abas and Zanzibar. Shy brides bound for Africa sit in a clump wrapped in folds of red saris peeping inquisitively through laaj masking their darting child looks. When lifting their laaj to enquire the scene, their black pearl eyes gleam below the sari's zari glazing over their foreheads. Standing alert over them are young men in white turbans waiting for their time to embark with their family luggage and their brides. Their eyes in quiet anxiety stay on the dhows.

Food vendors push hand carts over broken pebbles and cement; ringing bells, spilling steaming tea, and crying out in sing songs - hot bhajia…hot samosa ... sand roasted grams … juicy mangoes … fresh sugarcane. Smells envelop me like a bubble - piquant peppery fried and curried. People are dictating letters to scribes who would address them according to instructions. "Listen carefully and write precisely," they would tell the scribes. The letters are addressed to some lost loved ones with the hope they would be delivered to Daave's Veesi Eating House in Mombasa. Sometimes the photograph of a betrothed village girl or a young wife is slipped in with a note at the back. In pearly Gujarati, it says, FORGET ME NOT. SO MANY FULL MOONS HAVE PASSED IN LONELINESS. I BEG YOU COME SOON. SAVE ME FROM THE WIDOWS' ASHRAM. They hope a relative or a villager would see the letter, recognize the village of the sender and convey the message or at least send back home a word about the fate of their loved ones. Little does the betrothed one know that her fiancé may have drifted away to a faraway place in the interior while looking for work along the old slave and ivory caravan route. Or that he may have died, or that he may have already had a wife from Africa, and a family of his own.

Then there were Indian workers of all religions and castes arriving from the Arabian and Indonesian Seas. I see many people. So strange are their faces with skins that change colours like chameleons in the sun. I stare at the girls with pale white faces and narrow slanting eyes; young women with red, gold and silver hair, their skins pink under umbrellas over their heads though there is no rain. Some without lips, only painted lines around their mouths. Then suddenly, but cautiously, a shuffling of feet, people stepping back giving way to the English soldiers in tight khaki pants, khaki jackets with many pockets and buttons, and long leather boots, arriving at the quay. I too take steps back not knowing what is happening. Quietness falls over us as if a cloud of fear has fallen from the sky. What do the English soldiers want? The question is on everyone's face. They look around over us with master-over-slave eyes. They look through the crowds just disembarked and moving in hordes with their luggage in all sorts of packages, to the port's health check line-ups. Finally they come to the foreign women, call out names I have never heard before, and escort them like important guests to the Indian Army horse carriages. Someone says, "Cantonment women." It's the man in white Gujarati paatoloon like mine, whispering to his wide eyed wife. I notice he has two English suitcases and tucked under his arm is a wad of folded copies of *Bombay Samachar*. His wife like me and most of the other passengers carry potlo cloth-bundled luggage.

I hear Dadabapa's words and imagine the pictures of his mind. Ma joins me whenever she can. "Your Dadabapa's story reminds me of my own," she would say. "This is how it was when I climbed onto the dhow at the quay in Bombay. I joined a woman's group, of which there were many, as many sitting separately as there were castes and religions on board the dhow, and I stayed with one of Khoja women and brides all the way to Zanzibar." Then as if in self-talk, she would add each time, said differently, "There is no absolute new country in an immigrant's mind. Even when I say I have left India it is not without some part of it that I have come with within me that I return to in my dreams like your Dadabapa."

In the breadth of my girl's imagination, I would animate Dadabapa's tales into realms of adventure, unaware that in the thrills of listening to my family stories, there were hidden lessons of life. It was from such listening moments that I learned how to pass on the music of the story. Dadabapa was not only a teacher but also an artist of words. Even during his illness, he was a storyteller who came from another realm; every sentence from his lips flared my imagination. He spoke with passion as if suddenly, the illness freed his caged words that came out of his mouth with his caustic breath:

"Deep in my heart I have a hope that my sons, Noordin and Husein, will one day return to our ancestral village of Haripur and restore the dignity to their kinfolk and the land."

Dadabapa sighed in between his words but his sons were not around to listen to his hope. He was probably conscious of that because he had recovered enough now to finish a meal sitting crossed legged on his bed.

When I walked over the plank from the quay onto the dhow, I had no idea where it would lead me. The dhow was called NYOTA. I only knew it was going to Africa. It was a boat with a blue crescent moon and white star painted at the bow, where two boards carved in geometrically notched patterns, came together at its tapered nose. Later I learned that NYOTA YA BAHARI LA HINDI, the dhow's full name, meant STAR OF THE INDIAN OCEAN. In short, we called her Nee-ota. A wail of cries bidding farewell rises from the pier followed by echoes in sobs and howling laments of women walking back and forth from the prow to the sideboards. Families gather below us, crack open coconuts letting the shells fall and dissolve their offerings, pleading for safe voyage over the flexing waves.

It is time to set sail. The crew prepares to pull in the plank when a shrill whistle blow cuts through the pandemonium. From aboard the dhow, our eyes turn and fix upon five handcuffed prisoners walking in a single file followed by two turbaned guards with firearms. Captain Ahmed signals his men to let them on board. I hear the man in Gujarati paatoloon tell his fair wife that the captain was under obligation to carry this additional human cargo. He said India recently passed the much-debated COLONIAL PRISONERS REMOVAL TO EAST AFRICAN PROTECTORATE ACT that he had been following with keen interest. This man who had been by my side all this time spoke the act in English like a mantra as if to impress his young bride. However, it might not be, because he spoke loudly enough for those around him to cock their ears and tilt their heads to catch his words. I don't know if anyone understood the man but the attentive faces showed that the man was saying something important. We know from our village tax office that important government laws are spoken in English within the Gujarati sentence by learned office men. The man in the Gujarati paatoloon seemed to be such a learned office man.

Colaba Lighthouse blinks at the creek rocks, and then a haze covers its batting eye like laaj over it. The craft careens out of the white veil stuffing the funnel and into the waves of Kal-a Pani, Black Waters that come around us like muscled arms. Like Kal-i Mata, Black Mother, who lures human sacrifices into her embrace. Like Kal-yoog, Black Age heralding the transforming power of Black, the evil. One by one, the passengers drag into silence as if some impending dark cloud of destiny descended over them. What if what the Brahmins said about the dangers of crossing the Black Waters was true? What if we would have to live as outcastes, if we survived the Forbidden Sea? We were breaking the ancient taboo of India.

I look north to India through the haze. It is evening and my friends would be gathering at the mango tree to play hide and seek game of thapo. They would be standing in a circle and arguing how to continue the game we had left unfinished now that they were short of one runner, in fact the best runner of the team. Southwards, the gaze carries my tired eyes over to the mantle of green-blue-black waters holding the sheen of the red of dusk like rose petals in the worshipper's dusk palms. I turn around, fix my eyes southwards towards Africa, and see a crewman covering the crows' cage with a jute sack for the night.

11

There were three prostitutes at sea

Dadabapa falls into a deep slumber when talking exhausts him. On waking up, he asks for spiced chai and chapatti. He loves his chapatti rolled over ghee and jaggery that he dips in spiced chai relishing the taste with slush through his rounded lips. He wants to say more, quickly and continuously, in spite of Ma Gor Bai's hushed pleadings, "Rest after eating and talk a little at a time." Dadabapa would be quiet for a while but then it seemed like he had to talk to the pictures that were appearing to his awake and healed mind like how the artist sees colours in his head that he must paint. "It seems malaria has planted another mind in his head and now he cannot stop talking," says Step Mother Gor Bai. "His words thump my heart like his own. All immigrants share something that thumps our hearts in unison. Let him talk."

Dadabapa continues with his story when he was on board the dhow:

The craft rocks towards Africa in the light of the half-moon wavering over the waters. Gulzar Bai and Soneri Bai walk on their toes lifting their saris off the deck floor. They had no money to pay for their passage so they offered themselves to the captain. The

85

long journey tired the men and made them homesick. Captain Ahmed accepted.

Soon we began to gather in our caste and faith groups having thought about each other's names and villages carefully, and learned about each other from others on board the dhow. First, we shared stories here and there, building on comments and observations and learning to trust little by little. Then we observed what food each one had carried from home. We watched closely to read the ingredients, colour and textures. Later, when we were certain of each other's beliefs and castes, we ate together. We were suspicious and always cautious the way Indians are with other Indians on journeys, guarding the purity of our separate karmic paths because there were some criminals and some of lower castes on board who hoped to mingle and change their fortune. I learned that the man with Gujarati paatoloon, the one on whose private conversation with his fair wife I had quietly eavesdropped, is called Devji Momna, a fellow Satpanthi from the neighbouring village of Rajpur, who knows my family. I came to know the strange language I had heard spoken by the dark sailors at the wharf in Bombay is called Swahili. The people in Africa speak Swahili.

Rupa Bai, who is also known as Devdasi, waits until her son is asleep and then paces up to the lintel taking each step with a deliberate thud, jingling her ankle bells. She waits there below the flutter of the sail in the shadow of the mast hoping to make a few rupees that night. Her son sleeps alone, clasping a pillow in his arms. No man or woman on board would look after him because he is called God's child. Every morning Rupa Bai pays a little to the captain towards her passage to Africa. The captain does not charge her son.

The three women stay together on the dhow. I heard that they had arranged to run away from their destinies written on the walls of Ma Daam Begum's famous kotha in Bombay. They had planned together to escape to Africa but they had no money because Ma Daam Begum controlled the income of the brothel. They had heard stories of how other kotha women like them had managed to sail away in the dhow to the Indies, Fiji, South America and Africa. So they took a chance to freedom too.

From a dark corner of the lower deck, a convict sings to Gulzar Bai as she passes by him:

Tere pass aaneka iradha hey
Lakin aa nahi sakta
Mere pau baandhe huehey
Lakin dil awara hey
Aaj mey aa nahi sakta
Lakin ek din zaroor awunga
Tuje uthake ley chalunga

I have a desire to come to you
But I cannot come
My feet are chained
But my heart is free to wonder
Today I cannot come
But one day I will definitely come
Lift you up and take you with me

The song is lost on Gulzar Bai who wonders why someone should want to love her so much so, as to want to marry her, a prostitute. She was offering herself, not only because she had no money, but also because her husband betrayed her, choosing his new religion over her, making her impure absakan. Now she swirls in the cauldron of impurity, punishing her body, sometimes out of hate of religion, sometimes out of spite of society, but mostly out of sheer defiance against purity, as if in revenge against herself. She ignores the convict and treads quietly on. "He has no money to give me, only a song. A song will not pay my passage to Africa," she says loud enough for the convict to hear.

Two weeks go by and it will not be long before we would sight the African shoreline. The waters are calm, there is light rain and the gales fill the sails. A school of whales appears; they loiter about the waters contently basking their backs in the tropical sun. We wait for the sight of the first African seagulls and the smell of land to cheer up our spirits.

12

Deaths on Kala Pani

Dadabapa's eyes remain fixed at the space of the ceiling as though he were looking at the ocean. I thought the malaria that made pictures in the mind had come again even stronger than before with more vivid pictures. I had not seen the sea, but as Dadabapa narrates his journey, I imagine myself on the dhow, standing there on the rocking deck with him, holding his hand so I am not thrown overboard. I would watch the waves leaping at the bow and feel the moist breeze wetting my face. Thus, began the first great crossing of my family in the sensations of my body, sighs of my breath and sights in my imagination. The saga lived in me as I was growing up becoming a woman. Dadabapa continued his narration about the crossing of what he called Kala Pani - the Black Waters. I wipe the sweat around his neck and on his forehead. His voice is weak, his throat dry but he wants to speak. Sometimes only half a word comes from his lips, the other slips back over the tongue. Yet he continues to speak:

At first, typhoid, and then dysentery breaks out on that unfortunate craft in the middle of the Indian Ocean. It was no wonder that it was called Kala Pani. Aval Bai, the young wife of Popat Bhai from my neighbouring village of Kera, wakes up one morning to find that her bebli girl was not moving. She sobs uncontrollably dooska dooska and begins to tear off her clothes. Women come around the mother distraught with grief. Men put their heads down, chins on the chest, and sit with crossed legs in tight palothis in silent groups. With the dead infant pressed to her full breasts, Aval Bai pushes her way through the women. Weeping dooska dooska, she passes by the fender hangings, looking for a ledge or box to climb over the side lath and jump over with her bebli girl. It takes three Bais to pull her back and tear away the dead infant from her mother's grip. They wrap the infant in a white shroud, a pillowcase donated by an anonymous traveller. They wipe the bebli's hair soaking wet in her mother's milk. The Bais decide not to wash the body with fresh water that is rationed for drinking and cooking and not for burial rites. Captain Ahmed orders an empty gunnysack from the staff ration store at the lower hull. Immediately, Mari, the cook with two oblong smallpox marks on either cheek, spills out the onions from the gunnysack onto a spare sail, folded in squares and kept ready on the deck for stitching the ruptured hemlines. The cook then slips a stone in the gunnysack from a pile of stones on which deck hands sit while they chat, but was especially kept there on board for burial use. The Bais let the infant girl slide into the sack and spiral tie her with a jute rope, tightening the coil with each turn. They lift and put down the gunnysack coffin on the deck twice as if reluctant to let it go. The third time, they offer the unnamed baby to the sea and a silent prayer of peace.

Aval Bai spends the day with other women at Ambe Ma's shrine at the middle lantern above the trap door. Ambe Ma is the goddess of strength and the one you pray to for blessings of mamta motherhood. The three-faced earthen Ambe, clad in a red sari sits on a tiger. She is bright in her aspects of Mamta Mata, Shanti Mata and Santosh Mata – Mother of Motherhood, Mother of Peace and Mother of Contentment. She has a large red dot on the forehead between her thick eyebrows between her dhingly doll eyes and a smile that curves like a crescent moon just appearing. The rass, the pitch of sadness, in Aval Bai's muted wailing, flows into her body. She rocks forward and back to the rhythm of her chanting into the flutter of her pachedi held between her teeth like a tethered cockerel fighting to break loose. Where there should have been her bebli girl in her lap, there is a pillow. When she is not chanting, we see her caressing her cheek on the soft belly of the pillow. Or lisping lullabies into the pillowcase ear hanging bent over the corner. Then pushing out her burdened breast from under her tight sari blouse, she nurses the cushion if only to feel the baby's suction on her swollen nipple tender to touch. First, she must cover her bebli with her pachedi so no hungry eye would want the milk and cause stomach pain to her child.

Watching over Aval Bai's gestures are the three outcast women sitting aloof in the shade of the boat's brow within the protective gaze of Ambe Ma. When the three pray they also dance the garba - dha dhi na - dha tu na, 1 2 3 - 1 2 3. They call Ambe, their Mata meaning Mother. They ask Mata to dance the garba with them and let their grief pour from their hearts into their legs. Let their feet stamp out the past and be clean when they step on the virgin land. They ask Mata to be the witness to their freedom from Bombay, the city that kept them prisoners of shame called sharam. "We are going to Shree Ram Desh – God's Country," they would sing to Ambe Ma, "Give us a safe passage home." Like their dance, their song is worship when there is such beauty in their art and freedom in their hearts. Their names Soneri, Gulzar and Rupa mean Golden, Garden and Beauty. Rupa Bai is the eldest, perhaps sixteen or seventeen years old or maybe a little more, and mother of a two-year-old boy.

The days that follow are difficult to describe. So listen with a strong heart. At first babies died and then children died. Then adults began to die. Some said dysentery was what killed them. Others thought the food they carried had fermented and turned into poison. Some thought it was the dhow food and even stopped eating the daily ration of sticky rice and watery dal. Others simply accepted that the Black Waters needed a toll of human lives for the passage over what was forbidden. That was their belief as unshakable as Indian beliefs are. They said the Indian Ocean was a sister of Kali Mata, the Black Mother to whom human sacrifices continued to be offered for peace even though the English law prohibited it. The sun blazes fiercely and the children who survived the diseases and are strong, run about the deck playing and making noises such as the ones that we hear in the courtyards of homes. Then some of them dehydrate quickly. Lactating mothers express milk into kops and offer it to the children who are too weak even to open their mouths. Parting the little velvet lips with their two fingers, parents drip milk through the slit like eagles feeding wholesome white worms to their babies in the nest.

Then there are no more deaths and we rest. Waters gush and splash at the stern and the sun blazes. People visit each other's groups as though they were homes. But our hearts are heavy and we take comfort from stories of loss. We feel more together than ever before. Some break their caste and faith rules and share water. It is said that here the travellers on board the dhow make bonds of a lifetime like families of one ancestor.

A wind rises on the sixteenth day and continues to grow stronger in the days that follow. In the breath of the Indian Ocean, I hear the raga of guru-pir, the true guru and pir, the parent *mabap* of Satpanth faith. The swordfish that the black sailors called mkizi jumps high out of the water close to the bow, peering over the lower deck. It scoops up like a giant ladle and falls back into the sea running away as far as it can from the craft. There is a saying in Swahili that I learned on board HASIRA ZA MKIZI – the anger of the swordfish – BALA YA WASAFIRI – trouble for the travellers. Soon after, we watch the sea coagulating and beginning to churn seething in its mid-ocean chasms. The faces of the crewmen tense.

Captain Ahmed and the crew tighten the ropes. The sky darkens and a storm looks imminent. Growing in strength, currents of air growl around us, becoming forceful, almost violent. We lose direction. Nobody tells us but we know we are lost. Fear spreads like when in the dead of the night we know a marauding tiger is walking about in the village. No one tells us, but we know. Fear tells us. Villagers have a collective sensing of danger, because they care for each other like a family. It's the same feeling in every one who knows the whole village is awake, still and listening except for the children. My stomach tightens and then it hurts. The laughter, grumbling, arguments and singing subside. Gamblers' quarrels grating over card games vanish into the trepidation of the marauding storm as if it is telling the dhow not to come in its path. Like the tiger in the village. Only our eyes speak and that in fright. What shall we do?

Two days of not knowing what to do and what will happen accompany the turbulence at the sea and I begin to believe I will not live to see Africa. The Brahmins were right when they warned us that crossing Kala Pani meant death. Then I hear the women on board. Their prayers are loud, wailing prayers, imploring prayers like over dead bodies, same prayers said over and over again, endless prayers, beseeching prayers, "O Mowla return us to calmness." In their pleadings, I hear my mother's voice. Her wails sear the stillness of dawn, imploring Mowla for my safe return to her arms as I am leaving Haripur. Her wails assail my ears like the bereaved mothers' laments on board the dhow. Sea gales blended dooska dooska into communal weeping, feminine and painful. I touch my mother's silver anklets stitched into a double-fold secret pocket at the waist of my Saurashtran pantaloon. Worse was still to come at night when powerful waves hit the craft so hard that each time we would think we had run into a rock. That's when the cries pinged through the ferocious swashing at the prow. In the hull below the upper deck, lantern shadows dance like hashish elated Sufis celebrating God's beauty. Then an eerie calm comes over the sea and we thank God; the storm, it seems, has abated. People start walking on the deck again. Some rush to throw up, retching over the side planks on the upper deck. Women rearrange the family beddings, bundles and things. Children cry again. Shukhar sits on the lips of the Satpanthis. Then we begin to move gently as if pushed by a giant ripple. The potter kumbhar, holds tight to his wheel, Gajar Suthar to his bag of tools, the Goan to his Bible, the ayurvedic doctor to his bag of herbs and powder, the missionary to his tasbih and his wife to the books.

All of a sudden, the craft is heaved from below by a monster wave and thrust up into the void of pitch darkness. It stays suspended as if on the crest of the wave in mid-air. I hold my breath. We are in shock, frozen and helpless in a shroud of blackness, so black a night that you cannot see your hand held before you. My abdomen swirls inside. Then the abrupt fall so far deep that I feel my intestines rise as if pulled loose from the attachment to the stomach when a sudden thump shoots a shock wave into my head, and then comes a deafening crash of water like the Ganges flood. Every movable thing is knocked down. Every person standing or sitting is knocked over. Then abruptly, no sooner were we on our feet than a gale roars in through a wall of screams and slaps me on the face like a wet rubber mass. I find myself, hands clasped around a pyramid of limbs and bodies. The three outcaste women are seated in a tight hurdle, knotted arms and legs over each other and I over them. The child is in the middle of the three-woman embrace. Again, the gale roars into our ears and we are propelled up, and when we come down the second time, I find myself far away from the three women, now thrown around among the passengers scattered over one another. The craft swings side to side, shaken out of turmoil.

I see men, women and children rolling about the lower deck like empty bottles. Then immediately another gale rages over the dhow. This time the wind rushes in like a captive bull run amok and doing all it can to break free from the cloistered pen. Cutting through the sluicing deck waters at the lintel, comes a desperate, agonizingly sharp short shriek for help and then no more. You could feel an eerie silence in the dead darkness and the thrashing waves admonishing the boat. Parents run about frantically, calling their children's names – Ramesh, Surinder, Yezdi, Lila, Anthony, Hassan. They bring the children back into their embrace and hold them tight as the boat rocks from side to side as if it were a giant cradle pulled back and forth uncontrollably dole dole.

I hear a deckhand's shout cracking through the black silence between the gales and floods, "Woi reh! Kala Pani has taken her! She has fallen off over the toilet box!"

"Who was she? Who is she?" the men folk ask repeatedly, several times, braving the storm to gather around the deckhand, holding hands in tight grips in pairs or in threes.

"The one with a limp," answers the deckhand, just once, and the men begin nodding. Then they walk away to tell others how Paan Bai fell off over the toilet box in the dark.

I vomit instantaneously and then curl up my legs. Embracing myself in a tense grip, I shut my eyes tight and lay sick on the lower deck. This is how I used to stay in the courtyard when I was little and had strong stomach pains.

After the night of storm, calmness finally returns to the Black Waters of the Indian Ocean. The skies are blue and the sun shines on our path once again. It feels like a re-birth. Captain Ahmed yells to furl up the sail and raise it to allow sunlight on the waterlogged woodwork. The missionary and his wife spread wet manuscripts and holy books over the deck to dry. The potter wipes to dry his wheel with his wet dhoti on him. The suthar carpenter drains water from his toolbox, and touch counts each of his implements. The craft drifts in calm waters. There is a wind and it is gentle. Paan Bai's pachedi tucked tightly into a wedge and knotted between the planks above the toilet box, lifts and falls in the air, limp and forlorn.

Captain Ahmed scans the ocean from the high prow. "He is sniffing for land air. The air of Africa," says the boy deckhand at the bowsprit. The captain orders all hands to inspect every part of the Arab craft for leaks in the mangrove construction and ruptures in the coconut fibre cords woven into watertight seamless planks.

Every day then for the next three days we watch the captain's routine in the morning and at night expecting him to announce the sighting of Africa. First, he orders a bucket to be hurled overboard. Tied to the jute cord, the bucket is hoisted up filled with seawater and brought to him. Captain Ahmed dips his hand into the bucket with poise as if it were a habitual thing he did every day. "He is now feeling the temperature of the water and comparing it with the smell in the air," remarks the scrub hand at the bowsprit. The boy's eyes kept a scrutiny over the captain's every action and equated it with his expression before he made a comment for our benefit. "At night the captain will study the stars and put together what he sees with what he knows from the air and water," says the boy.

At night, I would often hear snappy commands of the captain at the stern. Once, I heard the deckhands say that, our Bhadala captain was from Kutch Mandvi the port of Gujarat known for its seafarers, among whom would be the descendants of the ocean guide who showed Vasco da Gama, the Portuguese sailor, the way to India and thus changed the course of Asian African history. After centuries of European rivalries and domination of India, we are migrating out of the

98

pit of poverty and violence to build yet another Empire for the English.

The following days and nights, we wait anxiously for something to happen that would stir the inertia that had come over the travellers recovering from the ordeal of leaving the land, the relatives, crossing over Kala Pani, the deaths, the storm, the hunger, the thirst. Then we hear the captain's shout, "Release the crow!" A joyous shout like a cheer in chorus in one voice shakes the stillness when the cage with six crows in it is brought to the prow and the first crow released into the sky. The black bird makes one circle above us, caws kaa-kaa-kagrow, its voice is dry and crusty like the papadam but he caws in delight. Then he dances to the air and flies away, free and straight in one direction. We watch the Crow Yama, the son of Surya, Father Sun God, with expectations, narrowing our eyes until there is just a black spot fading away in the immense blue. The avian being is carrying death away bringing hope. Yama is the guardian of directions; the regent deity of the Southward bound voyagers, son of dawn, and red splendour of the rising sun itself. Hope. I think of my mother. She would be offering cooked gluey rice marble globes to the ancestors for my protection. She would place the prayer food plate on the roof for the village crows to descend, pluck at her rice globes and take death away from the family. Every evening, she would be taking the food prayer plate to the jamat khana under her crocheted tablecloth, red where the flowers appear, otherwise white, four times folded over to keep away the dust, flies and hungry glimpses of the stonecutters returning home from the quarry across our street. Masts creak and the triangular sail flutters, two jovial men push at the rudder and the craft sails in the direction of the crow. We look to the sky and pray for the monsoons to rise gently and impregnate the sail because we have little food left.

After about two hours, a second crow is released. It makes one circle above us, caws kaa-kaa-kagrow with delight, dances and flies straight in the same direction as the first crow. The craft adjusts and veers in line with the flight of the second crow. Every eye on the deck is fixed on the black speck in the blue sky. Deep in us, we know the crow will not let us down because Rama made him to take us home.

Winds pick up by the evening, and then the next day the waves push and pull the craft, playing tug-of-war. Each second day one crow is freed. Winds, favourable to sailing south, blow continually filling the sail. Light showers pass over us. We are able to collect fresh water from the tarpaulins spread over both the upper and lower decks. We are able to bathe and even wash clothes and sheets. During the next two days, I sleep and sit in the same corner of the deck full of hope, appreciating the peace at last, knowing I will live to see Africa. On cloudless nights, I observe the constellations as if I were an astronomer carrying my eyes to a timeless space. When it's dawn, the breeze is tender, Saranyu's godly comeliness slips into Surya's enfolding splendour of red radiance and the morning raga immerses the galleon in the chords of the music of the Indian Ocean.

We hear Paan Bai's husband, Jaffer Bhai, a Khoja Ithna Asheri boy from my village of Haripur not yet twenty, singing to the sea. He sits at the prow staring at the waters like he is waiting for his wife, and if not her spirit, her dead body to surface. He waits in vain the whole day, day after day. A school of darting sharks appears in his scanning vision, cutting the smooth waters, fins upright triangles, but he does not see them. Aval Bai, the bereaved Khoja Ismaili mother, who is now known on the dhow as the 'one with a pillow in her empty lap' nurses Paan Bai's four month old bablo boy and hums looking at him in her full lap.

Khama mara vir
Mm…mm…mm
Gir na sih, raja mara vir
Mm…mm…mm

Comfort my man
Mm…mm…mm
Lion king of Gir, my man
Mm…mm…mm

She would say to the Bais that her breasts were sore to touch. On some days, she feels feverish. Her breasts are so filled that milk drips out through the brassiere and makes blotches on her dress, concentric circles, each day more concentrated than the one of the day before. Then the ringed patch begins to look like a cut tree trunk on her blouse. Bablo, covetous and strong-minded, digs into the sore breasts holding them firmly in both his tiny hands while he bites the nipples with his gums determined to draw out some milk. His greedy black eyes wander, fearful of being abandoned again by the breast. Bablo takes deep sucks and the Bais see contentment return to Aval Bai's face. They come around her and celebrate the return of her mother's milk with aarti veneration prayers to Hare Ambe, also called Mamta Mata the Guardian Goddess of Motherhood.

The Bais baby talk with bablo, lisping words and teasing him with sounds of his greedy slurping sucks at the breast. They sweet-talk and play with him dangling the braided ends of their hair in tightly woven coloured threads and silver jingles. They show his sister, the six year old they call Bebli, how to hold her baby brother supporting the neck; how to change his clothes and clean him holding his feet high while laying him down on his back, and so teach her to be a mother. Aval Bai now joins the women in the mid-day satsang song group on the upper deck.

As the sun begins to turn orange, Aval Bai's husband calls for her. Elders have been talking to him. "We too have lost children during the famines of Saurashtra when we were young and strong men like you and had young brides of our own," they would say. "When a woman is demented because of the death of her child, her man must give her the seed quickly so her lap does not remain empty. A woman's lap must be full with a child and that is a man's responsibility. Otherwise, her powers of mamta motherhood will turn evil and move towards Kali Mata. She will turn into a witch and be barren forever.

A woman is like a dhow," they would say, "her sail must be full.'

Aval Bai hands over bablo to Nanima, the oldest Khoja woman on board, who, during the day, sits at the bowsprit where there is the sign of blue crescent moon in a circle and white star. It's the signature of a Lamu craft builder. She sits alone here where the craft tapers into the open sea and smiles to the water, her mouth opening to the cold breeze on her face. She has no teeth and the wisps of her white hair fly dishevelled over her face. She is a widow, and she is going to Africa to be with her son, an itinerant bead trader, somewhere in the interior of the continent. She knows he is in Africa but does not know where. However, she knows he will take care of her once she finds him.

When darkness falls over the ocean and it is quiet except for an occasional wave resisting the prow cutting across its crest, Nanima takes Paan Bai's bablo boy and presses him to her body. She feels the warmth of his baby fat on her ribs. Bablo sucks and tugs at her rubbery breasts, and wails in protest until he falls asleep, tired. Finally, he lets go of the dry nipples. They both sleep in the corner close together below the deck in the middle hull.

Bebli puts her head down besides her bablo baby brother pressed into the curve of Nanima sleeping on her side. She sleeps under her mother's pachedi that she puts on over her head during the day. Sometimes she plays hide and seek with the pachedi to bring a smile on bablo's toothless face, and ask him, as her mother used to, "Who took your teeth away, hengh, my bablo boy?" Sometimes while rocking her brother on her one raised knee, sitting cross-legged in palothi, she lisps a lullaby imitating Paan Bai's fine voice. Everyone on board the dhow must have noticed how Bebli walks with a limp, but nobody says anything to her or even to each other. They watch only her with sadness in their eyes.

In the distant horizon where the sea flows into the night's skyline, an iridescent light wavers in the wind. On the upper deck, the sailors, the celestial navigators on the Swahili Sea, measure their position looking at the stars and calculate distance with a knotted rope attached to the captain's kamal. They whisper, "It's Paan Bai's spirit following us. Her heart yearns for her bablo baby boy on board." They know the mother's spirit stays with the child after her death.

13

Fellow traveller Devji Momna

As he feels better, Dadabapa frequently asks for water. He has been in bed for ten days and ten nights. Finally, he is able to sit with legs folded and say his two evening dua prayers by himself. When he has difficulty giving the testimony of twenty-one pirs that comes in the dua, I say the names for him. When he has difficulty while giving the testimony of the ten avatars to the present Saheb, which also comes in the dua, I say the names for him and he continues on to recite on his own. He asks for khichedi and butter for lunch every day. Each day it's the same. Ma prepares raab, the black millet porridge with jaggery and ghee, for his evening meals. As Dadabapa gets stronger, he no longer needs my support to walk to the pit latrine at the far end of the courtyard.

However, his mind is both here and in the past. "I am crossing over Kala Pani," he would say between asking me to help him to sit up or to cover him with a quilt. Sometimes he would point to the crows he sees at the ceiling and sometimes at the seagulls. Then he would say how hot the sun blazes in the blue cloudless sky and ask for water. He asks for tea at odd times of the day or night. On some days when he wakes up in the morning, he looks around wide-eyed as if he were in a strange house, someone else's home not his. His breath is weak and caustic. His speech is faint, half-words and half sentences, but he insists on talking. "Let him speak," Ma Gor Bai would tell me raising her hand when I try to quieten Dadabapa. "Only words spoken from the heart will break the rope that binds him to the past."

Dadabapa speaks drawing in prolonged inhales and deliberately lengthened exhales to show relief, the way old people speak between sighs on matters that affect them deeply. In the show of relief, there is often an intoned shukhar as he speaks now:

> The craft cruises closer to the coast, palm trees and mangroves appear. The sight of life, land and just the colour green bring joy to my heart. However, not all the immigrants are full of joy as I am. Some lost their loved ones who had embarked the boat with them in Bombay. The sadness in their eyes is profound. Some weep aloud, both men and women, calling out the names of the dead, pointing their fingers to the shore, telling them to see Africa over there. Mothers smack their heads with open palms, grieving their children they have buried at sea and are now leaving them behind. "I buried you my child!" they cry out aloud, "neither in India nor in Africa. Between the old country and the unknown country, I buried you in unfathomable depth, so dark, so wet. A nameless place where I cannot even leave a mark to say you lie here."

Fishermen's dugout canoes appear as the dhow sails into the creek whose entrance is guarded by a fortress standing on coral rock. The dockhands point to this sixteenth century bastion, yelling out its name, "Fort Jesus! Fort Jesus!"

The fort's walls rise into the sky where the sight ends and infinity begins, and where the blue above mirrors the blue below. The creek leading into the ancient sea port of Mombasa is a narrow passage where for three hundred years Portuguese, Omanis and the English have been warring for supremacy of the natural harbour and control of the monsoons - the secret of the passage to India. I learn about the port of Mombasa from Devji Momna.

Mombasa is a British colonial port, a small Bombay, with fine Indian mercantile houses. Here there are two and three storey wooden houses with latticed street balconies, exterior staircases and Saurashtran doors. There are spacious Swahili and Arab homes each one is known by its carved hardwood door suggesting the owner's ethnic origin. A Customs Office stands at the harbour. The port town is a huddle of red rooftops, the colour of earth among a lush grove of palm-thatched houses.

But we are not allowed to disembark for five days. We remain docked at a distance from the harbour because the boat was put under quarantine. A white medical officer comes close to the craft in a local canoe but he will not come on board. Standing on the canoe, he talks to Captain Ahmed in broken Swahili and Hindi. The medical officer takes notes about the number of passengers on board, how many men, how many women, how many children. He notes how many had died at sea and when the last death happened. The captain, speaking in Hindi lies about the number of deaths. He says there were fewer than the actual numbers of deaths. Then he asks for fresh water, vegetables and fruit. The white officer replies he will inform the mukhi of the Khoja jamat of Mombasa and other faith community elders. The officer enquires about the prisoners. Captain Ahmed tells him one drowned on board during the storm. The sea flashed the deck where he was seated chained to a post, which cracked. With the receding waters, the chains, the convict and the broken post drifted into the raging sea. It was dark and he did not call for help. If he did, how could we hear him? The storm filled our ears.

Within hours, two canoes arrive with fresh water. We had not tasted such sweet water before and there was enough for all to drink as much as we wanted to. At midday, hot cauldrons of rice and stacks of buttered chapattis, dal and bean curries arrive in more canoes, sometimes accompanied by bearded elders who speak kindly to us. There are separate cauldrons and food in baskets for each religious group on board. There were three cauldrons and three large food baskets for the Satpanth Khoja, the majority group on the dhow.

The following days, every day at midday, canoes arrive separately with the Khoja Five Brothers, the immigrant welfare association, bringing boiled milk for children, bananas, papayas and mangoes. Sometimes they also gave us some sweet mee-thai. We talk from the deck and enquire about relatives and people from our villages in Saurashtra.

In the evenings, the Satpanthis chant their dua prayers invoking names of the ten avatars of Vishnu. The men sit in a circle and the women sit in a semicircle behind the men. An elder unwraps a coarse cotton sheet and removes a framed picture of the little boy Saheb on the royal takht, a divan four times bigger than a divan, lined with bolster pillows. The takht of the little boy Saheb was like a throne, such as the one that Krishna sits on in reclining pose over his elbow digging into the cushion, his feet in half a palothi – one knee bent and up, and the other bent and down. A divine self, supine and relaxed, he who controls the world is sitting on his takht. His relaxed pose gives us comfort and hope. But little boy Saheb sits on the edge as if it were a chair. The old man kisses the photo at Saheb's feet and touches it to his left eye and right eye and then to his forehead. His head is bowed down showing revered veneration and homage. In this gesture is a prayer of shukhar for we have arrived. He props the holy picture up against a book on a red velvet cloth that covers a crate, a makeshift altar on the dhow for the boy avatar. The old woman, who spent her time on board the dhow smiling to the ocean breeze, places a stiff chapatti before the picture. It's wheat from the last harvest of an honest Satpanth peasant's labour in the fields of Gujarat.

I touch the picture and say a silent prayer of shukhar looking towards Africa. Then I pray for peace of my ancestors I have left buried behind in my village of Haripur. I know my mother would have her hands cupped in prayers at dawn, the last quarter of the night, the most promising time to pray, wishing that at least Mowla granted me daily roji. My eyes well. Then we hear Aval Bai sing but no one turns the head to look at her.

Guru-pir says
Sing the sacred song
Let your heart overflow
Every line a rass
So says guru-pir the parent

The next day at dawn when the horizon turns crimson, the colour of rose, my heart sings joy seeing the Bohora and Ithna Asheri mosques of our kin and the majestic house of Allidina Visram who I hear was from Kera, a neighbouring village to Haripur. Kera was also where Popat Bhai, the young husband of Aval Bai, came from. Screaming sea gulls crowd around the mast.

"There is an open square over there where stands the house of Allidina Visram," says Devji Momna pointing towards the port. Devji Momna lived in Mombasa and is now returning with his twelve-year-old bride. She is a shy girl and the fairest Gujarati I have ever seen. Whenever she offered me her home cooked snacks like thepla or bhajia, she would say, "Just to taste," with a slight smile under her red sari pulled over her head to the eyes in laaj. Sharing meals showed we shared the bond of faith and caste. It showed love and care like between two brothers, two hearts of one jamat, one family united by Saheb's love. Devji Momna knows my grandfather, the mukhi of

Haripur, because my grandfather used to sit with other Khoja elders to resolve the conflict over the ownership of their jamat khana in Rajpur. I heard people say there was a family feud after Devji Momna's grandfather passed away. His two sons decided to join the Ithna Asheri community while the other two, of whom one was Devji Momna's father, retained the Satpanth faith. All the four brothers claimed the jamat khana to be their joint responsibility entrusted by their father at his deathbed. "The jamat khana is my bequest to the Khoja jamat of Rajpur," said their dying father, "I wish all four of you, my sons, to honour my wish and live united." Then he gestured to his four sons to place their right hands, one over the other on his palm, and take a vow to respect and protect his bequest. Now, the question that puzzled the elders was to whom should the jamat khana belong, Ithna Asheri Khoja jamat or Satpanth Khoja jamat? "But both are Khoja jamats of Rajpur, are they not?" the brothers questioned the elders who were lost for an honest answer. So their deliberations, nodding and shaking of heads went on for months over many cups of chai. The problem was that no one could recall a precedent. How could they? The Khoja community had never been fractured so deeply before the coming of Saheb from Persia. Then there was the case against Saheb in the Bombay High Court by the dissenters who refused to pay the ordained tithe and claimed all jamat khanas for their own breakaway groups. There was no doubt that the elders would have gone on consulting all over India and pondering, had the solution not come from the brothers

111

themselves and had they not threatened that if what they proposed was not accepted, they would convert the jamat khana into a house for orphans as it had happened in Bhuj and Jamnagar.

The brothers asked the prayer house be simply divided into two to reflect their divided faiths. This greatly annoyed the Satpanth elders who cried out, "But the High Court in Bombay passed a verdict that all jamat khanas in India belong to Saheb!" The four brothers ignored the elders' rage. Today, they pray in one building, albeit separated by a wall but under one roof that the brothers say represents their one Khoja lineage. Then when communal meals are served, the two faith groups mingle that brings blessings of baraka of sharing roji. "Are we not one family, one people?" they would ask. "Should we not eat together in circles from one platter as was the custom of our forefathers?" Such an arrangement honoured the benefactor's wish and the brothers' vow to live united.

I stand on the craft's prow where Captain Ahmed used to stand to watch the stars at night and open myself to the land breeze. The draught carries the first faint calls to prayers like the verse of a chanter summoning the chorus to repeat after her. More song calls waft from over the island of Mombasa into the sea breeze and over the clanging church bell from the African mainland. Arabic summons to prayers from Sunni mosques of Yemeni and Omani Arabs, the Saurashtran Bhadala sailors', and the Memon traders' prayer calls sculpt the stillness of the old stone town. In the distance, I hear Krishna's temple bells clinging to the Moslem prayer calls.

"I live there below that red roof top. That's the jamat khana," says Devji Momna pointing far to the north-west to the rooftop at a grove of tall coconut trees over conical Swahili palm fringe roofs. At once, my heart lifts when I hear the word 'jamat khana'. Surely, I will have shelter and food at the jamat khana so big. I will sleep in an enclosure somewhere under the eave and keep myself dry from the pouring rain. At the jamat khana, I may meet someone from my village or a neighbouring village, who knows my family or my married sisters' families. My grandfather was a well-known mukhi elder, people would have heard of him. I stare at the rooftop of the jamat khana as long as I can. It fills me with hope and the warmth and comfort of coming home.

While lying on his back and while staring at the roof with wide-open still eyes, Dadabapa describes the jamat khana of Mombasa as if he were standing on deck of the quarantined boat at the creek of Mombasa in the year 1903.

I see the roof is ochre red, shaped like a pyramid over the prayer hall and it is the tallest of all the red ochre roofs against the deep blue of the Mombasa sky. From the craft, I can see the balconies of the jamat khana above the palm fringed rooftops of the Swahili town. Devji Momna defines the outline of the jamat khana with his finger. He seems to know every corner and pillar of the stone building. Pointing to the prayer halls, he says one is for regular prayers, and the other, on top of it, is the Hall of Meditation. The balconies are laced with banisters with high rounded arches and elegant stone columns on either side. The façade has a

113

rich rust patina in patches such as the one that moist salt air and warmth creates on the chalked coral.

Dadabapa lapses into a short sleep as if he were entering into the jamat khana and into the silence of the Meditation Hall. I let him sleep into his meditation, and go into the kitchen to help Ma Gor Bai make the evening raab. After he has said the dua and eaten the raab, Dadabapa says shukhar and immediately continues with his story. This time he looks at me as if the story was now meant for me, as if it were my story:

In the evening after the dua prayers, immigrants of all sorts join us - Baluchi, Afghani, Punjabi, Goans, Parsees and Sikhs. We sit in circles, mostly in mixed groups except the chura untouchables who sit at a distance and have to strain their ears to listen to the talk. The craft is rocking; hurricane lamps flicker in fishermen's canoes and reflect dimly on the caress of limpid waves licking the flanks of the dhow. Children sleep cradled in the laps of their mothers, sitting cross-legged away from the men. The three and a half weeks on the dhow formed friendships among us who had journeyed together over Kala Pani, its leisure and perils. Our friendships were bonded in the Indian way, the way of our forefathers, and ways of the villages we came from. If, of the same caste and religion, we ate together, and sometimes, sought a promise of a possible marriage match for our descendants. If not, we forged an equally close family like friendships, alike in all ways except for segregation at meals and of course having no aspiration to commit our children in marriage.

114

It was one such a quiet evening when Devji Momna tells his own story to me. When you survive a storm like the one we did, you grow close to each other. Devji Momna and I sit next to each other with our shoulders pressing to make room for his fair wife to stretch her legs and try to catch some sleep. This is how he told me his story:

"I am originally from Rajpur. I was born there but at the age of thirteen, I ran away from home because I had stolen mee-thai sweets from the village sweet mart. I feared my father's wrath. I paid my way to Bombay working as a ton boy on a caravan and then as a deck hand doing odd jobs on the dhow to Africa. In Zanzibar, at first, I worked fetching water for wealthy Indian merchant houses. A seth's wife took a liking to me and praised me to her husband. He told his brother, who took me with him to Mombasa. I worked as his bala-boy looking after the household children, fetching water, buying vegetables and cleaning the house and his shelf of beads on the veranda. The seth himself was an agent of Allidina Visram, a wealthy Satpanth merchant, and a kind of a manager of his inland trade. Sometimes, when we travelled together, the seth ordered me to sleep with him. Although, his wife found me loyal and hardworking, one day she told me I had to leave. I was becoming a man and a beard would not suit in her household. So the seth began to give me more responsibilities that kept me away from his house, wife and daughters. I made rounds of the warehouses and checked on textiles, spices and construction material offloaded from the crafts at the old harbour, and reloaded into his fleet of handcarts. I sold beads in the market to the Digo and Giriama when there was no work at the harbour. That was for me in my free time. In the years to come, the seth grew prosperous and old. My seth liked to sleep in the afternoon with his wife and leave the management of his business to me. I learned to write and add up numbers, and, in the course of years, I began to understand how to trade and deal with people of all religions, both businessmen and customers. By the time I was eighteen I wore a beard and when I went to the jamat khana, I was a respectable manager with a red fez cap and a buscot. My seth sent me to Nairobi on bead business errands. Then to the railroad shops, as far as Port Florence on Lake Victoria when the railway opened up trade and the white settlers began to arrive in large numbers from Europe and South Africa after their wars. When I saw the Great Rift Valley, I felt like I was in a giant's embrace. The sheer elation at seeing the expanse of the chasm seized me. I cried uncontrollably. I wanted to touch the rocks of the old volcanoes on the plains below; the floor of the Rift was immense grassland. As we descended the fault steps of the rift wall into the basin of the silent lakes, I cried again at the beauty of the infinity, the abundance of land and trees. But most of all, the abundance of fresh water in the rivers and lakes. The pink birds, the silk skinned antelopes, the giraffes and zeals of zebra. Truly, it was amrapuri, the heaven in bard guru-pir's ode to divinity. In the afternoons, thunderstorms filled this wonder. Pouring rain. I stood in the thunderstorm and let the water from the sky bathe me. Drenched, I felt born again, falling from the sack of my Indian mother's womb through the fluids of the Black Ocean into a new karma. Africa. At that moment standing in the downpour, smell of the earth on me – the scent of the red soil that the rain brings in Africa, I decided this land would be where I would live. Here, I would walk again and hear the earth speak below my feet. I would work hard to make a home and raise a family of my own.

"Now I am my own seth. I left my old seth and with my savings of over ten years, I bought a handcart. I pull my own handcart from early morning to noon in the streets of stone town Mombasa. In the afternoon, I go to the bazaar to bargain with Bhadala and Memon businesswomen in long dresses and pachedis, and coat button size diamond siris flashing on their noses. I take kitchenware on loan to barter with in the streets. Then I go to the old harbour to sell used clothes that I had bartered the kitchenware with. In the evenings, I serve Saheb at the jamat khana in Kuze. The Khojas know me as Jamat Bhai, the keeper of the jamat khana, but the people of Mombasa call me Khoja Hamali, the trusted pushcart hawker of old stone town Mombasa. I exchange water jugs, matching tea sets, knives and spoons for used clothing. I go house to house singing, *'Mali kwa mali … kutoka kwa gari la Khoja Hamali.'* Goods for goods from the cart of Hawker Khoja. Now I am retuning to Mombasa with my bride. She is from a respectable Khoja merchant family of Bhuj though I am a Momna. But I am rich and I am from Africa. Three matchmakers of Bhuj composed poetry in praise of her cooking, fair skin and virtues before

117

our marriage was arranged. I own my own hands and my labour is mine ... praise Mowla ... santosh ... shukhar. It's my karma. Santosh Mowla Naklank! O the Stainless One! Shukhar Sarkar Noor Mowlana Shah Saheb!"

So I listened to the story of Devji Momna and then Devji Momna listened to my story and we became friends. Friendships forged on the dhow are forever like gold to Indians. We became such good friends that Devji Momna who was ten years older than I was, insisted I stay with him in Mombasa as long as I needed to. He would even help me to find work and introduce me to the jamat as a fellow Satpanthi. This was important because at the time when there were so many conflicts and divisions among the Khojas that one could not always be sure if the new immigrant from India was a true Satpanthi or a pretender seeking to benefit from the Five Brothers Welfare Society that provided meals to the newly landed and the poor. Worse, if he were a spy. Many immigrants found their way to the steps of the jamat khana at Kuze that was not far from the old harbour. The stone of this jamat khana has embraced the lonely heart of many an immigrant. Here they lie down on the prayer mats to rest their tired bodies, listen to guru-pirs words and regain their strength to meet the new land when the sun rises.

14

Story of the Neem Tree

Dadabapa told me he was the eldest in the family of eight brothers and sisters and as it happened, he would never return to his beloved Saurashtra and to the responsibilities he had inherited being the eldest. The first thing he said he did on landing on the African shore was to buy a clay pot and in it, he planted the neem tree from his village of Haripur. On the dhow he watered the plant, a cupped handful thrice a week, and when it rained, he put it on the open deck. Every day he let the plant soak the morning light before the sun became fierce and when the water was rationed, he would keep a mouthful on his parched tongue for a few minutes before spluttering it over the seedling in the brown paper bag. Around the bag, he coiled his turban wetted in seawater, hauled up in buckets for deck cleaning, and covered the soil with the edge of the same turban to retain the moisture from evaporating in the blistering heat between the sky and the ocean that burnt the skin. Whenever he thought of his parents and siblings, and his village friends, he would look at the neem tree as if they resided in it, and talk to it. He would tell the tree to listen carefully and keep his words in its heart at the roots alive in the soil of Haripur. "You understand because we come from the same village, the earth that nourished me, nourishes you. We are brothers of one mother," he would say.

Occasionally Dadabapa did send some money home the first few years when he worked for Allidina Visram - first as a labourer at the old port of Mombasa and then as a boy serving Visram's managers in all types of jobs - as a messenger, a laundry boy, even as a house servant who made tea and cooked the daily meals. His loyalty and hard work won him the position of an apprentice to the most trusted accountants of Allidina Visram, the King of the Commercial Empire of Eastern Africa as he came to be known. Dadabapa's work as a store clerk included counting and memorizing the number of bead crates unloaded from the dhows at the old harbour and then their distribution inland to a web of Khoja bead stores, radiating from the stations along the newly completed railroad. As he began to understand the business, Dadabapa learned to write the numbers and add them up on paper. He also learned how the sizes, shapes and colours of beads differed from one ethnic region to another – Kikuyu, Kamba, Luo, Turkana, Nandi, Maasai and many more. It was his task to mark and ensure that correct boxes went to the inland bead stores spread between the ocean and the Great Lake and then to the Mountains of the Moon where they said the gorillas lived. He learned to write by writing names of the beads, their colours and sizes - olive-yellow-medium, seed-green-large, ring-blue-small, diamond-red-medium, and then against them he would write names of the customers – Mohamed Premji Brothers Beads and General Store, Kisumu; Hassanali Nagji and Sons Fancy Jewellery and Beads Store, Nairobi; Karmali Dossa Beads and Variety Store, Mombasa. His neat writing of alphabets and numbers impressed the traders. "His writing is

120

like the beads he sends us. Wonder who taught him to write?" they would ask.

Sometimes Ma Gor Bai and I talk in whispers about Dadabapa. We say he sighs and sniffs because of the hurt of humiliation from loss of face. Only once did Dadabapa mention that he had had to leave the island of Mombasa because his friend and business partner stole his money. Accompanied by his wife, Sohn Bai and two sons, Noordin and Husein, he came to Voi, a small trading town half way to Nairobi from Mombasa. In Voi, Dadabapa resumed his bead and blanket business with the little money he had but he did not do well. He pawned Grandmother Sohn Bai's diamond nose siri, the size of a coat button, and then, as months went by he sold all the other gold and silver in my grandmother's dowry chest but for four bangles each with a paisley leaf clasp. He never talked about this again. Ma Gor Bai said the shame called sharam of selling his wife's sacred adornments had turned to guilt in him. And now his guilt kept Dadabapa from repeating the story like the way he told other stories over and over again adding more or changing words like how the artist shapes and colours his pictures rubbing off and redrawing his lines, painting over yesterday's colours. Yet the thought of how the picture should be remains the same in his mind.

Dadabapa knew about all the different kinds of blankets and beads. That was his pride and joy. It was also his business. Then the Great War came, depression followed and the trade vessels did not come to the port of Mombasa as regularly as they used to. Dadabapa came to Nairobi where fellow villagers of my grandmother, Sohn Bai, had settled and there was a jamat khana. It was in Nairobi that he finally planted the stunted neem tree from the pot so it would grow free and tall rejuvenating in the sun, wind and rain on the African soil.

Part Four

Beatific Glimpse and Pir's Song

Indian Royal Splendour on Display

The Victoria and Albert Museum, London 2009

The vision of a king in all his splendour was believed to be auspicious. It was central to the concept of darshan, the propitious act of seeing and being seen by a superior being, whether a god or a king ... Although originally a Hindu notion, the idea of darshan became an integral aspect of kingship throughout the subcontinent.

Co-exhibition organiser, Anna Watson.

BBC News, Alastair Lawson October 27, 2009.

15

Chaikop

I remember the times when Dadabapa was in a loving mood. I remember how he teased me fondly. While caressing my hair he would say, "You had your eyes tightly closed for seven days after birth. Sometimes, I would mistake you for a kitten sleeping in my bed!" Such remarks by Dadabapa would keep my siblings and cousins roaring with laughter the whole day. I learned that for six months after my birth, I lay wrapped in a bundle with satin pillows on either side parallel to the tiled headrest of the Swahili bed that came with my grandmother's dowry of utensils and furniture from Mombasa. Later, I slept in that bed with my two siblings: Shamshu at my feet and Monghi by my side and watched the dying wick of the lantern throw shadows on the empty walls as if the room were on a swing. A single kerosene lantern hung suspended from the middle of the ceiling. The only spot that caught the flicker in the dark room was Ma Gor Bai's wall shelf spangling the glass of her English teacups. Or chaikops as we would say.

Ma Gor Bai lined her chaikops, each one turned over a matching saucer on a tracing paper cut in geometrical patterns trimming the shelf line. This array of alike English teacups and saucers was called a 'set'. Each piece matched. 'Set' later became a fashionable word to use in modern Gujarati. We talked of a set of jewellery, a set of spoons, a set of cooking pans and especially later the high-status sofaset. When you dressed up with matching dress, shoes and jewellery, we also said you looked 'set'. To look 'set' was to be modern. But you could have a 'set' of things only if you were rich and thus afford to be 'up to date', another word that crept into our kind of Gujarati. Ma Gor Bai arranged her set of chaikops with delicate carefulness, piece by piece, in an exhibition style on the wall shelf where the children could not reach. After all, it was our home's showpiece displaying our status as a progressive and prospering 'up to date' Nairobi Khoja family. I remember gazing at the 'set' with my eyes scanning the floral vines painted on opaque glass. Ma Gor Bai would serve Indian masala chai with satisfying pride in the proper way, meaning in a complete set of English teacups, each cup sitting in a pool of spilled over tea in the saucer. That was the Gujarati chai ceremony reserved only for the guests, who, as was the custom, all drank from the saucer. The three men folk in our home also drank chai from the saucer but it did not always match with the cup. Then, there were the remnants - kops with broken handles and cracks that ultimately landed as scoops in Ma Gor Bai's flour, rice and sugar bins. We, the women and children, had our chai in enamel and tin kops that burn lips. I remember my dented chaikop. It was not easy to cool chai in such a kop and my complaints were diverted to sweet-talk and magic tricks often by Dadabapa though not always. Dadabapa called my chaikop, kopo, big kop, because he said it looked like Jadio, the fat boy who lived down the street. Needless to say, Jadio's nickname was also Kopo.

That's how Dadabapa used to make fun of things giving them names of people.

Balancing chaikops on saucers while walking was a skill all girls in my family developed early in life. Taking small steps, I would take chai to Dadabapa, my father and Noordin Kaka uncle, one kop at a time, twice a day. I enjoyed the time away from the kitchen and home chores. I also liked to be in the shop because I could see the beads in the shop even though it was just for a little while.

When I took the morning tea, at around ten, I would stare at the multitude of beads on the shop's door panels. How they spangled the yellow sun from the east! When I took the afternoon tea at around four, the beads spangled the yellow sun from the west. I felt the sparkle of colours at those times was made especially for my eyes to see. Behind the bead panels was an assortment of objects, cans of different sizes; tobacco in dried banana leaf twists dangling from the low ceiling like dates on a palm tree; tin funnels, tin kops, tin taa lamps in groups of ten hanging on sisal rope looped through their handles; iron hoes nested in boxes. There were bottles of bitter quinine and sweetened cough syrups from England that stood on the shelf amidst Steamship matchboxes from Sweden, blue Vicks bottles, Ten Cents cigarettes and Manchester sewing needles and thread. At the corner of the glass counter was a stack of funnel shaped packs made of newspaper, each one carrying a quarter or half a pound of sugar that my stepmother prepared. Next to the sugar packs, lay a clutch of paper twists, each one containing one-spoon measure of salt that my Kaki Bai auntie made. She also made bigger three spoon cone packs of salt. Behind the counter on the cement floor there stood a pile of blankets, folded in neat rectangles, to the height of Dadabapa himself. It was here behind the blankets, that I hid myself on hot languorous Nairobi afternoons. Sitting on the cool cement floor, I dreamed about beautiful dresses and velvet hats in silver zari embroidery. I dreamed about how I would be a bride in red silk laden with shiny zari. Sometimes I would take my dhingly doll with me and dress her in stripes of red and bright zari cloth, left over bits and pieces from old frocks from Meethi Bai's lodge that Ma Gor Bai remade to fit Monghi and me. Then I would be the bride in my Gujarati dhingly doll.

The store was popularly called Duka la Ushanga na Blanketi, the Bead and Blanket Store. No one really called it by its real name paint stencilled in English on a plank below the rainwater gutter at the roof: NAGJI PADEMSI AND SONS, P.O.BOX 103 NAIROBI. Under this was a hand written sign in Gujarati: ખોટા મોતી ના સાચા વેપારી meaning, OF IMITATION PEARLS WE ARE GENUINE MERCHANTS. The ethnic people like the Kikuyu and Maasai, called Dadabapa Mzee Blanketi. They called Ma Gor Bai who worked on beads every afternoon, Mama Ushanga, the Bead Woman. My cousin-sister Malek, my younger sister Monghi and I helped Ma Gor Bai on some afternoons, sorting out the beads that came in box-full from Rajan Lalji's shop. We put the beads into smaller boxes according to their shapes and colours. Then we laid them out in clusters and strings on the floor, creating separate spaces for Kikuyu and Maasai beads. Each group's preferences for shapes, sizes, colours and hues were different from the other. All this was in preparation for the display on the panels of the shop's folding door. However, for this, we had to wait for Ma Gor Bai to guide us, bead string by bead string.

Dadabapa's store was diagonally across from the peepal tree at the temple. Under the sacred tree that a devotee, a pioneer Gujarati Hindu settler of Nairobi, had brought from

Saurashtra in India, stood a statue among others, of the female deity, Ambe Ma, the Mother of Strength and Motherhood. Was she not also called Santoshi Ma, Mother of Contentment? Would that not be shukhar in the Satpanth way? At her feet, in the evenings, every day just before sunset, Brahmin Devram lit a lamp, chanted the evening raga, and placed a large bowl of milk, an offering to the nocturnal royal python of Jugu Bazaar. Here, they say in Jugu Bazaar, is the site of the first Hindu temple of Nairobi.

There were many storytellers in Nairobi's Khoja bazaar that often mixed folk tales from Asia and Africa and animal fables from the two continents facing each other across the Indian Ocean. There were stories of the saga of migration where the past walked with the present, affecting karmas, and stories of one faith within many faiths. Good storytellers like my Dadabapa digressed and moved back and forth so their stories stretched on to the next day. When they saw how their words held our imagination, they made the story larger pushing the ending farther into the next day.

I lived among such captivating storytellers like Naaras Dai Bai, my Ma Gor Bai, and of course, Dadabapa, who like all good storytellers, always had one more story to tell. I am taken back in years listening to their stories while telling my own. I live the past as if it were today when I tell you this story.

16

Loving Gujarati

Like me, my younger sister, Monghi, and brother, Shamshu, were also born in Jugu Bazaar. We are three of seven siblings who survived malaria, typhoid and dysentery. Because of housework that is expected of me, I cannot go to Mrs Hajji's school for girls where Monghi and my cousin-sister Malek study. Saheb wants girls to go to school, so our parents send them to school like boys. But not me. I am the eldest and I am needed at home. In the afternoons when I have some time, I sit with my Stepmother Gor Bai, who is known in the bazaar for her skills in embroidery and cooking curries. I watch the needle at her fingers run like a fish swimming in a velvet sea. I am thrilled when I make my own stitches from dot to dot that Ma Gor Bai chalks on merikani cloth for me. The stitch has a little sound in it like a Gujarati letter sketched in Dadabapa's book of the Satpanth verse.

"To read Gujarati is to hear the sound on your tongue the way you see the zari stitch in your fingers. Every word is an incantation under the line. Now repeat after me," says Ma when she teaches me how to read, as she would teach me how to stitch. "Each shine is an incantation of a shadow under the zari," she would say. I also learn to write from Dadabapa and from Monghi and Malek who go to Mrs Hajji's school. They are all my teachers.

Monghi, Malek and I share a clay slate on which we trace Gujarati alphabets: kk - ક, kh - ખ, gg - ગ, gh - ધ, ch - ચ, tt - ત, th - ઠ. Shamshu has his own slate though he seldom uses it. I begin to see each letter as a zari stitch in a curl, a line, a stroke. A wriggle at the bottom changes the sound of the alphabet to oo, a curve at the side standing like a hook adds ee and a dot on the top transforms the letter into nasal nn. A quick stroke at the side adds an aa. Each mark on, below or at the side, by itself or in combination of whole and half alphabets captures a hum, a drone, a bustle, a nasal nn or a quiet purr in the vibration of the tongue and ળ said with the rub of the tongue on the palette. Or even a hiss through the teeth as in 'hass' for a smile, or a hit at the palate as in 'Nah!' for a sharp refusal, 'No!' I can change ch - ચ to cha – ચા, and cha - ચા to chee – ચી or chi – ચિ and to chu - ચુ or choo - ચૂ or even cho - ચો, and I beam with joy.

Ma says I beam like sun's rays at dawn knowing Gujarati. "The sun breaks the night in his excitement waking up," she says. "Reading is like embroidery. It is the raga wrapping the verse of guru-pir that awakens you." She knew because I know she felt the same inside her seeing me read and I was just beginning to know the beauty of reading from her. The beauty of waking up like the sun. But she would also caution me, "Good girls do not show the rass inside. Rass is a voice inside that calls you to the moment of timelessness, when you have no thought or memory." I understood rass was like a momentary thrill, something so personal that you could not share.

In the margins I draw zari motifs in florets and vine leaves like those on the borders of Ma Gor Bai's' pachedis to be the sounds of the alphabets. I want to sing as Dadabapa does and write like Dadabapa whose handwriting, people say, dances like a string of singing pearls on paper. Each sound silhouette on the slate echoes the music of the stitch of my floral embroidery and a line in the divine song.

"Gujarati syllables are shaped by breathing rhythms of sound that reach the heart like musical notes," says Dadabapa. "To know Gujarati is to know the music of syllables like sitar strings of the heart." Each time we sit down with folded legs to practise the art of writing, Dadabapa would show Monghi, Malek and me how to pick a point to start from the top of the syllable under the line. How to keep equal space between letters and twice that space between words. As I scrawl the letters into words and words into sentences, the clay slate sits in my embrace kneading into my stomach like our neighbour's cat, Naakty. The cat is so called because she is stubborn, looks mean and never listens to commands. Dadabapa gave her the name, of course. Nevertheless, Naakty is loved by all the women in the household and she likes to paw knead Kaki Bai auntie's rollover stomach before settling down into the warmth of her ample thighs. Thus, I learn to read letters in the song of zari needlework. I learn to read in the eye-sound-space-pattern letters close to my body like Naakty in Kaki Bai auntie's lap. Reading and writing Gujarati became methodical and as repetitious as breathing. Like my embroidery, like droning meditation into the melody of guru-pir's song, Gujarati letters grew with me like a mirror of Satpanth. Like an extending echo in the verse of Das Avatar as I became a woman.

131

However, every morning I burn with envy on Monghi and Malek when I see them making tight oil-shine braids, and then tying wide ribbons on them of the same blue colour as their pinafore uniform over a white shirt-blouse. Ma Gor Bai tugs the ears of each ribbon so the loops flare up and Kaki Bai auntie straightens the side pleat on their uniforms before they walk out of the house with a slate and a book in their cloth school bags. They wear black polished shoes with buckles and they are allowed to wear a shirt-blouse because they go to school. They look smart and so English children-like, so not like them of the shantytown that everyone wants to compliment them with gestures like picking a bit of loose thread, straightening a crease, brushing fallen dandruff off the shoulders, none of which is needed. Everyone wants to contribute to their smartness. Everyone wants to be a part of their education. Everyone wants to be a part of their schooling. Everyone is proud of Monghi and Malek as if they were receiving education on behalf of all those at home who had not and will not go to school. And I, in my jitherka scruffy hair and rag dress, scurry about cleaning up the breakfast mess that they leave behind on the floor. Even Hawa looks smarter than I do in her clean morning kanga with yellow flowers that smile at you. Nobody offers to brush off the ash from my hair.

Sometimes, I would pick a fight with Malek and even Monghi because I was envious. I would begin to tease and they would retaliate. When we have expended all the hurting words in our scope such as "you are fat," "you are a one eyed witch," "you are dirty," "you are smelly" and "you are black," we make faces at each other, pulling out our tongues. Then we tug at our ear lobes, twist faces, dance fingers on the nose and turn heads showing tongues from the side. Finally, when she

132

would have had enough of my unrelenting sassiness, Malek would bend her elbow until her thumb touched her shoulder. Then she would squeeze open the bump at her crooked elbow saying, "See your arse!" She would put shame in my eyes and when I could not think of a comparable gesture to put shame in her eyes, I would run away to complain to Dadabapa. I would be happy when he admonished my cousin sister.

17

Picture Darshan and the Song

Ma Gor Bai wakes up at five every morning to light the charcoal stove and prepare water for bathing, and then chai. After about an hour, Noordin Kaka uncle and my father shuffle out of their rooms and come into the courtyard to join Dadabapa. I hear an intermittent chain of puff-in-puff-out and then my nose twitches to crisp whiffs from Dadabapa's Ten Cents cigarette smoke drifting towards my bed. Noordin Kaka uncle and my father are smokers too. Everyone can smell tobacco on their clothes, but they do not smoke before Dadabapa. The men cough to clear their throats in the early morning cold; there are sniffs of a blocked nose and a few words. They sit there cross-legged on the stringed charpoy bed with tasbih rolling in their hands and blankets over their shoulders. Precisely at six thirty, Dadabapa begins to hum, partially singing the dawn raga, softly through some sharp khokharo, carving out a melody as if from a rock in his throat. He repeats his favourite verses over and over again, like the one about Mira Bai who drinks a bowl of poison that does not affect her because of her devotional rass - the mood of her

134

aesthetic bliss that comes from her unblemished love for the cowherd god-avatar Krishna. "He sings to match his melody to the pure colours of sunrise," Ma would tell me. The three men move their torsos under the blankets listening, and humming the chorus. My two sleepy siblings walk into the courtyard, and climb onto the stringed bed. They fall asleep again across Dadabapa's lap and he covers them with his blanket that sits over his shoulders. I wake up, look at Saheb's holy picture on the wall, my first sight, my darshan, and walk to the kitchen to help Ma prepare breakfast.

My story begins in colours of the dawn with divine verses and seeing Saheb, his deific image on the wall. In my home the three walk together like sisters and sometimes they embrace, like sisters. All divine.

My Ma pulls her pachedi over her forehead and over those black eyes that she uses to control us, smiling the approvals, frowning disapprovals. Her eye commands are stronger than her word commands. Walking in laaj, she carries the chai tray for the three men in the courtyard. Still sitting cross-legged at the same spot on the stringed charpoy bed, blanket over his shoulders and children in his lap, grandfather balances the saucer in one hand while he pours the tea from the kop into the saucer with the other. He sips in the tea with a gulp of air, followed by an exhale, appreciating the warmth clearing his gullet. Ma Gor Bai tells me the gasp-in of air cools the steaming tea on his tongue. "But from the sound of it," she would add, "it is the monsoon storm approaching." She breaks the silence of the morning. "Take chai to Bakari," she says handing me the chaikop.

My early morning routine, I take chai to Bakari, the Swahili watchman employed by four adjacent shopkeepers in the Jugu

Bazaar. He is known as Askari Bakari or Watchman Bakari in the Indian bazaar and in Majengo, the black Moslem township habited by communities of Somali, Nubian and Swahili, where he lives. Majengo is a township of corrugated sheet iron and mud walled houses far east towards the new airport and the white settlers' coffee trees at Eastleigh.

Askari Bakari is seated on an inverted crate, embroidering a cotton cap. I watch his callous fingers negotiating the sewing needle, executing a stitch in and a stitch out of pin-sized holes. My eyes narrow, tracing the brown silk thread in the pinhole crescents; some are inverted, some upright, some sideways. Bakari hums the same kasida hymn tune every morning about this time.

The movements of the watchman's fingertips marking the rhythm in the kasida's music captivate me. His voice rises up and down and pauses as his fingers go up and down, filling in a line and leaving out a space between the lines. I stand and listen to the hymn's melody and watch the needlepoint. I hear the beauty and then the elation. How his voice and fingertips work one into the other, the song into the art. Bakari the Watchman sees the wonder in my eyes, and says musically, "It's the Swahili Ibadi prayer, art of my forefathers carried from the old country on the Arabian Sea that opens its arms to the Indian Ocean washing the African continent." His coarse fingers continue to translate the song into the supple kofia cap embroidery in silk thread.

"This is the pattern of the crescent moon shining through the cashew nut tree. It's called Khorosho na Mwezi. Look through here. You will see the last of the dawn through these holes." Bakari pulls the unfinished cap up for me to peer into the rising sun. In the bowl of the half-finished cap top, there sparkles a myriad of tiny dots of red. Awestruck, I stay with my eyes fixed deep into the perforated sky's fading red becoming bright yellow.

When Hawa comes to call me, she finds my face buried in her father's cap and her eyes widen, wondering. Jets of light streaming through the pin holes fall on my face as the sun rises. I am exhilarated.

"A garden of His Light is paradise," Bakari says to me. He smiles letting me know that he knows I understand, though I am a girl, and girls do not embroider delicate stitches through pinholes to create patterns on Swahili men's prayer caps.

"Saki, Dadabapa calls you for the aarti prayers," says Hawa in Swahili. Hawa is the only other person besides Naaras Dai Bai who calls me Saki. Then she greets her father.

"Shikamo Baba," she says. "I touch your feet, Father"

"Marahaba," he replies without looking at his daughter, and sips the tea from the kop. "Seven times I bless you."

After his morning chai, Dadabapa gathers all his grandchildren around him at the Saheb's framed picture at the shop's corner altar. A slim garland of stale marigold roses and browned jasmine hangs on the picture that calls for veneration. Below the wilted loop are a handful of mung, a silver coin and a burnt-out incense stick in a silver peacock stand. A fresh tuberose. A broken tasbih. Some coins. Dadabapa replaces yesterday's incense stick and lights a new one on the peacock's head cast in silver on the incense holder. He lights another one holding it between his two fingers as if it were a long sewing needle.

"Remember life is a changing cycle of karma from yoog to yoog. We have been through eight million, four hundred thousand lives in four yoogs, each one a distinct colour - red, yellow, white, black. And there have been ten manifestations of the creator," says Dadabapa measuring his words as he looks at each one of us in the eye. Thus begins the morning lesson, and the song.

"Satpanth stories are in the four colours of the yoogs. Each has its own persona in red or yellow, black or white." I keep still, my eyes tightly closed. I thrill in the expectation of the rass of darshan seeping into my body, the devotional bliss in my ears, the magical picture in my eyes.

"I am at your feet. I offer this my aarti dua today," Dadabapa speaks to the picture. Then he turns around and speaks to us. "Children! Sing with me! Let me hear your voices loud!"

I open my eyes gradually to the holy picture and my heart to the coming bliss. Dadabapa draws incense smoke in circles around the picture in which all the ten avatars of the creator as fish, animal, man and halves of each - god the fish, god the animal and god the man stand before me. I look at each image, my palms pressed before me, my chants following Dadabapa, line by line. Shamshu mumbles by my side. He is impatient for his mind is elsewhere. Pictures of the avatars sing back to me. My eyes fall on them pleading darshan. Awe fills me when the chant of the fish-animal-human god avatar in the ten descriptions becomes one prayer to our unison universe. Behind the children, Ma Gor Bai and Kaki Bai auntie stand at a distance with their hands folded, eyes closed, all singing together. My father stands in the opposite corner, also with his hands folded, eyes closed and singing. Only Noordin Kaka uncle is not there. Even Hawa joins us.

I am Vishnu's machli avatar, the giant fish
I saved the Vedas from heinous demon
Behold! I am the Lord of the Age

When he comes to '*I am*' in the end verse, Dadabapa raises his voice. Repeating after him, we would call out '*I am*' in a chorus, shouting at the top of our voices. He would smile aside without looking at his grandchildren imitating him.

I am Vishnu's kurma avatar, the turtle
I deliver life when oceans whirl
Behold! I am the Lord of the Age

Awe grips me. So vast a Divinity before me. So vast the story of Das Avatar. So vast the Creation.

I am Vishnu's Krishna avatar,
Black and bare chested a lover
Behold! I am the Lord of the Age

Dadabapa pauses to hear us repeating each verse correctly after him, exactly as he wants us to, emphasizing '*I am*'. He would make us repeat if he hears a miss of a syllable or a slip in the rhythm in the harmony of our voices.

I stand my ankles crossed
And play my melodious flute
Behold! I am the Lord of the Age

Before me, Krishna tremors, a shimmering Light. I hear the music of his flute calling his girl murids to garba. His love of Saurashtran dance touches me - dha dhi na, dha tu na, dha dhi na, dha tu na. He is the mischievous god, native of Gujarat.

I am Rama, Vishnu's man avatar
Handsome prince god of the golden bow
Behold! I am the Lord of the Age

The divine epic is my dua. My skin bristles, breaking into a thousand pinheads. Water wells in my eyes.

I am Lord Narashima, Vishnu's fearsome avatar
A creature half man half woman
Half a beast half a human
I tear the royal demon apart
Behold! I am the Lord of the Age

Finally when we come to the last verse, we sing it all together raising our voices when we reach *'I am'* in the end line.

I am Ali, Vishnu's tenth avatar
Riding Dul Dul, Zulficar I sway
Behold! I am Naklank the Lord of the Age

My eyes rest on Saheb. I do not close them. With my palms pressed together, I stand still absorbed in the devotional gaze of darshan. In the centre of the great mystery stands Saheb wearing a hefty moustache, splendid in a grand red turban as becomes a raja. He is bedecked with jewels sparkling jug mug and a blue silk coat with epaulettes. A broad sash sports an array of gold and silver medallions on his chest, insignia of honour and distinguished service that decorate many an Indian prince in the magnificent pageantry of valour and fidelity to the English raj. In patchy arguments with Dadabapa, Noordin Kaka uncle would say how the glorious Empire possesses the magic to create friendly blue-blood lineages. How the Empire pampers its made-up rajas to relinquish Indian jewels to embellish English crowns. How the rajas then gift elephants, camels, horses, and their devoted subjects to battle for England. Thus are the allegiances to the great raj secured against a century of sporadic Wars of Independence. How they combat Indian violence with Indian violence in the old country that Dadabapa calls Desh. We, his grandchildren, imagine the Desh of his mind in his stories, in the movies and worship pictures.

Such talks of adults about the raj and rajas and the subject people-devotees of godlike rajas do not bother me the way they bother others in my home. All I see are beams of light radiating from Saheb to the nine avatars of Vishnu, Hari of Hindustan, in whose bosom, once the celebrated pir prince Saheb, an exile from Persia, sought a sanctuary. So the story is told of the coming of Saheb to Hindustan and about how he was the avatar before decreed an imam. The celestial mandala of nine god avatars pulsates in my vision. A halo of Light falls over Saheb, the tenth. Above him in gilded calligraphy is inscribed Om. My palms come together; my gaze turns inward becoming a prayer in me, his murid, a Satpanth devotee, an English subject. I wonder what it would be like where the ten avatars live together as one in a place that is beyond the cycles of karma. The after-karma world. The pure souls' only world. The ancestral world in the living present. The world where the karmas come to rest after a hundred thousand cycles of wandering. It would be peaceful all day. It would be where the colourful mandala is realized. Not a picture anymore because the avatars would walk out of their painted images. It would have many a dazzling Light, splendours in jug mug shine all around you, all darshan-deedar to celebrate. Such was my imagination when I was little. Such was my imagination sparked by the desire to be in the gaze of eternal darshan.

I grow up among a panorama of devotional sights, stories and songs of the Satpanth concealing the sacred within to nourish the atma meaning the soul. The vibrant images in the

Das Avatar mandala and ritual chants etch into my child head creating bigger imagination. I live in it.

From Dadabapa and Ma Gor Bai, I learn to hold the secrets of my faith close to my heart and drink the rass of the raga in the ginan songs of Kutch-Kathiavad and Sindh, the region in India that Sikander the Great called Saurashtra. Thus, my intimacy with Saheb grows large in the secrecy of my heart. He is my expectant bridegroom, my secret love, the one of the gilded sword Zulficar that tremors at his waist as he rides Dul Dul, his horse that's unblemished of any birth mark or battle wound, the one of pure white coat. As it was expected, he would come. As told in ancient scriptures he would come riding a horse, who would be white.

Part Five

Wasikia - Do you hear?

To listen to my story you must feel the words in your body
Like how you listen to the smell in Swahili
Wasikia harufu? Do you hear the smell?
Or listening to how the cold enters your body
Wasikia baridi? Do you hear the cold?
Or even listening to joy in your heart you say
Wasikia raha? Do you hear happiness?
To feel the pain in Swahili is to listen to the pain
Wasikia uchungu? Do you hear pain?

When you listen to my story in your body
And it smells and you feel the heat and cold
Joy and the pain like how you hear a song
I know then you are listening
When I ask Wasikia? Are you listening?
I also mean, are you feeling?

18

Chup Chap Whispers

Once a month or so, but always on Saturdays, the local Punjabi scholar, Gangandeep, visits Noordin Kaka uncle in the shop. He would talk for a long time with Noordin Kaka uncle while my father and Dadabapa would pretend to ignore their conversation but would in fact be listening. Gangandeep is aware of the men folk in the shop and he would speak softly, keeping his head in the direction of the silent pretenders. He handwrites a newsletter in Gujarati and makes as many copies between sheets of blue carbon paper as the determination of his hand would allow. When I can, I steal-read the blue smudged scripts from behind the chaikop shelf where Noordin Kaka uncle hides them. But I don't understand what I read. What I know is that what Gangandeep writes irritates the English because it's kept hidden like witchcraft. From men's talk, I know it's all about the injustice that the brown and black subjects suffer in Kenya and the rest of the Empire.

In that secret place behind the chaikops, there are other magazines with pictures of nude paper white women, and the ones with red covers. The red cover ones have line drawings of the same angry man raising his shackled fists as if he were boxing the air. Another one, also with a red cover, shows the angry man breaking his chain that flies over his head like an iron snake. All the red cover magazines have an identical image of a sickle and hammer on them, like a stamp as if it were their sacred Om.

"Gangandeep does not let the governor sleep in peace," Dadabapa would say after the Punjabi scholar leaves the shop. The news is about Indian opposition to the English raj, Gandhi, and about the attempts of the natives to repossess their land and acquire education in Kenya colony. Turbaned Gangandeep also collects funds for the Kikuyu Independent Schools that the natives have started 'to show resistance to mission schools in the reserves' as Noordin Kaka uncle puts it. I overhear the men talking in soft tones when I come to sweep the shop floor before the closing hour. Dadabapa is aware I am eavesdropping. He glances at me now and again with anger flaming in his eyes. My father and Noordin Kaka uncle are not aware of my presence until Dadabapa draws their attention to me. My father, looking in my direction, gestures to me with a sharp jerk of his chin to return to the courtyard at once.

Like most other Sunday mornings in Nairobi when men folk go into the shop late, say around ten, and begin the day's business, there is a noisy gaggle of family children at play in the courtyard. My brother Shamshu is imitating Dadabapa pointing to the crows at the rubbish heap at the back door that opens into an alley and open sewer gutters.

"Children! Come and listen to a story. Do you hear? Say yes, so I know you hear me. Come here my little demons!" Shamshu calls out faking a khokharo, a cough-and-spit out.

"Do you see the crows there on the rubbish heap? They are immigrant ancestors that came with our forefathers from India. When they spread their wings to bask and gap their beaks open, they are imitating the dhow's sail panting in the ocean sun." Then in a softer, controlled voice, he continues after one more throat grating, cough and spit, "You can make a living even from thrown-away scraps. Do not waste anything, particularly food, ever in your life." Shamshu makes more exaggerated guttural noises before lifting his stick and pointing at the girls. "Every grain is anaj, your roji, the baraka-blessing of food. To waste a speck of food is a sin. Disrespect to anaj, your roji meal. When you have two grains share them with the hungry and your roji will multiply twofold. Sharing brings blessings of abundance that is baraka." Then Shamshu does the crow walk moving his body from side to side, 61 – 62, 61 – 62, 61 – 62 … There is a hint of tease in his imitation of Ma Gor Bai's gait. He caws kaa-kaa-kagrow like papadam breaking over the tongue as he hobbles, exaggerating the side up, side down amble of the kagrow crow, his head moving dole dole from side to side. Standing at the kitchen door, Hawa, Ma Gor Bai, and my Kaki Bai auntie repress laughter behind clenched lips. Girls' muffled mirth wavers around the courtyard wall. My little cousin-brother, Bahdur, cousin-sister Malek's brother, laughs loudly, uncontrollably.

"Sakina!" calls Ma Gor Bai taking me by surprise, "Go to the karo and help Hawa with the dishes." She returns to the kitchen to prepare turmeric paste.

"Smear with care so the yellow marks don't show in the jamat khana," says Kaki Bai auntie to Ma Gor Bai. Her quiet voice wavering.

"They will not show. You are blue only on the back and upper arms," replies Ma Gor Bai applying the turmeric paste, gently tracing the red blue swellings with her fingers on Kaki Bai auntie's swollen body.

The previous evening, Noordin Kaka uncle had beaten Kaki Bai auntie with the kitchen ladle when she returned late from the jamat khana. Noordin Kaka uncle was hungry, and when he gets hungry, he is angry. "His fuse blows off like the street light if I delay serving food," says Kaki Bai auntie, nursing her humiliation while speaking in anger. Besides that, they have had some disagreements over my auntie taking food offerings to the jamat khana and singing the Das Avatar. It could be the real cause of Noordin Kaka uncle's rage, which Kaki Bai auntie tries to hide. Although she must know, their night quarrels permeate through our common walls. Noordin Kaka uncle calls Das Avatar a Vedic hymn like the ginans. He says our chanting is not Moslem, therefore kafir infidel, therefore sinful. But Kaki Bai auntie is stubborn when it comes to matters of her faith, and like Queen Suraja in the epic song of Das Avatar, she would secretly say the Satpanth prayers at home, and even carry prayer food to the jamat khana concealed under her pachedi. Besides that, she must honour her father's community standing as the mukhi of the Nairobi jamat khana.

"You should have decided to leave Satpanth before you sent the marriage proposal to my family," she would tell him whenever an argument erupted over the singing of the ginan that she said hummed in her ears like a call of faith.

Dadabapa is proud that his daughter-in-law is from a religious family, and therefore, a respectable loyal to Saheb, honourable family. In a quiet way, he protects Kaki Bai auntie

149

who is known in town more as the daughter of mukhi Dharamshi than the wife of Noordin Nagji Padamsi. Dadabapa never says a word when they argue, or even when Noordin Kaka uncle calls his wife a Saheb loyalist. Nevertheless, every morning when Dadabapa calls the family to come to the mandala of Das Avatar, he says Kaki's name clearly, distinctly and loudly as if to dare Kaka to stop her. No one can defy Dadabapa. He is the father and provider of the family welfare and protector of its honour.

Much later when I was older, and thought more, I would understand how during these times of divisions among Khoja families over matters of faith, some women were caught between loyalties. Their hurt deepened in their hearts aching under the weight of keeping the family honour, the faith of their conscience and obligation of wife's duty to the husband as the custom would want. Such was the fate of Kaki Bai auntie. The pain lessens when women tell women about their divided loyalties and secret lives, like keeping loyalties to both the faiths. However, just as Ma Gor Bai's words are fluid and light from telling secrets of her life, Kaki Bai auntie's words are restrained and heavy on her tongue from not speaking, especially when it comes to Noordin Kaka uncle's shifting prayer gestures and routines that she had noticed.

I feel Kaki Bai auntie's pain in my body for I am becoming a woman too. I hear her unsaid and not understood pain. I feel her worrying about her children. She tells Malek and Bahdur to love their father and Saheb. I understand her love for Saheb. One day, I heard Ma tell Meethi Bai how Kaki Bai auntie was torn between three loyalties – as a Satpanthi to Saheb, as an Indian wife to her husband, and as a mother to keep peace in her family.

Even as girls, Monghi, Malek, Hawa and I, would share women's torments, sometimes quietly without a word said among us, just sitting next to each other as girls do, their bodies touching and their hearts beating in unison. We are six women in the house and we must protect our family honour, our faith, and our duties to men, and not let a word slip out to the neighbours. Otherwise, the shaming will spread like the savannah fire when the land is dry, the sky is hot blue, and the grass is crisp. Then, as Ma Gor Bai would say, "Who will marry you?"

One day my cousin-sister, Malek, told me how she would feel the sound of Om when she pressed the symbol to her navel. So one hot afternoon when Dadabapa was having his after-lunch nap, I tried to draw Ali Om in floral Gujarati letters on my palm. I used a nib dipped in Quink inkbottle that Dadabapa kept on the shelf above his bed on top of his Satpanth books. Then I pressed the sacred letters to my navel and waited to feel the vibration, aa … Om … o-aa-m … Ali on my abdomen. Nothing happened. Perhaps I needed to re-write in heavier letters. However, when I looked at my palm again, it was smudged blue all over. I hurried to the karo where Ma kept the grey pumice stone to scrub her heels.

19

The Stone Jamat Khana

In Nairobi, our community life revolved around the three-storey jamat khana. The chiselled granite stonewalls stood at the corner of two main streets, Government Road that ran down from Kingsway, and Victoria Street that faced the Indian Bazaar adjoining my street, the Jugu Bazaar.

Behind the jamat khana was the legendary lane called Moti Bazaar, known as the bead market for the interior. It was also called Khoja Bazaar. Behind the Khoja Bazaar, was the Indian worker shantytown, descending haphazardly into the Ol-ng'arua swamp at the Nairobi River where you would see Punjabi vegetable farmers, men and women sitting on haunches, bent backs digging, harvesting or weeding side by side. In Moti Bazaar, you would see lines and lines of beads on display both inside and outside the shops on the veranda. More beads were kept in crates piled on top of each other in stores and stacked in packages under the beds in homes that were behind the bazaar stores.

Every day or every other day, when I would go to Moti Bazaar to do some shop errands for Dadabapa like returning loaned packets of beads that he had run short of or exchanging business notes, I would see rural bead merchants haggling over the prices of beads. I would imagine their daughters sorting, arranging and displaying the new stocks of beads when the merchants returned to their countryside homes along the old caravan routes of Allidina Visram and the new railroad. I would wonder if they would hang the beads in strings on the door panels the way I do in Jugu Bazaar, or would they display their beads differently. I would wonder about the colours that the far away ethnic people liked to wear. Listening over the conversations among the bead traders, I would hear about the distant cultures and imagine how they worked their art. I heard names of ethnic communities of the interior like the Kisii, the Luo, the Luhya, and the Taita. How would their beadwork compare with the Kikuyu and Maasai who come to Dadabapa's shop? Would their patterns and styles of beaded adornment be similar? I had not travelled beyond the Indian shantytown of Nairobi, so I did not know the land and its people. I could only imagine looking at the varieties of beads in Moti Bazaar. We had no relatives outside of Nairobi to visit to celebrate a marriage, or moan a death like my friends, Jamal Bhai's daughters, who would always be going here and there like to Kisumu or Eldoret or Arusha.

Sometimes when I went with Ma Gor Bai to clean the Meditation Chamber, I looked out of the windows of this third storey of the jamat khana. The windows were taller than I was and under the blue sky, I could see over Nairobi's valleys and ridges. I could see as far away as what my father told me were the Embakasi Plains to the east that slip into

Athi Plains. I saw the Ngong Hills surge in five blue humps like a passing camel caravan. On other side, my father, who collected magazine pictures of mountains, deserts, waterfalls and birds more than he read about them, told me that the hills drop precipitously into the cleft of the Great African Rift Valley. Above the Meditation Hall, the clock tower of the jamat khana was a shining metal diadem.

It would be to the religion school on the ground floor of the granite jamat khana that every evening, before the sunset over the Ngong Hills, I walked with my little sister, Monghi, and cousin-sister Malek, who was three years younger than I was. Bahdur, my cousin-brother and Malek's younger brother, always trailed behind us, deliberately keeping a distance because he would not want to be seen walking to school with girls. Sometimes we called the religion school Sindhi School because we learned Khojki in Sindhi-like alphabets here. We greet Meeshnari Shivji Bhagat standing at the door cross-ankle like Krishna, enjoying the evening draught from the Ol-ng'arua valley. My heart beats faster as I pass by him. Raising his hand, he stops me to ask the routine missionary questions about my family: How is your Dadabapa? How is your father Husein Bhai? How is your mother Gor Bai? And how is Malek's mother, your Kaki Bai auntie? Then he asks with an ironic tinge to his voice, And your Noordin Kaka uncle? He does not expect answers to these everyday questions. So I just nod after each question to be polite and step away when suddenly, he asks in a louder, more commanding voice, just what I dreaded he would, "Where is your brother Shamshu?" I stiffen up. Turning my head, I indicate Shamshu is coming behind me, though I know I have not seen him this afternoon after lunch.

Meeshnari Shivji Bhagat, the principal, spends his time between Nairobi and Bombay exchanging spoken messages, some letters, some gifts, some money and a few newspapers, between the two continents that churn and blend tales of travel, politics, faith, families, spirits and miracles like spices blending into curry in a cauldron. On the side, Meeshnari runs a small trade in religious literature, Saheb's wall pictures, tasbihs and trinkets – rings and pendants, coat lapel medallions with Saheb's image or his flag or his turbaned crown. "It helps to pay for my passage to and fro India," he would say as if to tell us it's not a business he profits from.

As always, the missionary begins today's assembly with a short prayer. It's Monday, and on Mondays, he tells a short story about sewa, the obligatory giving to the community and to Saheb. I enjoy listening to the principal's stories, especially the one about the sewa of one man who helped to build the Nairobi stone jamat khana. He begins the story with the stone of the jamat khana. The story of the granite stone is close to my heart because within its walls I am myself, at peace in the beauty of the chants and grace of rituals.

"The granite stone came from Porbandar at the tip of the Peninsula of Kathiawar on the Arabian Sea," the missionary would talk with much dignity and pride painting the scene of the waves crushing against the rocks on the Saurashtran coast. I actually believed he owned the jamat khana and I admired my teacher all the more. He stood tall in his black coat, white cotton paatoloon and red fez hat.

"The stone came from the birthplace of Mahatma Gandhi who leads the freedom movement in India. The Saurashtran stone was stacked by bare hands into vessels bound for Mombasa and it arrived by steam rail to Nairobi." As he

155

speaks, Meeshnari Shivji Bhagat arranges his red fez hat with a swinging black tassel, though it needs no fixing.

"I saw with my own two eyes how the stone was carried in bullock carts, handcarts, and on donkey carts trudging from the railway station all the way down to here. This very spot at the acacia forest where before there stood a wooden jamat khana."

Clearly, Meeshnari Shivji Bhagat is proud of the new jamat khana. It shows on his face. His description is so vivid that I feel I am witnessing the construction of the jamat khana.

"Virji Nanji designed the building, the finest in colonial Nairobi. Virji Nanji, they say, was an unqualified architect whose drawings were so professional that when they were presented to the Nairobi Municipality, the English architects could find no fault with them. They could not na-pass them, so they passed them all." As he continues to speak, the missionary points his finger to the ground with one hand while adjusting his fez cap with the other hand once again.

"I was here at the site where a dua prayer was offered to the new land and God. When the coconut was cracked and then the red African earth was broken to lower the stone from the old country. There it rested embedded in the African soil like our hearts. Now we pray on it, the foundation of our new lives."

The missionary's words captivate me. His lips are thick and look even thicker because of a fine moustache, so finely crafted that the girls believe it is lined on with Quink ink.

"All this was possible because of the dharma sewa of Count Kassam Bhai Suleman Virji and others. Sewa is the spring, the source of our faith and community. Your dharma is your religion. So, now for your homework this week, you will visit the clerk's office on this floor and look at the picture of Count Kassam Bhai Suleman Virji, and read about his service inscribed on the marble stone."

The missionary ends the assembly with a caution said with much authority as was his habit when speaking to children. "If you memorize well during the week and not skip classes, you will not shame your parents when you are called to recite the dua." He ends with his threat mantra, "Agonizing karma awaits you for your sins, and honey-sweet paradise for your good acts."

The very next day, eager to see the picture of Count Kassam Bhai Suleman Virji, I walk into the clerk's office at the Nairobi jamat khana. I am expecting this dharma sewa giver to be a white bearded old man in a robe holding a tasbih like the picture I had seen of Allidina Visram. Instead, my eyes meet a portrait of a young man, handsome with a healthy black moustache, wearing a tie under a buscot under a buttoned up English jacket with double rounded lapels. I look into the wet black eyes of Count Kassam Bhai Suleman Virji. A ray of light from the corridor strains through the stained glass door illuminating the Gujarati script in black ink. It reads that in his will, Count Kassam Bhai Suleman Virji, once the president of the Religious Council, offered sewa money to Saheb for peace of his soul and that he gave generously to build the Khoja Khana. On the right hand top corner is a symbol of a crescent moon with a star in it and on the left hand corner is inscribed Om. Our two religion symbols are emblazoned on the stone that built the jamat khana where I come to be at peace and where every evening my heart returns to rest in the sacred pictures and chanting. Chanting is like

157

embroidery. It brings me to my inner self as I gaze into Saheb's red robed portrait on the wall of the prayer hall.

When they prospered, our forefathers built more jamat khanas into the interior to bring the Satpanth merchants home to stay. Here they said shukhar after their long saga over the Black Waters and overland journeys by rail, donkey and bullock carts, and on foot. Here they would chant in the evenings and meditate at dawn so that they might come to know who they are. Then when the sun rose and made a new day, they knew they must build again because, as they said, "We have reached home. Shukhar Mowla!"

20

At the Religion School

As was his practice after the assembly, Meeshnari Shivji Bhagat goes around correcting our sitting postures on the floor. Boys sit in adap-palothi - hands folded at the chest, straight backs and cross-legged. Girls sit with knees together, hands in front and feet back. "The orphans at Naklank Ashram in India show more discipline than you do," he says. On the straw mat that runs from wall to wall, boys and girls sit separately and in circles, older boys teaching younger ones on one side of the school hall, and older girls teaching younger girls on the other side of the hall. Boys and girls are further divided according to their ages. At thirteen years of age, I am a senior student tutor of nine-year-olds.

I have memorized the dua text and can say all the names of the pirs without a mistake. And it is not difficult to know the names of the avatars of Vishnu in the dua because they are also there in the ginan of Das Avatar that we sing every month on the evening of the new moon in the jamat khana.

159

But, now Meeshnari makes us learn by heart, forty-eight other names, names foreign to my tongue. New, unfamiliar sounds to my ears. Forty-eight names of Arab avatars that he says are the names of the imams, Saheb's ancestors that he wants us to say now instead of the Indian avatars. "Because one day, we will recite them in our daily dua," says Meeshnari. I try, but find it difficult to put them to the rhythm of the dua I sing in Gujarati. Now before the jamat, I fault. To make a mistake while reciting before the prayer gathering means admonishment at home and shame to the family as if you have committed a sin. What I find hard to bear is the teasing of my peers. Before the night of recitation in the jamat khana, Ma Gor Bai gives me three almonds, a rare and precious commodity, to chew slowly, thoughtfully and thoroughly, releasing the good juices for the brain to help me not to make mistakes while saying the sacred texts. She understands how the intrusion of alien words halts the pulse of my song because she is a dua singer too.

Meeshnari Shivji Bhagat towers six feet tall over the girl's black velvet caps in my study circle. He bends down like a bow and shows me the assigned verses of Das Avatar to teach the girls under my tutelage. I look closely at his coat. The lapels have double pointed corners like fox's ears. On the right lapel, are three round thumb size medallions with Saheb's picture on one, Saheb's monogram on another, and on the third medallion there is a green flag with a red diagonal line, which I have come to know as My Flag. He displays different medallions on him each day as a kind of advertisement for his trade. Men see and can bargain a deal for a medallion they would want on their own lapels. I hold my breath and then I breathe lightly, diverting my exhales away from the missionary's rotund face blowing out words

160

with wind. I feel flushed and hot. My hands begin to tremble and I hold them together tight in knitted fingers.

"Will you sing the first two verses, Sakina?" asks the missionary.

I try to find my voice suppressed under the emotions surging in me. Then looking straight at the classroom mandala poster similar to the one on Dadabapa's shop shelf, I begin to sing the Das Avatar. Tears warm my eyes when I see the avatars dance before me like zari twinkle jug mug on velvet. Verses become vines interlacing my voice, the fruit. Gradually, I feel my body transform the sensations from the missionary to Saheb's eyes. He is the one I really love.

"Shabash! Excellent!" The missionary pats me gently on my head, straightens his back and looms over me. He stands tall in a well-pressed white Saurashtran cotton paatoloon and a black cotton coat that reaches his knees.

"And what is another name for Das Avatar?" he asks.

"Brahma Prakash," sing out the girls in a chorus. I feel proud of my students.

"And what did Lord Narashima say?" he asks again, excitedly, expecting the precise answer.

"Sitting on the threshold, neither inside nor outside, *I am*," chime the girls accentuating *I am*.

"Shabash!" says the principal again leaning on the yellow sandglass pane of the door that refracts golden light from outside onto his face. We made our teacher happy that day. Then as he walks away, I hear him hissing out air through his parted lips, whispering to himself as if he were suddenly thrown into a trance by some miracle, "Sitting on the

161

threshold, neither inside nor outside, *I am*." This was not the first time I notice such peculiar behaviour of adults so wrapped up in thoughts that they talked to themselves. They think children are not aware of adult behaviour, but we are observant and we would even imitate them, especially teachers, to entertain each other. "Neither here nor there, *I am*; neither this nor that, *I am*; neither a Hindu nor a Musalman, *I am*. A worshipper at the threshold of both, *I am*. My sewa service to Saheb is to teach his children. My duty to show them how to live Satpanth lives concealed between the thresholds of Hinduism and Islam." Perhaps Meeshnari was affected by the unending disputes between the Khoja factions: those who were loyal to Saheb and paid him the due tithe like us the Satpanthis, and three others, the Sunni, Hindu and Ithna Asheri Khojas who refused to pay him his religious owing. Listening to Dadabapa's peers one evening, I heard them discuss how the killings that happened in Bombay could easily happen here in East Africa and that worried many.

No sooner does he walk out of the hall than the silence breaks. Older boys challenge each other to stand up and some do, look around for a second and sit down quickly, defying the principal's rule number one, 'Do not stand unless told to.' The girls watch from the far side of the hall, amused, they chuckle. I cannot stop them joining in the classroom play. The boys feel heroic when the girls respond with smiling looks and cheering giggles, and they stand up for longer time defying each other. Some get excited and excite others just calling out girls' names – Gulshan, Gulbanu, Gulnar, the three of the fairest in my group, all sisters. Havoc breaks out when the girls begin teasing each other with boys' names, who called out their names. But where is Shamshu? He would be the first to stand up and call out girls' names. I look around and do not see him. My heart thuds against my ribs.

I know Shamshu has slipped away again. He is good at that. I also know he would be hiding in the dark side of the stairs that lead from the prayer hall to the Meditation Chamber. Shamshu would wait for the evening prayers to start so he could then slip out of the building undetected. He would rendezvous with Razak, son of Ful Bai, Shamshu's wet-nurse. Ful Bai is the daughter of Bebli, who is the daughter of the Ithna Asheri Khoja lady called Paan Bai, who walked with a limp, who was on the dhow with Dadabapa, and who was thrown off the toilet box into the raging ocean during the storm. The two boys are like brothers being nursed by the same woman they both call mother. Together, in a group of two, Shamshu and Razak would sneak around adult entertainment houses of Nairobi's shantytown. They would peep through the courtyard doors, and at windows from behind the whistling thorn bushes at Ol-debbei acacia groves. They would haunt around Meethi Bai's lodge that Shamshu tells me, 'is in the darkest patch of the street.' The boys peep a look at the dance girls swaggering about in pace with the rhythm of soft mujra tabla beat and flute tamasha.

After the evening of niggling around the bush around Meethi Bai's lodge, my voyeur brother loves to show off to me, Hawa and Malek how adult he is. He would describe the scenes so vividly to us that we would want to believe he had been in the lodge itself, and was actually entertained by the dance girls. He would even imitate the girls' swan walk and their seductive poses, standing cross-thigh in silk saris, pulled skin-tight over their hips, one braid at the front laden with champeli flowers, a henna red fingertip on the chin in a filmi vamp pose, big filmi eyes, made aghast with kohl seducing

163

men. We laugh at Shamshu's mimicking of the forbidden feminine gestures at which he is very good.

Unfortunately, for Shamshu, as I come to know later that day, Meeshnari Shivji Bhagat walks out of the class hall and comes up the stairs to collect chalk that he stores with other school material in the cupboard by the door of the Meditation Hall.

Shamshu is taken by surprise. Without a word and forgetting his errand, the missionary reels forward and grabs the crouched boy by the ear. Pulling him down the stairs by the same ear, he mutters repeatedly through his clenched paan-stained teeth into the boy's tender lobe, "Is this why you come to jamat khana, hengh? Is this what your parents send you to do at school, hengh? Why don't you be like your sister, hengh?" Meeshnari Shivji Bhagat has a habit of coughing out a 'hengh?' at the end of a sentence emphasizing admonishment in a question. Shamshu is short of breath and almost choking from the missionary's thick breath, its smell of bidi cigarette poorly suppressed into the fragrance of chewed over sweet betel nut paan.

The principal makes Shamshu sit in adap-palothi with both hands and legs folded, in a corner of the classroom. The rest of the evening, I keep my head bowed down in shame. I feel the girls' looks fleeting from me to Shamshu, back and forth. Some were giggling under their breath.

Meeshnari Shivji Bhagat sits at his desk. On the wall behind him are two posters printed ahead of Saheb's Golden Jubilee in Bombay to raise funds. Dadabapa would remind us that these pictures are the devotional labour of one poet-artist and Saheb's devotee, Major Abdullah Lakhpati. Meeshnari then fixes an angry look on Shamshu and takes a pause

164

followed by a sigh of some sort of pain that adults express as exasperation. Turning around, he asks both of us to stay behind while the rest of the class climbs up the stairs to be with their families in the prayer hall.

Once again, he lashes out at Shamshu. He fumbles at words and having found them, he at once stops himself from uttering them. He seemed to be now searching for words that would not be rude that come almost naturally to him speaking among his peer friends. Or he seemed to be searching for words that would be befitting a principal of a religion school. The missionary goes about speaking in a round about way in long sentences equally insulting. "You are a shame to the good family name of Nagji Padamsi. This girl, your sister, is the pride of the family. Why can you not be like her, hengh?" However, his questions have no answers nor does he expect any from Shamshu, because that would be disrespectful.

"Do you know the twenty one names of pirs in the daily dua? Do you know the names of the ten avatars of Vishnu?" questions Meeshnari Shivji Bhagat. These questions are meant to humiliate Shamshu and assert the principal's authority if not to vent his anger. Everyone knows that Shamshu does not know the names. He fumbles even when he sings the Das Avatar. Shamshu looks down and is silent, as he becomes a student before his livid master.

"And how many Prophets have there been? May I request the raja to answer this simple question, hengh?" asks Meeshnari Shivji Bhagat, again in a tone meant to ridicule. I am anguished inside. I want to run out of the school hall, but how could I? I have been placed there to witness and report home.

"One hundred and eighty four thousand!" replies Shamshu, his eyes brightening as he lifts up his face for the first time. Shamshu's correct answer surprises both the principal and me. But the missionary does not acknowledge that the boy has given the right answer. For a moment, he does not know what to say. He was well ready to give the next verbal thrashing.

"Here, take this and know your Das Avatar. You are lucky you are not in the Naklank Ashram. I taught at the ashram for five long sewa years before coming to Africa, only to meet donkeys like you," says the frustrated principal before handing the book to Shamshu demonstrating favour.

21

Shame called Sharam

Later that evening, while rolling chapattis, I hear my father drumming his fingers on the table as if he were playing a harmonium. He is sitting at the teak dining table on the courtyard veranda. Dadabapa is sitting opposite him, head tilted and bowed into *Africa Samachar*, pretending to read, but in fact, trying to hear what we are talking about in the kitchen. It is already past dinner time. Shamshu's chair is empty. I am whispering to Ma Gor Bai about the incident at the religion school.

"Your father gets impatient like your Noordin Kaka uncle when he is hungry," says Ma Gor Bai while removing the eggplant buried in the ashes under the brazier's grille. Gently, she strokes the mixed neem leaf and wood coal dust from the wrinkled eggplant skin, still mauve with a gleam. She taps it on the grey cement floor before blowing over it with a few rapid puffs. Then she throws the ash-roasted vegetable into the oil spitting mustard seed, and immediately covers the pot to allow the moisturized mustard seed smoke to flavour the eggplant. Before serving, she adds a few succulent garlic cloves, and spring onions together with fragrant coriander leaves with a pinch of salt. Finally, she stirs the mix lightly.

"Sakina, take the bharto and this green chutney to the table. They can have dinner now. Hawa will bring the plates and the yogurt bowl. It must have formed by now."

"I am afraid to go. Bapa will ask me what happened in class," I reply.

"Where is Malek today?" asks Ma Gor Bai.

"Kaki Bai auntie called her away," says Hawa.

Ma Gor Bai thinks for a moment and then she says, "I will take the vegetable and chutney myself then." She peels a tender white onion, places it on a wooden board and hits it with her fist. Thaak! A cold ting spurts from the onion onto my face, my eyes smart. Ma Gor Bai does not notice it. She drops the squashed onion into a teakop saucer and carries the roasted eggplant, the onion and green chutney to the table.

"What is the matter?" she asks father. He does not reply and looks away. He is not interested in a conversation. "Children will be children until they are married and have responsibilities," says Ma Gor Bai. Hawa arranges three plates on the table while Ma Gor Bai places the hot clay pot on a makeshift cloth ring seat.

My father removes the leather belt from his trousers and lays it on the table, the buckle dangling at the board's edge. Ma glances at the belt and then questions my father enlarging her black eyes. He refuses to speak.

"Please do start to eat before the bharto gets cold. I am bringing more hot chapattis in a minute. Here green chili-coriander-garlic chutney. Yogurt, hmm?" Roast eggplant with green chili-coriander-garlic chutney and yogurt is my father's favourite meal. However, Dadabapa is the one who begins to serve himself. It is also his favourite menu in front of him. None of the children likes bharto. In fact, any eggplant meal, no matter how it is cooked – roasted, curried, fried, steamed or pickled is liked. My father moves neither his hand nor his head ignoring Ma.

"Bring some cool water from the clay pot, Hawa," says Dadabapa while plucking at the chapatti. He turns the piece into a teaspoon size cup and swipes into the eggplant roast where the core is thick and luscious. He eats, relishing the taste on his tongue and the feel on his fingers. His three down pointed fingers hop-skip from the chapatti to the bharto, onion, chutney, yogurt, and then, nesting the combined bunch in three fingers, without a drip, he takes it to his mouth. There seems to be a long wait and there is no talk. Dadabapa says shukhar with a long spicy belch while washing his hands in the basin held by Hawa.

An hour passes by and Dadabapa is sitting in the darkness on the wooden bench in the courtyard listening to the cautious snubs of hyenas, as if they are testing if it was safe to come into the bazaar alley. The neighbours have already blown out their lamps. We hear the routine clang of the trap door fall back on the iron frame at the floor, under the raised squat toilet at the wall end of the courtyard. The Indian night soil man chura, sputter-empties and cleans the bucket with a quick splash of water. Then we hear him shooing his donkey to move on pulling the municipal cart to the next trap door at the gutter at the back alley. At that hour, Shamshu skulks in. Askari Bakari, the night watchman, is humming a kasida on the front veranda looking at the stars, as was his habit at this time of the night.

Finally, father stands up from the table. He takes Shamshu by the arm and without a word, begins brandishing his belt in the air while looking for a suitable place to lay him over. The bewildered boy gives out a shriek that rings through the silence of the night in the bazaar. Sitting on the kitchen patlo stool, I am listening, trembling. My heart throbs heavily. My legs are pressed to my chest with my arms around the knees. I bury my head in the space between. I am worried about my friends at the neighbouring bead shop listening to the commotion in my home. The shame it would bring in the morning worries me, not Shamshu's pain.

"You have dishonoured the family name. You have no sharam! I don't want to hear about this again. Understand? You will go to the religion school and follow the rules like other boys of your age. Understand?" My father shouts as he raises his arm and slaps the leather belt on Shamshu's bottom. Through the kitchen door, I see my father's hands are shaking, his eyes watery with rage and pain. He is too weak to strike again. I stare, aghast at the scene.

"Pirshah!" cries out Ma emerging from the kitchen. "Don't kill the boy!"

When everyone left the veranda, I come to clear the table and see that two plates are clean. Hawa follows to help and we carry the remaining food to the kitchen where the girls and Ma Gor Bai are waiting for their dinner. It is getting late and my stomach tightens and loosens involuntarily, but I do not feel like eating.

"The price of keeping family honour is not easy. When one errs, all suffer. Pirshah ... pirshah. Family shame is family pain shared," says Ma Gor Bai.

Monghi's eyes are closing when I carry her to bed. She lays her long neck on my shoulder. Meethi Bai calls her Gazelle of the Bazaar, but she is too slim, bony, and of wheat colour to be called beautiful. I am the fair one, chubby and called the beautiful. Cousin-sister Malek is even darker than Monghi

170

and not beautiful either, but she has thick black hair that at times, fills me with envy.

Immediately behind me, I hear Ma Gor Bai's footsteps going into the courtyard and Hawa cleaning pots in the kitchen. I sing a lullaby to Monghi, sitting by her on our bed.

Monghi mari nani
Lala, lala, lala
Harani dok wari
Lala, lala, lala
mmm...mmm...mmm

My little Monghi
Sleep, sleep, sleep
One with gazelle neck
Sleep, sleep, sleep
mmm...mmm...mmm

"Be quiet now! I want to sleep," says Dadabapa in a commanding voice as he enters the room. I stop singing though I feel defiant inside and want to continue to sing. The fear of shame called sharam that will taunt me with looks tomorrow, if not telling questions from the neighbours, turns to resentment. They would ask as if they don't know, "Sakina, what was that noise in your house last evening? Was it a thief?" Or, "We have not seen Shamshu for many days. Is he out of town?" Or that polite question, "Is all well at home?" The questions that beg for lies for the one answer that they know.

Dadabapa hangs his buskot waistcoat on the nail behind the door and sits quietly on his bed for a while, clearing his throat several times in a series of identical throat sounds. Then

171

he lies down, inhales a long drawn breath and a slow controlled exhale of shukhar. It is quiet except for the daring snigger of hyenas that are now close to our back alley door. Sometimes, Shamshu and his friends hide behind the door to wait for them to come, and then, they surprise them by banging tins, yelling, and throwing rocks.

Monghi stuffs her fingers into her ears to keep away the tittering snorts of the hyenas that Shamshu would mimic from the dark corners, exaggerating them into ferocious snarls. It terrifies me, but Monghi panics and she would run to hide in the cupboard, only to be laughed at by Shamshu. I cover my little sister with a light cotton quilt, hand stitched, patch with patch, mix and match pieces of discarded dresses. Each dress makes its own story in the home through its life of wear and tear. Each patch thus has its own dress story to tell. The red satin patch is from my dress when I was seven, the year I was scalded learning to fry puris, and the one with crochet cuffs is the one that Meethi Bai gave me. I used to wear it when we went to the Ladies Only film show at Film India, so Dadabapa and my father could not see me in the dress from the dance girls' sinful lodge. At the time, it was my favourite. Ma Gor Bai and I worked on the quilt when there were no orders for zari embroidery.

For a minute, I stand there watching Dadabapa lying on his back already snoring on his single metal bed. His hairy stomach, exposed below the vest, rises and falls with the purrs of his snores. He looks so different and sleeps so quickly, peacefully. Tiptoe-ing to his buskot hanging behind the door, I steal a tongolo ten cents from the inside pocket. That is to treat myself when we have our girls' satsang get together with Rani Victoria at her statue under the jacaranda trees. There we would pick the purple flowers and blow into their bell bellies until they popped. We would compete to make the loudest pop sound that we called topp the English cannon fired at German demons.

When I return to the kitchen to help Hawa wash the utensils and keep them clean for the morning tea, I find my father, Ma Gor Bai and Shamshu, all sitting in silence on patlo stools eating together from the same round copper senio tray coated with tin. I have not seen my father eating on the patlo stool before, nor have I seen him eating with Ma in the kitchen. He looked so little, like a schoolboy. It pains me to see his eyes are wet. I listen to Shamshu asking for forgiveness, his silent pulse of repentance throbs like my own heart calming down from fear and shame called sharam.

"Wash the small pot first, Sakina, and later make masala chai. Three kops," says Ma Gor Bai and she swallows a chapatti scoop dripping oil from the bharto.

That night when everyone had gone to bed, I go to the bench under the mango tree, adjust the hurricane lamp on the branch and open the book that Meeshnari Shivji Bhagat had given my brother that evening. Shamshu had slid the book behind Ma Gor Bai's English teakop set reserved for guests and rarely touched. Shamshu would not look at the book again, I know. I begin to read the first page by joining sounds of the alphabet to make a word. My reading is not as good as my stitching is, but I can manage one letter at a time. D દ, I read, - S શ – Mo મો with a stroke on top and at the side of M મ.

I read that the book was printed in 1924, almost twelve years ago when I was two years old. I read that it's called *Pir Sadardin's Das Avatar* published by THE RECREATION CLUB INSTITUTE on Jail Road, Bombay. That's where Meeshnari Shivji Bhagat says with pride that he took his training to become a missionary in Africa! I wish I could take the training in Bombay and become a missionary like a man. Then I could tell stories of faith and miracles like a missionary. Show a picture from the magazine like a missionary. Preach a long sermon on Fridays like a missionary. Most of all sing like a missionary. A girl could read many books if she were a missionary.

I know I would teach best what I want to learn myself. Taking a pencil and a tracing paper, I begin to know the book by first outlining the symbols on it, the sun, a glowing globe shooting rays into the darkness around it like a god avatar's head in a spiked halo. I trace every line of the prickly sun's ray, then copy the rounded Om from the title page and pencil it delicately in the centre of the sun's orb just as it is in the book. Every line sings a corresponding word-music to me. I hum singing back to the drawing as if I were embroidering a rosette on velvet, as if it were a musical note. It is magical, a spirit divine in art.

In the kitchen, Hawa is asleep. I hear her breathing deeply into the night's empty space. Suddenly, almost without a thought, I feel an urge to see her, to be with her. Hawa has her knees drawn up to her stomach, a child bundle on a gunnysack in the corner, wrapped tightly and completely in her kanga. The kanga that is patterned in paisley vines with a line of writing in a frame. It reads *MWANA NI UA LA NYUMBA* which means A CHILD IS THE FLOWER OF THE HOME. My father told me that the kanga borrows its name from the spotted hen of the savannah that makes lattice-like pathways along the grassroots, and like its cousin the ostrich, prefers not to fly.

22

Confession

Three days after the incident at the religion school, it is chandraat, the evening of the new moon and beginning of the new Islamic month. We observe the evening with prayers in the jamat khana, confessions and giving of the monthly tithe to the mukhi who represents Saheb. Mukhi Dharamshi beckons Shamshu with his finger to come to where he is seated in the prayer hall. In fact, I was expecting the mukhi to call Shamshu earlier after I overheard a conversation between Dadabapa and Meeshnari Shivji Bhagat earlier that evening. From time to time, I steal voices and make them my own to tell the story. In fact, listening into adult talk is a habit that knits into my day.

When we are back from the jamat khana, no one says anything about the mukhi whispering in Shamshu's ears. However, the word has spread and everyone knows, even the neighbours know that the mukhi summoned Shamshu, and now everyone waits anxiously to find out what the mukhi whispered into Shamshu's ears. But Shamshu says nothing when he returns home.

Before serving dinner after coming back from the jamat khana, we would wait for Dadabapa to finish the confession ritual that he performs at home every evening of the new moon. Dadabapa places the photograph of my Dadima Sohn Bai on the table and pleads on her behalf three times asking for forgiveness of her past worldly sins. Then dipping his tobacco stained fingertips in a bowl of holy water, he sprinkles three times on the photograph at Dadima's forehead. I feel Dadima Sohn Bai is always included in the cleansing ceremony that we all perform every chandraat evening at the jamat khana. We still live together with the departed spirits such is the belief of our Satpanth faith.

The next evening Shamshu waits for me to go to the evening school with him. That is not only unusual but also earlier than usual. He seems anxious.

"What worries you?" I ask.

"The mukhi wants to see me. Will you come with me?"

"Yes," I agree without a second thought.

I wait outside the prayer hall sitting on the hardwood bench with wrought iron legs shaped in lion's paws. A brass plaque fixed exactly in the middle at the back, reads: IN MEMORY OF LATE MRS MUKHIANI FATMA BAI BHOGA SAMJI DHANJI. Swallows fly in and out of the circular courtyard, chirping and twittering noisily. Under the roof space, they have made nests, in fact, a line of nests. I watch the birds coming home and wonder if there are any eggs or chicks in their grass laced baskets under the rainwater gutters running along the edge of the eaves, and over the line of light bulbs that flare up on festive nights. The keeper of the prayer hall called Jamat Bhai, walks in with live coal glowing in a cupped ladle over which he sprinkles loban gum resins from a rusted

176

perforated tin that rattles like a calabash with cowry shells. He ignores me and enters the hall just as Shamshu is emerging from the heavy hardwood door with frosted glass panes. I stand up instantly. He does not look as worried as when he went in.

"What happened?" I ask anxiously holding him by the elbow.

"It was not that bad," he speaks, smiling broadly, jerking back his arm. "I just signed a life insurance cover for myself. But you don't need one," he jokes. He makes me feel small and foolish because I worry. He does not know I worry less about him than about what talk would circulate in the town about our family. It's family sharam, the shame that kills me inside and the shame that steals honour.

"But what happened? Tell me," I ask again knitting his fingers in mine. His clothes smell of loban smoke.

"I was nervous when I saw the shadow of the mukhi seated in guru-meditation pose. Maari-geea! I said, I am dead!" Shamshu begins to speak, side smiling. He is not someone who can be easily scared away. I ignore the bragging streak in his voice. This is how he says what happened dramatizing his meeting with mukhi:

"I halt and stand at the door. Light slices through the crack in the door. It's an hour before prayer time. Dark. Quiet. I follow the sheen from the door running on the straw mat. White beards are seated in a line at the side wall in meditation. I walk on. A cough from one of them thunders through the silence. It shakes me up like a gunshot fired at me. Sounded like a warning. Eerie.

177

"Come closer. Here Sam-su." It's the mukhi voice. I recognize it. He calls me again, 'Sam-su'. I walk towards the voice in the shadow. A woman in a corner is stooping over, sweeping the mat softly with a green grass broom. Makes no sound. Only movements of a silhouette like a ghost minding his own business and occasionally scraping out caked su-kreet from the mat, then kissing it, before taking it to her mouth. I know who that would be. She would be the absakan widow who comes to Stepmother Gor Bai's satsang. She is the Bai who has given her life to Saheb's sewa. The one who says she is Saheb's daasi-slave, and the jamat khana is her home, her ashram in Africa until the day she would go to him, a bride in shinning bandhani shawl. The one who has given her complete inheritance, a fortune it was, to Saheb except her bandhani that she has kept so it may be laid on her when she dies.

"Now, Mukhi Dharamshi leans forward out of the shadow, motioning me to sit down. I sit down, adap-palothi, hands cross-folded over my chest, back straight and cross-legged."

Shamshu's gesturing and posturing makes me giggle but I don't want to show it, sucking in my cheeks.

"You have been up to something I hear, Sam-su," mukhi tells me calmly. His shadow is on the wall nudging his nodding head, but he is not angry and at once, I feel at ease. "You need not confess what I already know. I accept your mistake on behalf of Saheb and I will accept your confession. This vow will protect you from all …" he hesitates, "mischief." I am no longer afraid. I think he had a smile behind his put-on serious look.

"Repeat this after me. Say, I vow never to touch a cigarette in my life and to attend religion class regularly," the mukhi tells me.

"I vow never to touch a cigarette in my life and to attend the religion class regularly," I say quickly. I remain seated in adap-palothi crossed legs and crossed hands. Back straight.

"Now, say, I vow never to touch alcohol, cigarettes or do dirty things. Three times," the mukhi tells me.

I recite the vow three times.

"Aameen. Mowla forgives," the mukhi blesses me by stretching his right arm across the floor table and resting it on my shoulder.

Then Mukhi Dharamshi produces a cotton thread of twirled twines, coloured red and green, tied together with seven knots at one inch or so apart. He whispers a prayer over the thread and blows into each knot, one at a time, moving his head from side to side as if spreading his breath from end to end over the threads three times.

"Your head," he says. I bow before him. He puts this red and green thread around my neck and ties a knot.

Shamshu shows me the sacred thread around his neck, the twines and the knots. Ma Gor Bai told me the knots represented seven heavens of the universe when I received my first red and green cotton thread that I wear around my wrist.

"This will protect you from all evils, youth's temptations. Tobacco, alcohol, women. When you are troubled by the desire, say pirshah seven times and remember Saheb's name and your vow." The mukhi comforts me with such sincerity and gentle words that I pledge to myself to keep the vow to the day I die.

"And you may remove the holy thread when you bathe. Keep your body clean. Your body is the temple of prayers in unison with God and the ants, birds and fish. Earth, air, water and man are one temple of God. Man, God and the sentient beings live as one," adds the mukhi. "You know your Das Avatar, don't you?"

Yes, I lie.

"Pirshah!" I exclaim. "You lied in the jamat khana, Shamshu?" I was shocked.

He does not reply.

When we part, Shamshu walks towards Victoria Street to meet his friend Razak. He will not join us for the evening prayers at the jamat khana and he knows I will be quiet about it, though I don't like him skipping the prayers. It being Friday, there is no religion school today. The frogs of Nairobi are throat singing to the early evening moon. Tight-lipped pulsating jelly bulbs are cheering the night to come that will bring fresh water to fill their swamp in the valley of the Nairobi River. The Punjabi farmers who grow all sorts of vegetables here will also be happy like the river frogs, and say, "At last God answered our prayers." Then there will be mosquitoes in their hundreds.

Back from the jamat khana, Ma Gor Bai, Hawa and I step into the kitchen, as is our routine. I hear Dadabapa and my father talking while waiting for Shamshu to come to the dinner table. He is late again, but they are patient because they know he has been to see the mukhi. Most of the time, Noordin Kaka uncle prefers to eat, while he reads in his bedroom. "It is better that way," says Kaki Bai auntie, "so he does not spew out blasphemy while you are eating." Everyone knows food is anaj that is sacred, and so no child is sent to call Noordin Kaka uncle to the table.

Dadabapa and my father are quiet when Hawa and I bring to them chapattis, red chili chutney, raw white onions cut into slices, firm formed yogurt in a bowl and two curries - spinach and bitter karela. There is silence such as the one from suppressed annoyance. Ma calls it 'silence of tolerance'. I wonder if Dadabapa's irritation is not because we are late bringing food to the table. Not that we were late cooking. It was because we were hoping Shamshu would be coming soon.

After a while, when Dadabapa speaks, he seems more composed. "I do not like your wife's friendship with Meethi Bai of the lodge. Brings disgrace to the house. Brings shame of sharam to me in the jamat khana." My father keeps quiet avoiding Dadabapa's eyes.

The silence in the kitchen grows deeper such as the one from sharam or family shame. However, Ma does not look down or away in anger or sadness, though she did hear what Dadabapa just said. He intentionally spoke loud enough for her to hear. We, the children of the house, eat from one plate and share the kitchen patlo stool sitting two on one.

"Shamshu takes after his Noordin Kaka uncle," Dadabapa begins to talk again abruptly changing the subject. "That naastik faith doubter son of mine!" He speaks in contempt of Noordin Kaka uncle like he were spitting out a curse.

181

"And does Noordin not take after his uncle in India? Your brother, my Sunderji Kaka uncle," says my father. He surprises me. Nobody can talk back to my grandfather like that, especially not my father, his good son who follows his faith. Ma's eyes widen looking at me. But there is no anger or a question put to me in her look. The eyes that I have come to understand so well that I know what they want when they widen and when they narrow. They are not the same now. There is not even wonder or fear in Ma's widened eyes, just a quiet delight in a little surprise.

Dadabapa does not answer. Instead, he looks down, and up again agitated, muttering under his breath between, "Naastik! My own blood! Calling the Satpanth ginans idolatrous!" I am not sure if he is cursing his brother Sunderji or his son Noordin, or both.

Ma Gor Bai whispers to me, "Your Dadabapa's anger comes from his hot blood, stained because of naastik faith doubters in his family. Cursing over food will bring bad luck of kisirani to the house." She begins to transfer the left over curries from the cooking pots to smaller tin containers so Hawa and I can start the washing, and keep the utensils ready for next day's cooking.

"In every generation there appears someone in the family who is a faith doubter. All the prayers and sewa in the jamat khana cannot stop that. How can they?" asks Ma. Hawa listens as she brushes out ashes from the charcoal stove onto a tin plate. "Dadabapa's elder brother Sunderji, converted to Sunni Islam. That was not unusual because bewilderment, fear and anger continued to divide the community for decades following the first and subsequent lawsuits against Saheb. Reporting in the newspapers was discussed in the jamat khana and people took sides in my village as it happened all over India. The Satpanth secrecy became public, and those loyal to Saheb receded deeper into the silence and mystery of the Satpanth faith. They tightened the hidden hierarchies of devotees in every jamat khana. Then, accordingly, every jamat khana opened a register of the faithful, separated by columns of murids loyal to Saheb in hierarchal order. Dadabapa never mentions his brother who blemished the family name. His father had forbidden the family to meet or even speak about Sunderji. Have you ever heard him say the name Sunderji?" asks Ma Gor Bai as was the manner of her speech putting surprise in listeners with unexpected questions. "Sunderji was made an outcaste by the Khoja jamat and disowned by his own father, the mukhi of Haripur. His name was never again mentioned in the family as if he was never born to them. Your grandfather then was considered the first born son," says Ma without giving even a hint if she agreed or not with the outcasting of my great uncle Sunderji. This leaves me confused but I had got used to her 'not saying this way or that way' as Meethi Bai used to put it moving her open palm from right to left in frustration. "Satpanthis like your stepmother who are brought up in pir's house do not tell you what faith they believe in. That is their way, which is the Sufi way, which is Satguru pir's way, which is the hidden way." However, after her long narration, Ma Gor Bai, does let out a full exhale partly to express Dadabapa's pain as if on his behalf, and partly to indicate the gravity of the incident that seemed to weigh on her. She might have even said so to my father without revealing her own belief. Then changing the look in her eyes, Ma Gor Bai suddenly turns her face and stares at Hawa who had been engrossed in our talk. Startled, little

183

Hawa comes to herself and hurries up removing the ash from the stove.

"Now, Dadabapa worries about Noordin Kaka uncle," Ma Gor Bai continues to say, "if he disowns his son like his father who disowned his son, Sunderji, the stain in the family will be exposed to the jamat in Africa. It will bring shame of sharam to us all. Dadabapa's honour that he has tried so hard to uphold in Africa will be washed away. That will tarnish his genealogy, his children, grandchildren, and their children."

Hawa and I take charcoal ash in our palms, wet it and begin to scrub it over the aluminium and copper pots. We work quietly listening to the men's talk at the table. I hear Dadabapa raising his voice to tell my father, "And tell that Ravana brother of yours to take *Chiragh e Hidayat* back to his Ithna Asheri friends before I burn the sacrilegious book in your wife's stove."

Chiragh e Hidayat I later learn from my kitchen teacher, Ma Gor Bai, is the book that explains the principles of the new faith practices of Khoja Ithna Asheris, the breakaway group from the main Satpanth body. "They voiced fierce dissent in Zanzibar," said Ma. "For some, the new country opens minds to challenge the old. Away from ancient India, the immigrants breathe freedom in religion and customs. Yet, others seek comfort in affirmation of their forefather's beliefs and become even more stringent in their faith than they ever were in India. Such is the culture of questioning, confirming, and changing, which migration creates in its wake."

Part Six

Stories from Meethi Bai's Lodge

In the 18th and 19th centuries, British soldiers of the East India Company frequented Indian prostitution houses called kothas, patronizing the old cultures of sex entertainment, a heritage of both ancient Hindu and later Moslem civilizations. Following the Indian Wars of Independence from mid 19th century, thousands of troops from the British Isles were stationed in India. Their mission was to quell the sporadic non-stop native militancy for freedom that continued for the next nearly a hundred years. To entertain and meet the sexual needs of its armies, the colonial government brought large numbers of European women. However, their numbers were still not adequate for the growing number of British forces. Hence, Japanese women, the next best of the fair skinned, were brought to India exclusively for the non-Indian military camps. Some writers on the history of prostitution in India claim the numbers of foreign prostitutes may have run into thousands. All prostitutes were given numbers and to keep their numbers they had to report for regular medical examinations at prison hospitals. The problem of STDs was huge affecting the soldiers' health and consequently their fighting capabilities and sanity.

Townships, thriving on sex business, grew around the British cantonments of which Kamathipura in Bombay was the better known. Today, Kamathipura survives after more than seventy years since the

British soldiers left India and is considered among the largest sex worker areas in the world.

(SUDHANSHU BHANDARI: PROSTITUTION IN COLONIAL INDIA MAINSTREAM, VOL XLVIII, NO 26, JUNE 19, 2010; KAMATHIPURA HISTORY, WIKIPEDIA, HISTORY OF PROSTITUTION IN INDIA, WIKIPEDIA).

Women from the Bombay kothas as from other kothas in British India would have found their way to East Africa together with the absakan (inauspicious) ones to escape social stigma, and like all Indian immigrants they would have hoped for a better life in the new world. The absakan widows who voluntarily joined the indentured labourers to Surinam called the new world 'Shri Ram Desh' or ' God's Country' (ED: RAJESH RAI AND PETER REEVES, THE SOUTH ASIAN DIASPORA: TRANSNATIONAL NETWORKS AND CHANGING IDENTITIES, ROUTLEDGE, UK, 2009). South America like Africa was indeed God's Country for these ostracized women. In her book FROM JHELUM TO TANA (PENGUIN BOOKS, 2007), Neera Kapur-Dromson mentions women from Lahore's famous Hira Mandi kothas (historically linked to the Anarkali Bazaar created for pleasures of British soldiers in the Punjab) came to East Africa to entertain the huge railway Indian service and workforce. Thousands of young men in the Indian indentured and skilled labour force brought to build the towns and infrastructure of the British East Africa Empire were not accompanied by women. The Uganda Railway construction (1896 -1902) alone had a force of more than 38,000 young able bodied men of all categories from unskilled labourers to technicians and engineers writes Neera Kent Kapila in RACE, RAIL AND SOCIETY: ROOTS OF MODERN KENYA' (KENWAY PUBLICATIONS, 2010). As early as 1902 colonial health documents recorded existence of brothels in the racially segregated Indian worker town along the swamps of the Nairobi River (NAIROBI MASTER PLAN FOR COLONIAL CAPITAL, 1948).

23

Meethi Bai's Lodge

Months go by, short rains are over and the dry season sets in. It would be at least six more months before the long rains come with the monsoons from the Indian Ocean. Punjabi blacksmiths, Kutchi Kanbi stone dressers and Gujar Shuthar carpenters bring their skills to build the new capital of Kenya. They pull together with the combined strength of the Kikuyu, Kamba and Luo people, all workers, builders of the foundation of the Empire and a new country. A modern Kenya. Houses in the bazaar rise when the logs, stone, gravel, iron slippers and sheet iron, arrive in bulk from the railway auction. They sing as they work to the sounds of their hands beating the iron, cutting the stone, pushing-pulling the saws and bending the sheet iron, lifting by many hands. Knocks of the ball hammer and pick axe, cracking of timber, and the dismounting thuds of cement bags slipping off the sweaty backs, are marked by assorted language expressions of Ha! Hoi! Eeh! Ooh! Hai! Ya! Haiya! Aah! Gods' names, male and female, are called – Ram, Allah, Mungu, Yesu, Vishnu, Ngai, Ambe. . . All hands join to dislodge a granite rock in the red soil to the rhythm of one work song.

Hare Ambe! Mother of Strength!
Lift the demon bull!
All together! Pamoja!
Strength!
Hare Ambe! Warrior Mother of Strength!
Up together now, lift! Pamoja!
And up, up, up, and lift
Together now! Say Hare Ambe! Pamoja!
Hare-ambe! Hare-ambe! Hare-ambe!
Harambe-harambe-harambee pamoja!

Then all of a sudden, the workers stop singing, training their eyes towards the cloud of dust in the distance. Every morning and then late in the afternoon, the son of the white Boer settler speeds on a piki piki motorcycle to and from Colonel Grogan's stables at Chiromo and over the creaky Ainsworth bridge to Kingsway and into the Indian Bazaar. Passers-by stand along the street to watch this spectacle of machine, speed, noise and dust, crackle by. Children halt their heated fights and mischief in the alley play, and come running to the bazaar when they hear the distant crunch of the machine. Then they begin cheering the man coming in a blur of brown cloud even before he appears, "Kaburu piki piki! Kaburu piki piki! Motorcycle Boer!"

"An English invention, a bicycle with a power machine. It's a wonder," Dadabapa would say every time the piki piki runs through the bazaar. At the same time, the performance of the Kaburu, the Boer on the motorcycle, annoys Dadabapa because after he has disappeared, the dust from the havoc comes to settle on the veranda where hundreds of beads stand in arrays of strings. "Salo Kaburu!" he curses the Boer settler as he lifts the shop duster, a rag from an old white, discarded merikani bed sheet, attached to an arm-length tree branch.

No one, not even the neighbours, talk about Shamshu's shame anymore and I thought it was forgotten. The girls at school stopped throwing taunting eyes at me in a way that put shame on my family. But not for long. Ma Gor Bai hears from a trusted friend in the jamat khana that Shamshu was seen at Meethi Bai's lodge.

"Were you at Meethi Bai's lodge?" asks Ma Gor Bai when Shamshu comes from school and sits down on the kitchen floor waiting for his lunch to be served. I was roasting chapattis for him on the iron plate careful to keep them the way he liked without any black blister on them. Hawa pours out a couple of spoonfuls of lamb curry into a bowl plate for Shamshu. He does not answer and concentrates on the meal before him.

"You have been loafing again, hengh? Were you at Meethi Bai's lodge?" asks Ma Gor Bai.

"Yes, but I did not enter."

"Tell me the truth and I will not tell your father."

"True. I did not go in."

"Then why did you go there?"

"We were curious."

"Who was with you?"

Shamshu does not answer and Ma Gor Bai does not ask again. Probably he was with Razak. After a thought, she asks, "Why did you not enter?"

"In the dark, I heard a throat clearing sound followed by cough-spit out. We ran away quickly."

"Why did you run away?"

"Because it sounded familiar."

"Who was it?"

Shamshu hesitates playfully. I start to stir the yogurt, pretending I am not keen to hear the answer. Hawa suppresses a giggle as if she knows the answer. Ma Gor Bai looks at her and then at Shamshu and waits patiently. He teases her with silence. She is not sure if the boy will answer as he raises his bowl of yogurt to drink. She asks maybe because she wants assurance. Her suspicion cannot be correct, could it? Moments pass and Shamshu finishes drinking the yogurt. He burps and gestures shukhar like an adult, before saying in a calculated tone, "Dadabapa."

Ma Gor Bai looks away as if she had neither asked the question nor heard the answer. At the same time, she is aware of Shamshu trying to catch her eyes. Shamshu's eyes are smiling mischief and they follow me as I leave, pretending to look for Monghi. He makes us feel small. I find Monghi standing fascinated by the broody hen we call Mama Kuku. For a moment, I watch how Mama Kuku puffs pompously in the courtyard fussing noisily around her fourteen softball hatchlings. When I return to the kitchen with Monghi, I see Ma Gor Bai and Hawa have been waiting for me, sitting cross-legged around the pot, to begin the meal. Shamshu is still there quietly watching over us.

"Cut the chapatti into small pieces for Monghi. I will pour the curry on top," says Ma Gor Bai. Monghi protests; she wants to eat like adults, turn-twist-break a piece a time from the whole chapatti. "Here, take this teaspoon," says Ma Gor Bai. Monghi lets out a wail. She insists she wants to eat with her hand like grown-ups. "You will eat with your hand when you have learned how to break the chapatti with your fingers, dip it into the curry and take it to the mouth without a drop falling down. You messed up your new dress yesterday eating with your hand, remember?"

I look at Shamshu and he looks back, his eyes suggesting I play with them. He can turn a serious concern into a laughing matter so that he can show he is smarter. I know he stays in the kitchen because he wants to be asked more questions about Meethi Bai's lodge. I see his game. He wants to re-create the drama that he saw and feel bigger than us kitchen women. I pray Ma Gor Bai would not pursue further. I feel a relief when, after a while, Shamshu gets up and strolls out of the kitchen, looking disappointed.

Like Hawa's wrap called kanga, my story has pictures in it. Hawa told me her cloth was so called because it was spangled like the feral hen of the savannah named kanga. Like the hen, my story nods its head up and down. You wonder what corner it will go to now. Where will it hide? Where will it reappear? Where will it come to rest? However, kanga's head never stops bobbing. My words meander along the story path bouncing up and down like the nodding head. When I was young, that's how stories were told. Like the bird called kanga criss-crossing paths of time, moving up and down with each step, pulling past to present, pushing present to future.

24

Meethi Bai's Daughters

Meethi Bai, the oral artist of Jugu Bazaar, the one with the nightingale's cords in her throat, the avian voiced, is the songstress exemplar of marriage songs. Meethi Bai, who never misses her evening prayer at the jamat khana. Even on days when the monsoon rains are torrential, you see Meethi Bai carrying her slippers in her hands, walking bare feet through the red mud pools to the jamat khana. Ma Gor Bai once told me Meethi Bai's story in secret when we were alone, cooking in the kitchen as always, three times a day. If it were not cooking then it would be cleaning utensils to a shine or preparing lentils, chafing rice and grinding spices for storage in an array of containers. Hawa listened as she swept the floor and dusted around the house.

Meethi Bai's love and passion for prayers, music and dance nourished her youth when she made friends with the dance girls of the coolie lodge at the railway quarters on Landies Road down from the railway station. She was the eldest of six children, just turning thirteen when her father, Ton Boy they called him, died in a fatal accident on Thika Road. He was a labourer on the lorry that brought river sand for Nairobi's new stone buildings. Meethi Bai's widowed mother milled grain on their hand mill to support the family. However, her earnings were not enough even for one good meal a day. Willingly, she arranged with the dance girls for herself to make night visits to the coolie lodge by the railway station rather than be a burden of mothaj on the taunting community. Though an unwanted absakan, she was a proud widow, fiercely independent. She taught her girls to live with pride, and free of the community's welfare and the accompanying stigma of mothaj. After her mother's death, Meethi Bai took her place at the lodge and in time owned it.

Meethi Bai's lodge is on the 'donkey-horse-cow spatter-muck-sludge track' in the Indian shantytown. White people, residents on the lush hill groves and garden homes with red Mangalore tile roofs, thus describe the road. It is here, at the lodge, where the men folk are entertained on the weekends. People refer to the lodge as the bachelors' palace or the kotha, meaning the house of the dancing girls. On fortnightly paydays, the breeze carries the music from the kotha through the impenetrable darkness of the Nairobi nights. The kotha has many stories. The most commonly told are the stories of the three 'Bombay Ladies' as the townsfolk called them before they were married and left the lodge. I heard the stories of Gulzar Bai, Soneri Bai, and Devdasi Rupa Bai here and there, in parts, eavesdropping on adult talk. Sometimes, I heard from the neighbours or at the jamat khana. Then at the satsang meetings where the three women would talk about their inside pains and hold us all enthralled. Sometimes, I heard Dadabapa talking about them with his friends. He seemed to know them well because the three women were with him on the dhow coming from India. But he never mentioned their names in the house, let alone their stories, except when malaria made him delirious and speak out the secrets in his head. Most of all, I heard their stories from Meethi Bai. Theirs were the stories that men would make fun of while the women would press their three fingers to their lips, the way Indian women do, to show these women have no sharam that is shame. This gesture of utter horror shows it is something they should not talk about, yet they must tell you.

Gulzar Bai was from a reputable Satpanth Nangaria Khoja family who was married at nine years to another reputable Satpanth Nangaria Khoja family that later openly declared their conversion to the Sunni faith. That happened in the later decades of the never-ending strife following the Khoja Cases against Saheb in the High Court of Bombay. It was rumoured that, of the four Sunni Khojas killed by the Satpanth Khojas, one was from Gulzar Bai's marital family and of the four Satpanth Khojas hanged for the crime, one was from Gulzar Bai's paternal family, an uncle from the father's side. Such a marriage of families torn apart by faith was destined to fail, they would say. When Gulzar Bai refused to change her Satpanth faith, her husband drove her out of the house calling her a kafir bitch. To save her family honour, Gulzar Bai did not return to her father's home in Jamnagar and eventually found herself in Bombay's sex kotha where she met Soneri Bai and Devdasi Rupa Bai.

Soneri Bai was still a child when she ran away from her married home because her husband's family converted to Arya Samaj. That was during the time of dissent in the community. Dissent sharpened by debates, conflicts, killings and confusion among the Satpanthis, followed the years between the Khoja Cases against the Saheb in the High Court of Bombay. History of the Khojas shows how dissent and community break ups follow public trials regarding matters of the tithe, property and faith. In fact, Soneri Bai's husband was one of the leaders of the new Arya Samaj Khoja community and when Soneri Bai refused to convert, saying Satpanth was the faith of her guardian pirs, her mother-in-law and sisters-in-law with whom she used to play dolls, called her a flesh eater and cow killer. They spat on the twelve-year-old when they came to ask her if she was ready yet to re-convert. However, Soneri Bai was a stubborn child wife, the type who grows more stubborn when she is beaten, who sits in a corner, and who neither eats nor cries. She ran away with her neighbour when she reached puberty. The man promised to marry her, and she could keep her Satpanth faith, though he was a Sunni Moslem himself. However, when they arrived in Bombay, he sold her to Ma Daam Begum's kotha, the prostitute house in Kamathipura. Soneri Bai could not run away back to her parents because the family had lost face due to reasons of her causing. One reason was that she was married and that is to say, she had been given away forever to another family. The second reason was that she should accept her husband's religion. That was custom. The third reason was that she could have protected her honour by entering an ashram, or alternately, even death would have been more honourable. That too was custom. Instead, she chose to live in a kotha and that was the fourth reason. She had brought shame to not only her parents, brothers and sister, but the entire caste. Then one day, Soneri Bai learned from a girl from her town, who was married to the old man called Boothpalish who waxed and polished the long boots of English soldiers at the Falkland Road camp, that her parents had joined the new Swaminayaran Khoja group. Soneri Bai was not aware of her family's conversion. Was it because of her that her family abandoned the caste bound Satpanth community? The guilt consumed her inside. The chaotic times for the Khoja turned out to be advantageous for the Hindu re-conversion activists when the Satpanthis lost face, if not status in the caste due to their vacillating religious beliefs. These times were when the bewildered Khojas asked each other, "What sect of multi-sectarian Islam did Satguru-pir, the forefather of our faith, actually convert us to?" Some even argued there was no conversion, only a progression of Vedanta that now received Ali into its ancient fold and hailed him as one of its own Vishnu avatars. To support this belief there were those who talked about how Saheb quoted from the Das Avatar when he was summoned to give evidence of Satpanth's most sacred doctrine in the High Court of Bombay. "Saheb told the English judge," they said, "That though the Satpanth Ismaili faith was closer to certain Sufi orders, it was unlike any Sunni and other Shia beliefs. And he won the case, you see. He did not need to quote the Quran, did he? Yet, the judge ruled the Satpanthis were Moslems and therefore must pay the holy tithe to Saheb the avatar, just made imam."

Devdasi Rupa Bai's story was different. Her family had dedicated her at birth to Ambe Ma's temple in Bombay with a plea and hope that their next child would be a boy. Devdasi Rupa Bai grew up in the temple and was trained in the ancient arts of devotional songs, dance and sacred sex. They called her the blessed one because she would never ever be an absakan widow. She became the most acclaimed songstress and prayer dancer of Bombay. That was before the activists of the anti-Devdasi movement drove her out of her sanctuary together with the infant cradled in her arms. When she came to her parents' home, they refused to let her in because it was a shame to 'take back a daughter' as they said, 'whom we have committed to God.' The God who did eventually listen to them and gifted them a boy child. Most of all, they feared the anti-Devdasi activists. Devdasi Rupa Bai's coming to Kamathipura attracted wealthy patrons since her accomplishments in the triple arts of the temple centring on the Bharat Natyam dance, were rare in Muslim kotha houses that flourished on Kathak for entertainment. Devdasi Rupa Bai became so valuable a kotha artiste that Ma Daam Begum kept her locked in during the day, denying her the freedom of the bazaars lest she be kidnapped or enticed to flee to a rival kotha. However, Ma Daam Begum dearly loved Devdasi's son who was freed by the temple priests of all claims to a father in a fire ritual. The ritual was conducted in great secrecy on the night of the full moon and under the cover of bringing peace to the irreligious land. Then the boy was blessed as God's child and the three priests together prayed with palms pressed together, imploring the Supreme Deity that the boy's life be dedicated to the service of selfless sewa to the temple. This was the advice they gave to Rupa Bai when she had to leave her temple home. Ma Daam used to say how it was a joy to see the boy running around the kotha. "A home is not a home without the sound of soft pattering feet," she would say. "Like monsoon raindrops they cool our sleepless eyes." Devdasi called her son Vishnu though he had no official name given by the astrologer, as was the custom.

The three women lived at Ma Daam's kotha in Kamathipura along the Falkland Road cantonment. The English soldiers were always on mission in and out of Bombay because of the disquietude that had gripped the land after the 1857 rebellions and mutinies by Indian soldiers. It was also where European prostitutes entertained English commanders and Indian aristocracy in bungalows in the high-class area, and where, in smaller chambers and streets, Arab, Jewish and

Japanese women competed with the darker skinned native prostitutes for a night's love of the lower ranking Indian soldiers. Ma Daam Begum, an artiste of Lahore nobility herself, was able to procure a house in the high-class part of Kamathipura because of her connections. Here she ran a Hindu-Muslim Lahore style kotha, a song-dance brothel with the number 55 displayed vividly in a decorated photo frame on the front door. She was given this number by the English cantonment, an authority indicating her house was disease free and safe for the white soldiers to visit. Moreover, all in her bevy of ten girls were numbered in accordance with the cantonment health registry of Indian prostitutes. How Ma Daam Begum used to boast in the bazaar about her girls! How beautiful they were! How accomplished! How loyal! Also how punctual they were with their weekly medical examination at the prison hospital. "As punctual as I am with my five prayers. Never miss one," was what she used to say. When it came to keeping the standards, Ma Daam Begum, as an Indian, impressed even the top English officers. She preferred to present Gulzar Bai and Soneri Bai, both beautiful with firm bodies having experienced no childbirth, only to the English officers with ranks of colonels and above. Soneri Bai was dark but the sparkle in her black eyes combined with her bearing made her irresistible to the white soldiers. To them she was their goddess Kali, the postcard Indian beauty, dark alluring female, a savage in an exotic and mysteriously sexual way of ancient India. A deity, consort fit for gods. However, Devdasi Rupa Bai, a skilful singer and dancer, entertained only the Indian nobility visiting Bombay. "Her talents will be wasted on these uncultured white-cheeta soldiers," Ma Daam Begum used to say widening her eyes, looking askance, referring to the English soldiers as if they were in the next chamber.

Otherwise, Ma Daam Begum was known with affectionate wonder as the Ma Daam Begum of Kamathipura.

Of the three, Devdasi Rupa Bai was the first to be married and leave Meethi Bai's lodge. Not long after her arrival from India, she attracted the eye of Sufi Ebrahim from the River Road Mosque, a once-a-week client at the lodge. He fell in love first with her song and then with the singer herself. Once a week he brought a sweet ladoo for her son and played blindfold man with him. Meethi Bai called it a marriage of melodies when she gave away the bride.

Devdasi Rupa Bai sings at the Radha Krishna temple at the apex of the hill in the lane that connects Grogon Road and River Road. Her husband Sufi Ebrahim sings at the Sunni mosque with a green dome where River Road meets Victoria Street behind the new granite stone jamat khana. The townsfolk call the jamat khana, Khoja Mosque, a three storey building with a clock dome. Khoja Mosque stands at a four way stop where animal drawn carts, human pulled carts and rickshaws, bicycles, horses and the rare piki piki motorcycle and motor cars meet. Devdasi Rupa Bai and Sufi Ebrahim have seven children, including God's child. The three boys and four girls are brought up Moslems but they also go to the temple and visit shrines of Hindu deities before whom their mother offers devotion in songs. "My children are like Gandhi," Sufi Ebrahim would say with pride. "After all they are brought up in their mother's lap at the temple's shrine like Salim, the Mughal prince, son of Akbar the Emperor and his Hindu queen, Johd Bai, the Empress of India." God's child is renamed Salim and his mother no longer calls him God's child as he can now claim a worldly father. However, she continues to call herself Devdasi, God's she-slave, in honour of her parents.

Meethi Bai also gave away her two other lodge daughters called Gulzar Bai and Soneri Bai. Gulzar Bai married an ex-convict and travelled deep into the Maasai Mara plains where the couple started a bead business with the dowry in cash and gold that Meethi Bai provided.

"Meethi Bai offers a dowry suiting a princess," said the townsfolk attending the marriage feast, "who can resist it?"

In fact, Meethi Bai gave opulent dowries to all the dance girls at her lodge. She called them her daughters born out of the circumstances that they shared like sisters in a family. "They are my own flesh and blood, born of one mother called Circumstance, the maker of destinies," she would say, "whoever of my daughters receives a marriage offer shall have my mother's blessing and her wealth."

The offer of a large dowry tempted the poor man to better his fortune through marriage with the lodge girl and it gave the woman dignity that was her honour to keep and guard. "Africa is the land of second chance," Meethi Bai would tell the girls. "Embrace her and love her. She is your destiny. Your mother now."

Once a week, every Thursday night, Govindji Bhai used to sing to Gulzar Bai before he carried her away from Meethi Bai's kotha.

Tuje uthake ley chalunga
Din raat aankhohi aankhomey
Tera pyar sambalta raha chala hun

I will carry you away
Day and night in the eye of my eyes
I have kept protected my love of you in me

Govindji Bhai remained behind in Kenya when his mates, all three of them, returned to India having served their jail term at the Fort Jesus Prison in Mombasa. The ex-political prisoners had vowed not to marry because, as they said, they were married to the fight against colonialism. However, Govindji Bhai broke his promise when he first saw Gulzar Bai on the dhow. Nobody is sure if Govindji Bhai is a Satpanth Khoja, a Sunni Khoja, an Ithna Asheri Khoja or an atheist revolutionary. They know he is a Khoja of Saurashtra of Lohana bloodline and that is all that matters to Meethi Bai. They have twelve children together at the Maasai Mara where they have a flourishing bead trade started with the gold and cash given by Meethi Bai.

Soneri Bai, the dark skinned one, married some years later to an elderly Punjabi widower across the Great Lake. The widower was too old and feeble to travel to India to bring a virgin child home the third time. He had eight children from his two previous marriages. He needed a mother to look after the children and a wife for himself. Soneri Bai has no children of her own. She lives a widow now but owns a lodge where Indian merchant travellers rest before continuing their journey towards the Mountains of the Moon, the Congo, Rwanda and Burundi. She is known as Ma Daam, the Begum of the Lake.

Part Seven

Zari thread and the verse

Moghul art, language and attire were greatly influenced by Persia that had a long tradition of pattern weaving and zari embroidery. Abu al-Fazal ibn Mubarack, the well-known chronicler of Emperor Akbar the Great, writing in the 16th century, noted that the Emperor preferred textiles embroidered in beautiful patterns and that imperial embroidery workshops were set up in towns that included Ahmedabad in Saurashtra. Here they produced fabrics and patterns in a variety of fashions in an age when, writes Abu al-Fazal ibn Mubarack, 'the drapery of embroidered fabrics used at feasts surpasses every description.'

MUGHAL MAAL BY LOUIS WERNER IN SAUDI ARAMCO WORLD JULY/AUGUST 2011 VOL 62, NO 2.

Though it is said that there is mention of zari in Vedic literature, the art of zari embroidery probably began to take root in the villages of Saurashtra during the Moghul period from the 14th century. No doubt, the royal patterns would have been toned to local decorative and stitching traditions as they changed hands and integrated into folklore over the years. This would be about the same time when the Persian Sufi pirs began to influence Vedic liturgy in Saurashtra creating the Ismaili Satpanth Das Avatar and ginans or the sacred verses that often have Light or Shine as a metaphor. The Indian word zari (or jari as in Gujarati) comes from Persian zardozi art embroidery.

205

25

Stepmother Gor Bai and Me

During the day in the Jugu Bazaar, I help my stepmother to turn the stone mill. We take turns turning the stone round and round gr ... gr ... Then in the kitchen, we prepare food offering of milk and black millet bread for the evening prayers. On Fridays she calls the offering 'pir ji mani' meaning 'pir's chapatti'. Ma Gor Bai comes from the village of Superi where the legendary Kamar Bai lived in a house in which was a grave of a Satpanth pir. A legend has it that on Fridays after the morning bath, when Kamar Bai prayed at the grave, a fragrance rose from the earth, so enchanting that whoever inhaled it was healed of the pain of the heart and restlessness of the mind. Thus, on Fridays, villagers and others, people of all faiths from all over Saurashtra who were afflicted by illnesses of pain in the heart and restlessness of the mind that the doctors could not cure, came to Kamar Bai's courtyard in Superi. Each brought milk and black millet bread as an offering they called 'pir ji mani' or 'bread for the pir'. There they sat, chanted and offered dua prayers and inhaled the healing fragrance rising from the ground. At the threshold of

206

the courtyard door, they bowed down to the ground in reverence and hand kissed the cotton cloth that had the impression in turmeric of Meeshnari Kara Ruda's footprints. This Satpanth bhagat too had visited the shrine and inhaled its fragrance. This gesture, they did when they entered and when they left the holy house.

Observing Ma Gor Bai, I learn to spittle wet the cut end of the zari thread on my tongue and glide it through my lips. Then, before it dried, I would slide the spit-stiffened thread through the eye of the needle. Ma showed me how to pick the right colonial chenille from the little black paper wallet in her English toffee tin. The chenilles stood like slim steel-shiny soldiers in a line behind a black band. "He, Mr John James in England, makes the finest needles for Saurashtran zari embroidery," says Ma. "The finest in the raj and in all the needle and thread shops of Nairobi."

From Ma Gor Bai, I learn to embroider black velvet Khoja girls' caps that we make to sell, and, as a result, Ma Gor Bai has accumulated a little treasure of her own. "This will be for the two dowries of my daughters," she tells Monghi and me when a finished cap is sold. She deposits the money in an old English biscuit tin that has a print of the coronation of King George V, the English king who wears a beard like the imam of Jamia Mosque. I stitch silver threads into florets and leaf symbols of desert sprays in spinning spirals, and soon my skills surpass Ma Gor Bai's. Day after day, week after week, month after month, repeatedly, I make the same rice grain stitches — forward, back; cross, half cross, and copy them on the velvet cloth, singing, humming guru-pirs' songs in cantos that describe the pattern to my eye. Each tiny stitch, like the one at the ear tip of the floret, is of the identical sheen and smoothness of silver zari as is the word in my voice singing

207

the holy song. Passion to repeat, repeat, and repeat overcomes me. I repeat inlaying zari in the sacred. Each stitch runs a word, a line a verse. Each lift up from a stitch or two coordinates with a short pause in the verse I sing. It's a pause to take in the breath. A longer pause matches the space after a curved line that ends a stanza. The stitch becomes the word and the word, a stitch, in the play of the eye, finger feeling and my breathing. A rhythm flows in my gaze. I hear the beat of my heart. I have different sacred songs for different patterns in different rhythms. In the shine of zari, I hear guru-pir singing Light to me. A meditation. A thought. An imagination. "Imagination is embroidery of your thoughts," Ma would say to me.

From my dots like bard's puns
Of beauty is born the shine
I catch Lord's riches in my ode
Silver treasure in fingers between

Thus, I embroider, memorizing the stitch in my fingertips until I can fill the space with the exact length at the exact angle to create the exact light and shadow in the next stitch of the next floret, exactly three indices away, as if it were a measure of a verse. Sometimes, Hawa sits by my side and follows my stitches with her dark eyes, mesmerized by the rhythmic in-out movements of the zari strand, the appearance and disappearance of light and shadow on velvet. Rass of ecstasy embodies me.

"*Inanilewesha* – makes me drunk," she murmurs in Swahili, "*ferdausi imeniingia nafsi* – paradise enters my being." Looking into her eyes, I understand the bliss of rass in her. That is her nafsi, her being in Swahili. That is my nafsi, my being.

Walking about the courtyard, I see floral spaces in sunshine and shadows in nooks and corners of the house. The song shows me how to see patterns. The courtyard is patterned in florets and verses. The sky is a blue velvet cloak. At night, I thread the dots through the twinkle of the stars with one long silver thread like Askari Bakari's embroidery. Then I sing to the needlework of the sky.

"Stitch a stitch when the heart sings and the mind quietens into meditation," Ma Gor Bai would say with a smile when she sees me doing the zari embroidery.

Visitors come to our house to see, to chafe the rough edged zari borders in their fingertips, to admire and some would want to buy. "Sakina is married to zari. She is happiest singing in the shine gardens she creates. The child loses herself in the paradise of her imagination," Stepmother Gor Bai tells the visitors. Sometimes our visitors buy the velvet caps, but more often, they come to tell stories from the Khoja villages around Jamnagar, Rajkot and Junagadh in India, and the peasant fields around Mandvi, Bhuj and Kera. They talk about families of new immigrants coming from the twin towns of Savar Khundla, and also from Una, Bhavnagar and Vera. Their difficult journeys in the wooden crafts and stormy gales that drive the dhows astray, sicknesses on board, and burial of children at sea. Among the visitors are those who come to sell their jewellery to Meethi Bai or to another rich lady of the bazaar on behalf of the immigrants who, out of desperation, have to part with their heirloom of silver and sometimes reluctantly, even gold that they have been safeguarding for their daughters' marriages. The mothers know a bride's worth is measured by the weight of gold on her.

Stepmother Gor Bai's gift as an embroiderer and her knowledge of the song are companions that people say go with her schooling in pir's family and good heart. They would say she was born in the village of Superi in the house of the pir's shrine in the land where stitching in colours of the desert sunset and cactus green, is an art. Over time, I learn more about women like my stepmother. I learn from their memories of their embroidered dresses, pachedis, saris and shawls like the bandhani. "We come from the land of stitch embroidery, Krishna's garba and Sufi bard's mantra," they would say. "The land of panths that tread the paths of Hinduism, Jainism and Buddhism told again as pir's Islam. The land that accepts all faiths, and gave birth to Sat-guru-pir's children and his grandchildren, pirs again, but Indians now. The land that created the Sat-panthis, the makers of true faith and the hidden people."

To this, Ma would add, part in verse, part in prose, "The land where stitch embroidery twines folk tales in the wisdom of many a belief. Chants of the guru-pirs tie Sufi beseeching in Bhagti ragas when in the thirteenth century, Islam's young blooded zeal was halted, and then absorbed by the rock of Mohenjo-Daro, a civilization older than the Arabian Quran. A civilization guarded by gurus to whom the life of an ant, the lowest of beings, was sacred more than the ultimate ascendancy of the prophets of Abraham." I came to understand how such stories of faith intersperse family stories of my stepmother and Dadabapa – that's how our traditions are remembered, and that's how I learned lessons of life. "When I was nine, I was married," Stepmother Gor Bai would begin her teaching story. "My widowed grandmother was a gupti, which is a hidden Satpanth devotee at the shrine of the Pir of Superi. She wished to start prayo-pavesa at the hill

210

ashram but wanted to see me married before she took the vow to her final pilgrimage."

Part of my stepmother's story I heard from her. I am sitting on the kitchen patlo, stirring the curry of black lentil, the one that is white eyed. Malek and Hawa sit on the cold concrete floor, taking turns, slicing vegetables, washing dishes and kneading the chapatti dough. Monghi and Bahdur share a patlo floor stool and watch over our routine gestures in quiet manner of children before their hunger becomes unbearable, and then they are restless and tearful.

"I was married to a young man from my village of Superi. He worked at the port in Zanzibar. His name was Vali Premji." Ma Gor Bai narrows her eyes hinting past hate from her tightened lips, and sorrow in sniffs following words. We forget the hunger biting our stomachs when Ma begins her story.

"When after seven years of waiting, the young man I married did not return to Superi to take me to Zanzibar as he had promised. My family decided I should go either to the widows' ashram or to Africa to look for Vali Premji, my wedded husband. The opportunity to go to Africa came when I heard about the two girls from Superi who were travelling to Africa, and, like me, they were going to meet their husbands. But, unlike me, they were married by proxy. The marriage maker in our village exchanged their photographs across the ocean. Then the photographs represented the grooms at marriage. Their families studied the faces in the pictures, nodded, and gave their consents saying, "We know them now." My parents made me to take the craft from Portuguese Gujarat, the port of Diu. My mother sold her silver anklets to pay for my passage, and we had some money saved from

211

embroidery work laying weighty zari borders on the Satpanth bandhani. I was already sixteen by then and the time had come for my grandmother to prepare for her prayo-pavesa. She wanted to see me with my husband, in my own home or in the ashram, before she took the vow to journey to peace, her final pilgrimage to quicken her going to the next karma. She could not wait any longer because she had no more to do with her life."

Ma Gor Bai plucks out portions from the dough prepared by Hawa, masticates and presses each one in her lifted hand before she lays it on the chapatti rolling stool. Her shoulders are humped, arms moving back and forth, mechanically. The patlo stool rasps on the grey cement floor in the stillness of the kitchen. The stillness of watching over the evening meal about to be served. The stillness of hunger. From the remaining dough, Ma Gor Bai makes the last chapatti, the size of her palm, and gives it to Bahdur, the youngest of the children around her.

There is more dough that Ma plucks off the kneading plate and rolls it into a ball again before she continues to tell us her story. "Finally, I found Vali Premji but he was married and had three children by his Swahili wife. He lived next to the house where Gandhi, in his folly of youth, could not say no to the invitation of the white captain of the Bombay-Durban liner and visited a Zanzibari dame. That was wrong, he admitted later, and said he had remained fully clothed in the room. Thus, is the story of Gandhi told, and laughed about among the women of Zanzibar. I decided not to return to Superi because I could not face the dishonour of a broken marriage that would also bring shame to my family. And I was determined to defy my destiny and not to enter the ashram. Africa, they said, was the land of the second chance." Ma Gor

Bai pauses to look up and out through the door into the courtyard. "In Zanzibar, I lived near the jamat khana where widows gathered with other women who had not heard from their husbands. They said their husbands went to the mainland to join foot safaris into the interior to look for work. Each day we cooked meals for bachelors and earned a living that just barely gave us one meal for our children and ourselves, but saved us from the scorn of mothaj on reluctant well-wishers bound by taunts of faith and family obligations to give alms. I worked hard in the Welfare Cooking Committee and taught them new recipes. I was an absakan, cursed and childless woman, like the fourteen-year-old widow, Jee Bai, who threw herself into the water and people sighed, thanking God, for she had freed herself from the disgrace of lifetime mothaj on her community. They said she had the courage of a sati to die with honour. Many a time, I thought of throwing myself into the waters of the Indian Ocean like Jee Bai. But, Jee Bai's death frightened me and awakened the courage in me to live. Africa, I said to myself, is the land of the second chance. So I started to embroider velvet caps, pillows and dresses, coverings for the coffins and took them around the bazaar to shopkeepers to display and sell. I worked day and night. I had learned the art of zari embroidery from my pious grandmother, and she from her mother, who was widowed at twenty-one. She made a living from zari embroidery on the Satpanth bandhani while she sang the sacred verses into the stiches, and calmed herself inside."

Ma Gor Bai strokes my head as if it were a cat sitting. Then she traces the parting with her one finger scratching my skull with her fingernail as she talks.

"My marriage to your father was arranged by one Kheroon Bai, a wealthy lady, the only daughter of a clove and slave merchant in Zanzibar. She taught me courage and how to live in troubled times. She used to say my problem was little. That there were bigger problems, community problems. That I should always see the bigger problems. She was referring to the fragmenting Khoja jamat in Zanzibar. When tensions between the Khoja Ismaili and Khoja Ithna Asheri became intense in Zanzibar, Kheroon Bai's parents could not agree which group to join. They had business partners between both the sections and they were related on the two sides. Moreover, the man's family took an oath of loyalty to Saheb affirming their Ismaili faith while his wife's family joined the Ithna Asheri jamat. So now the question arose in which faith should they bring up their daughter Kheroon Bai?"

Ma Gor Bai looks at me and smiles the way adults smile at children when they tease them with a question knowing the children cannot tell the answer, and they cannot wait to tell.

"Thus her mother would take Kheroon Bai to the Khoja Ithna Asheri mosque and the father would take her to the Khoja Ismaili jamat khana. However, the father had his doubts. He read both the Das Avatar and *Chiragh e Hidayat* to be at peace with himself and his families. It was no secret that he did not sign the Book of Allegiance because he could not make up his mind. His was a family divided by beliefs but united by their caste kind. To this day, there are such families of one lineage but opposing beliefs. Now the question arose again when Kheroon Bai was ready for marriage. What could she do? What group should she join to find a suitable man? Khoja Ismaili or Khoja Ithna Asheri?"

Stepmother Gor Bai asks the familiar question again, then looks at me, and smiles, knowing I have no answer, only a question. "So what group did she join?" she asks my question followed by the answer she knew all the time.

"So Kheroon Bai on becoming an adult, attended prayer meetings on both sides, in the jamat khana and the mosque, and worked among all the women in need irrespective of their beliefs. She was a wealthy woman with her own independent income from the clove plantation that she had inherited and she lived outside of men's politics. Because of her wealth, she also had a free mind."

Ma Gor Bai pauses to masticate the dough ball using her fingers in one raised hand like she were telling her tasbih She divides the dough ball into four equal parts for Shamshu, Monghi, Malek and Bahdur to play with. Then she half closes the stove's door before continuing to narrate her story.

"Kheroon Bai was appointed the head of the Widows Committee in our Satpanth Ismaili jamat because of her devotional work among the widows of Zanzibar. She had taken it upon herself to seek out mistreated and shamed absakan widows in the divided jamat of the old port town. She arranged re-marriages of widows, which was Saheb's wish. She used to say, 'Saheb's wish is my command.' Bless her soul. She did not marry so she could serve those who did."

I watch Monghi making a miniature doll out of her ball of dough. Malek has made a cat with a long tail and Bahdur is trying to fashion a piki piki motorcycle without much success. Shamshu's figurine appears to be a gun.

My best afternoons are when the girls are called by Ma to help her with the new stock of beads just arrived from Rajan Lalji's store. We arrange the beads in different sizes and sets of blues, whites and reds for the Maasai. We make triangular newspaper packages of lustreless pink beads, all of the same

215

size, so tiny that the hole in them allows just the slimmest sewing needle to go through. These are for the Kikuyu women to make their ear haangi rings.

Some afternoons when Ma goes to her satsang meetings and Monghi and Malek are at school, I would be alone working with the beads. I remember the afternoons in the month of February in Nairobi when it is hot and there are no clouds above you, and you would see the sky an infinite blue awaiting water-laden monsoons from the Indian Ocean. I remember these afternoons because Dadabapa, my father and Noordin Kaka uncle would leave the shop to me to look after while they went for a quick nap as they said. Few people walked about in the bazaar and hardly anyone came to our shop except an occasional group of Kikuyu women returning from collecting firewood.

On such afternoons of the dry month there are cool wind gusts that tunnel through the store's veranda persuading us to be patient for the coming change of the season was near. The same wind would stroke, brace and cuddle the group of Kikuyu women as they drop the bundled firewood off their backs and stretch their weary limbs in the eaves' shade outside the shop. They come to drink water in their cupped hands at the tap besides the granite steps. It became like a routine for me to look at their beads from a distance. Their ear haangis were circular, each one the size of a wrist bangle. A bunch of these bangle rings hung in each lobe and were so many and so weighty that they had to be held by a leather strap over their heads massaged with natural oils. You would hear them talk over the gentle flapping of their muthuru skirts, ochred red and oil rubbed calfskins to the softness of cotton. The flutter of the skirts in the wind would usher a chorus of clinking one-cent coins on iron ringed anklets padding over the floor.

216

Copper coils rasp on their forearms and calves. Each bundle of sticks tied with a leather strap that sat on their shaven heads just above the forehead where the weight made a groove on some. The fashionable among them would have a black net stretched over their shaven heads. The mothers would then pad into the duka store, their eyes on new displays.

I see these farmer women of great beauty in their freedom drawn from the countryside under an open sky. Their lives are so unlike our lives. The women of my family are confined within the walls of the home-store-jamat khana, all in the shantytown of Nairobi. We are like the white women at the new Catholic nun-house in Loreto Valley where priests grow coffee. Stories about these nuns and coffee trees actually originate from the Indian carpenters and masons who build and fix their houses, churches and schools. Then through circulation of words, looks and whispers, they put astonishment in women's eyes at the jamat khana. Sometimes, I would marvel about these white women who keep secluded in an ashram, but mostly the Kikuyu women are the ones who captivate me. Looking at their dress and the beads they wear, their gestures and their embracing eyes, I often wonder what lies there beyond Nairobi on the hills where they were raised. Was Muthoni Nyanjiru not one of them, nurtured by the freedom of the open sky country? What made her, a woman, to throw a rock into the face of the mighty Empire? In the shop, the Kikuyu women would admire, discuss, joke and laugh aloud at amazing things English and Indian, but it's the beads that they come to see and maybe purchase some. As I watch, I cannot but wonder again and again how one among them defied the big raja-king, god-like emperor, a white avatar in the picture worthy of darshan. Sometimes, like Muthoni

217

Nyanjiru in my Dadabapa's head, they would have babies cradled in soft skin pouches strapped to their bodies with names like Njoki meaning born again. Over the stale scent of incense from Dadabapa's morning worship, I smell the aroma of red therega earth on their skin attires. Quickly, before the slight breeze pushes the earth's odour out of the store, I inhale deeply to know the fragrance of the red land beyond the Indian shantytown.

Nairobi is at the confluence where the eye meets the rich colours of Kikuyu beads on farmers descending from the hills and Maasai beads, similarly rich in colour, on pastoralists from the plains. Both neighbours, inter-relating the beauty of the sky country in their ethnic eyes, converge in the Indian bazaar like flows of two rainbow rivers.

26

The Offer

Hawa and I watch the crescent moon in the cloudless sky over Nairobi. The rains have delayed. The moon stalks the stars on a clear night like today. We are sitting on the steps of the shop's veranda. The day has been long, serving water and chai to the satsang widows' meeting. Behind the bolted doors of the shop, my parents are talking earnestly, with crisp yes-no whispers. Nights are warm in the shantytown before the monsoons sweep over the tin roofs puffing dust clouds in the air, as if to make it known it's on the way to fetch dark rain clouds for us. Then the short rains come and push the heat away out of the alleys of shantytown Nairobi. How we thank the wind as if it were a benefactor! In the stillness of the black velvet sky, a falling star is like a Diwali sparkler. Askari Bakari, the watchman, standing on the far side by the last wooden pillar of the veranda, is a silhouette shrouded in a shadow.

"If you look long enough at the sky's art patterns, you will hear the secrets of the universe," says Askari Bakari.

I see stars floating in the emptiness above marking the rhythm of the hymn of kasida that I hear Askari Bakari sing. Some stars are up and some down, some blink to the right side and some to the left. All silver zari stars hanging by an invisible thread that connects them all. The sky reveals its embroidered landscape so strikingly that each time I look at Askari Bakari's kofia cap, the heavens appear in my mind. I hear the music of the kasida hymn like a pattern made of sparkles in the sky's zariwork.

"I received another reminder of Sakina's marriage offer from the Momna family of Nairowua," I hear my father's soft voice at the shop window. "They say they have been waiting for two years now. Dadabapa had given his word to the boy's grandfather, Devji Momna, when they met in Zanzibar again after many years. They were good friends, like brothers. Devji Momna died of swollen legs before he would see the promise fulfilled, shukhar. Now Dadabapa urges me to honour his word to the fellow Satpanthi. This is a good offer. There is love in the bond of the two grandfathers. They had respect for each other. The boy's mother is impatient. She says she will not wait forever for us to let Sakina go. The boy is getting old, she says. He is their only son. Sakina will not have to cook and wash dishes for a large family. She will be happy," says my father. He is half speaking, half mumbling to Ma Gor Bai. Hawa is still and alert like a little bird in danger of becoming a prey of a large predator bird. She tilts her head to hear more, smiling at what she hears, blushes a little as if on my behalf, and with her alluding eyes hints to me to listen. She is observant and curious about all the little happenings in the family. She would always be aware of the hidden messages within the covert talk in the family intimacy. Except the children, everyone else dismisses Hawa as 'just a child.' She also does not speak Gujarati or Kutchi, and the adults say she is only a girl, only a little black girl they call toto. Or they would say she is 'just a servant'. Sometimes an adult is kind to 'the child' and gives her a penda or a ladoo that she loves. I do not respond to Hawa's eye hints. I am high up sailing in the firmament, brilliant with crescent moons, zari striped boats. Bakari raises his voice coming to a crescendo. In the sleepy bazaar, I muse to the lilt of the evening kasida, a lullaby carried by the night's breeze of the monsoon season, blowing to the rhythm of the slowing closing day.

"Sakina is not yet ready for marriage. Just look at her. Her body so frail!" replies Ma Gor Bai. "She is not ready yet to bear the weight of a man. And look at those breasts. Bottle tops! They are not ripe yet to nurse healthy children."

"This time they want us to say either 'yes' or 'no.' Dadabapa has pledged Sakina to them. We must honour the pledge."

"Say 'no' then, not now," says Ma Gor Bai curtly.

"Our business is declining and so is my father's health. He wants to see Sakina married so he can die in peace. We may have to go farther into the interior but we cannot take father with us. Noordin is thinking of going to the Congo where his wife has a brother. It will be better for the peace in the house if he goes. He upsets us all when he preaches about the true religion. Sakina will be a mothaj if there is no marriage soon. She is the eldest and we can marry neither Shamshu nor Monghi before she leaves for her destined home." My father's voice sounds like a plea.

"She is no mothaj to me. It is sinful to make your blood, your own daughter, feel she is a mothaj!"

221

"But what will people say? She herself will suffer the shame of mothaj even if you are kind to her. It's a matter of our family honour. It is good to marry Sakina while we still have this home and the shop. It will give us the respectability at her marriage and save face."

"You think only about your beautiful face! I am thinking about Sakina's life ahead! I would like Sakina to be with us for Saheb's Jubilee in Nairobi."

"We can weigh Saheb in Nairobi when the bequest offered by the jamat equals his weight in gold. It will take long. Can we afford to wait that long? Will they wait that long?" replies my father. "Meanwhile, let us agree to the offer. The boy is the grandson of my father's friend. They met on the dhow and my father lived with Devji Momna in Mombasa when he knew no one in Africa and had no money. We are indebted to the Devji Momna's family. We must honour the promise my father made."

"We will see the boy when the Nairowua jamat comes to Nairobi to see Saheb weighed against gold. No one will miss this auspicious occasion for his darshan-deedar. Let us decide then, but I still think it's too early to give away our Sakina to a Momna family somewhere in a bush town in the interior that no one has heard of," Ma speaks with slow thoughtful, perhaps even angry, words.

"Saheb does not want us to live segregated in Africa. We are all Satpanth immigrants - Momnas and Nangarias, Punjabis, Sindhis, Guptis, Kutchis, Gujaratis. Are we not one in worship? Did we all not take the oath of allegiance to Saheb? There will be one jamat khana for all. One big Khoja Khana. That's Saheb's wish."

"Saheb also does not want us to give away our daughters as child brides."

"No family likes to take old maids. Family has no honour when there is a spinster sitting at home. An unmarried daughter is a mothaj, an undignified load that sits like a disgrace on our shoulders. Moreover, we must honour my father's word, whether it's to a Momna or Khoja, it's my father's word. Give away Sakina and gain respectability. "

They argue no more but their talk kindled a fire in me. I want to be married. I want a husband. I want to be a mother. I want to be a woman. My story drifts into my dreams of my own home. It flows into the silence of the night's pulsating stars in my eyes expectant of a new day, a new life. My awakened body throbs with a desire to be loved by a man. Loved like Suraiya on Film India screen. Loved like them at Meethi Bai's lodge.

27

Haiderali in English Sports Jacket

Jugu Bazaar, Nairobi

A week before my fifteenth birthday, my father surprises us. We had just returned from the jamat khana and were clearing the table of the khaki shirts and brown woollen coats. That afternoon Malek, Monghi and I had been making buttonholes on the British army uniforms under Ma Gor Bai's stern eye. For each completed garment, she gave us one tongolo ten cents that we carefully tucked underneath the lining of our velvet caps.

Outside, the street is lighted and shops are open on this Diwali night. Vedas are recited and goddess Lakhsmi's name praised. Her auspicious presence into the bazaar and account books called upon. The books are on low floor desks or on boxes covered with bright saris. They are the centrepiece of Lakhsmi's makeshift shop altars. The pages that will carry the accounts of the coming year are garlanded with orange marigolds, showered in rice, crossed with the blessed su-astik in red kum kum paste and spotted with saffron dots like the bride's brow. It is a welcoming sign heralding the lucky bride, incarnate she-deity Lakhsmi bringing energies of abundance over the threshold of the old into the New Year. In all, the money books are made auspicious. At the propitious moment in the galaxy's dance, a rupee of pure silver with the head of Rani Victoria, Empress of India and East Africa or a thaler of Maria Theresa, the Empress of Austria, is stuck on the Gujarati account book covers. The Empresses endorse all fair trade of the Indian and Arabian seas. The two sovereign female silver heads have more strength to draw in goddess Lakhsmi than the African shilling of the Empire bearing the heads of Victoria's male heirs. Demons stay away this night, terrified of the ceaseless whip-snaps of firecrackers and the dazzling shine in the Jugu Bazaar.

Inside the house, my father announces it is time to accept my marriage offer from Nairowua. Men sit at the table and women are in the kitchen. Ma Gor Bai and Kaki Bai auntie on the patlo floor stools, girls sit cross-legged on the cold cement. Father puts a photograph on the table, pulls up a chair and sits down. He folds his hands as he calls out, "Hawa come and take this." Hawa picks up the photograph from the teakwood tabletop that has absorbed several years of curried oil spills leaving patina patches of uneven shapes. She walks to the kitchen in deliberately unhurried steps, head bowed low down over the photograph. Eventually, she gives the photograph to Ma Gor Bai.

It is a studio shot portrait of Haiderali Devji in an English striped sports jacket and a dotted scarf loosely wrapped around his neck. The first thing I notice is Haiderali's eyes. They are sharp and narrow, probably with a shine, and then I wonder if he is dark or fair of skin. He looks fair in the photograph for sure. His wavy hair is neatly parted in the middle. This is the first time I see what the man I am going to marry looks like. I am overwhelmed with shyness to say anything. "You can keep the photograph with you," Ma Gor

Bai tells me. My heart leaps. I will show off the photograph to the Jamal Bhai girls in the next bead store. I will be married. I will have a husband. I will be a mother. I will be a woman. I will place the photograph on my China handkerchief and sprinkle rose petals and jasmine around it. The photograph has taken the place of Meeshnari Shivji Bhagat in my heart where it pulses. Meeshnari Shivji Bhagat, anyway, did not return from India and his picture in me was fading with the days.

"Look at him for a long time and you will love him," Meethi Bai would tell me later in private.

"Keep peace between you and his mother. Peace is more important than love," Ma Gor Bai would say later in the kitchen with Monghi, Malek and Hawa listening.

I am frustrated, because at home I have no privacy to look at the photograph and be with Haiderali alone. I steal moments to be with Haiderali hiding behind the stack of folded blankets in the store as I used to when I was little. With my pachedi over my forehead, to the eyes in respectful laaj, I now look at Haiderali from below the veil's edge, speaking mischief, "Come get me if you can!" I do not smile and bite my lower lip lightly, seductively, at the side like in a love-tease look in the film. He does not talk so I say, 'hmm-hmmh' for him and reply to his 'hmm-hmmh' with my eyelashes in filmi surprise eye talk. He says he loves me. I twitch my nose and shrug shoulders, teasing him, as if to say, "I don't know about that!" Putting my fingers on his lips, I catch his love whispers on my fingertips. I take a vow, "I will always be faithful to you in this world, and through the cycle of karma in the worlds to come where we shall wander in bliss, hand in hand, forever. Forever I shall be your bride and you my bridegroom. We will wear rose garlands and red silks." I imagine myself lost far away behind the Indian trees and flowers, the moon and the clouds, in the stillness of the filmi meadows where Haiderali would come looking for me in the magic of hide and seek love play. I know I was born to dream. Meethi Bai says dreams come true. A dream, she says, is a gift from the other world.

A month passes by in expectation of the announcement of the marriage day. I am too embarrassed to ask when it will be. Sometimes, Ma Gor Bai whispers to me, "Soon you will be at your own home caring for your husband and your own family." Sometimes Meethi Bai teases me about Haiderali with eyes asking, "You like him, no?" She makes me blush. I enjoy the moments and her teasing endears Haiderali all the more to me. News goes around the Jugu Bazaar. My father has accepted the offer from a Momna family in Nairowua, a one street town on Kenya Tanganyika border. Men shake their heads, and women cover their mouths with three fingers. "What a Khoja girl given to a Momna?" they ask in disapproval. Relatives and friends, especially women, come home to see the photograph anyway. At the widows' satsang meeting, the picture goes from one hand to another. Women look at it with such intensity that I think their stare would tear a hole in the picture. "Don't look for too long. Pass it on," stepmother would say, afraid an evil eye may cause kisirani and then a withdrawal of the marriage offer. Widows turn their faces away from the picture. Their eyes look to the blank wall where they would do no harm. When the Jamal Bhai girls, my childhood friends, see the photograph of Haiderali in an English striped sports jacket, they would exclaim in breathless surprises, "You are so fortunate Sakina! Your husband is so fair, so English looking, no? Does he speak English too?"

I keep the photograph hidden in my black velvet cap behind the cotton lining where I had pulled out the stitches to slip it in. "Shamshu will not lay his hands on my velvet cap," so I thought. I do not like him to tease me. Sometimes he also calls Haiderali, topiara, the man with a hat meaning an Englishman, and sometimes mzungu, the one who wanders around, also an Englishman. Mostly, I am afraid he might blackmail me into giving him my tongolos and dhururus I have been collecting in an old English toffee tin for my marriage.

In the evenings, after school but before my family gets together at the jamat khana, I sneak into the clerk's office at the lobby of pillars. There I sit under the painted photograph of Suleiman Kassam Virji and pull Haiderali's photograph out from my velvet cap carefully, lovingly, as if it were him. I look at it in the light streaming from the corridor chandeliers and bring the picture to life placing it in my lap, rocking it like my dhingly doll. The one that's made of clay with a painted black plait, a long pleated sadlo skirt and a short choli blouse that ends with a red hemline above the navel. This Gujarati damsel is dressed like Krishna's milkmaid, his lover and murid. She is I and I am she when I make her a bride. She has a red dot on her forehead between the eyes. I am milkmaid Radha. The one of venerating gestures and darshan filled feminine looks. Like Indian filmi actors, we play pretend game called, 'Come and get me if you can.' That is the moment of magic in the rass of dandia dance with the avatar. Haiderali smiles at me. "I will come and get you my little milkmaid, my bride," he says. I look into his eyes. I am a teenager, in love with a picture.

"But first you must buy me Charlie's ice cream," I reply to the picture in my lap assuming he is asking me to go out with him.

228

I continue to dream about Haiderali Devji in the photograph. Throwing alluring teenage glances, I lay a trap for his eyes in mine and when he catches my look, I turn away and pretend to be lost in thoughts. I am on the screen at Film India. He too is on the screen with me. I ignore him for a minute, and then put my finger on the chin in a rehearsed actor pose showing doubt. Half veiling my face under my upbraided hair lively in latka pose, menacingly. I peer at Haiderali through my curls, eye teasing like an actor. We play filmi naakhra – speaking gestures and talking eye-thoughts. Like the actor, I dream to be loved and to be a woman.

Ma Gor Bai and Meethi Bai meet more often now, mostly in the afternoons, discussing my dowry of furniture, carpets, clothes, copper vessels and kitchen utensils. I listen filled with family pride and feel pampered.

"We will put the clothes and jewellery in a new suitcase with leather straps and shining buckles like those that the memsahebs at the Norfolk Hotel put on rickshaws. We will order one from the English Bazaar on Delamere Avenue," says Ma Gor Bai.

They talk about the days of marriage and revise the order of rituals.

"I would like you to be the song leader," says Ma Gor Bai to Meethi Bai.

"Hai reh! But what will people say? You know they consider me the impure one. My coming to the marriage will bring bad luck. I am the absakan one in their eyes," replies Meethi Bai.

"Well in that case, so am I the impure one. My first husband deserted me, you know," reminisces Ma Gor Bai while she looks away through the window into the busy street. Mkokoteni, Nairobi's famous pushcart men jostle along mud tracks behind a horse cart loaded with boxes. On the boxes are two natives in ragged English clothes, leather shoes and settlers' hats. An elderly Kikuyu man with a giithi fleece cape walks leaning on his muthegi staff of African peace tree. Carefully he selects dry patches in-between red muck puddles to put his next step. Red cream mud churns under the feet of men and women, horses and donkeys. The elder on hearing the familiar machine hum, waits for settler Kaburu's son to pass. Then the youthful white man comes on his piki piki motorcycle spluttering through the mud pools.

"I lived an outcaste Satpanth widow in Zanzibar. They called me the polluted one, the unfortunate absakan. But they liked my embroidery. My art is my verse, a cry of longing to be free. The pain I put to art is nature's gift to the artist. Without the art, her mind becomes a prey for spirits. I am blessed with fingers of an embroiderer as you are blessed with the throat of the nightingale. Are you not called the koiyal bird?" asks Ma Gor Bai. Meethi Bai looks down at her nails, fingers moving. Ma Gor Bai would not have expected a reply to what is well known. Besides that, it would have been boastful. One has to be humble about one's talent. Such a compliment needs no acknowledgement as the town people would say. Or they would say in other words, the Satpanth way, "Do not test her humility for she does not have the strength of Gandhi's humility to bring down an Empire."

"And also bring your dancing girls from the lodge to sing the chorus. At Sakina's henna night, I want Nairobi's nightingale to celebrate the Satpanth bandhani. That will choke the bazaar's gossip in the throat," says Ma Gor Bai. The look in her eyes suddenly turns stern.

"With all my heart I shall sing *Evi ruri che mari rehsham bandhani Saheb-jine* - so soft is the silken tie, my binding with Saheb," replies Meethi Bai stressing the pun on bandhani meaning the wedding shawl and a spiritual tie with Saheb the bridegroom. "The bandhani ties colours like how my heart ties my love for Saheb. He will be my groom when they take me covered in my bandhani to him waiting at the threshold of his house in heaven." It was this love for Saheb that created a hidden wall of silence from those who did not know him and spoke in khus khus whispers of his Krishna-gopi-mischief in the English world.

"I will send a message to Devdasi Rupa Bai to come and be your accompaniment. She is an old grandmother but her voice is young like a girl's. She sings in colours of Sam Veda," says Ma Gor Bai.

"Did this Veda not birth Satpanth melodies?" asks Meethi Bai. She is thinking aloud, asking questions to pose doubts, seeking answers from herself, the singer, not Ma Gor Bai.

My story is a song.

28

Song of Satpanth Bandhani

The rainy season in the month of November that we call 'Short Rains', is almost over and the jacaranda trees in Rani Bagh stand like a parade of purple bouquets under the blue sky over Nairobi, the town between rivers. Sitting on the floor, on a mattress covered with a clean white bed sheet, I watch through the wide open door. Ma Gor Bai, standing at the threshold of the courtyard veranda, is ceremoniously receiving the women of Haiderali Devji's extended family. No sooner did they step into my home, looking over everyone else as if in search to claim me, than I notice Ma Jena Bai, Haiderali's mother, my mother-in-law to be, my sass to be, coming towards me. My heart thumps. I look down and gather myself in stillness. She places a nose siri of seven tiny diamonds in my lap and then, immediately, like a mother casing her child in her pachedi from the cold, she covers me from the head down with the Devji family bandhani. It's a silk

232

shawl of dark purple-crimson almost black tie and dye dot patterns. It's framed by a weighty border of pure silver zari thread worked into a leafy vine on which sit florets. I remain still, motionless, half in a fantasy world, half in fear of the unknown fate that awaits me in the new fold. But I am adorned like a jewel in a crown and Ma Jena Bai is beaming over me having taken the bride. Everyone around is celebrating me, the jewel, while my heart beats with trepidation. I seek to hide into the bandhani's desert landscape of florets. I seek to run into the tracing of stitch in, stitch out creating one floret into another in the timeless flow of my imagination. I want to hide in the richness of its shine in the border. I want to hide under henna's patterned network on my skin. I want to hide into the seven diamonds of my nose siri. I want to hide in their sparkle. Then quickly and suddenly, completely unexpectedly, Ma Jena Bai flicks open a miniature silver box and press a pinch of bajar tobacco powder into her nostrils, sniffing in with contentment before returning the box into the cup of her brassiere. She hums to herself and talks excitedly in a commanding voice, "Keep the gold set near here! Spread the velvet and the shoes over there!" She has brought my wedding clothes and jewellery to be shown, to be bragged about, and they have to be placed under her watchful eyes, fully exhibited. The beautiful bandhani shawl bears me down like a load of an unknown future on my shoulders. I begin to shiver but no one notices yet all eyes are on me.

There are whispers that Ma Gor Bai has invited Meethi Bai to sing the marriage song. The lady is famed for her marriage songs, which she composes and sings with her dance girls from the lodge. However, she is also the proprietor of the dishonourable Indian house. The keeper of prostitutes is an outcast but the Satpanthis, the lovers of Sufi chants, say, "The nectar of her voice in the ear softens the curse on the tongue." Meethi Bai carries that dilemma.

The olive henna paste absorbs the heat from my body and I am cold. Ma Gor Bai has hired the best-known henna artist, Kulsum Bai, the only daughter of the Bohra tinsmith on Victoria Street. Kulsum Bai adds black tea to the henna paste. She knows how to keep the precise consistency for working the henna into fine line patterns on a warm night like today. Then all eyes turn to the door. Meethi Bai arrives in a flaming red sari, prepared for an evening of singing while paisley and floral patterns are sketch-pasted on my feet up to the ankles and on my hands up to the wrists. The carousing excitement of the evening temporarily numbs the apprehension that has been building in me since the morning.

Meethi Bai sings setting the tempo in six beats, 1 2 3 - 4 5 6, moving her head dole dole. She stretches her plump ringed fingers forward with the first beat. Then she withdraws her hand, fingers curled in, back to the chest with the second. At the third beat, she places her hands cross-folded on her chest. The hands I know so well and loved them raking through my hair looking for lice eggs to crack between her two painted thumbnails. A silence follows every third beat long enough to take in a deep breath. My heart races.

Honour the bride, her female self
Adorn the mother she will be
Sangaar, siri and the Satpanth bandhani

The response wavers in a limp echo, like the sound of a receding tide, *Sangaar, siri and the Satpanth bandhani.*

Meethi Bai, the koiyal songstress, continues, her eyes playing about the room, her head moving from side to side telling me to be proud for this long awaited day is here. But I am looking down holding in the feelings I have never had before. Meethi Bai claps, accenting every third beat, and nods to others to clap with her. She is in charge of the evening. The women clap, the chorus mounts becoming louder, filling the air, *Sangaar, siri and the Satpanth bandhani.*

Meethi Bai continues moving her head dole dole, her eyes are lighted and a smile sparks up on her red lipstick. Devdasi Rupa Bai picks up the next verse.

Laksmi, she will be
Wealth shines in Devji family
Sangaar, siri and the Satpanth bandhani

The women clap and sing in unison while Ma Jena Bai with her hand touches the cup of ceremonial sweet milk to my lips. I sip a little, not enough to make a gulp. Warmth spreads over my tongue. My body stiffens, the warmth entering chokes me. What is it to know a man? Nobody has told me yet. Taking the cup from Ma Jena Bai, Meethi Bai wraps her arm around me and with the other hand, coaxes me to take a little more into my body. I feel like an infant comforted in mother's lap being persuaded to swallow bitter quinine. I reject it. Meethi Bai brings her head close to mine. I feel her breath hang in the funnel of my ear.

"When the man covers you, let him," she says. My eyes widen. I want to hear more. "When he wants to be inside you, let him." My heart thumps gripped by fear. I want to throw up the sweet milk. "It will be painful, my dear child, but let him because he has the right."

"How? Why?" My eyes question Meethi Bai but she says nothing, yet she knows what I ask. Instead, she looks into my eyes with intensity of a sadness that deepens the anxiety surging in me. When tenderness returns to her kohl-blackened eyes as if on an impulse, she tugs, turns, sucks at and pulls out a ruby ring from her little finger, sliding it onto my middle finger, all in one continuous movement. I feel the warmth of her spit as the ring glides down over my cold knuckle creamed with henna. It's the ring that my sister Monghi Bai used to play the bride with and Meethi Bai used to tell her that she would put it on her finger when she was really a bride.

The milk is hot and heavy with pistachio and almonds under a thick salve paste on which stand stripy bright orange saffron halos. Women sitting around me, cross-legged on mattresses, soft chew the honeyed nuts, relishing saffroned warmth of the full cream milk. Some are offended by the presence of Meethi Bai and they whisper chup chap under their breath. Some will not sit near her. Some feel she has no right to sing. Some feel she should not be at any wedding let alone this one. Though all like to listen to Meethi Bai's lyrical stories and marriage songs, not many would talk with her in the bazaar or even at the jamat khana. In fact, she is never invited to sing the ginans for she is the inauspicious one, the absakan unlucky one of Nairobi. She has many names and is often the subject of men's talk, joke and love. They would call her the bazaar's night bird while women despise her as the husband stealer.

"If you sing to the song you will hear its story in the music," says Kulsum Bai holding my henna laden hands at the elbows so they do not stain the bandhani shawl. Her voice is fine like the patterns she paints, words connected without a pause. Meethi Bai begins moving her head from side to side again, horizontally, like an elegant temple dancer. I watch her apprehensively through side looks as she begins the next verse.

Sangaar, siri and the Satpanth bandhani
Blessed is one born of beauty

Covering her face partly with the edge of my bandhani, she veils one eye and sings from behind the silken mask, moving her head. She plays with me the way mothers play hide and seek behind their pachedis with babies in their laps. The same way I played mother with my dhingly doll behind the blankets in Dadabapa's store when I was little. Now she sings as if she were the bandhani.

Bandhani I am Brahma's lotus
From my dots like bard's music
Of beauty is born the shine
I catch Lord's riches in my ode
Silver treasure in cupped hands

The diamond in her nose plays winks with the lantern's light each time she turns her head showing a jasmine bunch perched on her perfumed hair clasped by a silver clip in the shape of a parrot in a cage.

"Her song is like the weave of the fabric of your bandhani," says Kulsum Bai.

Women steal happy-sad looks at each other like the swishing savannah wind hesitating to come closer lest you discover a storm in its wake. What are they thinking? They add to the uneasiness in me such as the one that comes from suspicion of someone you trust, yet you know she is hiding something from you about you. I turn to the song of the bandhani to seek an answer but instead its rass takes me away into itself, and I cannot understand the compassion and pity in the joy of celebrating me. The confusing feelings of the bride at an Indian wedding come from the women's hearts that know the uncertainties that lurk ahead behind the glitter. But if they could talk, the women would say the girl must wed whatever future holds for her meaning happiness or unhappiness is not in her parents' hands. That is destiny. Meethi Bai's neck muscles tense and her veins swell over splinter bones at the neck as she sings, trapping and elongating the vowels in her voice.

Sangaar, siri and the Satpanth bandhani
The dyer strung me in knots, some small, some big
Pressed my tender skin in his fingers two

The tempo steps up. Meethi Bai claps to the rhythm of six beats, 1 2 3 - 4 5 6, leaving a space between like dots jumping, patterning the bandhani. She motions others to pick up the rhythm.

Unwinding strings
Knots break radiating dots
Colours bright inside,
Shadows curl outside

She holds up my bandhani once more half screening her face, teasing a look at the women with her dark contoured eyes in mischief, as she would play with men wanting her. She stretches her legs out forward and, tensing her fingers, cracks her knuckles at my temples. Then she relaxes, aware that she has captured the audience. Her words flow in calculated unhurried strokes of her hands, sometimes clapping and sometimes slapping her hips.

O ye Kutchi Kathiawari folk!
First is the art of spinning the thread
Thread into thread weaves the bandhani
Three arms long the width of loom

Meethi Bai nods around like an Indian peacock, her red English lipstick lips inviting smiles. She continues her song, attended by a constant resonance of clapping, sometimes sharp smacking, and sometimes soft thudding of palms on sitting thighs, and sometimes an appreciative murmur in-between the lines to stress a pun or a metaphor.

Pour colours pure in a dyeing pot
Let embroiderer's zari sting the eye
Line by line blaze silver the desert bloom

Women exchange looks to hush each other to listen, and then turn, all facing Meethi Bai, expecting to hear more of her melodious voice. She sits leaning on the wall. I am the bride in bandhani shawl with the henna lady fanning over my freshly painted feet and hands. Ma Gor Bai gives Meethi Bai a pillow, which she accepts with a thankful look, without a smile or a word, and places it between her back and the wall. People say Meethi Bai has the voice of a classical Saurashtran singer of the age of Mohenjo-Daro, and for that reason, they would also want to call her the Koiyal Rani, the comforter of men of Indian Nairobi.

Words cascade like dance steps into musical beats. Six beats, and then a miss beat. Meethi Bai stretches out her feet again and her toes tap the air. She has a ring on the middle toe of each foot. Both her feet are cracked with lines at the heels, like erosion furrows in pictures of faraway volcanoes in the

Rift Valley. Heads move from one side to another like cobras stunned by music. "Wah! Wah!" they blow into the air.

It's Devdasi Rupa Bai who sings again.

Saurashtran cloth traded Indonesia Sea
Adorned black princes of Zanzibar
Sangaar, siri and the Satpanth bandhani

Beyond the mountains of the Golden Dawn hailed Sikander
Yavana king lover claiming rule over the land of the loom
Then came Sufi bards singing Mohamed, Ali and Nizar
But to Vedas their hearts pulled, pirs becoming guru-pirs
Sangaar, siri and the Satpanth bandhani

Meethi Bai turns towards Devdasi Rupa Bai and nods, and continues her story of the bandhani, clapping, and at the same time with her eyes motioning all to clap after her. Her kohl-lined eyes between twirled up lashes specked with Ponds powder, make her eyes look larger than they actually are exaggerating her telling looks. At that moment, Ma Gor Bai walks into the room with a wide smile exposing her gold plated tooth otherwise rarely seen. She goes around the room with Hawa, Malek and Monghi by her side, offering sweet milk with one hand and lifting her long frock with the other as she takes each step forward. Oudh scent of arean wood wafts from her pink velvet dress with tightly smock-stitched waist, over which sways her plaited hair in a silver-silk knotted tassel. Women exchange melodious looks with eyes shining the music in their bodies.

In a few stylized, showy movements of gathering, pleating and feeling the weight of the bandhani in her hands, Meethi Bai throws it half over herself and half over me. The hefty four inch border in zari lands diagonally across her bosom and stays stretched from across my shoulders. She continues to narrate the story of the bandhani, calling the song back and forth while the women sip the milk relishing the saffron flavours of masticated almonds and pistachios cooked in a cauldron of sweetened milk over slow wood fire and steady stirring, so that no cream congealed on top. Ma Gor Bai had assigned the stirring job to Hawa, Malek and Monghi, who took turns the whole day long, passing on the mwiko ladle as tall as they were from one hand to another like a relay baton.

"We enter the divine through beauty," says Kulsum Bai suddenly as if to herself. I think about my bandhani, as if awakened inside. It is my own now, part of my body. No, it is my body. My hands and legs stretched out in front are cold from henna. I think about men. How different are men from women? Nobody has told me. I have seen no pictures of naked men. I withdraw into myself with chilling anxiety, and shiver. My pulse radiates with the pulse of the bandhani. Meethi Bai runs her fingers over bright and dark dots in the silken cloth before finally closing her eyes. She sings lengthening the vowels as if releasing the imprisoned sounds from the depth of her throat. When she concludes, her voice quakes.

Sangaar, siri and the bandhani
Guru-pir dyed the soul's cloth
In dots of colours fast and bright

Ma Gor Bai comes closer and sits besides Meethi Bai in the empty space. Devdasi Rupa Bai repeats each verse after Meethi Bai, like a mirrored reflection in an altered raga. Her eyes are also closed. Listeners fall silent, rapt by the nightingale duet. I feel dazed and let it be.

241

Dot in bigger dot the cloth makes bright
So to yourself, your word to deed
Dot in bigger dot, colour in deeper colour is bright
Zari of your words glimmer in deeds

"They are like two pilgrims walking along a path unaware of all that is around them but their walk. Their song, like the pilgrims' stride, is their meditation. That is the Satpanth way," says the lady with plastered hair. A sliver of silver hair at the parting in the middle of otherwise black silk catches the eye when she bows forward with her hand raised to the forehead, partly in humility and partly appreciating Meethi Bai, the way Indians appreciate great artists at musical gatherings when seized by the rass of musical ecstasy.

Guru-pir dyed the cloth
In dots of colour bright
He dyed in many a dye
Lesser light shines in greater Light
Lesser soul lives in greater soul

"*Wasikia raha?*" asks Hawa with a mischievous wink. Do you hear happiness? Do I feel happiness? Yes? No? I don't know because the song has not ended. It will end at dawn tomorrow when my marriage contract will be sealed in the jamat khana after Ma Jena Bai, my father and Mukhi Dharamshi have together viewed my dowry and noted its value. Then the tithe will be agreed upon before the mukhi accepts the money on behalf of Saheb and performs the ceremony.

Part Eight

The Patterned Country

The old man said that this was the true religion of all peoples, that all Kavirondos, all Buganda, all tribes from as far as the eye could see from the mountain and endlessly farther, worshipped adh`itsa – that is , the sun at the moment of rising. Only then was the sun mungu, God. The first delicate golden crescent of the new moon in the purple of the western sky was also God. But only at that time; otherwise not.

PASSAGE FROM THE BIOGRAPHY OF CARL GUSTAV JUNG
FROM HIS FIELD NOTES IN EAST AFRICA, 1925.

29

Land is the Ornament of God

At age sixteen, my parents give me away to the Devji Momna family in Nairowua. Nairowua is one day's drive away from Nairobi over the savannah country in the south towards Kilimanjaro and Tanganyika. It's one day if you leave before dawn, you would arrive around midnight. Haiderali and I have not met before but we have seen each other's photographs. Now we sit next to each other in the back seat in a car they call Ford. Ford is written on the bonnet. Like a picture of a flat topped acacia in an ostrich egg. In the one empty seat next to Haiderali is my dowry packed in a bulging suitcase, press fastened with two broad leather straps, and buckled. Embossed on two sides in gold ink in English it says GENUINE LEATHER. "Genuine leather hengh?" Haiderali reads it out to me, partly teasing and partly in compliment. It was his way of complimenting by teasing, which I would get used to. I wait for Haiderali to say something more so I can respond and start in on our courtship like in the movie at Film India. Like two actors in love riding together and courting at the back of a bullock cart below the haystack. He teases, she responds with eyes. However, Haiderali says nothing and does not even look at me. He is reading *Chakram* and chuckling.

My eighteen-year-old husband, Haiderali Devji, has hired the Ford, together with the driver, Amirali Bhai who came late in the afternoon to collect us. He said he was late because he needed to change a tyre, fill up the petrol, clean the car and what not. Ma and the Devji Momna family left early in the morning for Nairowua by Merali Bus. Ole Lekakeny, my husband's assistant at the bead shop, sits in the front seat next to the driver. Like the Kikuyu old men who come to chat with Dadabapa, his lop ears weigh down in copper prisms. The car is a mechanical box on wheels. It moves with such a hard-headed heat that it frightens me. I feel locked into its sheer speed and determination. I have never ridden in a car before, let alone one that moves with such fury, grinding the road like a stone mill gr … gr … There is no way I can jump out and escape if I want to. My husband is dumb. I sink down into the spring sofa seat and peer through the window from under my pachedi pulled over my eyes in laaj, and over the hair that Meethi Bai had combed in filmi fashion with a cautionary note, "Make sure these laatka locks are there when you arrive in Nairowua." The exhilarating haste, the heat of the machine, trees running, it's scary but beautiful like an adventure into the unknown. I gather myself.

Memories of the care and love of Meethi Bai and my Ma fill my head. Sometimes we slept together in one bed during the afternoon nap when it was hot. The men slept on the other string bed, all together, in the courtyard. My Ma used to massage my head with coconut oil when it hurt and then combed my hair when we went to the cinema. "When your hair is long and thick silky black, everyone wants to comb it," she used to say.

247

On Wednesdays, Ma Gor Bai, Meethi Bai and I used to sneak out of the back door when Dadabapa, Noordin Kaka uncle and my father were engrossed in after lunch soft talk in the store. We would take the back road so no Khoja shopkeeper would see us cross the jacaranda and bougainvillea bushes of Rani Bagh and pass by the wild fig tree with 'Jafro loves Sheru' carved on it in a heart shape. We skirted the jamat khana to come to the Imtiaz Ali Sufi mosque and then through the slip road shamble into Victoria Street and the bustling River Road. We queued for the Ladies Only matinee show at Film India, the cinema by the alley on the ridge above the Ol-ng'arua swamp. Across the swamp, on the other ridge that we called Nagara, were the new stone bungalows of wealthy Indian merchants and another bazaar known for its meethai sweets.

I look away out of the window because I do not want Haiderali, riding triumphant in high spirits, to see my cheerless face lost in thoughts of the home I have just lost. But he stares at my face when I turn. He makes me uncomfortable. What is he studying? My three dot tattoos on the chin? When I was nine, Ma Gor Bai finally took me to the sonara's grey-eyed wife on River Road to etch three black tattoos on my chin. At first Ma Gor Bai refused but I was stubborn and insistent. One day I even cried and complained to Dadabapa how much I wanted to look like my mother. But what does my husband want looking into my face like he owns it? Anxiety creeps into me. Worrying thoughts about living with Haiderali's family spiral in me, and fear swells up in a whirlpool of suspicion. I do not know why I fear Haiderali. He has not even said a word to me. "The beauty of the land will absorb the pain in your heart if you gaze long enough into it." That's what Meethi Bai, the woman's best friend and

248

artist, the lover on our street, used to say. I fix my eyes on the savannah. The landscape calls me to her arms like an artist to her art. I touch the ruby ring on my finger. Monghi Bai cried when she saw the ring on my finger. "One day I will give you this ring. Don't let envy burn your heart now. If jealousy eats you on my wedding day, it will bring bad luck kisirani into my life," I said to my sister calming her. Then I gave her my Saurashtran dhingly doll so she would make her a bride, dream about becoming a bride, and ask Saheb for a good husband. When I am gone, she would be the next to marry and leave home.

The vastness of the land grips me. The absolute infinity. This is my first journey out of Nairobi. The vehicle is delving deep into the savannah like a craft ploughing into high waves of the Indian Ocean in Dadabapa's stories. I watch in wonder at the movements of shadows as big as the mountains intercepting the evening light on the grasslands, shift like the pulse of a giant. Above are the tinted clouds retreating in the setting sun's shafts of yellow, orange and crimson. The sun is over the distant five rises of the Ngong Hills waiting in deeper blue in the waning light of the sky. I had heard from the Kikuyu women who came to Dadabapa's shop that there in the hill's shade nestles the coffee shamba of the storyteller mama of Kenya, the storyteller memsahib, the storyteller called Kaaran. In the foreground is a muthuri euphorbia, tall to the height of a house, its ascending fingers pointing to the sky, its stem perched on a red-pinnacled termite mound. Ma Gor Bai would have been ecstatic looking at the beauty of this land at this hour of the setting sun. She clutched me in an arm lock holding me secure while we said goodbye. Then she opened her arms pushing me out in the world and speaking words that hurt, "I throw rice over my shoulders. With these hands that raised you, I send you away from my house." Ma Gor Bai wept, remembering the day she was pushed out of her mother's clutch embrace to be sent away. "Do not return a divorcee or widow to dishonour your birth family." She wept for me and herself, and all the women wept remembering the day when their mothers turned their backs on them. Their hearts were one with my own at that moment of my departure. "That is custom. Cruel is the ritual," said Meethi Bai. Smudged kohl spread below her eyes. But in those eyes, I read envy. Was she resentful because she had no husband? Because she had no marriage? Because she had no child? Did she resent her destiny as I was fulfilling mine? She too let me go into the world all alone to be a wife somewhere nowhere in Africa.

"Indian custom is the Black Mother, Kali Mata. She demands the sacrifice of pure girls. On this day the mother kills the daughter in her to keep family honour and she weeps for her dead child and herself." I hear the bitter words of Meethi Bai behind me.

In the far distance, my eyes rest on a herder. He watches our car, the Ford with brown wooden sides, polished, and all four tyres, black solid rubber spurning red dust off the murrum track. As I watch him, he strides into infinity at the frame of the grassland that lies between the horizons, east and west, north and south, each way touching the sky. In his view, the far away Ford would appear a dudu, a shiny brown insect shell bustling on grass root paths beneath the crispy sheaves. The scurrying noise of the lone machine traveller hums into the setting sun and expands the evening's solitude. In this solitude, I see beauty, crimson quietness that echoes the immensity of this land that I would later learn the inhabitants called the Ornament of God. My breath fades. My skin stiffens struck by the moment of wonder that seizes me from within.

Haiderali has not spoken to me yet. Our eyes have not met in love like in films I have seen. Yet he stares into my face so close to his that it scares me. What does he want? We are going to Nairowua where I know no one. My heart is heavy with the sorrow of leaving my brother and father, Ma Gor Bai, sister Monghi, cousin-sister Malek, and Hawa in shantytown Nairobi. I will miss Dadabapa's stories, Meethi Bai's stories, Noordin Kaka uncle's stories. I look intently into the land beyond the car but it does not soothe the loss of the family in me. Peering through my pachedi, pulled over me, I walk with the animals of the savannah. The Ford jogs along the broken murrum road parallel to the railroad. My head turns to thoughts; my heart breathes sighs while my eyes feast on the land.

So large a paradise exists on earth for these animals and earth-painted people. It's a civilization of man, plants and animals living in kinships tied by the emptiness under the sky of sunset colours like the beads at Dadabapa's store. My thoughts in pictures merge with questions I ask myself. My heart thumps, my body is in elation. Is this not the universe of man, beast and plant in unison? Is it not the shine of prakash, the hour of the Light at the threshold of life and death? Is it not the mantra - the picture prayer of Das Avatar that reverberates in me painting ten pictures of the divine?

I close my eyes in worship. O savannah! Fabric in shades of wheat! You are the beam of Light, the Om prakash, Brahma prakash, the Noor, Pirshah, Pirshah, Ali Om! My eyes carry me far into the land to the herder again. He stands amongst his cattle and zebras, feral in zeals of six to ten patched all over the land as far as the eye can see. I imagine myself walking the earth with him among the sheaves, the herder, keeper of zebra and cows. Keeper of free land and free animals. I feel as if I am suddenly bursting out and away from the Indian shantytown Nairobi, cramped, noisy and grimy, into the boundless purity of Kenya. The steward of the land looks upwards and watches the sky's diminishing gleam at dusk.

"Day begins in the darkness of the womb like how life begins," says Ole Lekakeny in Swahili from the front seat. I feel he speaks for me. I feel my life is at the threshold, passing through the darkness to come to life again. A moment of rebirth. Ole Lekakeny stretches his eyes and they rest on the nomad, his earth ochred body, and the staff on his shoulder. I had seen Maasai men carry such staffs of the wild olive tree when they descended from the Ngong Hills, walked about Nairobi, and shopped in the Jugu Bazaar. "Light is conceived in darkness like in the Maasai bead pattern of dark blue beads, the pattern narok. It's the pattern of my age mates that I wear on my ankles." Ole Lekakeny begins to describe the evening. "In the band of dark beads, there is a line of bright red and orange. The line cuts the darkness, and from the slit emerges a new day." Bouncing copper earrings in his lopped ears exaggerate the movement of his head. "The man of the savannah sings to his cattle about the setting sun's homestead where in darkness begins the new day. At this time when the evening fire is lit, legends are told of colours of Maasai lineages." But I am not listening, my thoughts are with my father and Ma Gor Bai discussing my marriage offer. I was sitting on the steps with Hawa and sailing in the sky, brilliant with sparkles. The evening had captured me. Even if I had listened, it would have made no difference, for my destiny was made that night while I walked the stars.

As the sun descends into the coolness of the valleys of the Ngong Hills, it reflects orange rays on the Ford's lacquered wood panels. We, the foursome in the car, travel along the Mombasa road going East, running parallel to the railway line. The road and rail are like two lone companions, pathfinders in the wilderness of the African savannah. There is a pervading fragrance of oudh perfume in the car, vaporizing from my long pink velvet frock and pink silk pachedi that covers me, the bride from Nairobi. When Ma Gor Bai drew the pachedi of a married woman over my head, she prayed for me.

Ya Mowla! Ya Sarkar!
I ask only three things for my daughter:
Keep her happy
Keep her in good health
And keep her free of mothaj
Let her tint not our family honour

"Did you find all the beads we need for the coming season of graduation ceremonies?" asks Haiderali suddenly jerking himself half up from the back seat. His coarse voice booms through the monotonous murmur of the Ford startling me.

"Yes, bwana. All but one. There is a shortage of the tongolo size, the white one with a spiral on it. Many people use that one," replies Ole Lekakeny without moving his eyes that are fixed in the direction of where the herder has just disappeared. He speaks fighting the Ford's drone.

"Did they, at the Rajan Lalji store, make a list of what we want?"

253

"Yes, bwana. All beads for the graduation rituals."

"I will write to them then."

The road narrows into a murrum track and departs from the railway line. I feel a loss of companionship and the loneliness of two travellers, the railway line and road, now moving on their separate ways. The Ford turns south into the vastness of plains towards Tanganyika Territory where the Germans ruled before the British. Squat thorn bushes spot the grassland. Feral herds of wildebeest and zebra spread like wind seeds across the grassland moving into Mara, Serengeti and Kilimanjaro.

"The zebra is a gift of beauty to the land," mumbles Ole Lekakeny. "And beauty is peace."

Shadows of the zebras are dark now, almost black blotches, pacing southwards in droves in the dusk's last rays behind them. At the moment of beauty, the land is at peace.

"See!" says Ole Lekakeny pointing out with his full arm through the window. "In the setting sun the landscape is a sea in the sheen of saen beads. The grass sings golden blonde bowing farewell to the departing sun. The rain clouds heave at the old caldera's broken shell. God walks the land." He hums for a while, as if in private to the beauty before continuing, "The Maasai count the new day at the setting sun. It's the hour now. Time begins when the animals are at rest; at peace in this land where men descended from the sky." Only I listen to his self-mumble in Swahili over the pouncing clatter of stones hitting the axle below. "And the woman gave birth to two sons."

"Last season's short rains have thrashed the top soil and exposed the lava rocks underneath the murrum," says Amirali

Bhai, negotiating the rocks along the way. "It will be some time before they start grading and resurfacing. By then it will be the season of the long rains again."

Haiderali sings *Meeting in the Rain* from the film Barsat, smacking a tabla beat with his two fingers between the knuckles of his other hand clenched in a fist. His head moves from side to side absorbed in the music he is making. He feels exhilarated by the speed and rain but is oblivious to the landscape. Tropical rain heightens romance in an Indian man like in an Indian movie. He sings like an actor.

In the rain
Thum…dina…din…thum
I meet you
In the rain

"Wah! Wah!" compliments Amirali Bhai.

Thum…dina…din…thum
You meet me
In the rain
Thum…dina…din…thum

Amirali Bhai chimes into the chorus:
Thum…dina…din…thum.

"All animals - wild and domestic, humans and spirits go into the womb of night. Grasslands and the sky descend into darkness," Ole Lekakeny speaks again to himself. Shadows retreat into the quietness of the African savannah and calls of the night. Amirali Bhai switches on the headlights. Soon the predators will prowl and their shadows will loom darker than the night encircling the horizon. Then the scavengers of the night will stealth into the scene. Amirali Bhai pulls the car to the left side and over the shoulder of the murrum road. It slides into a shallow trough under the canopy of a tree that I hear Ole Lekakeny call Ol-lerai. The headlamps beam on a rust tree trunk, fissured and rough. The trunk curves upwards into many branches and cleaves into multiple kindling. An umbrella of foliage of dark shades and shadows now cover us. Here in the lap of Ol-erai we rest for the night.

Haiderali puts his arm around me. I feel him weighing down on my shoulder, the hair on his forearm tingles my skin below the ear. I begin to shake. He presses his head on my shoulder bone as if to hold down my shakes. I feel the warmth of his breath move, intermittent flows from the nape of my neck to my chin and then below the chin, into my frock, in the middle. I keep my face straight staring out of the windscreen over the shoulders of the two men into the darkness. He moves forward and buries his nose into my dress through an opening at the neckline. Everyone else in the car is asleep or pretending to be asleep. Dim silhouettes of zebra and wildebeest continue moving south, free willed in the slight moonlight. After a while, Amirali Bhai snores lightly with his head backwards. Ole Lekakeny breathes heavily, leaning forward, his chin pressed to the chest.

Haiderali hums faint tunes in my ears leaning his body on me. I see a slanted grin on his lips in the dim light of the night as I watch ahead wide eyed into the black country. He begins to unbutton my dress. I shudder and keep looking ahead anchoring my body to the night's stillness. He slips his hard-skinned hand into my dress startling me.

"What is this?" I mutter under my breath so the men in front do not hear while pushing his hand away from me. Then

I turn my head on the other side away from his prying eyes on my chest. I have never seen such behaviour not even in films!

He laughs softly and obeys. However, after a while, again, I feel his hand crawling into my dress. First the pads of his finger tips, then the long nail on his little finger, the gap under his humped fingers and then the heel of his palm.

"Bhoonda!" I blurt out.

I call him a vulgar! Grip his wrist out of me and shove him away with all my strength a second time. The bad word just slipped through my lips. I did not intend to call him that. My first communication with my husband! I am not a dance girl at the lodge, am I? He has no sharam.

Haiderali is amused and laughs from the throat as if he were the ruler, not the romantic filmi hero I imagined who would cry tears seeing me sad and worried. Meethi Bai did not tell me about this. She only said with her hand over her mouth, "When your husband comes over you, let him, and when he wants to enter you, let him. It will be painful," she said "but let him because he has the right." Then she pressed a ball of cotton wool into my hand. "Hide it under your pillow," she whispered. There was mystery in her hushed words that only time would unravel to me because nobody spoke of it not even Ma Gor Bai. I wrap the bandhani tight over me and hold the edge in my fisted hand so he cannot put his hand through my dress.

Haiderali then circles his arm around me over the bandhani, pulls me to him and presses his body on mine. I sit leaning half over him, stiff as a log. Now he begins to draw circles on my head and thin straight lines on my body. A chill runs through me. Why is he doing this? His unknown expectations weigh on me. The fear of not being in control

257

grips me. I have hidden the ball of cotton in my brassiere for now. Will I need it now? I wish I could escape into the arms of the Ol-erai acacia covering us. A whimpering, complaining hyena limps around the car and sniffs holding his nose high. I had not seen a hyena so close to me before, yet I was not afraid. At night, in the alley behind our house in Nairobi, I heard them gruff and bark like ogres that consume children. I imagined them and was terrified.

Haiderali is not a friend like my dhingly doll or the photograph that I could talk to and play love games with and be in command. He frightens me, holding me so tight that it's difficult to breathe. He is not even the actor singer dancer I imagined, holding my hand among flowerbeds. I am not in charge of my dreams anymore. He behaves as if he owns me. I am determined to keep awake.

The car is enveloped by the chill of the night. Inside, our breath clouds the windowpanes. It is a long night between dreams and vigilance, between wakefulness into faraway darkness and slumber into silence. Haiderali has lodged his big head between my dress and the bandhani shawl, his salivating mouth already down and wetting the silk of my brassiere through the velvet of my dress. His rounded lips over the hardness of my nipples like rubber seals. He is baring his teeth like a determined hyena raking into the softness of my breasts. A fathomless numbness descends into me. What is happening? What shall I do? This was my first night with a man sitting in a car with my body pressed to his.

30

Rainbow on Zebra's Neck

In the half-light of the new dawn when it is neither day nor night, the bare rock top of a dead volcano comes forward before us gleaming red. I peer towards the east searching more of the dawn below the mountain but the mist has subdued the colours of sunrise into a receding blue grey. Amirali Bhai starts the car and leaves the motor gurgling. My heart throbs with the whine of the engine idling when the fear of the sudden change in my life returns to anguish me. Before the day ends, I will be in Nairowua where I know no one I can call my family. Above, in the shredded rays of the rising sun through the treetops in the mist, Ol-lerai's canopy turns bright in bits - a myriad of starry clusters like beads on the people of the savannah. Below the tree, the Ford is webbed in floral netting. A line of acacia flowers, each one perfectly round pink-white and hairy, sits on the lip of the black rubber that holds the windowpane. Amirali Bhai swerves the Ford out of the trough over a nurse log cracking it into splinters, and then once again we are jogging along the murrum road - the lone artery through the heart of Africa. We are on the famed Cape

259

to Cairo road that Noordin Kaka uncle once said, jokingly, how the Englishmen would walk to prove their love to the disinclined memsahebs.

Haiderali slept with his head in my lap. He had his feet on my dowry bag that had moved, and now it stands sideways, wedged between him and the driver's seat, too big to fall through the gap. The suitcase is all I have. It's my dignity, my security. It has my things. The people on the other side will judge me by the size of my dowry case. The rest of the dowry – furniture, kitchenware and carpets – will come later by Merali Bus.

The road towards the Tanganyika border is much smoother now as we continue to move south. In the haze of the morning mist impala does hop around in circles while the only buck stands still staring uneasily at the intruding machine that carries us. He is of perfect symmetry and bears the majesty of the Kamba ebony carvings of his shape like the ones I would see displayed on the pavements at the European Market for the white memsahebs to buy. Morning light probes through the grey shroud and falls on Amirali Bhai's hands alert to the sudden shudder of the steering wheel. When the tyres hit the next crack, it spits out gravel chips.

As we travel south, the mist clears and at once, I see Mt Nairowua behind a rainbow beyond a screen of light drizzle. The old craggy caldera looks up farther away to the snows of youthful Kilimanjaro, its white top lifted up in a halo of clouds. During the years to come, I would learn that in Maasailand, women are the architects of the houses they build. That it is a land of primordial legends of the origin of man told in the sacred geography of mountains, trees and rivers. That here are created wisdom proverbs and the poetry about

260

colours of Africa. That here they said bead art is visual knowledge and that is beauty which is peace. Soon I would be in the shadow of Kilimanjaro, the pulse of Africa. The Maasai call it the House of God, unaware that Rani Victoria's generous heart bestowed their sacred mountain upon her cousin Kaiser Wilhelm of Germany, because English Kenya had two snow mountains at the equator and German Tanganyika had none. So the story is told in English books about how benevolent the Empress of India was. English, Indian and native African legends run parallel in tri-partheid East Africa, and like their customs and houses or hotels or even seats in the train and bus, neither one touches the other. Only Noordin Kaka uncle knows because he reads books and newspapers in English, Gujarati and Swahili. I don't read all that but I am good at listening and re-telling what I hear like it were my own story like this tale of Rani Victoria and her cousin Kaiser Wilhelm of Germany.

"God pulls down his blanket down waking up to a new day. Soon he will stride the land and there will be brightness all around," throat whispers Ole Lekakeny gathering his wrinkled face into a smile. He composes such a calmness around him that I am drawn to breathe in the rhythm of his breath. Like him, I look out of the window. Anguishing thoughts of my marriage and life ahead are absorbed by the vision of Africa in the pure light of dawn.

"We, the Maasai dress in ochre. Colours of the earth are dyed on our skin." Ole Lekakeny is aware that I am listening though I do not say anything and he does not turn round to expect a reply. "We evoke blessings in the time without end like the sky. God's peace is in the beauty of his infinity, the sky and his ornaments of lustre and order, in the richness of grass we hold in prayers for peace. The rainbow pauses

261

between the horizon of life and the abode of the ancestors below. God walks in colours, black and red; Enkai Narok and Enkai Nanyokie, are her names," says Ole Lekakeny before he begins to hum a melody. Such a melody I have not heard before.

They are approaching home, the three men in the car not me. Fear seizes me again and I go numb. The car has taken me far into a wilderness by the mountain where I know no one. I breathe in deeply, inhale-exhale, and meditate the way Ma Gor Bai had taught me, how to awaken my senses to the beauty within. But my head feels hot, too hot to meditate. I want to open the door and run into the coolness of the dew, barefoot, and quickly, before the sun picks it up. I want to throw myself on the dew and roll my face on the cold wetness of mother Earth.

"These people are always singing," Haiderali speaks in a groggy voice, lifting his head from my lap and looking at me in the eye. His tousled black hair is scented with my wedding oudh perfume. I feel relieved he is not angry with me. I loosen my bandhani shawl around me and the smell of yesterday's bridal grooming oozes out - fragrant arean wood oil dabbed at the joints and under the breasts, its staleness mixed with overnight sweat and warmth stuffed between my skin and petticoat. The smell is so much that it fills the car.

"So do we," I reply. But in my head, as I return his look, softly feeling relief from the encasement of the night's clothing and my husband's clasp.

Haiderali offers me bhajia for breakfast. I eat quickly - one, two, three, four. Tightness grips my stomach. The smell of oil-cooked food makes me sick. Fear returns. I feel nauseated. He forces me to eat more. Quietly, I push each bhajia through the slit between the seat and the door.

Ole Lekakeny takes his eyes to the far distance ahead. I follow them. Occasionally he looks up to the sky to whisper a prayer and spit moist vapour on his open palms. Then he recites an ode, his prayer to the colours of the sky in the sun's first light through the rain. I hear the colours like in Satpanth ragas. I hear them like embroidery on my fingers:

God beads the rainbow on zebra's neck
Emankeeki of the sky
Ti-ti-ti drops the rain
Stripe-stripe-stripe falls the rain
Dot-dot-dot each drop a bead
From emankeeki on zebra's neck

31

Su-astik at the Threshold

I step into the Devji family home, a sixteen-year-old bride
in a pink velvet frock on which flows zari vine at the side
from the ankle to the shoulder. People of the town come to
see me, the wife of their own Nairowua born boy with
smallpox marks on his face. Haiderali was born of Khoja
Momna African bead merchant parents on the border of
Kenya Colony and Tanganyika. Tanganyika was once a
German colony, now it's called a Territory assigned by the
UN to the English to administer when the Germans lost the
Great War. These words are Noordin Kaka uncle's words, not
mine. He would say how European emperors and empresses
in their hasty greed for Africa separated many an ethnic
people like the Maasai of Nairobi and Nairowua. These were
communities of one culture, one language, one landscape and
one economy, he would say. One people, territorial keepers of
spiritual shrines, were split into two political halves as
Kenyans and Tanganyikans. No ethnic elder was present when
the deal over his ancestral land was sealed at a conference in
Europe.

"She is the wife of my first born son," proudly says Ma
Jena Bai to the women of her jamat khana volunteer group

called the Nandi Committee. The Nandi Committee receives, sorts out and arranges the evening's food offerings at the veranda where the evening draught pushes the fragrance of the cooked curries and smoke of loban over red hot coal into the open courtyard. "She is a blessed Saurashtran devi," someone at the back whispers. Yes, I am beautiful like the ancient women of Ajanta, fairer than all the men and women of the Devji family. I am of narrow waist on broad rounded hips and a noticeable backside bulge under my long velvet frock.

"In pregnancy such women develop large breasts like Bombay mangoes. Much milk," says Ma Jena Bai with a measure of pride while sniffing in a dash of bajar tobacco. She is sitting cross-legged on the grey cement floor in front of me, tracing a su-astik with rice. "When I saw her in the jamat khana in Nairobi, I asked Meethi Bai about her character and she sang praises. Women with such a gift of body can carry many healthy boys. Nurse them for full two years. Grind rice and lentils without aborting."

I stand on the patlo stool, like a statue on a pedestal at the threshold of the Devji home, listening to my sass, Ma Jena Bai, bragging about how she found me. However, she knows my Dadabapa gave me to Devji Momna, her husband's father, to seal their friendship with a tie of their grandchildren's marriage, forever. She talks about my accomplishments as a zari embroiderer and teacher's assistant at the religion school. "She is shy," I hear someone say. In truth, I felt lonely. Uneasy among the people I had never seen before. I was not shy. I keep my eyes down, screened by my pachedi pulled over my forehead in laaj, avoiding any eye contact. Eyes that are studying details of my symmetry. I feel like a prey, circled by a pride of lions whose hungry yellow eyes are fixed on the impending kill and feast. I tense my body, push my shoulders in and hold myself together standing on the patlo stool. In my hands is a coconut, the seed of life awaiting fertility to birth. Meethi Bai told me I would be bringing new life into the Devji family home to continue their progeny, honour and name. Haiderali stands by my side on another patlo stool. He is laughing and joking with the women who in turn laugh at him in fake mockery, lisping audible whispers, "You are such an ugly toad. You are black. You are short like an eggplant. Your nose is a trumpet. Your hair a mesh of wire. You don't deserve this bride! This jewel of Nairobi!" Cold sweat trickles down my nape under the pachedi. Zarina, Haiderali's little sister, holds my hand, and that comforts me. She is admiring the netted line drawings of leaves, crescents and flowers in freshly painted henna of deep ochre on my fair skin. How the cold olive smears turned into such bright warm earth colours on my hands? Stepmother Gor Bai's words echo in my heart, "Earth colours your hands, marking a new beginning. You are re-born of the earth as you were born of her. Let the sprouting seed of the soil be auspicious." On my wrist gleams a gold bangle as wide as the digit of my thumb. The bangle with a paisley clasp is a creation of the Saurashtran craftsmanship of Surat. It is a piece inherited from Grandmother Sohn Bai's ensemble of ornaments that Dadabapa kept within folds of cotton cloth. He slept on it under the mattress. To keep my dowry gold, Ma Gor Bai gave me her own sandalwood box that lay hidden deep inside the top shelf of the bedroom cupboard under her velvets and silks. It is inlaid with a Mughal floral pattern in ivory like embroidery on velvet.

"Jari, come and sit here beside me," Ma calls Zarina her daughter. "The rice is for fertility," says Ma Jena Bai to Zarina, instructively, as she goes over the su-astik with a second line of rice trickling from her funnelled fingers. She performs the ritual of describing the su-astik before us speaking in resolute sentences. "It's the su-astik that connects the ancient religions of Saurashtra - Jainism, Buddhism, Satpanth and the many panths descending from the Vedas that hold pirs' words sacred. Here in the centre where the four lines meet, we place a piece of silver, the mark of Laxmi and Light of the pir. Put it here in the centre of the su-astik," says Ma putting her finger on the point at the union of the four sides of the su-astik. "The union is propitious. It's the meeting of the four directions. Marriage is such a union." She gives Zarina a fifty cents silver coin with the head of bearded King George, crowned and cloaked in fur. "Now take this betel nut and stand it on the fifty cents sumuni. The hard seed protects the shine of prosperity in the house. Keeps evil away." I know the su-astik is the chakra's centre of life's energy from all directions and a welcoming sign to the lucky bride, the incarnate Lakshmi who brings abundance as she steps over the threshold into her new life. "You are the symbol of su-astik, the goodness of life, like su-kh, the goodness of happiness and su-ndar, the goodness of beauty." Ma speaks to the symbol as if it were a living being and flicks out her little finger that she dips in saffron paste and makes an orange-red dot on the temple of the betel nut. "With this mark of auspiciousness I adorn thee," she tells the su-astik. "Like the su-astik, saffron embellishes the home linking all the divinities of Saurashtra – Jainism, Buddhism, Hinduism and all the in-between panths of the pirs of Persia. Guru-pir's wisdom seeps like spring water to the roots of the peepal tree on African soil," says Ma Jena Bai. Her words bring me closer to her. I listen attentively as if they were meant for me to know. Then Ma seals the su-astik under clay saucers.

I step over the threshold with my right foot and crash onto the inverted clay saucers revealing the su-astik sketched in rice. Suddenly the sound of crashing clay under my feet awakens me into a new life. Consummation of my marriage? I ask myself. I step over my childhood and enter into the Devji home, a woman. I have accepted the ancient sacrament of my forefathers and made a covenant with the Earth below my feet to take me home.

Neighbours and friends gather around this ancient Aryan symbol on the African soil under my feet. They watch and sing welcoming songs, celebrating Haiderali, the warrior, the conqueror, the bridegroom while I feel like I have just made a leap into an unknown space and severed the umbilical cord that tied me to my father's house. Fright grips me again, suddenly this time, when I realize there is no turning back. "Even looking back will bring misfortune." Ma Gor Bai's words echo in my ears when she showered me with rice for the last time with her back on me. With fisted hands pressed to her temples, Ma Jena Bai cracks her fingers, a prayer to break all my torments at the threshold before entering her home and beginning in a new life. It's a gesture to crack du-kh, meaning unhappiness, taking it onto her while beseeching su-kh, meaning happiness, to come to me. I touch Ma's feet for her to accept me into her home. She places her hands on my head and then points towards a corner where she has laid out footprints of Haiderali's father on a clean white merikani cloth. Haiderali and I pay our respects to the yellow turmeric impression touching it and then taking the hand to the left eye, the right eye and the forehead. Rising up, we bow together before the father's photograph hanging by a frail wire from the moulding. Haiderali's father was clean shaved, a dark skinned man with wiry hair, wearing a black coat and a fez hat with a tassel.

The next day is Tuesday, my second day in Nairowua. My body aches but I cannot say that to anyone. I remember Meethi Bai's last words to me as she bade me farewell. I was weeping in her arms. "You will heal from the sore of the man in you when the red henna on your hands fades." I understand Meethi Bai now when I walk and it hurts, when I sit, it hurts, when I sleep, it hurts. I can tell no one; no one wants to know. Why did I get married? Could I have said no? Could I have said I don't want to marry? Did I have a choice? Is this called kismet, destiny of a girl born an Indian Satpanth Khoja?

32

Mama Khelele

Each day at sunrise, Ma waits for me in the kitchen. She is there before me and makes me feel self-conscious if not guilty. As soon as I step in, she begins her day's instructions on household chores. Day in day out, her sentences are continuous monotones, eating into my head. Light the stove-- taak taak. Don't take too long at the back door talking with the milk woman--taak taak. Put chai on the stove soon–taak taak. Just two pinches of tea leaves-taak taak. Money does not grow on trees-taak taak. Add coal to the samavat-taak taak. Be sure the men's bathing water is hot-taak taak. Serve breakfast to men folk first-taak taak. For breakfast today, fry yesterday's chapattis in ghee and serve them hot with sweet mango pickle and cream-taak taak. Keep some fresh cream for me--taak taak. You will have chai with me after the men have gone to the shop--taak taak. Don't forget and be quick because we don't have the whole day to make breakfast-taak taak…taak taak… taak taak…

Each time, I nod in measure of her taak taak instructions, looking down, respectfully. I was expecting to be told about the housework and was eager to start what Ma Gor Bai and Meethi Bai had cautioned me would be my duties in my new home. But the tone of Ma's unending taak taak commands is eating into my head.

When the milk woman arrives, she stands at the back door to the courtyard, "Mama! Mama!" she calls.

"The milk money is there," Ma directs me, pointing to the open windowsill with her chin. Then again, she begins her taak taak. Take the milk sufuria - taak taak. See that she fills it to the brim – taak taak. Make sure the sufuria is clean – taak taak. Hurry now – taak taak. The sufuria should be full - taak taak. We don't have the whole day – taak taak. Don't spill the milk. The same monotonous taak taak knocks on my head like knocking on the door, and eating into my head.

When I first saw the Maasai milk woman at the back door, I could not take my eyes away from her carriage and beads. She was middle aged, with a brown complexion and skin that glowed. Her teeth gleamed when she smiled at me. Her baby was in her front apron, asleep. She, with the grace of an impala, emptied two long and narrow gourds of milk that were decorated with beads too. Then she replaced the raw cowhide tops and slipped the gourds into a pouch in her clothes at the back.

"Mama Khelele?" she asks about noisy woman.

At first, I did not understand her. What noisy woman? Who was she? Soon, I gathered she was referring to Ma. I smiled, turning my head to the side, indicating Mama Khelele was inside. She smiled back. That morning, I made a friend.

After breakfast, Ma continues to instruct me taak taak. Wash the breakfast dishes and then start sweeping the bedrooms. We don't have the whole day … taak taak knocks, eating into my head.

When Ma returns to the kitchen after her morning routine sitting in the sun, she has a strong smell of coconut oil in her open hair. She noticed that I had almost completed the chores – more taak taak knocks eating into my head that end with the usual, 'We don't have the whole day.'

I nod obediently. I am keen to show Ma my willingness as well as my ability to work in the house. One day, Ma's response to my quiet obedience startled me. "We waited too long for you to come. There was no reason for you to wait until you were an old maid. I was married when I was thirteen, you know. Now I feel old and tired. I needed young hands to help me in the house many years ago." Then without a pause, she continues her rhythmic taak taak again, "I need hot water for my bath … the samavat coal must last the whole day … taak taak - taak taak."

I feel she is screaming at me and I feel like screaming it out to the air. I cannot put my feelings into my embroidery in this alien home. Ma's home. Without the art, the artist in me feels homeless. Ma has not yet smiled once at me since my wedding day.

When Ma emerges from the bathroom, her body is hot and her grey hair falls in thin strands, wet and sticking together, her white scalp showing between the strands. She starts again - I will be going to the vegetable market … taak taak talk.

I sigh, relieved that I would have a little time away from my mother-in-law's vigilant eyes and relentless flow of taak taak knockings on my head. The mornings seem long and tiresome. How am I going to be able to live in this house? "When you remember us and your heart pains, keep on working and sing in your heart. Singing absorbs pain," Meethi Bai said to me before my marriage. But I am not able to work and sing with Ma over me. "When you feel humiliated, work. If there is no work, find work. Work hard. See work as your gift. Your kismet." I want to ask if housework is atonement. Atonement for what? My last karma? Is marriage atonement?

However, Ma Gor Bai said it differently, "When you are in pain remember your embroidery. See how each stitch runs. See how a stitch in stitch makes a stitch line shine. A straight stitch line. A curved stitch line. A circular stitch. A loop stitch. A loop in loop stitch. Work your eye into the stitched lines and stitched lines into stitched patterns. Art sees the pain in your heart and absorbs it and that's what makes art deeper. Art holds emotion. The more pain you feel the more art you make." But I have no time to myself to embroider in this house and I dare not ask Ma if I can, even if there was a little time to myself.

Bees buzz astonishingly loud around the honey bottle on the table on the veranda. Some glue onto the old English strawberry jam jar along the sticky honey line where the top is screwed to the smudged glass groves. It is half-full with honey, speckled with crumbs of bread and butter. There are more bees coming in scattered groups of twos and threes. I fill the enamel basin with water and submerge the honey jar into the water. It sits there while I go about my chores. The bees disappear unnoticed by the time Ma returns from the market.

No sooner does she step in, than she begins her one line non-stop taak taak song. First, sort out and then wash the fruit and vegetables in here. The menu for lunch today is spinach and chapattis. Start cutting the spinach, put it in this pot and for the chapattis, use three kop hands of wheat flour. This

273

size, not more. I will teach you how to cook just enough for the family and the day's prayer offering. Do not be wasteful. For the spinach, a drip of oil, one finger pinch of turmeric, thumb and two finger pinch of powdered coriander, half an onion, three cloves of whole garlic, two potatoes and one tomato. No salt. Taak … taak … taak.

It's the same talk every day, day-in-day-out. Sometimes it is accompanied by crude gestures like thrusting potatoes into my hands to peel no sooner than I have cut the spinach. "Watch me," she says as she stretches her hand into the spice bottles one after the other nipping the yellow and brown freshly ground powders with her fingers - she opens her fingers over the hissing steam below a heap of green spinach - a mixed pungent, moist smell of turmeric and coriander rises with the vapour – she covers the pot. She is quick with her cooking and precise in her recipe. She watches me like a voracious Nubian vulture crouched on the acacia before it plunges down spread winged to kill. I roll the chapattis and roast them. I serve lunch each time with yogurt, lime pickle and freshly cut onions. - I roll, roast and bring hot chapattis, one at a time to the table serving Haiderali, and Kabir my brother-in-law - Ma feeds Zarina with her hands while following me in and out of the kitchen with her eyes. I feel confused. Am I doing things the proper way? Ma eyes me suspiciously, her rotating chameleon eyeballs follow whatever I do, quick to pick on a mistake. Should I carry with the right hand or left, or both? Is this the right way to serve food? Every house has its own way. How do I know what is the right way in this house if Ma does not tell me?

It so happened that, one day at lunchtime, having cut the papaya, I was carrying it in both my hands to the table. I was not used to walking in a long dress. Rasping over my nervous

274

footsteps on the cement floor, I tripped over, lost my balance and fell, squatting down on my haunches. The papaya spread in squashed red and pink cubes over the grey floor. I heard Ma mutter 'kisirani' loud enough for all to hear which was as irritating as it was humiliating. Narrowing the eyes did not veil her superstitious thought. Tightening the lips did not lessen the pain of the insult I felt. I was blamed for throwing food, the sacred anaj, someone's roji, on the floor and bringing ill luck of kisirani to the home! Ma did not come to help me clean up and stopped Zarina by putting her foot across as Zarina rose up instantly from the floor stool to come to me. The men just ignored me sitting on the floor as the chill of the concrete floor snuck up my feet and I was cold and angry.

After lunch, my mother-in-law and the two brothers retire for a nap. I do the dishes, then go to the courtyard, and wash my hair of the smells of steamed turmeric, garlic, cumin and coriander. Standing in the sun, I lift my hair. With fingers raking at the scalp, I feel the warmth of the afternoon sun filter through my wet hair to the skin. I close my eyes to be alone within myself. This time of the day is when I allow myself a selfish moment, when I do not belong to anyone. I grant this to the sun on my face, hair and a little wind.

"Sakina!" Haiderali calls from the bedroom as if it were the one and final call. With my hair still moist, I hurry towards the bedroom. My heart is reluctant. My body wants to be in the afternoon sun. Zarina smiles goodbye, as she leaves, half running for school. I smile back. There is one person in the house who smiles to me.

Sitting on the bed, Haiderali is singing filmi songs and drinking from the red and gold-labelled bottle with a picture of a short stout Englishman on it. The picture is walking, lifting his tall hat and smiling broadly.

"What are you drinking?" I ask.

"Johnny Walker. It's called whiskey," he replies. His face stretches in a grin. He sings a filmi courtship song and moves his head dole dole.

"What does it taste like?"

"Sweet and sour, bitter and hot and sweet. Very hot."

"Why do you drink it?"

"It heightens the rass when I sing." Then, with one hand clutching the glass, he pulls me down with the other into his face, "and when I make love to you."

I do not want to be with Haiderali at this time of the afternoon. Really, not at any time, but I know Ma would be up and about soon. I would rather be away from Ma's taak taak and her floating chameleon eyes. I soon learn that the natives call her Mama Khelele, the noisy mama. Khelele is a loud noise like the bell, kengele in Swahili. Mama Khelele, can also mean a quarrelsome woman.

It would be from Ma Jena Bai, Haiderali my husband and his brother Kabir, and from the friends I make at the jamat khana that I would learn in bits and pieces, here and there about Nairowua, the two streets town, on the savannah where my home is and where I will raise a family.

33

Nairowua Jamat Khana

Nairowua, two hundred kilometres from Nairobi, is still Maasailand. Here, is a spring whose waters flow over a volcanic rock into Engare Nairowua, the Warm River descending from Mt Nairowua that gives the name to the town. Throughout the day, herders from far and near bring their cattle to lick on the rock salt at its confluence. It was here that the English established a border observation post during the First World War to keep vigilance over smuggled goods and collect the Kenya-Tanganyika trade levy. The post also had a white administrative officer who monitored over the collection of the Hut Tax or Family Tax as some called it, which was paid in cattle. The Maasai called the man DC, short for the District Commissioner of the Nairowua locality. In fact, nowadays, they call all white men in khaki shorts and sun hats DC because they wear the DC's ethnic dress and have similar customs, faces that change colour in the sun, temperament and smoking sticks. Two neat lines of chalked river stones stand on either side of the path up to the DC's office. This, the people believe, is white magic. No people in Africa chalk stones white as milk. The white stones stand in perfect lines, like how the English askaris stand at the Empire Day parade, in straight lines like white shields. Any man who walks up to see the DC today turns into a woman and shakes before him. Next to the DC's office is the tax cattle kraal surrounded by khaki mud walled and grass thatched quarters of African guards locally called Black Legs. They are so called because of their dark blue, tightly gartered, ankle to knee legs and no shoes or stockings.

Every morning, the Union Jack is raised to the triumphant call of a lone trumpeter and salutes of the DC and Black Legs standing behind him. The flag stutters before stretching out to the morning breeze as if returning the delayed salute.

Jadavji Bhai, the man Haiderali called Kaka uncle because he came from the same village in Saurashtra as his father did, started the first beads and general store below Mt Nairowua on the track that became the main Nairobi to Nairowua road. The road's surface varies from ankle deep muddy sludge during the rains to powdery dust that spirals up with the ground wind during the dry season. Later, the store expanded when the Greek coffee growers, and the English and Boer fruit and dairy farmers, arrived and employed farm labour. They then razed the hushed emerald forest and built mansions on the hills rolling into Mt Nairowua. New regimented rows of khaki mud and grass thatched quarters of their plantation labourers gave birth to a number of fenced villages pitched on leeward sides of the rolling hills. A Catholic Mission was quickly established to rein in free souls, and in the course of time, one could buy not only beads and blankets, but also tea, sugar, salt, matches, tobacco, English cough syrup and medicine for bad stomach and medicine for headache at Jadavji Bhai's Nairowua Beads and General Store. His wife, Puri Bai, hung bead strings on rows of nails on the folding panel doors. She also cut and hemmed cotton shuka wraps that the men put on their bodies long before their women did.

More Khoja trading families arrived in Nairowua after the First World War when the depression led to bankruptcies in the bazaars of Nairobi, Kisumu, Mombasa and even small towns like Thika and Machakos. Tanganyika, across the border, became a British Territory and the Khoja businessmen foresaw markets, especially bead, shuka cloth and blanket markets, opening up. Indeed, the Maasai prospered because the rains over the savannah were plentiful in consonance with the regime of their ceremonies that required plenty of beads. Their cattle and goats multiplied. The need for meat products for the soldiers of the vast stand-by military in service of the ever expanding Empire, led to animal slaughter houses and canning factories on the savannah that the nomads' herds replenished. With the growing prosperity of the animal keepers of the savannah, their bead art of self-adornment flourished. It was put on the Bead Bais to unpack, separate, arrange and display the range of beads in growing quantities. As a result, the Khoja bead merchants prospered to having three full meals a day. Some could even afford to buy imported household furniture from German settlers leaving Tanganyika across the border after Germany's defeat. Crateful of beads from Czechoslovakia began to arrive by rail and buses, and astonishingly, in as many varieties of colours, lustres, sizes and shapes as were the likings of a hundred ethnic peoples of Eastern Africa. New assortments of opaque, transparent, two and three coloured, and spotted beads arrived in separate wooden crates marked SAMPLE to test the preferences of the people not seen before by the Indian merchant. The astute bead trader then dispatched information on precise types preferred by the different ethnic communities to the wholesale importers of beads in Nairobi and the coast. Then they waited for the correct stock to arrive, which took at least six months and much longer if it were a completely new variety. Jadavji Bhai brought a wide range of beads liked by the Maasai from Rajan Lalji's bead store in Nairobi and kept them well stocked for the ceremonial times, such as marriages and graduations from one age group to another according to the order of the Maasai calendar of rites. He also purchased and stocked discarded khaki army blankets and army kabuti coats, and merikani cotton sheets that were red ochre dyed and worn by the pastoralists. With the arrival of more Khoja families in Nairowua, there also grew trade in Zebu cattle, hides, skins and honey of acacia flowers - Ol-debbei, Ol-erai and Ol-jarbolani, each distinctive flavour that I learned to distinguish. In time, with collective community effort and fund raising, the jamat khana was moved from the back room of Jadavji Bhai's home to a new green painted corrugated iron sheet house with a cement floor and veranda.

The sun is setting and will disappear in a few minutes as I, carrying the day's prayer food led by Ma, enter the Nairowua jamat khana garden. There is a twelve-foot tall wall of corrugated iron sheeting all around, also painted green, and it stands in contrast to the red-earthed courtyard and roof held on posts. The zari shine on my blue velvet dress and aroma of oudh on my skin lifts my spirits. I look bright and festive though inside I feel exhausted after the day's chores, and listening to Ma's relentless taak taak that rings in my ears through the purr of the breeze. Here in the garden's compound, a mango tree has grown to be fifteen feet high.

"Its fruit is paisley shaped with a tapering head. People come from afar to ask for the seed to plant in their courtyards," says Ma pointing to the mango tree. "Haiderali's father dried and preserved the seed to give away for his santosh, meaning satisfaction of his heart that is shukhar. He would not sell the seed even when we had nothing to eat because he said such a fragrance in the mango is the fruit of Desh, the old country, and is not for man to make profit of her gift," says Ma. She looks at the tree contemplating before speaking again. "The seedling of this mango tree was brought by Haiderali's grandfather, Devji Momna, from his ancestral village in Saurashtra. He planted the seedling in Mombasa. It now bears fruit at the causeway dividing the sea and the island. Here in the evenings children play thapo under its shade. It was Devji Momna's wish that the seed of the fruit of the first tree be planted wherever the family settled in Africa. When his grandchildren and great grandchildren rest in its shade, and eat the fruit, relishing its sweetness, they will remember where they come from." Ma Jena Bai talks to the tree now as if it were Devji Momna himself. Then she turns and continues to say as if it were the tree speaking from its ancestral arboreal memory, "Haiderali's father, Khimji Bhai, planted one seed in Zanzibar where the staunch faces India across the Black Waters. I planted the seed of that tree that his father, Devji Momna brought all the way from India, in a ghee tin and brought the seeding here to Nairowua." Ma picks into the cup of her brassiere and with her two pinnacled fingers removes her pakit pouch. Her pakit pouch is as large as half the size of her palm and it bulges like a rubber ball. In it are her tasbih, tightly pressed in and zipped up together with some coins in a small square handkerchief. "We are a religious family, honourable family," she says for the tenth time that day. Then she opens her miniature silver box and purrs in bajar tobacco pressed between her two fingers up her nose over twisted lips exposing her canines. Its sweetened scent puffs up in the air over me. I wonder what it would be like to sniff her tobacco up my nostrils.

281

Ma and I have come early. We sit on the bench made of hardwood mvuli and wrought iron back, armrests and legs shaped in lion's paws. I put the food plate down beside Ma.

A lady with round rimmed glasses greets Ma Jena Bai and puts her food plate next to mine. Then she sits on our bench. The familiar pungent odour of freshly fried spicy tilapia creeps out through the yellow-oil-blotched *Colonial Times* wrapped over her dish and pinches my nose. It's her food offering for the day like my own, a portion of her family's daily bread, like my own. This thought brings me closer to her. Later, I come to know that the name of the lady with thick glasses is Khanu Bai, and she is the Captain of the Nandi Committee and a mother of two boys. She is also known as the funeral chanter and the jamat calls her the keeper of Saurashtra's melodies and in that, they say, Nairowua's Satpanth faith. Later, I also come to understand why the people say that when she sings, the air pulsates Vedic verses rising from the depth of her heart. The pulsations fill the chamber of our remote rural jamat khana in Maasailand. In the layered wail, moan and tremble of many voices, resonances awakened by the chanter, I search my soul as my voice merges into the chorus, becoming one body of one heart with the people of Nairowua, my new community.

My eyes rove around, picking up details of this new place when they fall on a teenage girl with a bad leg who had hobbled over to sit by Khanu Bai's mother-in-law. "She had polio at age six," Ma whispers to me. "Cannot sit crossed legged. How can she?" Immediately then, her next thoughts came in questions, "Who will marry her? How can she cook? Bap-reh-bap! Mowla, what kismet have you given this girl? She cannot sit on the kitchen patlo with those metal legs. How can she? Pirshah, pirshah, pirshah." More disabled and aged people arrive and occupy benches on either side of the door

282

to the prayer hall. I see how the evening on the jamat khana bench is a respite for the aged and disabled of Nairowua. Each one of them rolls a tasbih through the fingers; some fingers are bony and crooked.

There is a copper plaque on the bench where the three of us are seated. The writing is in English but none of us read English. "We donated this bench in the memory of Haiderali's father. There was an old wooden plank on stones right here where he used to sit and say his tasbih," Ma reminisces. I listen patiently to my mother-in-law as she continues to talk aloud, making sure that Khanu Bai, the keeper of the sacred song and faith, can hear her, "Haiderali's father too knew the sacred songs, one hundred of them, all in his head. He used to say that we Khojas do not make use of the wisdom in the divine songs. 'All the guidance and rules of life are contained in the holy chants', he used to say. The poet-seers gave us the melodies to safeguard our faith and life's code for living side by side with all Moslems and all Hindus." Ma pauses and studies my reaction. "You will look for a time to recite the chants in the jamat khana. Singing the ginans is our family tradition."

"I hear your fair daughter-in-law sings music," says Khanu Bai. "We expect to hear her sing guru-pir's songs soon. They say her voice is as sweet as her skin is fair."

"Even an ass has fair skin but have you heard her bray?" snaps my sass. "Sweetness of the voice is nurtured by the faith in Saheb in your heart not fairness of your skin. Haiderali's father was dark skinned but when he sang, he held the jamat in a trance. Like black Krishna who made sweet melodies."

When Ma Jena Bai remembered her husband, it was his faith that she extolled not his looks, and she took the opportunity to inculcate the heritage of oral wisdom in me that her husband had bequeathed to the family. "Haiderali's father used to tell me if only we could see the pearls that the guru-pirs gifted us as ginans. But," she would sigh, "we are lost to the pleasures of Kal Yoog, this black karmic age." Ma talks with pride and rolls her tasbih, at the same time shaking her suspended foot under her long faarak. "The jamat loved Haiderali's father. His name was Khimji but the entire jamat called him Bapa. You know, like how Gandhi is called Bapu. At home, he was Bapaji. Bapaji came to the jamat khana every day, morning and evening. Never missed a day. He was an honest man. Helped many. Very religious, like his own father, Haiderali's grandfather Devji Momna."

Two elders arrive together, both in loose Gujarati paatoloons, bearded and wearing red fez caps. They remove their slippers, unlock the jamat khana door, fix their red fez caps and enter. Khanu Bai shifts her eyes, indicating to Ma that it was time to be at their volunteer duty post at the food table. However, Ma's dangling slipper has slipped off her foot and fallen to the ground upside down under the bench, somewhere irretrievable for her worried foot. She continues to roll her tasbih as she toes the ground, searching for the slipper under her long faarak while we wait. Finally, she stands up, pretending she has completed a quick prayer and we move towards the veranda of the jamat khana. Ma has more to say as we walk.

"The natives called Haiderali's father Kabuti because he wore a brown coat because of cold, you know. It was made by Da Costa, the Goan tailor at Jugu Bazaar, three shops from your grandfather's little bead and blanket shop. He made the kabuti out of military blankets from the auction after the war ended. The Goan was a dear friend of his," says Ma. Then she pauses for a while before continuing, "When malaria killed Bapaji he left the coat to his two sons. It should be well taken care of by you now - the way I used to take care of it for Bapaji. Wash it once a month before the new moon with the Lifebuoy, not Panga soap, as you would clean your own skin."

Before entering the prayer hall, I bow down to touch the floor at the threshold imprinted with the bare footprints of generations before me, the Satpanthis of Nairowua, who had bowed down to this floor on the red African soil and in reverence kissed the hand that touched the ground. I wonder how many would have been young brides like me who would have been starting a new life and lived to become grandmothers in this little town, in their little shops on the savannah. Like them, every evening for the rest of my life, I shall bow down low to hand kiss the floor before crossing the doorsill over their footprints into the realm of rituals and chants, prayers of shukhar and silence of the hall. I shall sing and hear incantations that hold memories of pirs of my childhood. I shall inhale the thick smoke of loban, the healing tree gum, waving my hand through scented clouds that veil over my face and bring me peace. My tongue will relish the sweetness of sugared semolina fried in pure ghee of suk-reet. I shall offer my kissed on hand to fellow Satpanthis, and accept theirs in return similarly kissed on, reciprocating mutual respect that murids offer each other in the jamat khana. I shall look into Saheb's smiling eyes in the picture on the wall and let him know I have come to his house today. How the jamat khana embraces all my senses! If I let it, it will absorb me wholly into its consciousness.

34

The Coat called Kabuti

Ma continues to tell me the story of the family as if she were completing a lesson on the heritage bequeathed to me by marriage. Both of us sit on the patlo stool on the kitchen floor, facing each other. She stirs the kheer and I fry the puris. "Listen carefully, as I told you earlier," says my mother-in-law. She is now the storyteller who must speak.

"Haiderali was born in Zanzibar. His father, Khimji Devji Momna, who we called Bapaji, lived on Mla Ndege Street in the stone town where my parents were born and where I grew up. On that street once resided Chandu Nancy, the well-known Saurashtran accountant employed by wealthy Omani merchants of the dhow fleet. It was on this street that we, the Khojas, traded in the kanga, the speaking cloth of the Indian Ocean.

"People say that Haiderali's grandmother was the second wife of Devji Momna, the pushcart hawker of old town Mombasa. The town people called him Khoja Hamali, but in the jamat, he was known as the Jamat Bhai, the caretaker of the Kuze jamat khana in Mombasa. After his first wife eloped with an Afghan butcher, Devji Momna lost face, and subsequently, his business declined because he could no longer look at his customers in the eye. Neither could he live with the shame as Jamat Bhai of Mombasa. To make matters worse, no Khoja family of Mombasa would want to have a Momna for a son-in-law even though, like them, he was a Satpanth Ismaili. Thus, when he heard that Jamat Bhai in Zanzibar died of asthma, he sent a message that he was willing to take his place and serve in Saheb's house. Devji Momna was appointed the new Jamat Bhai in Zanzibar and he started a new life in a new town. Within a few weeks after his appointment, and with the encouragement of the mukhi, he sent a proposal to marry the dark girl he saw coming to the jamat khana. Every day they exchanged looks and smiled at each other, secretly. People said in whispers that the dark girl was a slave child. They said she was abandoned at the base of a clove tree, and a Khoja couple, who did not have children of their own, found her in the fragrance of the clove flowers in season. They decided 'to sit her in their lap' meaning adopt her. We, in the Devji family, do not speak about her past or even mention her real name. I still don't know what she was called, but in the family photograph, you can see she is of black blood. She is wearing a faarak and a pachedi pulled over her head, and she spoke Swahili-Kutchi with such a melodious voice that whatever she said sounded sincere and sweet like music from her heart. We called her Mama-ji. In the town, she was known as Mama Biriani because when she cooked biriani, the aroma from her kitchen filled the streets of the Stone Town Zanzibar. Devji Momna and Mama-ji had one son, that's Haiderali's father, Khimji, my husband. And they had three daughters who are married along the coastal villages of Zanzibar and Pemba.

287

"Khimji, Haiderali's father and my husband, was of dark skin and wiry hair. When Devji Momna contracted elephantiasis and could not walk, twelve-year-old Khimji scrubbed and cleaned merchant vessels docked at the port so he could feed the family. He was a hard working boy that he was! He had the responsibility of looking after his mother and his three sisters. Mama-ji was a shrewd businesswoman who cooked biriani for the local hotels and even started making lentil bhajia, selling them outside the jamat khana in the evenings. People bought her bhajia because she was a widow who supported four children but later her bhajia became as famed as her biriani in stone town Zanzibar. Her daughters went to the waterfront every evening selling bhajia. From the profit, Mama-ji expanded her little business to buying and selling cloves and nutmeg from the plantations. She taught her son and her daughters to trade and soon the family became as skilled at bargaining with the spice merchants as the Khojas of Muscat who visited Zanzibar. Gradually, they began to prosper.

"When Mama-ji sent an offer to my parents for my hand in marriage to her son, they quickly agreed. When I protested because Khimji was not only a Momna but he was also black, my father said to me, "It's a thrifty, honest and religious family. Yes, he is black but you are no fair-y from the last karma either. Yes, he is Momna but you are no blue blood princess either. I cannot wait forever for a fair prince for you to descend from the sky." I was turning thirteen and Haiderali's father was sixteen when we were married.

"Haiderali's father, my good husband, was known as Khimji Bhai son of Devji Bhai in town. However, he was not so lucky in business. One day, only a month after our marriage, in the month of June when the Indian Ocean turns mad with rage, he lost his first cargo of cloves destined for Muscat. He had invested all his savings in that batch of cloves. The dhow capsized in the storm. My good husband was reduced to selling all the family adornment that honoured women. That included my own. I had hardly had a chance to wear all the gold from my father's house that was meant to last us my lifetime and lessen the burden of poverty in future. My good mother-in-law and I sat in the street where I was born, milling flour and spices for the rich merchants' wives. We lost face.

"Bapaji, my husband, decided to move to the mainland of Tanganyika. He knew of a man from his father's village in Saurashtra, who his father talked about, who he would call his Kaka uncle as was the custom, and who had done well in the bead trade in the interior. Kaka uncle's name was Jadavji Bhai. They said Jadavji Bhai had settled at a spot where the river waters are warm along the northern bead route towards Kilimanjaro, the pulse of Africa and traveller's compass. Here at the cattle salt lick near the DC's office, he rented a mud hut from the DC, where he slept and kept his bead stock. Then he would travel south towards the old slave and ivory caravan route from Bagamoyo to Ujiji on Lake Tanganyika carrying small quantities of beads to find what ethnics of the interior liked. He found the people already knew exactly what colours they preferred narrating them in their histories of migrations and traditions of ceremonies and adornments of their forefathers. That they had not only the words for different colours in nature but also the tones, and that beauty was a primary part of their life. They said societal welfare was peace that they called 'utu', differently in many languages, meaning humanity. They would say to him, "Where there is not beauty, there is not peace." He felt so safe in the civilizations of the inland people that throughout the year, Jadavji Bhai, while sleeping in the villages, travelled across Tanganyika selling beads along the paths that crossed vast grasslands and highlands. He took notes, and made sketches of their body art and the beads he saw on people. When back at his mud hut in the DC's compound, he would write a letter to the bead import agent in Dar-es-salaam describing the colours, shapes and sizes of the beads he needed. Jadavji Bhai wrote a letter to persuade my husband to join him on his foot-trade-safaris and help him to expand his bead business on the savannah among the ethnic people where no bead merchant had reached before. He had all the papers from the German colonial office in Dar-es-salaam and knew the routes but now he was growing old and needed a young man to walk his walk.

"We left Zanzibar, arrived in Mombasa, and then took gari-la-moshi, the wagon-that-smokes, to Nairobi. Bapaji, my good husband, invested all the remaining money he had in a stock of beads from Rajan Lalji store in Jugu Bazaar, and then we left for Nairowua with a trunk full of beads.

"In Nairowua, we lived with Jadavji Bhai's family for almost a year. In the house, there was Jadavji Bhai's wife, his two sons and two daughters, his parents and his wife's three younger brothers and a sister. Orphans all. Bapaji, my good husband, helped his Kaka uncle with accounts and plans to expand the bead business. Jadavji Bhai agreed it would be easier to import all the beads from Nairobi now that the war was over and both Kenya and Tanganyika were one British East Africa.

"In just two months with Mowla's grace, Bapaji, my good husband, was able to sell all the beads at the market. He returned to Nairobi and brought more beads from Rajan Lalji and sold them all again. Then he went repeatedly to Nairobi, and in time, we were able to have our own little bead store and rent a room at the back to live in. It was a patched tin house on the only street by the river in the new town that was coming up on the Nairobi road away from the DC's office. You can see the house by the river. A Somali family from the north lives there and runs a hotel. That was our first bead shop in Nairowua."

Ma shows me the Da Costa tailored long black coat that hangs at the back of the veranda door on a wooden hook. "It now belongs to my two sons,'" she says. "Whoever needs to go to see the DC wears it with his red fez hat. There are two red fez hats in the house but only one coat. In a few days, it will be chandraat, the evening of the new moon. Wash the coat today and dust the hats."

I carry the coat to the karo and sit on the ledge while I empty the pockets of some copper one cent coins, forgotten pieces of half chewed betel nuts and dried up su-khreet wrapped and pressed thin like flattened dough paste in ghee soaked jamat khana tracing paper. I look at an English playing card, the Queen of Hearts. She is bejewelled in English ornaments and white animal fur rolled around the neck, blonde-haired; skin white as paper, blue eyed and red lipped. But she has no clothes on! I stare at her naked body, her straight back, her drawn up wormy legs and up turned paisley mango breasts. I had never seen naked white woman without sharam before or any woman for that matter. The mixed smell of snuff, su-kreet ghee, sweat and bitter paan, stale bidi tobacco and bangi marijuana, strikes me. I indulge in the sweet pungent mix of odours. Sad, it has to be washed away together with the red dust of the month and all the pocket stories! In its place now, there will be a fresh smell of

Lifebuoy soap. I always wonder why the brick redness of the soap does not dye my hands or the clothes.

On the evening of the new moon, chandraat, Haiderali looks smart and starched stiff like the DC. He strides proudly to the jamat khana before Ma and me, and refuses to carry the prayer food in his hand. He is wearing the long black coat, a brushed red fez hat with a swinging tassel, trimmed hair and closely shaven cheeks. I feel proud of him.

It is Tuesday again. I have been in Nairowua now for three weeks. The whole time I have been feeling tired and tense, and hoping Ma would go to the market every day and stay there. My groins hurt. My head bursts with Ma's taak taaks. I look at the henna on my hands. The patterns are still faintly visible. It will take time to heal my heart, and then the henna too will fade away. My head is teeming with praises of the Devji family and I do not want to listen to the family's noble heritage any more. No one asks me where my family comes from though all know that my mother is from the twin villages of Savar and Khundla and that my father's family came from the village of Haripur, in Saurashtra as well. When my mother died, he married an absakan woman from Superi who brought me up. Here they would talk of my stepmother with awe. Partly because she is an absakan who can bring kisirani bad luck to you, and partly because she was raised in her grandmother's house where a spirit habits and where people go to heal inhaling the fragrant smoke that oozes from the grave without a fire.

Only when Ma goes to the market can be myself. I go to the courtyard and look at the savannah sky. The clouds, like grass, change moods during the day, resounding to the glares of the tropical sun. This is the blue sky country. I dream, creating shining zari patterns in the pulse of the clouds. I see the landscape of kofia patterns and zari florets. Sometimes I see the white angel horse, carrying Saheb flash by, and I offer a prayer, my devotion to his image in the sky.

I imagine singing my first ginan chant in the jamat khana of Nairowua. I would be greatly admired and envied. My sass would brag to her sewa service committee about the Devji family tradition of singing devotional poetry that comes from the love for Saheb. "Deep love only can give a voice like that," she would say. I am coming to know Devji Momna, my Dadabapa's friend and fellow traveller. My marriage is the emblem to their friendship forged on a voyage on the dhow coming to Africa.

35

Beading the Sky

Routines set in like it were a cycle of movements around the home during the day, and to and from the jamat khana in the evenings.

"Follow me to the courtyard. There is something you have to learn to do," I hear Ma's words when she emerges from the bathroom scratching her scalp and rubbing in coconut oil at the same time. Some months have passed by since my arrival in Nairowua and not once during the month has Ma called me by my name, Sakina Bai. She addresses me as 'tu' as if I were a child.

I follow Ma into the courtyard where in a corner; there is a heap of empty bottles of all colours and thicknesses. She takes one bottle from the mass of glass and half fills it with dirty motor oil from a dented rusted drum. She strides to the samavat and from the coal plate underneath, pulls out an iron rod and plunges the hot shaft into the bottle. The oil sizzles and bubbles. A sharp crack and then a snap. With a dextrous hit and tilt, Ma has broken the funnel top off the bottle leaving the three-inch bottom full of oil.

"That's how we make drinking glasses to sell in the shop. That's how we survive the war. Whenever you have a little time in between housework, you will make glasses here. Make some this week and get used to it. They give us our roji meals in these hard times," says Ma as she walks back to the kitchen. Suddenly, almost as a second thought, she turns around saying, "Smoothen the top on the grinding stone. It's under the table near the paraffin tin there." She points at a battered tin. Looking confused, she then asks me in a soft polite voice, "Have you seen my bajar tobacco box?" She goes into the veranda and disappears, not expecting an answer, not expecting me to know anyway. I had thrown her silver tobacco box under her bed.

More months go by. I try to cope with the work under Ma's chameleon eyes and make a few drinking glasses every week and lay them out on the shelf in the shop. One morning while I am mopping the veranda, Ma calls me from the kitchen, "Vavu! You will go to the shop in the afternoons from today. Ole Lekakeny will show you how to work with the beads." I stop mopping and sit on my heels, holding the dripping gunnysack in my hand. Ma watches me from the kitchen while she stirs the curry pot on the stove. Breeze through the kitchen window pushes the steamy spice aroma of green pea and potato curry into the house. "You and Ole Lekakeny will manage the shop in the afternoons. Learn about the beads from the old man. I need to rest longer in the afternoons. Beads are our roji of the blessed meal in these hard times. Be sure to have your pachedi over your head all the time while you are in the shop. Maasai age group graduation celebrations are near. Ravana war will never end but it does not bother the Maasai." She calls Adolf Hitler the demon king Ravana. I cannot contain my joy. At last, I shall be free to indulge in the colours I have been watching on display on the store's veranda.

I come to the shop that afternoon after I have washed the dishes and mopped clean the kitchen, and even made one glass from a green bottle. I walk in quietly, apprehensively, and sit on Ma's armchair.

"Jambo mzee," I greet the old man.

"Jambo, mwanawangu," he replies calling me his loved child.

That afternoon we do not talk except for greetings. I do not know how to communicate with Ole Lekakeny sitting there by my side, or if I should. He gives me a copper bowl in which are broken strings of seed beads. Then he shows me how to sort out different colours, picking each bead by the eye with the pointed tip of the sewing needle and dropping it in a different English jam jar marked by colours red, white, blue, green, and orange. My eyes fix on the spangle of seeds. Each bead colour touches or lays over another, yet each one is an independent hue in itself, sovereign and free in the art it makes together with others as if in stitches, a landscape spotted with dot darts merging into one another. Tears start welling in my eyes. I press and widen my eyes, then blink to make the water disappear. But the more I blink, the more water comes flooding into my eyes. I thrust my chin to the chest, instantly the pachedi border falls down over my ears. No one can see how I cry.

That afternoon, the next two hours, I work in silence bead by bead. I need no one to talk to me now while I talk to my thoughts strolling out to the memory of my days

296

embroidering. Is it the fingers that evoke the talk? Is it the blood in them or the skin over them that tell me to talk to my embroidery while they work with beads? Or is it the eyes that direct the fingers to reminiscences of the body?

Every afternoon I would sit in the lap of beauty, building on memories in my fingers. Sometimes, I would stretch my eyes to the distance, to the grove where the Ol-debbei bead-trees are absorbed in tree talk. Hollowed circular beehives sit wedged in their cleaved branches like pregnant women at the market place. Before me, I see the brown murrum Nairobi Road on which stands the KHIMJI DEVJI MOMNA AND SON BEADS AND GENERAL STORE. There are three other Indian shops, wooden frames on granite stones and red tin roofs. In between are grass spaces visited by goats, cattle, and children. On the hot, indolent savannah afternoons, I would dream I am playing with the goats and children born free on these grasslands. Then I would take my eyes as far as I can see along the earth road to Nairobi. I would imagine myself walking barefoot into the infinity of the savannah, feeling the heat of the afternoon sun on the powdery volcanic dust under my soles, the cool breeze filling my hair intentionally left open to it. Such bliss in the heart that only freedom in nature gives if you were to let all your senses open to it.

"We sell beads in strings not in patterns, because that is the work of artists of the savannah. But the pattern keri we make here," says Ole Lekakeny. "You will learn how to bead the bead in your fingers and let the colours sing to your eyes. You will know Maasai art when you start beading the sky." Ole Lekakeny brings me back from my dreams to the beads in my lap and the song on his lips. I try to understand his words — *beading the sky?*

When Ole Lekakeny sings, I remember the first time I heard this song was in the Ford coming to Nairowua when I was a bride.

God beads the rainbow on zebra's neck
I see it blossom on his beaded neck
Be peaceful in the blue sky
With emankeeki on your neck

36

Mariam's Kismet

Though it is many months later after our marriage, Haiderali has not forgotten I had asked him to show me the town. So one afternoon he borrows a friend's car and takes me on a tour. He is proud of Nairowua where he has grown up and he is proud to introduce me to the town he knows so well. He calls Nairowua his town.

We drive down the Nairobi Road and take a turning into a side road. Haiderali explains pointing with his eyes as he drives, "The DC allocated free plots here to each Asian community to build their houses of worship. There is the Krishna temple, Sunni mosque, Sikh gurudwara, Ithna Asheri mosque of our kin, and the Ismaili jamat khana. This road is called Temple Road." Between the five houses of worship, I see Indian shops. Most are tin structures built on cement floors with slopping veranda roofs supported by wooden poster poles. Shops with shelves full of blankets and sheets, grass brooms and kerosene lamps, shiny aluminium containers and hoes, maize flour and red beans in open standing sacks.

Temple Road ends at a stone and cement mixing plant where there is a natural spring and a pool. Haiderali takes a turn around a smooth faced granite rock through whose cleft grows a wait-a-bit thorn bush. He brakes unexpectedly, as if shocked, into a large drove of Zebu cattle. Their coats are in browns, reds and mustard-grey patches, sweaty and gleaming health in the afternoon sun. A Maasai boy with a slim stick taller than he is and wearing a shuka cotton sheet across his chest down to his thighs follows, commanding and talking to the cows to walk straight. He would be no older than seven years.

Back to the arterial Nairobi Road and we take the second track on the left. This cattle-goat-motor road runs behind our shop called KHIMJI DEVJI MOMNA AND SON BEADS AND GENERAL STORE.

"This is Market Street. It's a short drive up the hill. Do you want to see more?"

I nod.

Market Street leads to an open place where Chaga, Taita, and Kamba women sit with legs stretched out on a grassy patch eroded by the constant abrasion of human and animal feet. Their sisal and baobab root basketry, clay pottery and fresh tomatoes, beans, potatoes, local leafy vegetables and onions from the silted riverbanks are laid out before them in neat piles of threes and fours arranged in straight rows. Haiderali parks at the side and tells me to walk with him. As soon as I open the car door, a whir of voices and activities engulf me.

Haiderali talks with the men as if he knows them well. You would not think he was the same man I lived with. His Swahili is not good but he speaks Maasai with ease. He jokes with the

300

women under what Ole Lekakeny would call an old Ol-lerai male acacia. Their elongated milk gourds, mellowed deep brown, shiny with butterfat, lean against the solitary tree trunk. They shift the gourds to the shadier side of Ol-lerai's awning shade as the sun moves west in the warmth of the cloudless blue sky.

"Pretty woman, will you not be a co-wife at my homestead?" Haiderali jokes. A peal of laughter follows excited chattering. Then a response comes from one in the group. "My father will ask for a hundred cows to marry such an ugly man, hairy like a baboon." More laughter. The reply came from the milk woman who comes to the courtyard door every day! I smile at her. She smiles back and says something I do not understand.

"What is she saying?" I ask Haiderali.

"She is asking if you will agree to be her co-wife."

I stand there shocked, not knowing what to say while they laugh and prattle, expecting a response from me. Their coffee brown breasts bulge under the front aprons becoming slightly visible and shaking when they chuckle.

"I will have you bedecked with beads from head to foot and give you a space to build a house of your own, and ten cows, all sampu!" Haiderali talks like an aroused warrior, gurgling throat words in controlled courtship. He quickly translates for me as he speaks. Envy enters my covert eyes and I cover it up with hearty greetings, "Jambo! Jambo! Jambo!" between broad smiles. But my words are no match to the spirit in the language and open laughter of the women under the Ol-debbei canopy. They do not speak Swahili.

"But who will marry a mushroom? My children will look like mushrooms too. Enkai Narok! For the sake of the Black Merciful God! No! No!" Says the milk woman with shaven hair, clear complexion, and lustrous teeth. The women laugh again and chatter natter heartily, noisily, among themselves. Some are chewing sugar canes, ripping open the stiff knotted skin at the side of the mouth with their canines, and biting into the stalk.

Scratchy gramophone sounds over guitar twangs, over hymn chorales, from bars and tearooms that skirt the market square screech into the air. Haiderali walks towards a nyama choma bar butchery, leaving me suddenly, wandering about the vegetable, milk and honey market. I observe how like other ethnic women at the market distinguishable by differences in their beadwork and attires, the Maasai women sit with their legs stretched forward. I wonder how long they would sit in that position and if their backs hurt because they have no backrest. Town people come to them to buy milk that they pour sitting down from their elongated gourds into empty Guinness and Tusker beer bottles that they plug over with leaves. Women in animal skin aprons who I think would be from grassland forests, stand by their casks carved from tree trunks, full to the brim, overflowing with honey, hive wax, and a flotilla of dead bees. People buy yellow waxy combs to suck the honey, and then they chew the wax while they work and talk with each other. Elders are pacing about looking for mature honey that will ferment well to make beer. Flies and bees whiz with aggression around fresh milk and maziwa lala meaning sleeping milk, and they paste themselves on clammy honey containers. It's all women, their talk, their laughter, their businesses. In one corner tethered goats of mixed white, black and brown patched coats bleat distressingly under the mid-afternoon sun, while their masters quibble and haggle with local butchers over their prices. When Haiderali returns, his breath smells of Tusker beer and he is carrying a brown paper bag. This habit of his annoys me.

Market Street ends at the Catholic mission on the hill where there is a church, a hospital, and a school. In the town, we can hear the bell toll from the hill calling the people to prayers. Haiderali parks the car at the shady side of the meadow. A path leads to a clump of Ol-tepesi acacia hill trees. In the copse, partially hidden by trees and vines, I am startled when suddenly I see a white stone standing on a pedestal like a person. Coming closer, I recognized it to be a shrine of Mariam like the one at the Holy Family Cathedral in Nairobi. Kneeling before her are three paper white children, one boy and two girls, all made of plaster. Haiderali goes into the trees behind the shrine to find a place to urinate. I look at pensive Mariam, her mother named her tuberose, the fragrant flower of Arabia, and she is the mother of the miracle maker Prophet Isa. I ponder how quickly my life has changed and what I am doing in the Devji home. I wonder if my life will always be lonely like Isa's mother in the holy stone. Though all day long, I move from the bedroom to the kitchen – courtyard – veranda – shop and back to the kitchen – bedroom, inside I am lonely Mariam. People see me as a quiet, hardworking wife, but I am raging inside. Singing in the jamat khana brings beauty to my heart and that is peace when the day is closing into the first hour of night. When the Nairowua jamat, sitting communally in meditation, falls into silence, it is beauty too, and that brings peace to the heart of every Satpanthi. And beads give me joy in the afternoon. Otherwise, I live between the torments of kitchen – courtyard - bedroom. Always the bedroom in the end. I want to run away from Ma Jena Bai and

Haiderali but the afternoon at the market has awakened me to how much I want my husband to myself.

Mariam's eyes look down to the ground, not at me. I wish they would look at me and we could talk, woman to woman eye talk. But her eyes will not talk. Her thick pachedi comes over her forehead in modest laaj like a Satpanth lady in stone. She is cloaked in a long faarak like me. She stands quiet, thoughtful, and patient. Her posture reminds me of Jena Naaras, and her words ring in my ears. "We cannot change the kismet we come with, so we must accept our destiny with contentment of shukhar." I look at Mariam again. Meeshnari Shivji Bhagat once said a chapter in the Quran honours her name. She stands dead white before me, a tall stilled grace carved in stone. She is without any colour, her hands folded loosely at the waist, palms together in a limp namaste. Her tasbih crawls over her fingers before drooping down in a loop. She has turned her woman's endurance into strength of patience, grace and contentment of shukhar to bear her everlasting pain of mamta motherhood. She is like Rani Victoria in Nairobi's park, but taller, slimmer, and much humbler. I complain. She listens. My hurting heart bursts out, "My sass, Ma Jena Bai and husband Haiderali give me no time to embroider ... when I sing in the jamat khana, Gujarati script blazes in zari singing to my heart, my fingers twitch to adorn ...they ache to create the shine. They yearn to be the shine of the Light, be free and at peace ... Haiderali drinks alcohol. What shall I do? Haiderali hurt me hard the first time he slept on me. I am frightened every time he takes me into his arms. It is his right, I know, they told me so, but I don't like it. I don't want it. Every time it's the same. Ugly, shameful, hurtful. What shall I do? Yet I want my husband and a home of my own. What shall I do?"

It is Mariam's kismet to be eternally standing, a stone woman listening, absorbing pain in prayer, and complaints of her worshippers. Each day, forever. Mariam, the mother of fragrances, the tuberose in God's garden, remains still. "I hear your heart child," she would say had she been able to move her lips. "Bear your destiny with mine. Be with me. Take my patience, take my courage and endure with me, endure with contentment. Shukhar."

37

Rama made Dhinglo Dhingly Dolls

After two hours or so, I find myself climbing up onto the shop's veranda. Stillness of the afternoon prolongs. Sitting down into the armchair, I put my eyes and fingers to the beads. Ole Lekakeny dozes in his chair. Haiderali opens the books to enter the day's sales. After a while, I hear him rake a cough, beckoning me to the back. How can I say no? If I ignore him, he will continue raking his throat until he scrapes it out.

"Ma does not want me to come to the bedroom in the afternoon," I come to tell him quietly so Ole Lekakeny will not hear. However, Haiderali does not reply; instead, he pulls me by the waist, at once breathing heavily at my neck. Froth spills out and over the Tusker beer bottle on the shelf corner.

"Ma will come to know. Not here Haidu, please. Ole Lekakeny is at the veranda," I whisper. My heart races, partly because of fear of being seen, and partly because of shame also of being seen. How can I escape?

"Ma is asleep, snoring," smiles Haiderali. He breathes over me in coarse whispers. His eyes are avid, his back arched. He holds me like a vice in his embrace.

"I am afraid, Haidu. Let me go. Not here."

"Why?"

I cannot reply, how can I? What do I say? He removes my pachedi, and lets it drop to the floor. Then he lifts my long dress and holds it over his arms around my waist, pinning me to the corner below the shelf lined with boxes full of beads, recently arrived from Nairobi. We stand clutched together, crammed in the angle of the cold cement plastered wall. My spine presses the wall safe where Haiderali keeps cash and I have my gold wrapped in double folds of merikani cloth. The cold of the iron box runs through to my legs. It is dark in the back store and it smells of cardboard boxes and decomposing chalk on plastered stone. I begin to shiver. Our shuffling feet disturb the shop's black-white banded cat, Paka Minima, who keeps the rats away and who sleeps below the shelf. Gradually lifting her pregnant belly, looking annoyed and worn-out, she paws out to a safer resting place.

Minutes later, Haiderali too walks away through the courtyard to the bedroom, saying, "Make kheer and puris tonight. I have an urge to taste kheer made by your hand today." I pick up the pachedi and walk back to my chair, softly and deliberately taking in deep breaths. Ole Lekakeny wakes up with a start, realizing he was about to fall off the chair.

About half an hour later, around four in the afternoon, Ma enters the shop.

"I need tea. Put some ginger in it for me. I don't feel well," she says. "I want to sit."

"I will make your tea in a moment."

"Tonight we can have parotha and mango pickle with chai."

"Haiderali wants to eat kheer and puris tonight," I say trying not to sound defiant.

"But we just had kheer and puris last week! The mango pickle will turn fusty if we do not eat it soon," retorts Ma. "We cannot afford using so much sugar for kheer every day. There is another war coming soon. Did you not hear Khanu Bai? She came back from Nairobi yesterday. She says people in Nairobi talk about one Hitlo waking up. That German Ravana has been restless to avenge the English after the shame of their defeat in the war. A wounded lion will always rise to attack the hunter."

I get up to vacate the chair for Ma. Zarina, who has just returned from school, enters the shop from the veranda. "After all, the humiliation led both the angelic devtas and wicked demons to avenge their hurting pride in Rama's war." I let Ma finish the sentence before stepping into the courtyard.

At around six in the late afternoon, Haiderali and his brother, Kabir, bolt the shop's front doors as soon as Ole Lekakeny leaves by the back door. Then three of them - Haiderali, Kabir, and Ma, start counting the day's earning, first separating the silver in two piles of one shillings and fifty cents. Then they make separate piles of the copper one, five and ten cents. Finally, they count the bills and Haiderali announces the total sum, "Two hundred and sixty two shillings and eighty eight cents." Haiderali divides the day's cash by eight calculating orally in Gujarati 260/8 is equal 32 and 3/4; 88/8 is equal to 11. No sooner he announces thirty two shillings and eighty six cents than Ma begins counting the exact eighth part of the day's earning from the cash on the table. That tithe will be the one she will carry with her to give to the mukhi in the jamat khana that evening like every other evening. That will be for shukhar for the day's earning and baraka for more in the future. She leaves with the tithe money wrapped in a cloth. It's already sacred that no one but she will carry to the jamat khana.

Meanwhile, Kabir pulls out a glossy copy of Charles Atlas from the cash drawer, removes his shirt, hangs it on the doorknob and walks with his arms bent to the back room where Paka Minima lives. I return to sweep the floor while Haiderali works on the books at the counter. He turns his head to look at me sweeping. I try to sing inside to be away from his predatory watch over me. My back is bent and my braid sways in front at my stooping breasts. I sulk and show it on my lips curled to the side.

On the courtyard veranda where there is the usual evening dressing up bustle before the prayers of the first quarter of the night, I find myself always the last one to dress up. From the samavat in the courtyard I bring bathing water for everyone except Zarina, and pour it into the debe tin. The tin's rim is bent outward on two sides to make handles to help carry the weight. As if it were a song he could not withhold, as if to placate me because of the afternoon, or was it that he simply wanted to say, "Rama made us for each other." I hear Haiderali singing:

Rakh na ramakada mara Rame ramta rakhya reh

Dhingla dhingli eh ghar banthyia reh

My Rama made ash toys to play

Then boy doll and girl doll made a house

309

I do not look at him though I know the song is for me. He has a towel around his waist and he is wearing a netted vest.

"Do not bring naandi food today from the jamat khana. We shall have kheer and puris," Haiderali says to Kabir who has just stepped out of the bathroom. That was a comment for my ears, a way of cajoling me ahead of the night. I keep my face straight.

"Yes. Today I will make kheer and puris after jamat khana," Ma snaps in to my bewilderment.

Haiderali ignores Ma. Perhaps he was not aware that Ma was listening. Perhaps he is annoyed but has to keep quiet as he enters the bathroom. Meanwhile, Kabir, also in a netted vest and towel at the waist, fusses over his Yardley-peppered hair at the washbowl mirror on the courtyard veranda. The Devji brothers' grooming is irritating, especially when I have to clean the combs, brushes, razor blades, face towels, and the washbowl after them.

After days of frenzied searching, Ma found her tobacco box under her bed, a likely place for it to have fallen into while she slept, so she thought.

38

Zera Bai and Khanu Bai

In the evening, at around seven, the family walks to the jamat khana. Ma, Zarina, and I, walk together with the day's food offering behind the two men. In time, I begin to look forward to walking to the jamat khana that is about twenty minutes away on foot. It became a routine like the morning routine when the milk woman comes to the back door. First, we exchange greetings and then friendly eyes. When we talk, it is in small words, half Swahili, half Maasai, and the rest in gestures. She told me she lives near Mt Nairowua pointing her finger to the mountain and herself. Showing her four fingers, she said she had four children; two like her were girls, she said, showing me two fingers of her one hand, and one finger of the other hand on her chest. The walk to the jamat khana frees me from the chores, and from Haiderali's lust and Ma's vulture eyes. Even when I talk to people in the jamat khana, I feel those eyes on me. Young women smile and come to talk to me. Like there is Zera Bai who is from Kisumu and recently married to a young man called Rhemu Bhai, who like Haiderali, was born in Nairowua. The henna on Zera Bai's hands like how it was on my hands has faded from bright orange ochre to faint red, and then into disjointed brown lines that looks like some vague aging marks. Ma somehow has a dislike for Zera Bai. "That Kisumu girl is full of naakhra perks, moving her body like a peahen dancing to mate," I would hear Ma repeating like a mantra.

Ma's mantra about Zera Bai affirms the chup chap chatter in the jamat khana, "Must have been an outline girl in Kisumu, you know. Imagine a love marriage!" Although Zera Bai was married in the jamat khana, her father, who owns the Lake Victoria Cotton Ginnery, was not pleased because Rhemu Bhai's widowed mother, "Stretched out her hand to the Welfare Committee," he said. Such a base act of begging would blemish his family lineage through marriage. But the truth was that Rhemu Bhai's mother was poor and an absakan widow. "One day the father's nisasa-sigh of pain from a broken heart will strike his ungrateful daughter." That's how Ma Jena Bai saw young Zera Bai's future.

Kabir Devji, Haiderali's younger brother, and his young men friends often joke about coy Zera Bai's peahen naakhra. "It's garam masala hot, hot spices," they say. "Sleepy Nairowua needs more of such hot stuff to wake up to modern times." Kabir's head is full of filmi 'modern' times. I learn that Khanu Bai, the funeral chanter and chairperson of Ma's Naandi Committee, is a neighbour and a friend of Zera Bai. In spite of their age difference and the varying reputations, they have become very close, so close that they wear exactly the same frocks to the jamat khana on new moon chandraat evenings. That is their sumph, like an oath sworn to their eternal friendship, an overt show of companionship between women so intimate that they make dresses out of the same material purchased, and tailored jointly in the exact pattern. They are like sisters in dresses sewed for an occasion by a loving mother. Identical in all aspects but for the sizes. They even have a photograph wearing their indistinguishably alike dresses and hairstyles with their arms curled over each other's shoulders like sisters.

"I was told that your father-in-law was known as Kabuti because he liked to wear his long black coat. The black coat also came to be identified with Devji family's thriftiness in all matters worldly," says Zera Bai while looking at me with a tease in her tell-tale naakhra eyes. It is not only Zera Bai who does eye naakhra. In fact, eye naakhra is an art accomplished by Khoja girls from remote corners of East Africa. One would think they have had training in this mischief, especially when it came to directing their eyes at boys who would be bewildered by their looks, and not sure whether to respond or not for fear of becoming victims of some rude feminine language, such as, "Say that to your sister!"

"And for his generosity in all matters of faith," adds Khanu Bai adjusting her spectacles. She had known my father-in-law Khimji Devji Momna well.

"These are the qualities Haiderali has inherited from his father and which he tries to keep," I say jokingly in reply, not meaning what I say. I say that to bait for more information on the Devji family background from the two women.

"It is whispered that when Haiderali's father was alive, neither the adults nor the children were allowed to eat from the meal that was cooked only for the prayer offering at the jamat khana," says Khanu Bai. She opens her palm and offers us su-kreet, a golden knob on a square tracing paper. Two of us, one after the other, pinch into the sweetened semolina dough and lick off the ghee on our fingertips saying santosh-shukhar. Khanu Bai eats the rest and licks up the film of ghee on her palm to clean it. She crumples and holds the tracing

313

paper in her palm, squeezing it in an attempt to absorb the ghee off her hand, releasing the sweet aroma of su-kreet into the air.

"What I heard was that food offerings were prepared with such diligence and precision that there was nothing left over for the family to eat," adds Zera Bai looking down noticeably exaggerating the whole affair.

"Well, I am married into a religious and honourable family. Perhaps a little thrifty. But am I not the lucky one?" I respond with a side smile that carries a hint of quiet sarcasm, begging for more information.

"Mamdu, my husband, you know, told me that when the father died, Haiderali removed the ten cent copper piece under the basin of the scale. It was so discreetly attached for gaining a few more illegal cents on sugar and maize flour that no one suspected cheating … " No sooner had Khanu Bai started to add than she fell silent like a hen that suddenly senses danger in the sky and stays frozen and alert. Ma was approaching hastily.

"We cannot be here whole night giggling thee-thee-thee," says Ma Jena Bai. I feel embarrassed. Her voice carries a rebuke.

As we amble-stroll back home, Ma's voice becomes even sharper. "When one hyena laughs, others join in, showing their teeth thee-thee-thee not knowing why they laugh."

I wonder why she does not approve of me talking with Zera Bai?

39

Storyteller of the Savannah

KHIMJI DEVJI MOMNA AND SON BEADS AND GENERAL STORE

P. O. BOX 6 NAIROWUA   KENYA COLONY   BEA

ખોટા મોતી ના સાચા વેપારી

I feel like I have lived in Nairowua all my life, yet I don't know the new person that I am becoming. The person that is being shaped by how I am viewed - a wife, a daughter-in-law, expectant carrier of family name and honour, a cook and servant in the house, but an adorned lady of Devji family in the jamat khana. What tells me who I am, speaking to the spirit in me, is the two hours on the veranda of the shop with Ole Lekakeny. I remember in the beginning how I used to trace the shiny blue flies chasing each other aimlessly on the wing. They did not annoy me the way they annoyed Ma. The flies would settle on the long milk gourds that the old man's nieces kept in the corner while they went about their business in the town. The milk was their food while they were in town for a day or two, and for their journey to and from their homesteads. They walked three days to come to Nairowua, stopping at homesteads of their cousins, age group friends and aunts, refilling their milk gourds. I enjoyed this time of

315

sluggish quietness of the afternoons away from the rattle of pots and pans and Ma's constant taak taak. Sometimes a stray bee buzzed in and caught my attention. Sometimes, the elusive black wasp that had made a nest in the roof under the rain gutter came to look around. The collective buzzing of the insects quivered into the sound zz … Om … o-a-m … mm. I would join in their humming zz … mm … zz…. Mm … Om … mm … zz … mm … Hari … mm ... Om … Ali … Om … mm … the afternoon meditation of the insects at the store's veranda. Ma Gor Bai had taught me how to trap vibrations between my tongue and pallet like a throat hum from the heart trapped in the high ceiling of the jamat khana. She had taught me how to meditate like the bee.

One afternoon Ole Lekakeny teaches me how to compose a Maasai bead pattern. His name, Ole Lekakeny, means dawn, for he was born when the colours of the sky were pure.

"This is the first composition of beads. It's called keri," says Ole Lekakeny stretching his arm down to pick beads from the box he keeps by his feet. "These tuntai beads in the shop come in four colours of red, white, yellow, and black. These beads compose keri, the only pattern that we make in the shop."

He shows me a cluster of shining olive shaped beads in his hollowed palm. I see the four colours of yoogs, the four cycles of human civilization – red, white, yellow, black in Ole Lekakeny's open palm. They buzz in my eyes like the meditation hum of the bee at the ceiling.

"The pattern is made in two tones, one dark and one bright. Hivi, it is so, the pattern keri. Black of charred wood with white of milk, or black with deep blood red, or black with sun yellow – that's how it goes. Hivi, it is so. The pattern keri." Then Ole Lekakeny tenses a piece of wire and straightens it as he continues to speak, "That's how the story of life goes. Sometimes there is love, and sometimes hate. Sometimes happiness and sometimes unhappiness. See how the sky reads the feelings of the land in tones of the clouds that pattern joy and sorrow. There are white clouds and black clouds in the sky. Black clouds bring us hope for life – rain, and rain brings green grass for our cows. Black brings us abundance. Black God is abundance – *Enkai Narok!*"

I listen with my eyes absorbed in the gaze of the four tuntai colours nested in his palm. I feel a sensation descending to my fingers. I want to touch the beads. But the old man is looping a stiff wire around my chair's armrest.

"Thread the tuntai beads into this wire. I have cut it to the size of a neck ring," Ole Lekakeny speaks while arranging the beads in three lines of white, red and yellow on the short one foot by one foot square table before me. In-between each line he places a line of black beads. I watch his fingers as he puts the beads together. How his fingers and eyes are one. I look at his eyes picking the colours in his finger pinch and I see how the affection in his gaze repeats in the care of his fingers. He works so ardently that his feelings for the beads come to me. Exhilaration captures me such as the one that comes from a long awaited expectation of conceiving a child. The pattern buzzes like bees at the ceiling. My sight meditation merges with the sound of tuntai bead colours. I hear their heart beat in the rhythm of bright-dark--bright-dark--bright-dark, making the pattern keri as I would in zari, making a floret to the rhythm of light and shadow on the bandhani.

"It is also the pattern of the leopard of the savannah and the mountain we call Ol Donyo Keri that you call Mt Kenya.

This is the land of patterns. Like ostrich patterns. Our neighbours, who cultivate on the other side of Mt Kenya hurting the land with iron tools, call the same mountain Kiima-ki-nyaa, meaning the Ostrich Mountain. They see the snow and rock on the mountain like feathers on the ostrich. White men learned from them to say Ki-nyaa and now they call the land Kenya."

Then Ole Lekakeny stands to arrange the strings of beads on the rack on the veranda. He opens a banana leaf packet and takes a swift sniff of tobacco, pushing a pinch of snuff pressed between his fingers far into his nose until his nostrils swell standing horizontal on his lips. He looks aside over his shoulder, head down and brings up a sneeze, and wipes his nose with the back of his hand feeling a relief.

"The time of marriage is the rite of passage of the pattern keri. Because there will be good days and bad days to come like the bright and dark sides of the mountain, Ol Donyo Keri. Like the colours of the clouds in the sky. That is the pattern of how life is." I listen, and then I nod. That is also how a good storyteller tells the story, in words that echo light in darkness and darkness in light, moments of joy in days of sorrow, and moments of sorrow in days of joy. Just as how an embroiderer creates her embroidery in bright and dark spaces on the bandhani and a bead maker the necklace.

I select the colours of tuntai beads under the teacher eyes of Ole Lekakeny, as I would pick embroidery threads under Ma Gor Bai's teacher eyes. I thread the beads one into one as I would a stitch, one into one. Seeing me thus engrossed with beads, Ole Lekakeny tells me the story of origin of the Maasai in the colours of the land and the sky:

"The Maasai descended from the blue depth of the sky into the dark depth of the Valley of Keri-o. And then we climbed out of it on a tree of peace." Elder Ole Lekakeny speaks as he works the beads. His lopped ears carrying lumped copper weights sway as he speaks.

I can see in his heart that he is pleased, for he sees the feelings coming to the light in my eyes that my tongue cannot shape into words.

"When you want to tell a story in Maasai, you say *a-inos enk-atini*, that is to say 'eat a story.' Listen to my story like how a Maasai listens to a story. Eat it and absorb its flavours into your body until it fills you and nourishes you the way grass nourishes the cows, makes them healthy and happy and their udders heavy. A good story is nourishment for the body of your community. Eat it well. Chew it well. Regurgitate it like a recitation in repetition. We descended with our cattle into this patterned landscape of this country called Kenya, whose geography of mountains, valleys and waters, we say, is the Ornament of the Creator."

"When did the Maasai start to make bead patterns?" I ask. This is my first question to the old man. I spoke so spontaneously that it surprised me. Such questions that hang on the tip of your tongue do not wait for the mind to say when to ask.

Ole Lekakeny does not reply. The pause makes me feel uncomfortable. Should I have asked? Ole Lekakeny begins sniffing ground tobacco in long drawn inhales. The sharp smell of raw tobacco fills the air and enters me. The snuff feels assuring, it brings a comfort I cannot explain … like the comfort of being near an old person. Like a grandparent. The smell on Dadabapa. The smell on Ma Gor Bai.

Then finally, Ole Lekakeny replies with a firm, "Always."

"How do you know?" I dare to ask again encouraged by the tone in the old man's response.

"When you are a child and you listen to your grandmother Koko tell you the story of origin of man and colours, you hear her heart not her words. And you see a picture inside her. Then you begin to understand the meaning under her tongue. It's the picture in her feelings that she wants to give you, not the words she speaks. Words without picture feelings are empty of meaning in a story. It's such a sense I had that said to me the story had always been with me like the spirits of my ancestors," replies the old man. "The story comes to us from our feelings in the colours of the land and animals, and it lives with us like our breath. Like life, the cows are in movement in search of pastures. Wherever they go, their shadows follow them between shafts of sunlight at their feet. But they are one herd.

We know our mountains and rocks by their colours, and we know the kinship of the cows, the zebra, the leopard, and all the animals of the savannah, with man by the patterns of light and shadow on them. We know God by the colours of his body. When he shows us his face in red and black he makes himself known to us. We are descendants from one homestead of bright and dark colours. We are descendants from one homestead of the pattern keri of the rock of Mt Kenya. We are the colours of the mystery of day and night, of ups and downs of life. We are the colours of light and darkness, of rain and drought. We are the colours of the emankeeki, the necklace."

When I bathe in the evenings, Ole Lekakeny's words touch my thoughts. I watch the old man working vigilantly, following his articulate fingers pricking each bead in the eye and threading it through the string. The warmth of water from the kopo cascades down my hair to the waist in black latticed mantle. I am a young woman. My breasts are firm. How deep are the thoughts that the sensations of warm water bring to me! For a moment, I live in a world of seclusion of my thoughts in the embrace of water, away from the demanding husband and harassment of my mother-in-law. In this moment of seclusion in warm comfort, I seek beauty, remembering the beads throbbing colours like the belly of the river frog, breathing and alive.

There is freedom in my heart when I imagine the afternoon, beads flowing through my fingers, my heart listening to lyrics of Ole Lekakeny explaining the emankeeki and the origin of colours and man. He reminds me so much of Dadabapa singing the Das Avatar and how God came to be fish and an animal before becoming a man. Dadabapa also told me stories of how we came to Africa, cramped in a wooden craft in the company of crows and the black ocean breeze. That's when his mind was sick with malaria. Ma Gor Bai let us sleep in the courtyard with Dadabapa when in February, Nairobi nights were crisp, dry and warm, and there were no mosquitoes in the air. During this, season of in-between the short and long rains that we called the spell that parched the throat, she would line surma dust into our eyes to cool them. My eyes would smart, and then I would feel the coolness seep into my eyeballs, tired by the day's yellow glare and stained red because of rubbing to relieve the itch of the invisible dust. I would nudge my sleepy head into Dadabapa's palothi lap and stretch my legs out on the stringed bed to sleep.

Dadabapa would tell us to watch the moon in the cloudless Nairobi sky and listen to our breath. Like a song, he would narrate the saga of the first crossing in the dhow. He would say how the immigrants watched the moon over the ocean at night as they sang and told stories of where they came from. And he would be gentle, moving our heads backwards and forwards on his rocking lap. We stared at the moon floating in the melody of the black ocean swaying the dhow back and forth in inhales and exhales of our breath. I would hear the hiss of the sea's breath, in-out, and I would strain to listen to the song between sleep and dream in my ears. Listening to Ole Lekakeny as I gazed into the beads in his palm pulling in the colours from the sky, mountains, animals of the wild, and epic tales, was like that too, a song between sleep and dream.

40

Losing my Name

It is the evening of another new moon in Nairowua. The evening we call chandraat – chand is the moon and raat, night in Gujarati. As usual, as on every evening when we come back home from the jamat khana, Ma Jena Bai, her daughter Zarina, and I enter the kitchen immediately to prepare dinner.

Ma looks directly in my eyes and says, abruptly and authoritatively, "It's the beginning of the new month today. You must forget Nairobi. All that is in the past. You have a new life and a new family now. Your name will be Moti Bai from now." My eyes widen and my lips part. Sass continues to say, "You are now one of the Devji family and you will maintain the Devji family honour as Moti Bai, my daughter-in-law. I expect a son from you soon. Do not waste time. You are fortunate to marry into this honourable family. Outside the house, you will always cover your head and screen your face with your pachedi in laaj, and no latka-girlish-perks before the elders. Like your friend Zera Bai. In fact, not before anyone. You can now remove this old bangle. Give it

323

to me for safekeeping. I will give you two new bangles, the Devji family ones. Married women should have two bangles. One on each hand." Ma leaves the kitchen with my mother's red gold bangle and comes back with a pair of yellow gold bangles that together are half the weight of my one bangle. Then she says, "I will make two new long faaraks for you for the jamat khana. I have saved some good tough cotton cloth from hamali the pushcart hawker. Your kismet has opened up marrying Haiderali," she reminds me. "I will give you two of my old dresses for the house. I don't wear them any more. Too tight to bend over to make chapattis, you know, at the stomach."

It was past midnight and I was in deep sleep. "Moti! Moti wake up! I am thirsty," calls Haiderali, sitting naked to the waist on the bed. He startles me, calling me Moti. I get up with a start, wide-open eyes, and without a thought walk to the courtyard and into the drizzle to fetch water from the clay pot. It is pitch dark, so thick that I thought I would hit my face on the black pane. I take my direction from the blinking glow of coal in the samavat. I wish I could walk on through the drizzle and the dark out of the courtyard into the savannah. To the freedom of the grass in its inviting openness. The walk is demanding me to come into the fathomless black. I want to ask the earth, *Wasikia - Do you hear? Do you feel what I feel?*

"Ma took my bangle, Haidu!" I burst out sobbing when I return. "Tell her to give it back to me, Haidu."

Haiderali ignores me, drinks the water, turns around and quickly falls asleep, snoring lightly. I feel like hitting him with the empty glass by the bedside. I lay awake and inch away from his sweaty warmth to the edge of the bed. My wet hair, warmed by my body heat, presses down humid into the pillow. It becomes tepid, and then goes cold. I begin to shiver. I do not get up to dry my hair though I am shaking sporadically. Instead, I turn over the pillow and pull the quilt over my head, tightly like a pachedi, and press the cold in. I pull up my knees snug on my abdomen and into its warmth. I think of Hawa sleeping on the kitchen mat like an embryo in the mother's belly. The marriage has stolen the dhingly doll in me dancing to the filmi song, 'Come and get me if you can.' The marriage has stolen the photograph of my betrothed in the English sports jacket in my lap. I turn my face towards Saheb's picture on the wall. I cannot see it in the dark but I imagine the beauty in his face and that is peace. I keep my eyes fixed there where his face is in the space on the night's velvet.

I have been coming to the shop every afternoon except on Sunday now for over three months. Each afternoon I watch Ole Lekakeny work with beads. He holds a bead between two fingertips and passes a sewing needle through the eye. I watch him and feel the zari thread between my fingertips passing through the eye of the needle. Ma Gor Bai's words ring in my ears, "Sakina, let zari glitter in the shadows of velvet. Darn dark threads amid the sparkle to flame the cloth. Life has some blissful days and some, which are sorrowful. But there is always hope in the floret that glows in darkness." That glow is fragrance to the eye. I long to be there in the walk of the paradise, my artwork, when they try to make a new person I am not. Sometimes I ask myself, "Am I a woman imprisoned in a girl's imagination?" Sometimes I doubt myself, "When will I grow up?" The despondency chokes me. Like the avian scavenger of the savannah, I fly away into sight meditation far up in the sky, where the Maasai were born, not touching the ground. Life will always be a pattern of joy and sorrow, light and dark, like the pattern called keri that cloaks Mt Kenya and the leopard too. I dig my face deeper into the pillow, listen to the story of the origin of colours in my head, and allow it to darn the fabric of my broken life. I want to eat the colours of the sky and land in the story of beads.

41

Kini and Ntinti

From the shop's veranda, I watch the weaverbirds at the acacia grove while my fingers pick out the olive tuntai from pinhead saen beads. The beads need to be placed in measures of soda bottle tops, first by their shapes and sizes, then by their colours. A light drizzle sweeps by with the cold wind lisping shukhar from the south and leaving a million sun sparkles on the trees across the red muddy road. Within its foliage, the weaverbirds droop vertical from their ball nests like yellow marigolds, like the garland on Saheb's picture in our jamat khana on Temple Road. How I wish I were a yellow weaverbird sheltered in the copse of the Ol-debbei men trees! Ole Lekakeny gathers his blanket over his right shoulder and throws the end over his left shoulder so that it sits like a muffler around his neck while the rest sags loosely over his seated body. I pull my pachedi tighter, twice around me. In August, it can still be cold in Nairowua when the wind blows onto the veranda where we sit.

Housework and cooking exhaust me because of the monotony of movements of the body and that hurts, not work. I am not lazy. Washing clothes and standing for the next hour ironing clothes breaks my back. But I do not complain. I move the chair on the veranda at an angle to let the afternoon sun fall on the side of my face. Sunlight filters through Ol-debbei acacia across the red muddy road, brightens one side of its milk dappled red-brown bark and exposes white thorns in V shaped pairs hidden among feathery foliage, the colour of fresh lime. I watch how the man tree nurtures the birds and bees of the savannah as a father would. I watch how they live in harmony on the tree like a family.

The sun warms my cheeks and fills the hollows of my tired eyes. The chair on the veranda is my home, my own quiet place to myself. It is an old wooden frame of a once snug armchair that Haiderali bought at a house sale at the Greek coffee plantation. Now a cotton pillow at the back and another to sit on, both discarded from Ma's bedroom, substitute as cushioned upholstery. In Nairowua, even my bed is not mine. Ma Gor Bai and Meethi Bai did not tell me that. When I am seated on the makeshift upholstered armchair, I can be me for the next two hours. I do not have to cook and serve, wash and iron, and be on my toes answering to calls from Haiderali and Ma. I do not have to share my armchair.

A group of young Maasai girls bedecked in layers of beaded neck rings and broad bands from neck to chest pass by the shop every month, or two if the rains are heavy. They climb up the granite stone steps onto the cemented veranda to look at the bead display that Ole Lekakeny and I set up each morning. The girls take my thoughts to how I used to walk with my friends and cousin-sister in Nairobi. I often wonder about their lives in marriage. How we walked hand in hand from Government Road down Ngara Road. Then we turned into Moti Bazaar on the right before the bridge, climbed up to River Road, and then to Victoria Street where at the jamat khana corner we would buy bhajia with tamarind sauce from Ruchuru's Ismailia Hotel. With the bhajia neatly wrapped in *Africa Samachar*, we would go to the Rani Bagh. While having a picnic at the foot of rani's statue, the boys from the religion school would appear as expected and hoped for. Though not an arranged meeting, it would appear to be so because when one of them spotted us, he would let the rest know. While sitting at a distance, the boys would whistle some romantic filmi tunes, say our names in catcalls and even sing a filmi song. We would giggle, steal glances at them and guess who was who in the group while pretending we do not hear them.

Two in the group of Maasai girls are relatives of Ole Lekakeny. Every time they come, the first thing they do is to respectfully walk up to Ole Lekakeny and bow their heads. The girls are between twelve and fourteen years old in my estimation. In the sunlight, their shaven heads shine of red ochre mixed with sheep fat. They have anklets made of star grass. That is custom of Maasai brides. They are blessed and they would bring blessings of plentiful grass and peace to all on Earth where their steps fall. Elder Ole Lekakeny places his hand on the girls' heads accepting their greetings. Then he blesses them with prosperity and children. The girls give him milk in long oval gourds with leather covers decorated with sampu bead patterns.

Every time I marvel at the wreaths of beads around the girls' necks and their bead embroidered olkila skin skirts. Often I wonder how they made such striking patterns as I watch them talk with Ole Lekakeny with eyes lowered. In my heart, I wish I could work with bead embroidery on leather like how the young Maasai women do.

After one more visit from the girls, I cannot refrain any longer and ask Ole Lekakeny about his visitors. I look at him to catch his eyes. The old man does not raise his head or show surprise or interest, as if he were expecting the question. In fact, now that I think about it, Ole Lekakeny was aware of my curious eyes observing the girls.

"Who are these girls?" I ask.

He does not answer for a while, letting me know it's not polite to ask an elder about his visitor. While I wait, I watch the sparse leafed Ol-debbei acacia branches stoop low, burdened with avian families. The boughs move in the afternoon stillness penetrated by the cold breeze. As I watch, I sway with the yellow weaverbirds.

"They come from distant homesteads on the plains of the dry lake in the shadow of the White Mountain where Seneeta stays," says Ole Lekakeny. "They belong to the age group of other girls with whom they come to the town. Nine months ago, this age group healed from circumcision and came out of seclusion from the Black Forest. Now they are women and married." As he speaks, Ole Lekakeny pours equal amounts of beads from the English jam bottle into three chipped cups with broken handles that Ma had discarded from the kitchen. The rest, he then arranges in soda bottle top size heaps by the side. Having organized his table for work, he continues to say, "Their names are Kini and Ntinti, and they belong to my mother's lineage. I am their great uncle and therefore, also their father. You see they bring me fresh milk of their cows." Ole Lekakeny looks at me, "They are of your age group. You are sisters and friends when you share the same time of marriage into womanhood. The bond of your marriage time and birth time of your husbands are strong." There is a longing in my heart to be with the age group of fellow women friends, sisters, walkers of the savannah, with whom I share the times of marriage and birth of our husbands, and therefore also the two doorways of life of a woman.

"Mzee," I address Ole Lekakeny with respect, "tell me how long does it take to walk across the plains from their homesteads to come to Nairowua?"

"Three days on foot."

"Three days on foot is very tiring!"

"Not on the savannah where the walk is a song. You walk to the rhythm of your heart, and that's the Earth's pulse. They are one. You are sad when you stop walking, and when you stop hearing the pulse of the Earth. The pulse is keri: black white - black - white - black – white - black, 1 2 - 1 2 - 1 2. You are sad when you do not hear the pulse of keri anymore in nature."

"Is there no other transport?"

"Sometimes they come with Seneeta, and they come before the spit spat at sunrise dries up. Bwana Haiderali keeps Seneeta's guns locked in the back store. They talk like friends. They talk about hunting."

I listen while picking up saen beads one at a time through the eye with a needle, not aware of the frown on Ole Lekakeny's face. I have heard of Seneeta, the stout white man with a beard who comes to the store to keep his tall hunting guns in the vault for safety.

"White men hunt animals for pleasure. That is strange to the Maasai," says Ole Lekakeny. He studies my expression because I am puzzled. He pauses to look at me. He reflects and then talks under his breath. I listen. "We say the land is God's skin. The silent ones who tread on God's skin are one with him." Ole Lekakeny speaks softly stopping in-between his breath. I want to say I understand what he means just to please him but I hesitate. I heard Haiderali talking to Kabir about planning a hunting safari over the weekend. I imagine guns, bullets, blood from fresh red meat dripping over open campfire and a crateful of Tusker beer. I keep quiet. Ole Lekakeny does not speak any more.

After a while, I feel uncomfortable because of the silence. "Where do Kini and Ntinti eat and sleep on their journey here?" I ask.

"At the homesteads of their clan relatives and age group friends. The pathways of kinship and age group families across the savannah are wide and they thread our lives as beads thread the necklace. Many belong to my mother's lineage on this side of the White Mountain. They are my blood."

"Are they sisters?"

"Kini and Ntinti are sisters as daughters of half-brothers, both married to the sons of the seer Ole Lenana. Kini is married to the son by his third wife of the Red Cow, and Ntinti to the son of his fourth wife of the Black Cow. Their husbands also belong to the same circumcision age group, so they are brothers two times over." Ole Lekakeny appears to be pleased to tell me about his family.

"I would like to meet them when they come next time," I say. I long for the companionship of women of my own peer group. We are speaking softly. That is respect.

"They will be happy. They ask me who the woman is with a winking nose, who watches, but does not greet them. I tell them you are a good woman, wife of Bwana Haiderali, and your husbands are age mates." Ole Lekakeny had noticed Indian women did not greet strangers, even their own kind, if they did not know them. He did not try to explain that Kini and Ntinti wanted to be greeted by me first. In Africa, one must greet all around you, men, women and children, even a new born baby. That is custom.

That evening in the privacy of our bedroom, I tell Haiderali about my conversation with Ole Lekakeny about hunting. Haiderali is more interested in getting into the bed and reading *Chakram*, his monthly magazine of jokes, but he does make a quick remark as he turns the pages. "The Maasai only eat the animals at their homestead. Don't you know that? That's why the world's largest numbers of wild animals are in Maasailand. One day I will take you to the Mara and Serengeti." Then suddenly as if moved by a vision, Haiderali puts *Chakram* down half opened on his bare chest and looks at me, "Imagine God's country, the Serengeti, where man and his animals, and the free animals live together in an ancient caldera. Where the blue wildebeest roves." My mind wanders over the grass plains of the Mara and into Serengeti's caldera. I am walking with Kini and Ntinti. We are three specks of red in the vastness of creation, like the herder I saw in the distance from the Nairobi to Nairowua road that brought me here when I was a bride.

42

Talking Colours

I walk slowly and deliberately to the courtyard and pour a glass of water from the clay pot for Haiderali for the night. I want to enjoy the night's breeze, feel it on my face, and listen to the sounds of the animals of the night. "My last chore for the day," I sigh. I am feeling more tired than usual but do not have a desire to go into the shared bed. I hear a lion roar at a great distance in Tanganyika, across the border. I wish to be alone and away in my chair on the veranda, and left to slumber listening to the sounds of solitude of the savannah at night. I stay in the courtyard as long as I can, feeling the night air and watching the night sky. A flood of sparkles cross the sky. See how Askari Bakari's crescent moon patterns make a canopy above me!

"Moti Bai!" calls Haiderali. "Switch off the light. I want to sleep. Where is the water?" I am awakened and thrown out of my dreaming with the stars.

A month passes by before Kini and Ntinti are again at the shop talking to Ole Lekakeny while also stealing looks at me. Beaded emankeeki necklaces sit on their shoulders, two identical chest collars in patterned colours, far larger than any other adornment on them. Ole Lekakeny calls it 'Kenya Bus' because of the emankeeki's size, and teases his blushing nieces who he calls his daughters. Short rains have ended, and the sun is a soft dazzle in the overcast sky.

The girls come to me smiling broadly and they are not shy. I touch their adornments and olkila skirt, turning the hem side over to see how the stitches are done and how the beads are attached to the calfskin. My curiosity makes the girls chuckle, and they talk excitedly to each other. I wonder what they are saying? I think they are saying something about me.

Kini and Ntinti feel confident enough to tap my nose siri with one finger, one after the other, and they giggle. "She has a winking nose," I think they tell Ole Lekakeny.

On their next visit to Nairowua, Kini and Ntinti first greet Ole Lekakeny. I am standing at the glass counter looking in their direction and observing the girls who do not look up to the elder when they speak to him. That is custom. I feel tired that afternoon. "It's the heat," I say to myself as I walk to my chair and sit down. "We are talking about the weather and enquiring about the health of people and animals," says Ole Lekakeny to me. As Kini and Ntinti turn towards me, their expressions change. They look up and they are smiling together like twins.

"May I touch your ornaments?" I ask. I feel the texture of Kini's beads. Tactile beads.

"Emankeeki. Talking colours," says Kini, touching her beaded collar.

"Do you hear the colours talk?" asks Ole Lekakeny.

"Emankeeki. Talking colours," I repeat as I begin to count the lines on the emankeeki by each colour, white red blue -

335

white red blue, 1 2 3 - 1 2 3. I wonder how many beads are threaded into the stiffened wire rings to make the emankeeki of a size that one can put on over the head through to the neck to sit on the shoulders?

"Would you like a beautiful neck like this?" asks Ntinti. Ole Lekakeny sees I am undecided, so he comes closer and says, "The head obeys the neck but does not know. Adorn the neck and the head thinks itself beautiful."

"Look at my emankeeki," says Kini as she throws her chest up with a swift thrust. Her neck ring, the entire splendour of colours resting on her shoulders, jumps up.

"Look at my emankeeki" says Ntinti. She tosses her beads up from her shoulder blades. I notice Ntinti' emankeeki is of exactly the same pattern as Kini's. Its richness fills my eyes. The colours warm my heart.

"Sidai! So perfectly beautiful!" says Ole Lekakeny. "The emankeeki pattern is one in the *muain sidain* art of making beauty in colours. Muain sidain has many arrangements in colours that please the eye. The pattern keri is one. Muain sidain is sidai, so perfect that God is jealous and schemes how to be a woman." He laughs, which is rare for an elder before not only women, but also a much younger age group than his own.

Kini and Ntinti blush together, spreading their catchy joy into our hearts. Ntinti steps forward and flips her emankeeki up with a thrust of her shoulders three times while making sonorous sounds from the throat. Kini does the same. Each time the emankeeki jumps up a little higher and the third time, it touches her chin. The two young women then toss up their emankeeki in unison and make sounds from the throat like short exhaling snores in harmony. Soon a rhythm develops

336

and they fill the space between the rise and fall of the emankeeki with song words, while also bending their knees with the tempo. They dance standing on one spot.

It is a mesmerising blend of musical words, echoed in a droning guttural gruff, coarse clatter and rasp of glass beads thrown up and falling on more glass beads. The bending of the knees suggesting the rustle of skin skirts and clinking metal anklets on thumping feet. All reverberating the sound of the two emankeekis talking on their chests, colours talking, dancing, and together making a melody.

Saen beads colours five
Sun red milk white sky blue and fire orange, grass is green
Tuntai beads colours four
One dark as night one bright as day

A cold shiver grips my body for a split moment as I watch Kini and Ntinti, a pair in such complete harmony in the rhythmic movement of their bodies, song, and rasping beads. I stand entranced. Their song is absorbed into their own spectacle, the upward thrust of emankeeki, the quake of the body and pulsation set by words, and measured in deep throat rumbles. The grating of the beads again. The chord of the separate components of the dance coming together. Ole Lekakeny's eyes brighten; otherwise, he does not say or show any feeling of pleasure.

Before they leave the store, Kini and Ntinti ask me again, "Do you wish an emankeeki for yourself?" The expression on my face tells them I would like an emankeeki like theirs. They need not ask again. "We will make one for you," Kini says. "Keep the beads ready. We will come again when the moon is green." Emptiness fills the shop when the two depart as if a warm spirit has passed by, taking away the colours of the afternoon. "Make the neck beautiful, and the head will brag that he is the beautiful one," says Ole Lekakeny when the girls are gone.

"Shall I have an emankeeki?" I am unsure. Again, I ponder about it and then ask Ole Lekakeny, "Shall I? Shall I ask Haiderali if I can have an emankeeki made for myself?"

"That is what women of the age group wish for each other when they make friends. When you share beauty, you share hearts because you share peace. Emankeeki beads are in the likeness of hearts and that is what threads the savannah. It is osotua, the relationship of peace among people." The elder's comment makes me wonder. Ole Lekakeny's expression does not change, but I feel his heart is singing the song of emankeeki:

Saen beads colours five

Sun red, milk white, sky blue, and fire orange, grass green

"Osotua means the gift of relationship. My daughters want to give you the gift of their art, which is the gift of a bond with one of their own womankind." I feel the warmth of tears swell in my eyes and I try to dab them with the tip of my pachedi. "The pattern does not reveal itself quickly. You must know the patterns in the sky, the mountains, and the animals of the grassland first. You must know their rhythms: 1 2 - 1 2 – 1 2 – 1 2 or 1 2 3 - 1 2 3, 1 2 3 – 1 2 3. Then you will see the emankeeki like the Maasai landscape in your mind's eye. When you see yourself a bead in the adornment of God that is the Maasai landscape, then that's when you will know the emankeeki. You will know then, when the beads talk, why beauty is called osotua and osotua is called peace. And why both beauty and peace reside in nature."

43

Beading the Savannah

Two afternoons later, Haiderali comes to the shop and brings down a box of beads from the top shelf in the storage room where Paka Minima lay leisurely with her head and legs stretched, eyes blinking, partly sleeping, partly awake. A litter of five wool balls, black, white and banded black and white, play with her downy tail.

"Why are you being dapandayo – doing things unnecessarily? Is there a need for this extra work?" Haiderali asks more in way of rebuke, telling me I was wasting his time, than to know why I needed the box down. Haiderali does not speak again nor does he help me to open the box of beads. He glances at me, indicating g he has done his part and leaves. Now I can do whatever I need to with the box. Haidu appears not interested. His breath smells of sweet paan chewed over the stubborn tang of Tusker beer. Ole Lekakeny has noticed that Haiderali comes less frequently to the store in the afternoons. He has been observing how Haiderali has been rebuking me by his silence when I want a favour from him, like today, to bring down this box of beads. Ma is not different. They behave as if they have cooked a conspiracy against me. I am not barren. I wish I could hide in the Ol-lerai

339

tree and stay in its canopy whose waft would be its green branches and weft my torments.

"Hodi! Hodi!" A woman's voice comes from the veranda. It is Mama Bisekeli from the white settler's orchard at the foothills of Mount Nairowua. Mama Bisekeli is wearing a maxi skirt of thick grey cotton, an arm length blouse and a broad rimmed straw hat. Every Wednesday during the harvest season, Mama Bisekeli brings peaches to sell to the shopkeepers. The Indian dukawalas are reluctant to purchase her peaches because they say she charges too much. However, they would invite her into their shops hoping to attract white farmers to their stores, and keep in good relations with the otherwise self-segregated race that looks down on the Indians because they rule over them.

"Come in, memsahebu, come in, and come in!" Haiderali waves his arm speaking in English. "Moti Bai, make a cup of tea for Mama Memsahebu." Haiderali turns to me and commands in Gujarati, "Bring your arm chair." Mama Bisekeli puts down her basket and sits down on my chair. She removes her hat and wipes away the sweat on her brow with the napkin that she has over the basket.

"Thank you," she says in Swahili.

"No, no, not to worry. You like tea?" Haiderali asks in English.

"Yes, thank you," she replies in Swahili.

"Not to worry! Hot today, no?" Haiderali asks in English.

"Yes, very hot," Mama Bisekeli replies in Swahili.

"Hot tea good on hot day. Heat cuts heat," says Haiderali in English again. Mama throws a puzzled look at him.

340

When I return with a cup of tea, I find nervous Haiderali smiling and standing over Mama Bisekeli sitting relaxed, laughing without opening her mouth. You could hear her broken laughter that does not go forward out of her throat to move her lips. Her face is both pale white and red, lips stretched to the extreme. She is the spinster daughter of Kaburu Kali, the Boer with an angry look who came with the Grand Trek from South Africa, and who carries a Bible and a gun, quite ostentatiously, wherever he goes. I bend down to select a dozen ripe peaches. Sweet fragrance of freshly picked fruit rises from the basket. Both Haiderali and Mama Bisekeli ignore me. They are talking about lazy African farm labourers. I glance at Ole Lekakeny. He is staring at the beads, looking down and listening.

When I return to the box of beads at the back of the store, I begin to tear open the brown paper packs with my bare hands, clumsily and rudely. Making noise. There are two dozen tightly pressed double lines of strings in each brown paper rolled pack from Czechoslovakia. Remembering the emankeeki colours of saen beads is overwhelming because of the sheer variety and great number of beads in the box. Mama Bisekeli thanks Haiderali for the tea, not me, and she steps down the veranda steps with her basket. She carefully ties the basket to the rack on the back of her bicycle. She smiles at me now as she leaves, as if to say goodbye, and then at Ole Lekakeny like a man to a woman. In Africa, white women wear trousers, and act like men to other women, and above men, black and brown.

"I wish to learn the colours of the emankeeki when we prepare the beads for Kini and Ntinti," I tell Ole Lekakeny with hesitation. Should I, or should I not ask the favour? Haiderali brushes by me, upset because Mama Bisekeli interrupted his afternoon nap. It's not my fault, I want to say, and ignore him as he steps into the courtyard, swollen faced, on his way to the bedroom.

"First listen to the colours. Then put them inside you. Place one string each of white, red, and blue, in that order at the corner there." Ole Lekakeny points to a space on the floor below the window. I sweep the grey cement floor at the corner and lay one strand each of white, red, and blue in that order.

"Now listen to the numbers. One string of white ... to three strings of red... to one string of blue." Ole Lekakeny speaks in a rhythmic sentence. I lay the strings accordingly.

"White red blue, 1 2 3 – 1 2 3," says the old man, my teacher.

"From here the numbers reverse like this. Three strings of white ... to one string of red...to three strings of blue." I feel unsure, but nonetheless, fetch more beads from the box and expand the lines on the ground. This is a different way of seeing bead art from the zari embroidery I am used to. I try to feel the textures and colours of beads in strings to know them. With my fingertips, I feel the smooth roundness of shapes and holes in the white, red, and blue beads. The weight of a string of beads in my hand is light, like a third of the weight of my wooden tasbih. The sensation of colours resting on my palms touches me tenderly. The hand's knowledge of beadwork is different from embroidery, yet there is a common feeling in the eye with zariwork. I feel the pulsations in this patterned bead art as I do in the silver thread of zari, but I cannot shape them in words. A zari rosette is created stitch by stitch at the tips of three fingers, the eye and the heart. The emankeeki is created bead by bead with the tips of three fingers, the eye and

342

the heart too. My fingers move with the throb of my heart. They are the silent hums in unison vibrations, as if they were the raga of colours. The sensation is bodily, a divinity that grows in the heart not said in words.

"That is good," Ole Lekakeny assures me. "Now place one strand of orange after the three of blue. See the landscape in your mind's eye. See the dawn breaking through the crest of acacia." I lay the strings accordingly and try to imagine the sunrise over the savannah, her trees, mountains, birds, and the blue sky.

"I must write this down so I do not forget," I tell myself tearing off a corner of *Africa Samachar* and producing a butt of a pencil from beneath the flattened pillow on my armchair. I think about how I made my first stitches, joining dot to dot on a piece of merikani that opened up a whole world of art to me. At first, Ma Gor Bai pencilled the dots far apart after every two-finger widths. Then she measured the space between the dots with the index of her little finger and the dots came closer. Next, half an index apart, and when I had accomplished connecting the pencilled points, she marked the specks a pinhead apart - dot, dot, dot. She gave me threads: red, blue, orange, and green. I made one line each of red, blue, orange, and green. Then I made double lines of red, blue, orange, and green. Little by little, I felt like I was bringing the rainbow from the sky down to my lap.

"I want zari," I would complain when I was six, wishing now to catch the moon and stars with silver threads into stitches of my own.

"Not yet," Ma Gor Bai would reply, "your stitches are still raw. You will waste zari."

As Ole Lekakeny speaks, I begin to write in the margin of the newspaper *Africa Samachar*.

1 string white

3 strings red

1 string blue

I draw a line here before continuing to write. "Now I must reverse the numbers."

3 strings white

1 string red

3 strings blue

I draw another line and then begin to write again, when Ole Lekakeny notices me putting down the words as he speaks. "Do not put away the words from the mouth into the paper. Keep them in your ears. The ears and eyes are in one head. They tell each other. They help to keep words in your body." I stop writing.

1 string orange

"This is half the *omuatat* pattern of emankeeki," says Ole Lekakeny.

My eyes widen, looking at him, "Only half? This is so complicated. Let's continue tomorrow with the other half."

Ole Lekakeny's eyes smile when he says to me, "It's not difficult. Now repeat the half pattern, except replace the orange string in the last line with a green one. That's all."

I take time studying the first half pattern. Then I complete the configuration in sequence of their colour numbers that make the second half, though I am not sure what I am doing. Taking a step back to view my composition from the top, I stand looking down on the emankeeki like a bird, and gasp at its eloquence of colours.

"The colours vibrate. They seem to speak to each other," I say quietly to myself. Then I say aloud, "Look, it's a prayer in colours!"

"Sidai! Good! You have now made the omuatat pattern of emankeeki. You have learned one bead paragraph of eye knowledge to read. Today you have made osotua of friendship with your age mates. Tomorrow afternoon we shall continue." Ole Lekakeny is pleased. "With this you have also forged osotua with the land. You can now walk the rainbow that connects the horizons. That's divinity, that's beauty, that's peace. It stirs the divine in the body when colour is itself the divine." He pauses before saying, "Watch the sky at dusk and dawn, at the time of worship when it is quiet. See how the crimson red of the sun in white strips of clouds stands closing the gap in the blue. That is omuatat, the prayer beads."

44

What did Gandhi say about Art?

The next afternoon, Ole Lekakeny is standing at the corner of the cement floor below the store's window. He has stencilled fourteen concentric circles with a white stone. He says the innermost circle is an inch bigger in diameter than my head. I am astounded by the precision with which Ole Lekakeny has drawn the circles, like art of a secret prayer ritual described in mysterious orbs. He judges the dimensions with his eyes, without an instrument. Then he draws lines, a pinhead apart, making circles. His hand holds the memory of beads, colours, and patterns like a long prayer chant.

Next morning when Ma notices circles on the floor below the window, her face contorts disdainfully, even before she greets Ole Lekakeny. "What is that?" she asks pointing at the drawing with her arm stretched out. Ole Lekakeny keeps quiet and continues setting up the racks for the display of beads as he does every morning. He is smiling inside. We both know Ma thinks it is witchcraft. She lives in awe of Ole Lekakeny's knowledge of, if not companionship with, the spirits.

"I am learning to make the emankeeki," I respond and then quickly add, "Haiderali says it is all right." I had come to sweep the shop floor that was one of my morning chores after preparing breakfast.

Ma shows she feels relieved with a sigh and an exhale. Her old face softens. She thinks for a while before sitting down. "Well, it's alright, I suppose, to make one, maybe, but don't wear it. In our family, we do not wear fake beads … only real ones and gold."

In the afternoons when I am alone with Ole Lekakeny, while Ma and Haiderali are having a nap, I add a line or two more of beads over Ole Lekakeny's drawing of the emankeeki circles on the floor. There are so many saen pinhead beads that it's impossible to count them. Ole Lekakeny shows me how to know the quality of beads required for each colour segment in fist sizes. Red, white, and blue beads are measured by full fists, while the green and orange go by half closed fists. I spread newspapers around the lines of loose bead strands so no one would walk over them. Each day, at the end of the afternoon, the floor mosaic grows bigger and brighter, and each morning, Ma looks at it before she sits down and shakes her head, but does not say anything anymore. Haiderali and Kabir see the emankeeki prototype on the floor, and on their perplexed faces I read, "What is she doing?"

"It looks perfect. Just like the way *they* make it," says Haiderali every time he looks at the beads on the floor. But I know in my heart, he is neither impressed nor will he ever be interested, even if I put it on. Kabir does not comment, but it is obvious that he does not appreciate it either.

"It takes too many beads to make the emankeeki of that size. They are expensive, these Jekosalavika beads. Make a smaller size," suggests Ma, "after all, all you need is a sample, not one to put on."

"Emankeeki of this pattern is only in one size, the size that fits through from the top of my head," I answer, gathering courage, something I have not done before.

"Maybe you can try to make *it* half the size. After all, it's all repeated patterns," comments Haiderali.

"It's the given number of repetitions that completes the pattern of emankeeki like all the other patterns of muain sidain," I try to explain in defence if not defiance. "It's like saying half a tasbih. Half a tasbih is not a complete tasbih, though the beads repeat, is it? Each bead of the emankeeki counts even if a repetition. Like the prayer beads, they look alike but each bead needs to be told separately to make a prayer." My sudden burst of eloquence surprises me!

"There are some other cheaper beads that you can also use," suggests Ma.

I keep quiet. Haiderali notices I sulk. His mind has been far away these days. There has been the talk of another war soon. People say the Second World War will bring the end of the world. One afternoon after school, Zarina comes to look at the bead montage. Standing over the patterns she exclaims, "How beautiful! How very beautiful!" I help her with art homework once a week or so, whenever I have time. One day I heard Zarina telling Ma, "You know, Ma, Moti Bai is better than my art teacher." I was elated, but dared not to show it.

"And what did Gandhi-ji say about art? Remember? I told you not to forget!" I ask Zarina.

"All true art is an expression of the soul," she replies with a glint in her eyes.

"Shabash! Well done! But there is more that Gandhi-ji says about art. Do you remember?"

"Real art, therefore, must help the soul to realise the inner self."

"Shabash! You can have my su-kreet sweet from the jamat khana the next chandraat new moon evening."

45

Sampu the Gift of Beauty on a Cow

During the coming days, I fill the remaining empty spaces on the floor circles, drawing with beads according to the colours in combination of the emankeeki as described, sketched, and explained to me by Ole Lekakeny while he showed me the fitting beads in his palm. Then I wait for him to comment and if not to nod his head before I can continue. As I watch over the pattern on the cement floor constructed so precisely bead by bead, by their sizes, shapes, and numbers, the emankeeki comes to life before my eyes. The colours now begin to hum into my ears like Satpanth ragas. They move in circles like the garba dance, 1 2 3 - 1 2 3, white red blue, white red blue. They are so much like colours on the emankeekis of Kini and Ntinti! Exactly.

Ma, however, continues to show her quiet dislike to my floor art. She is also getting impatient because it is taking too long and I am giving too much time to it. Then one day she says to me, "It's like rangoli that we, girls in my village used to make with powder colours." Her eyes brighten and she seems lost as if in a dream. From that day, the hard stillness in her eyes changes to softness such as the one that comes from a distant memory spoken by the look in the eye, not words.

Perhaps my emankeeki created a covert envy in her. She too would like to make one, but it does not become a woman of her age and status in the jamat to work on meaningless art on the floor. They might say it's not serious work when it does not make money. She even stopped me to work on zari embroidery because it was not profitable in Nairowua. "Control the child in you. You are a woman now," she said. When the art in me is stifled, I feel suffocated. Then I steal patterns from the sky, trees, the land, and from whatever I can, wherever my eyes wander. I catch them and I put them in my mind. At night, sitting on the bench under the mango tree in the courtyard, my fingers re-create the patterns on the velvet sky, as Bakari the Askari would, and let the musical colours play in my ears.

"Ma thinks you are wasting time in the afternoons," Haiderali tells me one evening after coming home from the jamat khana. I don't know if what he says is true. Does he say that just to pick a quarrel with me? What have I done now?

"But, Haidu, I also do other work in the shop and make tea for all in the afternoon," I plead in defence.

In response, Haiderali adds, though with some hesitance, "Ma complains about the work that needs to be done in the shop before the coming ceremonies of the Maasai." I feel frustrated because my joy in creating the emankeeki is denied. There is a spirit in me kindled in my childhood that feels silenced by my husband's words. "They are about to start the Dance of the Red Ochre."

To whom could I tell my inside feelings that come like an impulse to create art? I feel I am the emankeeki in the geography of patterns. I feel I am the zebra galloping in the sky. I feel I am the song of the emankeeki. I wish, at that moment, I could fly away in my song with the weaverbirds to Nairobi and be with Ma Gor Bai and Meethi Bai, who would understand why I cannot be kept away from my art. I am so angry that I want to throw the table at Haiderali.

'Have you no mind of your own?' I want to ask Haiderali. 'I too want to be listened to.' I walk out of the room to sit on the bench under the mango tree. Haiderali sees me upset. Baby mangoes like green ping-pong balls look down on me. They have sticky sap as if it were their umbilical fluid from the womb of the mother tree.

"Anyway, complete your emankeeki as soon as you can," Haiderali calls out when he notices my lips pressed together. I do not respond, nor do I feel obliged to because of the favour that he grants me now. He thinks he has all rights over me by marriage.

"I can send a goat to your friends' homesteads," Haiderali says to please me, but I do not reply. At such moments, only the art matters not words that I hear. Thoughts about running away taunt me. The charisma of the night sky stars, land breeze, and the emankeeki call me to come and hide within them. They ask, "Do you hear?" Yes, I hear you but how do I reach you? I hear you but I cannot come to you. I hear you but I cannot touch you. The anger in me wants me to be you, but I am chained to my marriage.

Kini and Ntinti are delighted when they see the draft design on the floor. The three of us pick up tresses of beads, one at a time and put them in five colour coded newspaper packages folded into triangular pockets. Kini and Ntinti talk eagerly about making the emankeeki for me that would be just like their own.

"The emankeeki is for the respect that we give as décor of a woman of cattle wealth. It makes her noble," says Ole Lekakeny after Kini and Ntinti step out of the shop veranda, and start their journey home towards Kilimanjaro carrying the newspaper packages in the folds of their leather clothes. The next afternoon in the store, I ask Ole Lekakeny, "Haiderali thinks we should give your daughters a goat as a gift. Is that appropriate, sawa sawa?"

"Perhaps a calf would be better. Later they can share the milk for their children to come," replies Ole Lekakeny. Then he adds, "A calf with the pattern sampu makes a beautiful gift."

"What is sampu?"

"It's one of the most liked patterns of muain sidain. Sampu is like the ornament that appears naturally on the lucky calf. It's God's gift. It's a pattern of dark lines on a mustard stomach. A natural ornament."

"I will tell Haiderali. But what actually is sampu?"

"Sampu is the most beautiful gift of nature. It's a gift of beauty to the homestead where such calf is born. Sampu cow is adoration. A pattern art that also appears on rocks and trees," replies Ole Lekakeny. He bewilders me and enthrals me in the same way. "A cow of a sampu pattern is a gift of nature's heart. We cherish it for its beauty. I used to sing to my father's sampu cow when I took his cattle to the pastures along the banks of River Nairowua. That was many years ago. I used to sing to her beauty. She was the only one in the herd that carried the gift that God gave my father. A sampu cow is never mistreated, or even slaughtered for food. In fact, just last year, a man speared the white DC because the DC took his sampu cow by force for tax money, and then he sent her to the government slaughterhouse with the rest of the tax cattle. The Maasai was hanged, but the song praising how the warrior died for the love of his sampu cow lives on."

"Can this be true?"

"Yes. So deep is a Maasai's love for beauty of patterned art we call muain sidain."

Months go by. Each time when Kini and Ntinti pass by the shop, they show me how close they have come to completion by measuring the emankeeki on them with an open hand. First, it was about a quarter, then about half, and the last time, almost three quarters already made. I am thrilled. I feel honoured. I feel respected. I feel noble.

Then one day, when they came to let me know that only the final tuntai beads were remaining to close the emankeeki with the pattern keri, Kini asked me if I was carrying a child. She surprised me. "No! Not yet!" I replied quickly. They did not stop smiling while talking between themselves. I could tell from the tone of their voices that they did not believe me. The two girls study my ankles and limbs and talk to each other, nodding their heads as if confirming their suspicion. However, Kini and Ntinti are doing other strange things to me, like touching my hair and saying nothing. Later, Ole Lekakeny tells me that his nieces said they felt that they were touching a zebra's tail on my head. After the girls leave to walk back to their homesteads, I go to the back courtyard to wash the red ochre and animal fat off my hands and hair.

The long rains are over at last and the grass is luxuriant and green from horizon to horizon. Ole Lekakeny says that all his storage gourds are full of maziwa lala that is, sleeping milk. Then one afternoon, he informs me about a message that he received from Kini and Ntinti.

"Your emankeeki is ready," he says, "and you are invited to come to the homestead of Ole Lenana to collect it and also visit them." My eyes widen, as I could hardly contain my joy. I smile inside.

"You smile in your heart like the morning sun behind the clouds," says Ole Lekakeny.

Haiderali arranges for a sampu calf to be delivered to the homestead of Ole Lenana in secret, so Ma would not know about it. I wait anxiously for the response to my gift, but receive no word. When Ole Lekakeny repeats the invitation, I understand it is a response to my gift of the sampu cow. I must visit Kini and Ntinti at their home. I want to see where they live.

I wait a whole week to ask Haiderali when he is happy and singing filmi songs.

"I have been invited by Kini and Ntinti to their homestead. Can we go? When can we go? I have not been past Nairowua. I want to see the land. When is a good time to leave the store? Ole Lekakeny says they stay beyond Seneeta's camp."

"You ask too many questions at once! That's far to travel!" he exclaims.

"Who is Seneeta anyway?"

"A white hunter. In America, they call him Ernest Hemmingway. Here we call him Seneeta, his Maasai name. I keep his guns for him in the iron box at the back of the bead store."

"We can go whenever you have time. My emankeeki is ready to be collected. Both Kini and Ntinti are very heavy now to walk to town anyway. Then they will be busy nursing their babies. It will be some months before they will come to the town again." As I speak, I think of Kini and Ntinti, both pregnant, sitting by the evening fire with their legs stretched out before them. I wonder if they are praying for boys, the way we do. I wonder if they give birth to girls, would their husbands and mothers-in-law be disappointed the way it is among us? I wonder what their mothers-in-law would say if they had only girls?

"I have never been into a Maasai homestead. I want to see Kini and Ntinti at home. Ole Lekakeny would like to come with us to show us the way, and meet his family."

"First, I will ask Ma if it's all right. She does not like to be left alone in the shop. She can come with us."

Haiderali noticed at once that I was quiet. Suddenly, as if hit by a stick, my enthusiasm about going to the homestead dies.

"Perhaps Kabir and Zarina can spend more time in the shop that day," he says indifferently, as he walks to the toilet on the far side of the courtyard.

"Kabir should spend more time in the shop instead of acting like a taxi driver of Mama Bisekeli's sister," I call after him.

He stops and turns around saying, "It's good for business to do favours to the white settlers. He is pulling customers to buy farm tools we have just introduced."

"What favours? What customers? He is smitten by the English girl. Driving her around and showing her off, feeling superior to his friends with fair wives and fiancées ... he has the fairest of them all," I yell back.

"She is so white, so dhori rupadi," Haiderali says on purpose. He makes me burn inside when he talks like that. I am also fair, but not that fair, not English white!

"Dhori toe gatheri bee hoi - even a she-ass is white!" I spit back. The envious black Kali in me is inflamed.

The whole day I imagine the bead pattern on the floor, decoding, deciphering its metrical configuration and counting the beads in sets of colour. However, my body does not respond to the mind's memorizing, parroting and rote learning colours in ratios and combinations. I cannot see the Maasai landscape the way Ole Lekakeny sees the Maasai landscape in the emankeeki. At night, after Haiderali has lain on me, claiming his right, pinning me down with brisk thuds and claps that last a few uncomfortable minutes, I lay awake, sleepless, wounded because my body is stolen from me. I am wide eyed, still stretched out on my back pondering and feeling the cool air over the sweat warmth of sheets. Then my eyes take my body to the emankeeki. It's a windless night. Haiderali leaves the bed, stumbles into his Bata rubber sandals, scuffles to the bench under the mango tree in the courtyard and lights a cigarette. Through the door, left half open by Haiderali, I watch the moonlight at the threshold, too shy to enter. Otherwise, the pitch-black air in the room is so still that everything around me seems timeless, nothing moves, not even time. With my finger, I scratch the pattern of the emankeeki on the black slate of the night. From the multiple lines of the beads, I slip into visions of the bandhani. The raga of the bandhani and then the song of the emankeeki merge in an echo, blurring the two as one. Suddenly, like being lifted up into the air, a sensation comes over me in a moment of a beautiful seizure of my senses. I dissolve into the shine of zari rosettes and the beads begin to gleam. Ragas descend like colours from the sky. Vision of omuatat shimmers in a melody. Colours dance as sounds.

My eyes fill with water. I am in Shiva's creation dance. I am in the eternal song of Das Avatar. Art is my worship. I am the song and the picture divine. The emankeeki swings before me, its rass and the temperament of dance-song-shine-colours-picture divine are one body. Whirling with the wind, I feel the emankeeki's pulse in my own. It speaks to me in colours. I hear its colours in me. Are the colours not inspired by the sky and land that dye God his colours too? It asks. Yes, I hear you. Yes, I feel you in me. Yes, I see now how a bead does a bead. How a musical note does another. I replicate the design in my mind, bead by bead, as I hear it. My fingers move, just the tips. They move on their own, sounding the colours, making a pattern, and tapping to the music of the song-dance of the emankeeki. My hair bristles on my arms. Scalp sweat tinges. I shiver. The pitch-black silence of my brick-wall-thoughts crack. I see the Maasai landscape open up in emankeeki's shimmer at the horizon in colours of omuatat, the dawn in white red blue, a streak of orange, and then the green sliver of grass where Kilimanjaro shades the plains and the sky mirrors the savannah changing hues. The song of the sky, the song of the savannah is the song of emankeeki, all one song that breaks through the solid stillness of the dark into colours, white red blue – orange and green. Colours fill the room over the soundless dark. They buzz over me. The beads are speaking to me. Talking beads, I hear you now, painting pictures in my heart like Koko the grandmother storyteller.

46

God's Mountain and God's House

The road to the homestead of Ole Lenana is rough and it goes into Tanganyika. It passes by where Ol Donyo Lengai, God's Mountain, puffs prayers to the sky and where the car heaves over volcanic dust. The fine dust filters in through the rubber lining of the glass windows as gruelling tyres of our Mini Morris spurs over the road. Arrogant, black and angry, though tiny in the Maasai landscape, the car complains like a protesting child. I fan myself with the school notebook that Haiderali uses to keep an account of mileage and petrol. When I look out of the rolling dust-ball machine's metal shell over me, it's all serene and green. Impala flick their leaf ears at us, twitching in silent gaze. Zebras too gaze at us and graze, and gaze and graze switching their tails like happy puppies.

A sudden jolt of joy, such as the one that strikes a hungry man seeing a feast, fills me. I breathe freedom in the freshness of savannah's early morning air before the grass-warmth rises from underneath when the sun is bright. I am out in the sky country. The patterned sky country. Over the patterned land. My eyes indulge in the infinity of patterns all around me. Haiderali is my filmi actor, my hero of the new, big blue screen and golden grassland. Today, I have him all to myself away from his mother. I am his dhingly doll frolicking like the impala doe around her stud. My thrill exaggerated by the car jogging, sends tingling sensations to my belly. I chuckle inside at the thought of what Ma would have said had she been with us. She would have said, "Stop this thee-thee-thee at once!" I chortle a girlish thee-thee-thee, intentionally, aloud, three times inside. Is it in spiteful defiance as if Ma were here? Maybe. Wherever I go, her presence is there. The taak taak. The chameleon eyes.

"Bhenchod! What pothole is that?" curses Haiderali swerving the car to avoid an opening on the road.

"It's not a pot hole, Haidu, mari jaan – my life! You are going over the Rift Valley! Can you not see?"

"O my stomach! Pirshah! This time I am surely dead!" Haiderali mimics me in girl's voice when the car hops over the next crack in the road.

"Mowla! My intestines are about to burst out!" I add approvingly. He laughs.

Between our mischiefs, I turn around and look at Ole Lekakeny. He sits regal. I am embarrassed. Ole Lekakeny is absorbed looking at the textures on the hills and water in the streams at the pastures of his childhood. Perhaps he is praying while looking up at the snows of Kilimanjaro. They flash in the morning sun as though in response. Haiderali pulls up at a roadside bar kiosk and returns with three brown paper bags.

"Shall I sing a song for my dhingly doll?" asks Haiderali as he hands me one brown bottle while also pointing to the glove compartment where he keeps the opener. I open the Tusker beer bottle for him.

"Yes, my dhinglo doll," I reply avoiding his eyes in mock shyness as Indian actors do.

"So I am your dhinglo, hengh?" Haiderali pretends to look amazed. He laughs. Then he looks at me with slanted man actor eyes in love, suggesting want and domination like a peacock on the screen. He takes time to compose a verse:

Toje hathjo ramakado ayn-a
Hee dhinglo tojo
Kutch jo vir, Khojo ayn-a

I am a toy in your hand
This your boy doll
Man of Kutch, a Khoja am I

The verse in Kutchi both surprises and amuses me. I look back at Haidu with slanted actor eyes in seductive submission. Filmi love, teasing lips, suggestive eyes, evoke Lord Krishna in him. Like the god, he cannot resist courtship. He is my Indian man. My teen girl giggles become uncontrollable and I suck in my cheeks to the teeth until they hurt. We are players in Film India movies. At last, I have found the husband of my childhood dreams.

"Haase teno ghar waase, the one who laughs, furnishes her home," he says. Appropriately said at the time I am making a home and it stirs the woman in me. I want a home and family of my own. I don't want to live in Ma's home. I don't want to cook in her kitchen for my husband and me.

Haidu continues making up verses from filmi melodies in garba tempo, 1 2 3 - 1 2 3, his head moving to the beat, his fingers drumming the steering wheel, his eyes smiling askance, into my feelings. He is a proper filmi actor who knows how to romance, keeping a respectful distance from his lover. Feeling safe, I chuckle aloud now, frisky laughter that I cannot control anymore. The laughter that hurts me in the abdomen. The laughter that gives vent to stuffed anger in me. Haiderali sings more mischief. I imagine him chasing me around flower bushes, my blue sari fluttering in the breeze. Courtships made in haven are enacted on screen. He is the master, the lost lover who filled my youth. I find myself hee-hee-thee-thee-ing in high spirits ready to give myself to the desires of my hero. I feel a woman turning seventeen.

Then, all of a sudden, Haiderali thrusts his left hand across over towards me while steadying the car with his right hand in a tight grip on the steering wheel. At first, I thought he wanted another beer. But no! His hand crawls over me. I freeze instantaneously as I do nowadays whenever I am touched. For a moment, Haiderali's filmi songs deceived me. I thought he would be the proper lover like the singer he was, like the new young Dilip Kumar he would be. But no! The reality of marriage rebukes the girl in me. I was in love with him. Love as it should be. The only love I knew and that lived in his proposal photograph. The man in an English sports jacket. I look out through the window and see a zeal of placid zebra, collectively a raw hairy hide of striped black-white bands. They are a group standing in one pattern that the Maasai call engoiteeko. Engoiteeko is like cloud lines across the sky after the rains have washed away the haze, dust, and the hot air. Then you can smell cool freshness in the air. It's one art in two colours. I yearn to merge into the patterned animal assembly. Into the beauty of the herd so calm and eating. Their collective beauty in one body décor. I want to be the stripes of engoiteeko that move like one wave little by little grazing into the infinity of the savannah.

47

E'sikar

At the homestead of Ole Lenana, we are told, much to my disappointment, that the seer had gone on retreat to Ole Donio Lengai. When junior elders come to greet Haiderali and lead him away to their house, Ole Lekakeny disappears into the house of the senior elders without a word. Only then do I see Kini and Ntinti come dancing and singing, greeting me from afar. I am equally delighted to see them both. I too want to dance and sing for them as they do for me. Three other young women join us, and all together, they escort me like a bride to a house where there are children and an older woman they call Koko. To my astonishment, Koko is the milk woman who came to our back door every morning when I had just arrived in Nairowua! We have not many words to tell each other now as before, but with several handshakes, fingers bending over back palms, consistent smiles, and audible laughter, we greet each other and say in gestures pointing at the other, "I know you," and, "how are you?" and "I know you too," and "also how are you?"

At first sight, the house looked like an oval mud hollow. Its walls are round smoothened by hand plaster, a mix of cow manure and brown earth. Inside, it's dark and cool. A smoky fire produces multiple shadows from a single flame, bobbing like heads of guinea fowl over the grass. My eyes take a little while to adjust to the darkness before I see more of this house where the emankeeki is born. This is where they talk of life in patterns. This is where the song of engoiteeko the zebra is sung when the rains come. This is where the legend of the origin of colours and man lives in one story. This is where geography is threaded in colours of beads. This is home on the savannah.

Air and sunlight stream through a pipe hole in the earth wall. The sun's beam is cloudy, shining like a bicycle headlamp through a fog, and it spots an assortment of milk gourds hooked on a partition screening a bed covered with a patchy brown-white haired cowhide. All around me there is earth smell and mixed smells of cattle manure and rawhide. Sheep fat smells waver in whiffs of smoky wood, hay and red ochre. My eyes smart. I close, tighten, and open them a few more times.

Then Kini puts the emankeeki on me. The beads sit on my beige cotton dress printed with large red flowers. Over my long faraak, I have my pachedi, plain brown colour with a large cotton border. Kini begins to sing. I recognize the melody is of the song she sang with Ntinti in the shop the other day. Other women join the chorus. Smoked curdled milk goes around in a long bead decorated gourd. Everyone sitting in semi-circle around the hearth takes a sip between the song lines, talk and laughter. Their legs are stretched out in front of them facing the fire with their eyes focused on the flame, the only bright spot in the darkness. Kids bleat and some whine in the pen by my side. Koko pats the baby lying by her side and it stops crying. The other baby, on her other side, is asleep.

Koko says the grass that nourishes the cows that nourish the Maasai made the lines of the song of emankeeki. "It's the savannah that beads the emankeeki that gives us the verses to sing and dance," she says in Swahili speaking to me.

Saen beads colours five
Tuntai beads colours four
Rainbow sits on zebra's neck

A resounding guttural chorus surges from the sitting shadows. Kini stands up to the song. "The song of emankeeki is the dance of emankeeki. *A-rany* to sing is *a-rany* to dance in Maasai,"

They begin slow breathing movements in unison, steadily thrusting their shoulders up, chests forwards and back, building to a tempo until their emankeekis jump to touch the chin as if competing whose emankeeki would jump the highest.

Colours of my land are coats of animals
Mountain rock, grass and wood of trees
My universe is she-sky the One Supreme

Three more women stand up, one at a time and join seamlessly into the rhythmic breathing, bending and straightening knees in dance. The unison rasp of toss and fall of several emankeekis on the chests merges into their expirations, becoming audible only in-between husky music from the throat.

Red is Her displeasure, drought and famine
Black, Her beauty, peace and plenty

On hearing the song, some girl children who are playing outside enter the house. They step into the dance imitating the adults lifting their bony shoulders, bare without beads, dropping them, and moving their heads forwards and back like the guinea fowl of the savannah. Little women wanting to be like their mothers.

Tell me the story of origin of colours again
First the man and his wives in houses two
Red and black

I feel the emankeeki on my shoulders with my fingers. It embraces me as if it were a child with arms around me touching my breast to show its want. I feel its colours, waves in rhythm, the body-breath-tempo, rise and fall of the chest. As if it were a lover's warm breath, his firm body on me. The emankeeki is rich in exhibition. It mesmerizes me looking at it stealing the lustre of the hearth's flame. I am bewildered by its smell of the kraal, redolent with burnt Ol-orien wood. Smell of smoked milk and earth, mixed odours of sweaty cow udders and rich grassy manure. I run my fingers over the beads in circles and press the emankeeki to my ears to hear the language of colours of the land.

Deep in the emankeeki, there is a language I yearn to come to, like Koko, like Kini and Ntinti – the way they say when you sing, you dance. The way they say to listen to a story you eat it. Sitting by the fire, I am a witness to their moment of *e'sikar* in the house dimly lighted by the glow of the hearth.

"The Maasai say e'sikar is beauty in its splendour, a deepness of joy that is adornment. And that is freedom." This is what Ole Lekakeny said to me when I completed the emankeeki's first set of beads on the floor.

"When you come to the moment of rass in the art of zari, all your senses meet at the tip of delight. That is the horizon on the vision of beauty," Ma Gor Bai used to say. "There is freedom in that sensation that comes from all the senses of your body. It's a numbness of all pleasures yet a great pleasure itself." E'sikar, I think, is like that. Like *rass* in Gujarati.

48

Sleeping Milk

Haiderali and I meet again at the cattle kraal where we are shown the sampu calf. It's a beautiful young one not ready yet to give milk. I want to touch the sampu on her patterned sides to know it with my fingers, but the calf stands with other calves in a pool of mustard manure-liquid in fresh urine.

"I cannot stand the stench here. And these flies!" Haiderali whispers annoyingly to me in Gujarati waving his hands frantically. I suppress my laughter in a way to let him know I am laughing at him inside. That's when I see Koko waddling towards us. She gives me a gift of a beaded gourd full of curdled sleeping milk. The maziwa lala type of milk that my stomach is full of. That's all I had been drinking in the house.

"We must bid farewell and leave before the sun sets. The journey is long," Haiderali says abruptly to the junior elders in Maasai. He is getting impatient and irritated, and he shows it to me in his side looks, as if it's my fault that we are getting late. As if, it's my fault that he is here. As if, it's my fault that the smells and flies irritate him, yet he was born in Maasailand, not me. No sooner is a little boy told to inform Ole Lekakeny to come than he runs as if shot from a bow. Immediately thereafter, Haiderali starts with goodbye handshakes - three times tight palm presses with each handshake, while also thanking everyone, over and over again.

Then before we leave, Kini and Ntinti admire my emankeeki for the last time. They both have gleaming eyes, affectionate and alert like the beads. Their hearts speak to me in the emankeeki I wear over my heart.

The car speeds on snarling up the road. Between my gazes at the grazing fields, I look at the emankeeki on me, my own emankeeki. Haiderali drinks his last bottle of Tusker beer while steadying the steering wheel in the tight grip of his left hand.

Kilimanjaro emerges tinted crimson in the setting sun. Cirrus clouds clear space for the puffy ones hovering by the mountain like magnified white reflections of the animal walk below. Feral zebras move on paths that connect pastures of the plains of the Mara and Serengeti to those of the Athi and Kaputei towards Nairobi.

"Moti, why don't you sing?" asks Haiderali twitching his nose and changing his look from the road to the emankeeki on me. His eyes are telling me that the smell of the nomads' homestead has worked into my clothes.

It's dusk, the time for prayers of the first quarter of the night. I keep quiet. I don't feel like singing filmi songs. I feel tired. Haiderali questions me with a look. He seems puzzled.

"It has been a long, long journey from sunrise to sunset," Haiderali remarks casually, unwaveringly.

I listen to the humming of Ole Lekakeny and fall asleep.

369

We were approaching Nairowua when I wake up feeling sick in the stomach.

"I should not have had sleeping milk from the gourd. I feel sick, Haidu," I can barely speak. I feel like throwing up.

"I also drank from the gourd. I am not sick, just tired. It's the heat and the dust," responds Haiderali indifferently.

"There was a smell in the milk. Some kind of a smoke, something that makes me nauseated." I burp a few times. The taste of the rancid curd in my mouth makes me sicker. "Perhaps it's the bumps ... and the milk too."

I remove the emankeeki from my neck. Suddenly, I feel its weight taken off. The kraal taken away. Suddenly, as though sucked into a bubble of vacuum, a feeling of emptiness comes over me. "Where shall I keep the emankeeki?" I ask Haiderali. He keeps quiet. Then I ask again and let the question hang in the air, "In my dowry suitcase under my bed?" This question has the answer.

Ole Lekakeny listens from the back seat, quietly with his eyes to the land and the mountain he calls God's House.

The next day it is hot and tranquil. It is one such an afternoon when people doze off while sitting and then they snore and sweat. I have had nothing to eat that day because my stomach feels sick. It pulls and pushes me from inside as if it wants to jump out. Suddenly, almost as if I were pushed, I fall off the chair on the veranda and a mass of beads spill over running in all directions over the cemented ground.

"Mama! Mama! Bwana!" Ole Lekakeny is calling out. Haiderali, awakened from a deep slumber, walks to the door, upset. He is shaken when he sees Ole Lekakeny in the courtyard carrying me. I whimper like a wounded gazelle in his arms. Then Haiderali's eyes fall on a wet red wad on my dress. He panics. "Ma! Ma! Come quick," he yells.

At once, Ma Jena Bai takes control and appears to be the most composed. No sooner does Ole Lekakeny put me down on the bench under the mango tree, than Ma covers me with a thick military blanket. She tells Haiderali to fetch Ba, the traditional midwife of Indian Nairowua who lives on the same street behind the paanwala's kiosk. Then turning abruptly to Kabir and Ole Lekakeny who are standing over me looking aghast, she howls out, "Go! Go! Out of here!" Without saying a word to me, she hurries to heat the samavat leaving me bleeding on the courtyard bench. She returns, running and panting, with steaming towels in a basin and begins cleaning me.

49

Zebra the Storyteller

Finally, the European war ends, and the Empire rejoices the defeat of the enemy Adolf Hitler. The District Commissioner at Nairowua, we call him DC for short, hosts a plush tea party on the lawns of his hill residence. His guests in the foreground are the white citizens, who are the planters, senior civil servants, and descendants of the makers of the now truly Great Britain. In the middle ground, stand the brown men, some with turbans, and some with their wives in simmering silk saris and colourful Punjabi dress that stamp spots on a plain of British military khaki. They are the returning Indian war veterans, workers, clerks, junior service staff and repairmen. And in the background are the black war veterans, carriers, watchmen, and workers, all loyal colonial subjects of the king. Having fought the war jointly, as one people of one great Empire, under one great king, the citizens and subjects of the United Kingdom now stand separated from each other to celebrate the victory in three enclosures bordered by flowerbeds. From their segregated spaces, they sing *God Save the King* in unison when the Union Jack is raised to the thunderous sound of drums of the Kings African Rifles band.

Later the DC walks towards the Asian enclosure with his wife, elegant under a wide brimmed hat with a ribbon that flops over the side in fluttering loops. The wind is warm under the afternoon sun. The DC shakes hands with Haiderali. His wife smiles, looking down on us kindly. They are both tall people. Haiderali bows so low that his coconut-oiled head touches the DC's starched white tunic-like coat at the elbow. I stand frozen, not knowing what to do when he comes to me. Hash! He does not shake my hand, just nods, and then compliments us as loyal subjects of His Majesty the King. He says the Devjis, the Jadavjis and the Patels represent the oldest shopkeeper families of Nairowua. "Hats off to you Indian shopwallas!" he says. "As Governor Sir Edward Grigg once said, 'We could not have made Kenya what she is without the Indians'." His wife confirms the compliment with simultaneous smiles and nods.

Both Haiderali and I blush inside and can say nothing, standing there feeling grateful, our hearts captured, first by the invitation and now by the darshan of the blue governing eyes.

Several days after the garden tea party and we would continue to talk about meeting the DC, his wife under the umbrella hat, the carpet like lawn at his bungalow on the hill and what he said the governor, Sir Edward Grigg, said about the Indians of Kenya.

Light November showers continue to fall at night, and in the mornings, there is a breeze. At midday, one sees fine lines of milk-white clouds at Mt Nairowua like pachedi borders trailing on the wash line. When the line clouds stay in the sky through the afternoon, Ole Lekakeny calls it a parade of zebra over the land like marching soldiers returning from the War.

"White men's war has ended and now there will be peace between them. They have leapt over the dark and come to light and they will fall into the dark again. Like zebra's stripes. That's how the story of war is told … like zebra's stripes in patterns of keri. The zebra is the storyteller leaping over narratives of light and dark like his stripes. Our elders say when the white men step into the dark again and there is another war, we must not interfere in their hostilities," says Ole Lekakeny.

"Why do you speak like that old man?" I ask. I feel more comfortable asking Ole Lekakeny now about things I do not understand.

"The elders said no to the English when they came to recruit Maasai warriors to join the KAR - the King's African Rifles. We told the English to leave the Maasai alone because we did not see why we should die when the white men fight among themselves over our land," says Ole Lekakeny.

In the afternoons, such talk with Ole Lekakeny takes me away from Ma's taak taak tolling into my head like the church bell on the hill. Like the other day as I entered the kitchen, how she taunted me about my second miscarriage and that hurt. It was only two months ago when I felt my body falling apart and I have not felt myself again. A voice inside me tells me the loss of mamta motherhood never leaves the womb. It's never empty because the cries of the aborted fill the space in the sack like an echo of a departed soul. "Look at your friends," Ma said to me, "Khanu Bai, two children, both boys! Look at Zera Bai. Even *she* produced a boy!" I know Ma resents the attention Haiderali shows me after I lost my second baby. He too cried and has changed. Sometimes he takes me out, like the other day to the DC's tea party, and sometimes, for Saturday afternoon drives to the countryside so we can be together. Together we share the pain for each other in silence looking out at the beautiful land. Calling the beautiful land to heal the other.

I know Ma also resents my spending Sunday afternoons with seamstress Roshan Bai. Haiderali told Ma the other Sunday when she began grumbling that he, in fact, approved of me visiting the seamstress. "Roshan Bai is Mamdu's sister. We know the family," he said. Ma does not know I make buttonholes and stitch hemlines at Roshan Bai. That I do not go there to just sit and chitchat. Haiderali knows I get paid a shilling for every four buttonholes and a shilling for two hemlines. Occasionally, there is a rosette to hand embroider below the neck, usually on the left side where the broach is pinned. For this, I earn a shilling and fifty cents. And while I wait for Roshan Bai to finish making a dress before she hands it over to me, I watch her in wonder bent over her amazing Singer Sewing Machine that is the talk of the town. The up and down movement of the piston, and the accompanying whirr mesmerizes me like the steam engine passing by on iron rails. I ask Zarina to come with me to Roshan Bai, partly so that the town people would not gossip when they see me walking alone on Sunday afternoons when husbands nap. And partly because I would like to teach Zarina embroidery. I have seen how keen she is about art that she learns in school.

"Stitch art shapes words that the tongue cannot say. They carry feelings of the body not said in words," I tell Zarina. "We can put thoughts of the mind and feelings of the heart into stitches." I find myself repeating Ma Gor Bai's words that slip onto my tongue whenever I try to teach Zarina as if my teaching hands were Ma Gor Bai's not mine. As if they know how they learned embroidery not me. "Stories embroider our lives, Sakina," Ma Gor Bai would say to me when I was little and angry, and stubborn, and refused to eat because of little upsets. I would be upset when not allowed to listen to the radio at dinner time, when the just introduced song request programme, *Aap ki Farmaish*, on Kenya Hindustani Service was on. I repeat the words to Zarina showing her how to make a stitch in and a stitch out by bringing her eyes and tips of her fingers together in the art of the thread. But, like my sister Monghi, Zarina's eyes and fingers do not always agree with her heart. I see on her face how the patterns do not speak to her. I show her how to implant Gujarati sounds in a stitch – the syllable, the vowel, the nasal buzz and the throat hum as in Om. A stitch of kind for each sound. "Each stitch has a personality," I tell her more and coax her to listen, how a straight line has a severe look and the curved one is gentle and polite. Then I show her how to make a line of zari in harmony with any verse of guru-pir that comes to her told by her fingers. But such work tires her. She says such embroidery is old fashioned. It's desi from the old country. Her straight lines are spidery. How can I teach her more when she cannot make a straight line in ten stitches? She slumps into the chair, shoulders inward diminishing herself in a gesture that rudely demonstrates boredom. Her placid hump is the result of Ma's constant reminders not to keep her back straight because such an arrogant posture pushes out her sharp nipple teenage breasts. "And that will pull the dirty bhoonda eyes of all the loafers of Nairowua towards you," she would try to discipline young Zarina.

I have come to know my heart is a zebra too. Whenever the linear white clouds appear in the blue sky again, my heart gallops over the blue field of stories. The savannah sky is the cobalt infinite in time as in space. She is eternal overlooking all joys and pains over the earth. Kenya is a sky country. Her patterns descend from the sky. I put the painting of the zebra, the wandering storyteller of the sky into the pain that weaves into my story and wait for black days to leap over to white. I am zebra the storyteller. I am his gallop over the storied sky in clouds of patterns over Maasai country.

Part Nine

Venerating Arts

The object of art is to stir the most divine and remote of the chords which make music in our soul; and colour is indeed, of itself a mystical presence on things, and tone a kind of sentinel.

OSCAR WILDE (1854 –1900), A LECTURE TO ART STUDENTS.

50

Light Bulbs and Paper Verses

After the two evening prayers, we gather around Rhemu Bhai, my friend Zera Bai's husband, to listen to what he has heard on the BBC about the king and how Great Britain is welcoming her colonial subjects with skills to re-build motherland after the war. Sometimes, as I listen to Rhemu Bhai, he reminds me of my Noordin Kaka uncle. Like my Noordin Kaka uncle, Rhemu Bhai turns fervent when talking politics. Like my Noordin Kaka uncle, he wants to show how much he knows and like my Noordin Kaka uncle, he actually does know more than people want to believe how much he knows. However, unlike my Noordin Kaka uncle, Rhemu Bhai also likes to listen to what other people have to say, including women. He has a PYE radio at home and he understands a lot of English though he cannot speak much of the colonial language. He talks about a thousand people scorched by a bomb that blasted like a volcano in Japan. He talks about Japan's surrender and the disappearance of Hitlo who we say is the demon king Ravana of Europe. He also

380

mentions Gandhi, his simplicity, his stubbornness, his imprisonment, his burning of English clothes, his walks across the Indian sub-continent and his persistence for independence of India all in one sentence. Rhemu Bhai is excited about the election of the Labour Government in the English Parliament that would for sure lead to freedom for India. There is celebration in the air and people talk about the end of shortages of sugar, matchsticks, onions, rice, wheat and especially spices and tea. We talk of soldiers finally coming home.

There is another reason why the end of the Second World War brings great excitement to the Satpanth Ismaili families at Nairowua. Saheb wishes to be weighed against diamonds in Africa to mark sixty years since he became the imam at the age of seven at a ceremony in Bombay. People say the spectacle that will be in Dar-es-salaam promises to compare Queen Victoria's own Diamond Jubilee that the rajas of India emulate to re-enact their own glory and rule. I remember Noordin Kaka uncle say at the time of Golden Jubilee before my marriage, how such celebrations had become as fashionable as they were competitive among the proxy rulers of Britain's feudal India, cultivating habits of loyalty and beatific manifestations of their darshan for their subjects. The English safeguarded Indian thrones, he would say with contempt under his cheek, against Indian hordes screaming freedom.

"These hordes are led by half naked people like Gandhi," my Dadabapa would taunt Kaka, "whose white cotton dhoti is as close to what the hungry farmer wears as the royal's silk is distant."

"It is an auspicious gift to the African jamat," says Haiderali, "to weigh Saheb against diamonds on the red African soil!" The picture of boy Krishna, happy, bejewelled and garlanded, an adoration on the swing, comes to my eyes. Blessings pour on us when we thus esteem an avatar in diamonds glowing jug mug and his darshan divine in Africa, our homeland.

"The jamat prepares to return to the shoreline of the Indian Ocean where our forefathers first landed. I hear Saurashtran Khoja families will come to Dar-es-salaam from South Africa, Mozambique, and even Madagascar," says Kabir with great excitement ambling about the courtyard veranda in a bath towel wrapped around his waist.

"Yes, they will come from all over Africa. The Saurashtran jamat of Africa will be meeting again. Families have been in Africa for three generations and some have not met since their grandfathers left on the great migration in wooden crafts," adds Haiderali.

"I have requested five jubilee passbooks for the family," says Kabir sitting down at the dining table.

"Also make the passbooks for your father, grandfather and grandmother," calls out Ma from the kitchen.

"But they are dead," says Kabir.

"Not their soul spirits. They will come with us too," answers Ma.

At home as in the jamat khana, our spirits find jubilation in the art, dance and song venerating Saheb sitting on the scale weighed against diamonds. While decorating Saheb's picture with red rose and white jasmine flower tubes, intricately woven blossoms and sacred verses binding petal with petal in zari thread, our hearts in one voice sing his adulation. It is in these jamat khana arts that my memory of worship lives. At such moments, I am the embroiderer, the garba dancer, the bead maker, the singer, the floral artist, the paper artist and in all that, the worshiper revering sacred beauty of his Light.

Badru Dapandayo, the electrician, is called to fix six dozen Phillips light bulbs that run round the perimeter of the jamat khana, along the roof, just below the rainwater gutter. He makes the circle shine like a halo around the jamat khana wall. It was Rhemu Bhai who donated the bulbs. Inside the jamat khana, there are celebrations every weekend starting on Friday evening and ending on Sunday evening. Women come in their finest velvets and silks, some in their wedding dresses and gold jug mug. Men walk proudly in stiff red fez hats, newly sewn long kabuti coats, and sleeveless half coats, called buskots, over shirts.

Two Jamat Khana Decoration Committees are appointed. I am in charge of the women's committee. We meet every night after supper to discuss and plan colour configurations, sizes, and design styles in crepe and drawing paper. What lengths do we require? And how many paper chains shall we make? How many twists, how many curls, how many stripes, and how many stencils, how many this, how many that shall we need to cover the ceiling of the jamat khana? Rhemu Bhai volunteers to bring the paper stock from Nairobi's DL Patel Press. I start making paper flowers to string and circle around each wooden post of the prayer hall while also leading the women artists in the singing of celebratory songs venerating Saheb.

My heart dances in the lyrics of colour and song. We create intricate paper cuffs and banners as if woven to the melodies, as if each were woven in flowers for Saheb's garland. I tell the women to whisper a verse that touches their heart at the moment into each paper shape. I am overwhelmed by the exhilaration in the eye meeting the fingers, twirling, twisting, and twining creasy crepe and silky tissue tracing paper in multiple colours. At that moment, I feel the art in my eye and the poetry on my tongue are one in Satpanth worship. Then the women lace the jamat khana ceiling with floats and paper bouquets. Some sing the jubilee celebration songs composed by master poet Gulzar to the haunting lyrics of the hit film Ratan. This film was recently shown in Nairowua over ten consecutive weekends in two warehouses, relaying the reels from one show with a head start of an hour to the other. It was because of the songs not the story that the film ran for ten consecutive weekends in a small town like Nairowua. Some men like Haiderali and Rhemu Bhai saw the movie over and over again, every weekend, until they could remember all their favourite songs in it – everything about the songs, not just the words and the melody, but also the hand gesturing, the head movements and the eye talk. We dance the garba every night until midnight singing adoration of Saheb while the children, exhausted from the evening's play and excitement, sleep on the prayer mats hurdled in one corner of the hall. Among the children are Zera Bai's boy and Khanu Bai's two sons. Then we eye Khanu Bai walk in with hot kadho chaikops crackling and spilling over on the tin tray. She works in the kitchen with Zera Bai, who heads the all women Kitchen Committee.

On the last night of the new moon before the long journey to Dar-es-salaam and the grand jubilee, we eat the much craved for Marie biscuits, an English delicacy, instead of the usual crispy bland sata condiments. The biscuits were announced as the Devji family donation. I try to hide my haraakh meaning joy not meant to be spoken, brimming over shyness that pleasure brings to girls like giggles held inside. But my smiles on lips pressed under my front teeth betray me. My happiness mirrors the pride in giving charity. "A Devji family sewa service tradition," I tell myself. That evening, it makes me proud of the family that I am married to.

One day, Haiderali comes home with a printed poster picture framed in glass and hardwood mvuli wood. Every Khoja home in Nairowua wants this poster picture of Saheb by the artist poet, devotee and volunteer, Major Abdullah Lakhpati of India. Ma decides to hang the Diamond Jubilee poster on the wall of the courtyard veranda, in a space of honour, between the two other older framed posters of the Golden Jubilee that are almost ten years old.

In the new Diamond Jubilee poster, Saheb's face emerges from the facet of a crystal rock radiating the geometry of refracted light that's so real that it desires to be Saheb's living persona. The Light in Light. Green and red 'My Flags' on both sides cushion the portrait. On top is a Persian crown studded with pearls and more diamonds. My reverence is awe intoned in pictured Saheb and secrets of magical writing in Arabic and English. My darshan is the mystery of veneration that withdraws into a hidden distance when friends who do not know him ask, Is he God? The three poster pictures call adulation to my eye. The expectation of his glimpse darshan-deedar is exhilarating when he would be weighed against diamonds in Dar-es-salaam.

Haiderali also gives me a gold pendant and two silver coins embossed with the Saheb's holy profile to keep in my sandalwood jewellery box inlaid with ivory. That's for baraka of wealth. Haiderali slips the jubilee stamps into the groove between the pages of Nooran Mubin, the sacred book in Gujarati print and pictures of conquests and downfalls of Nizari Ismaili Imams. The stamps profile Saheb in a smart English suit and bow tie. Here between the pages you would also find browned newspaper picture clippings of Saheb at the racecourse, his sons in English suits and military uniforms, and English begums in fairy tale dresses and diamonds jug mug. In the holy book, fixed at the groove between the pages, are also pictures of Queen Victoria, Kings Edward VII and Georges V and VI, and their English queens in fur collars and diamond tiaras *jug mug*, and the royal children in pretty shoes with shiny buckles and frilly socks. Among the pages are other pictures in envelopes, covert pictures, scissor-cut from filmi magazines – fair Indian women in shimmering tissue skirts, voiles over bare stomachs and hard pointed silk bodices. Kohl blackened vamp eyes and redone plump Indian lips in English lipsticks.

I count my family, people I will see in Dar-es-salaam. We have not met since my marriage. Dadabapa is not with us anymore but my father has made his pass booklet with his photograph in it so his spirit soul may also come, celebrate, and more importantly do Saheb's darshan-deedar with the family.

51

Blessings of Darshan-Deedar

The Devji family, like all the other Nairowua jamat families, travel to Voi by bus and then to Mombasa by rail. At Kilindini harbour, the Mombasa jamat hosts us to meals and we rest for a day. People say they will never ever forget in their entire lifetime the sewa service of the Mombasa jamat and they praise the men volunteers in khaki uniforms, thick leather belts and red fez hats. They thank the women volunteers in frock pachedis who tended the fires in the makeshift kitchens and cooked the meals over firewood. They would say, "That is service to the jamat, which is sewa, which is devotion, and that is love for Saheb, and that is our faith. That is what matters." From Kilindini harbour, we board the SS Vasna, the British India liner, to take us to Dar-es-salaam on the coast of the now British Territory of Tanganyika.

People would say going to Dar-es-salaam to see Saheb weighed against diamonds would be a blessing of darshan that comes once in a lifetime. But it was a tortuous voyage. SS Vasna heaves and falls in the ocean's gigantic waves. Some older men and women remember their voyage in wooden crafts when they migrated as children from India to Africa. Their voices quiver when they speak about the harrowing moments on water. I shake with fear and feel sick. Suddenly like a raider, the wind blows over the group of women on third class deck and suffocates me like it were a cold rubber pillow pressed into my face. I turn around gasping for air and crying aloud in panic. Khanu Bai comes to comfort me, reminding me that the passage of Bawan Ghati to the gates of heaven and into the next karma will not be easy either. "All transformations are difficult to bear. We are but mortals who are made to suffer," she says, "meeting Saheb is a transformation. We are tested if we are deserving of his darshan-deedar, his pure vision in our eyes, his return look, and his blessed glimpse to the murid yearning for Light. We must pray for this. Persevere through this test. The true believer will be saved. Pray! " The jamat on board prays together in one voice for the sea's madness to pass. Ma Jena Bai becomes frantic, and prays aloud holding her tasbih in her fisted hand above her head. Her voice rises above the sonorous canto of the thrashing waves and gales of the Indian Ocean gone mad.

"Mowla Naklank, O Stainless One! You have brought us so far over rugged terrain. We endured hunger and exhaustion so we may receive the baraka of your darshan-deedar. O Mowla, Lord Naklank of the Seven Skies, Ma-Bap our one parent! Will you let us down now? Have you not tested our faith enough that you send us these perils at the last minute?

"Mowla Naklank, impeccable sovereign of avatars! Are you teasing us now with the sight of Dar-es-salaam there, so close? Is this your game or do you wish to drown us? Is it your wish that I do not see a grandson? If this is your desire, then I submit to your command before my daughter-in-law has her lap filled. Is this what you want? My death in madness of the sea? I give my life to you. I obey whatever is your command."

The storm is short and it abates as quickly as it had started. The waves come to calm and SS Vasna cruises towards Dar-es-salaam that has no harbour deep enough to berth her. Native hand paddled boats wait to ferry the jamat to the shore.

Satpanth Khoja families arrive in Dar-es-salaam from the market towns and from isolated parts of this wondrous continent; from the thick rain forests and vast expanses of water; from the savannahs, highlands and deserts. They travel by bullock and donkey carts, buses, pickup trucks, and the railroad with their families of feeble grandparents and robust new-born babies. Bedford lorries arrive jam-packed with families from Iringa-Korogwe in the North and Ujiji-Dodoma-Morogoro in the west. "Upcountry roads are a nightmare," they say, "the corrugation, the dust, the blazing sun, the torrential rains and the cold nights under the tarpaulin at the back of the trucks are all a test of endurance of our faith in Saheb." They come in boats and ships like pilgrims from the islands of the Indian Ocean - Zanzibar, Pemba and Madagascar. They come from the Congo, Mozambique and South Africa. They come exhausted, thirsty and hungry, but their hearts are singing. Hearts soaring, expecting to meet their relatives from the villages of Saurashtra; friends they made during the migration voyages and travels across tropical Africa looking for a place to work and live.

We are the colonial subjects of three great European Empires and I hear Kutchi and Gujarati in the wind mixed with English, French and Portuguese. Those from remoter areas speak African vernaculars and use words from Bantu, Cushitic and Nilotic languages in their native Indian dialects. Coastal Khoja talk in Swahili and the Zanzibaris speak lyrical Swahili Khoja Kutchi to each other. In the babble of voices, I hear about two women from Nairobi asking for a Nairowua family at Camp Akbar in the Upanga section. At once, my heart misses a beat. I know, my body says so, that it is my family looking for me.

I see Ma Gor Bai and Meethi Bai coming towards me. Ma Gor Bai takes my hands in both hers. I bow down and kiss her hands over mine. Words fail my tongue as I take her right hand to my moist eyes and touch my forehead to it, and kiss it again in respect. The hand that raised me is sacred to my heart. She is my mabap, the parent mother and father. We weep with joy and sorrow, but I would not let her take me in her arms and that surprises her. Meethi Bai and I shoulder touch each other on the right and left sides. I feel the familiar beat of her heart, her stiffened brassiere, her oudh perfume, her Pond powdered skin and the weighty bangled arms. I feel the comfort again in the softness of her sagging muscles grooved by bindings of the sacred thread on both her upper arms. They bring memories of how I sought sanctuary in them when Ma Gor Bai scolded me because I had left the dust unswept under the bed, or the curry pot greasy. Ma Gor Bai would be most cruel with her words when I delayed coming home after the evening prayers at the jamat khana. Sometimes I would sneak out with friends to eat chana-bateta in tamarind sauce and sometimes I got carried away playing hop-step-and-jump when the night was warm and the moon was full. But I pushed her away when she wanted to hug me. Why? I see her eyes question me.

Kaki Bai auntie and my father appear after a while and they all kiss me lightly on the forehead. Happiness that cannot be expressed in words flows in tears. We shall eat pilau in one senio plate as a family, and dance the garba together, all night long. That too is worship. Only Noordin Kaka uncle is not here and I do not ask why.

It's not until after the communal prayers of the second quarter of the night that I see Shamshu briefly for he has been avoiding meeting my father. I am with Monghi and Malek holding hands, both together, one on each side. The Karachi Khoja Scottish Band marches into the cheering assembly, crisscrossing the ground followed by Bwana Picha, the photographer of Nairobi, clicking their every move. They are wearing chequered kilts, matching berets and blankets over their shoulders held by one giant safety pin. They play English military music with their bagpipes and march smartly just like the Scottish soldiers along Government Road at the Empire Day parade in Nairobi. The cheering and clapping grows thunderous, and the excitement ecstatic. Then the band pipes God Save the King and we stand still. Calmness returns. Finally, the band thunders Noor-e-Rasul-illah, Light of the Prophet of Allah. Love for Saheb brims over our hearts like floodwaters. We stand still in elation. Salutation to the music of our people by our own Kavi Dilgir, the grand poet beloved of the Sultans of Zanzibar and Saheb. Men weep openly, holding their heads high and singing. Women shelter under their pachedis. Some have their palms pressed together in revered salutation to the anthem as they would in prayer.

Shamshu is with a group of friends, all chewing juicy bitter paan and I see his mouth is striped with stains of dark brown tobacco minced to powder. Two of his friends wear English caps sitting crooked on their heads, front shades at the ears. They wear dark sun goggles and look like filmi loafers. I touch Shamshu on his arm, I cry. He is my little brother but I would not take him in my arms as I used to, to cradle him to sleep.

391

52

Diamond Embroidery

Having wished each other blessings of Saheb's darshan-deedar, and having given hands to each other over the shoulders that ritually closes the evening prayers, Ma Gor Bai, Meethi Bai and I join the concentric garba circles. We swivel in perfumes of Dar-es-salaam in women's hair and the ocean breeze - jasmine, rose, frangipani, langi langi, queen of the night called raat ki rani and kilua, all native floral fragrances of the Swahili coast. We move in spheres, in rhythmic steps to dadra beat set by thumps of a hundred palms cup clapping in unison. Saris swish and swell at the ankles; chiffon pachedis soar over torsos and velvet frocks reel funnels. We swoon like desert dervishes, the dua dancers, the dance prayer makers inebriated with the morning's darshan-deedar. Ma Gor Bai, Meethi Bai and I sit together, my fingers are locked in theirs, and I cry. They do not ask why I cry because they understand there is so much one can moan and complain about or tell that as women we can do nothing about. And they cry too, pressing their fingers even harder knitting into mine till they hurt. The hurt makes sorrow bearable.

When the tabla pattering begins and the harmonium buzz overlaps wails, we join the dance circle and sing the garba song with one all-women voice. In the song, we call the Begum seated high up by Saheb's side on a dais to come and dance the garba with us. The patron of the widows, known for her collection of regal saris, consents and steps down from the rostrum into the garba circle in a space between Meethi Bai and me. I swing. My eyes are moist. Bwana Picha, the photographer, rushes by me. The begum is showered by a thunderous echo of ecstatic clapping that envelope us at her every movement in the garba. Like when her back arches and her hands come together in a clap, like when she takes a half turn stepping back and like when she takes a full turn rearing her shoulders, holding her sari over her head after each clap with two steepled fingers. The jamat's gaze freezes on the Begum's grace, and her perfect Saurashtran dance decorum, her magical steps patterning ins and outs of the garba loops. In her posture, a stately matron, her compassionate benefaction of absakan women for she is the widows' patron. We call her Mata Salamat the Mother of Wellbeing. Patron of all the welfare societies for the poor and immigrants in Africa. Her feminity graces the garba circle. Saheb guru-pir Naklank, in garlands of rose and jasmine, composed and divine, is seated on a gaily-festooned dais. He watches over the garba like Krishna over his dancing gopi-murids in spinning saris and whirling frocks.

In the morning at the ceremony of weighing Saheb on a golden scale twice his size - he sat on one plate, feet above the ground and diamonds glittered on the other, I could not take my eyes away from the Begum. She walked a step behind

Saheb, serene and taller than Saheb in a sari laden with one thousand five hundred diamonds shining jug mug in the African sun. The mystic moment of the Begum's appearance onto the red carpet left a spark of brightness in my eyes, weary after three days of travelling and sleepless nights. I thought about the embroiderer of the diamonds on her sari when the Begum passed by me sitting behind the rope barrier. How the embroiderer's fingertips must have felt the touch of dot diamond one thousand five hundred times over? How her eyes would have met the fingers to create patterns in silent twinkles shifting sunlight with the Begum's every step and nod of her veiled head? Would the diamond embroiderer have had the same feelings in her heart that I know Kini and Ntinti had had for me when the dot beads slipped between their fingers to make the emankeeki for me? I feel something deep in me like a touch of the artist-makers' embrace when I put on my emankeeki in the solitude of my bedroom. I wonder if the Begum also hears the artist's heart when she wears the sari? So affecting had been her presence that day that till today it stays like a sparkle in my mind's eye.

Then when the Begum leaves the dance circle to rejoin Saheb on the rostrum, a tumultuous encore fills the night sky. We continue the garba without the Begum - footout-footforward – footin-footback, hipupleft-hipupright, shoulders-halfturn, bow and clap.

Aaje mareh angane
Hai reh mari!
Harakh na mai reh

In my heart today
Oh my mother!
Joy flows over

Woi rey! More men, their heels bouncing over toes, enter the dance circle. Dandia sticks whack to dadra music, 1 2 3 - 1 2 3, women sway and the play begins. Men lift-drop shoulders in seductive peacock walk heaving their chests. Saurashtran lyrics put to cyclic strikes of sticks and jingles of tambourines emerge from pitched notes of harmoniums like popping heads of kingfishers out of water. The air in the royal pavilion feels pregnant with music and perfumes of hair oils and fragrances fanned by swaying saris, pachedis and frocks. Saheb's gaze is upon us. He is seated on the dais on a high throne-like seat. Our eyes blessed with his darshan-deedar look. I feel his eyes over me and a chill runs through my body.

Foot out - foot forward – foot in; hip left - hip right; this side, that side; shoulders- turn-lift, drop; this side, that side; whack the dandia stick; turn around, once again foot out - foot forward – foot in ... 1 2 3 ...

I see dandia is a male performance weaving footsteps. It's an act of male elegance. Women frolic like maidens around Krishna weaving floor foot designs. Struck by feminine naakhra, the men exaggerate their hop steps to energetic jumps; roll their heads, smacking the sticks in swift twists of their wrists, curt strokes, snap touch and jump step. Under the spell of expectant courtship, each man swanks a style and feels Krishna in him, the god in courtship celebrated. His chin up, his shoulders thrust forward, and his body in a dance trance. He is the Lord of Dance, full of himself. He whirls bursting of music, lost in the movement's crescendo. That's when Kavi Kathiawari bellows a deep-throated note prolonging the reverie of hop-skip-step rotary. Women chuckle haraakh haraakh under their breath. They are in control, their dandia

395

sticks click, their nude waists mock in teasing under see-through saris and then turning to male eyes, their flower heads spin like tops. Girls taunt slant eye embraces, lift sari folds—the delicate ankle peep lift mock, the little glitter of slipper straps over painted toe nails and nimble steps, covert beckoning to the beat pounding in the heart.

"Such a courtship style is a heritage from Saurashtran village days on full moon nights," Dadabapa would have said. I sense his presence at moments like this that he loved. Ecstasy of rass possesses some of the dancers. The song-swirl-step dance swings in the measure of the tempo. I listen to Kavi Kathiawari's verses fluttering to the lure of the bandhani complimenting the feminine lead in a masculine feat. My heart sings to his voice.

Eh Kathiawari Khojan!
Tari bandhani no latkho tofani
Maro dil lalchai

O Khoja lady of Kathiawar!
The curl of your bandhani is mischievous!
My heart grows tempestuous.

I am enthralled by Kavi Kathiawari's Gujarati poetry. How it mingles into the musical codes, how it patterns the dandia steps, how it ripples over torsos curving under heads moving from side to side; how it pulsates to the rhythm of my heart!

Around midnight Meethi Bai is called to the rostrum. Her melodious drawl soothes over the quiet Kutchi-Gujarati rivalry challenging the celebrated poet Kavi Kathiawari.

Room joom faarti
Garbe ghumti reh
Eh Khojan, tu aayn Kutchan!

396

Whirling circling turning
Rotating garba dance
O Khoja lady you are from Kutch!

A thunderous applause from the Kutchi audience accosts us. The dandia dancers repeat the chorus with a bounce, steps doing steps, bringing the tempo to its pinnacle mesmerized by the movements of their own sweaty bodies.

Buoyant Meethi Bai continues singing in Kutchi, each line a measured mathematical verse-step inlay. My heart soars and wants to fly into the melody, high up like the vulture. More dandia dancers join in singing the chorus. The circle grows larger; the echo deafens the stillness of the night like no other night at this port on the Indian Ocean where the Satpanthis were nourished with sumptuous meals, love and sweet water. That day when their eyes were filled with the radiance of Saheb's darshan-deedar, a joy comes to them from peace of shukhar, contentment like no other. That's when you would hear the murid say how his heart is the *Abode of Peace*. That is Dar-es-salaam in Arabic.

Part Ten

Magical Days Wandering

In 'Eternal Echoes', John O'Donohue, the Celtic philosopher poet and a Catholic priest, says that the English word 'wander' can refer to the movement of persons, animals, objects, thoughts and feelings. To this, one could add imagination, the mind, art, poetry, spirit, travel and storytelling. The wind is a wanderer, he writes, wandering over the universe. In fact, he thinks the word 'wander' itself comes from 'to wind' and is allied with the German word 'wandeln' meaning to change. Reflecting on John O'Donohue we know a storyteller is like the wind, a wanderer and her stories allow the listener to wander about the universe of the known and unknown, earthy, magical and the spirit world. Stories too wander like the wind, like the spirit, and they change, changing thoughts and moods of the storyteller as of the listener, from the present to the past and vice versa, transcending realities over magic like faith.

53

Hunger bites Stories glitter

The excitement of meeting friends and relatives at the Diamond Jubilee lives on during the depression years that follow the end of World War II and the jubilee. In Tanganyika, the depression combined with famine, led to food shortages and families in Dar-es-salaam survived on ration stamps while we feted. We heard how the African residents were angered, and they nearly rioted when ten thousand of us descended on their town, and began eating into their emergency stock of rice. Shortages of milk were so acute that lactating Bais fed each other's babies, giving their breasts time to replenish. That was custom. The Bais would continue to speak in wonder how they saw with their own eyes the Begum's sari that held one thousand five hundred diamonds glinting jug mug in the African sun. They brag among themselves with much haraakh, not always overt, yet slightly visible delight at the spectacle of her beauty and richness. She was the patron of the widows; she was called Mata Salamat the Mother of Welfare; she was also the patron of the poor, was she not? Shyly, they would say with pride how the Begum danced the Saurashtran garba with them *just like them*.

Memories of seeing such abundance turn magical when times are lean, living on half-empty stomachs. When tales of magic transform to awe, they grow bigger as years go by. Zera Bai and Rhemu Bhai fascinate each other and us with stories of faith, devotion and miracles. One such a tale was of Mohamed Chel, the Master Magician of India before whom Fateh Meghji, the Master Magician of Mombasa, looked a learner, they said. On hearing the magician brag that he was the greatest of all the magicians of India, Saheb put him to test. He threw his walking stick on the ground before the magician. Quietly, the jamat watched. Saheb then asked Mohamed Chel, the Master Magician, to pick the stick and bring it to him. However, the magician could not lift Saheb's stick off the ground! The jamat was astonished! How can Mohamed Chel the greatest magician of India not be able to lift Saheb's walking stick when he can make the elephants stop walking? They asked each other. Mohamed Chel tried again and again, mumbling magic words and sweating. Saheb then asked a little boy to return his walking stick to him. Lo! A miracle! The boy lifted the stick without an effort and brought it to Saheb. Mohamed Chel stood before Saheb perplexed and embarrassed. "You see your magic is child's play," said Saheb. The jamat went wild with excitement. Thunderous clapping filled the pavilion. The magician, who was reputed to stop not only elephants, but also moving trains with his magic, was defeated to lift Saheb's stick! Mohamed Chel bowed his head as low as he could before Saheb, whose power he now knew, was greater than his own was. Saheb is the greatest of all magicians.

At last, there is peace at the Kenya-Tanganyika border though there are still the wartime roadblocks and restrictions on movement of people and vehicles coming into town.

401

Except for wheat, rice, tea and sugar, other foods such as milk, meat, vegetables and fruit are in plenty at the Nairowua market. However, not all the Indian shopkeeper families have money enough to have a square meal a day because businesses other than in beads have not picked up. Moreover, prices of sugar, flour and rice have gone so high up that some families can hardly afford these anymore. There is a stern warning from Nairobi to the Indian wholesalers all over Kenya not to hoard the commodities. The fine for hoarding is severe and could even be imprisonment. We remind ourselves of the African proverb, 'Poverty is better than war.' In the jamat khana we say prayers of shukhar for the war is over.

The rainfall had been regular during the war years and there was no starvation in the Maasai homesteads scattered over the savannah. Only I, Haiderali and Ma Jena Bai know that I have now carried sweetness in my belly for more than three months. I had two miscarriages but I cannot speak about them, lest I lose this one too. My 'Filling of the Lap' ceremony in the coming month of my pregnancy is a much awaited joyous occasion for the Devji family. Sometimes on lazy afternoons when the bees buzz at the acacia tree and the wasps fly over me and as my fingers work the beads, I dream of mamta motherhood. Such happy dreams glide over the distress of hearing stories of hungry households of the Satpanth Ismailis. As Ma grows old and feeble her taak taak has increased, not lessened; her voice has become louder not softer. She is losing her hearing but her sight is sharp as ever.

My story wanders like the wind blowing back and forth, as if it belongs to neither the past nor the present. Like aging memory, it's a wanderer over the vast mindscape of life that no longer separates the time between childhood, youth and old age.

402

54

Paper Flowers and Embroidery

At Nairowua, the rain continues to be plentiful, and the pastures for cattle, sheep and red Maasai goats are lush. Milk is in abundance for the herders of the African plains, and the bead traders know that the rituals of the coming generations will be grand events. Both men and women will be buying beads that celebrate their rites of passage and new statuses in the societal life cycle of the savannah. There will be ceremonies and feasting when the boys of the right-hand group are circumcised. There will be ceremonies and feasting when the boys of the left-hand group are circumcised. There will be ceremonies and feasting when the young men drop their weapons, becoming junior elders and marry. Here the savannah hosts sacred rituals of peace when the warriors abandon their hair locks and spears, and return to transcend to the loins of their mothers. The mothers then anoint them with milk and honey, the symbolic umbilical fluid of rebirth that they pour on their sons' shaven heads. Now, as men, they will hold the peace staff of the African Olive Tree, Ol-orien, the sacred tree of Black Africa. The Devji family prosperity depends on such uninterrupted ceremonial routines that come with the rains and celebrations of green grass. The green grass brings peace, and peace is beauty that in turn is fêted with muain sidain in bead wealth displays on the body. Like the muain sidain displayed on the emankeekis of hundreds of beads on the shoulders of Kini and Ntinti. "Like the muain sidain perceived on God's skin," Ole Lekakeny would say, "the Beautiful One is the Colourful One at dawn of every new day that breaks into the horizon over Maasailand."

Large amounts of beads are needed for the coming Maasai year of changing of the age set. Soon after, large amounts of beads will be needed again after the girls' circumcision because their marriages will follow as soon as their wounds heal. Elders are travelling and consulting across the land to fix the dates of the coming celebrations. For now whatever profit Haiderali makes, he hides from spendthrift Kabir who has a habit of plunging his hand into the shop's cash box. I complain about our bulging mattress but Haiderali ignores me and stuffs more bills each night.

"Looks like a pregnant cow. It's more pregnant than I am," I say.

"We can pay all our debts and purchase new stock to meet the needs of adornment during these days of prosperity," he replies.

Then fortunes change for the worse. Cattle plague breaks out. Many domestic and wild animals of the savannah are killed, and if not killed, weakened so much by this epidemic called rinderpest that they produce little or no milk, and their babies are born still. More than half of the Maasai cattle die. Ole Lekakeny mumbles his worries to me. One afternoon he says, "All the celebratory rituals are postponed until the families and animals have recovered from the disease. Until the young have the strength to be circumcised. Until there are enough animals of fitting colours to sacrifice." Then on another afternoon, he tells me, "For now, our rituals are prayers to appease Earth's anger. Seers sacrifice the remaining few white cattle, each one pure of colour and of perfectly curved horns. They meet on Ol Donyo Lengai, the sacred mountain that speaks from the depth of Earth. The anger of the Earth needs to be cooled," he says. "We must Heal the Earth so we too may be healed and prosper again."

Each passing day I hear from Ole Lekakeny how in the countryside more and more homesteads are being razed, and how the women are gathering their calabashes, cooking pots, sleeping skins and frames of their demolished homes loading them onto donkeys. Soon, he tells me the migration will begin. They need to leave the angry land polluted by disease that kills the cattle. They would erect new homes where the grass is blessed and the land carries no curse that kills cattle. One day Ole Lekakeny tells me that Kini and Ntinti have moved their homes into Tanganyika towards the Amboseli plains on the other side of the Kilimanjaro. I wanted to ask him if the sampu patterned cow, my gift to them, survived the plague. But I found myself suppressing a sob that came suddenly as if thrust up from the heart at the thought of their collective loss. Or was it a cry of guilt that I chocked in my throat?

The bead trade drops until the time comes when there is absolutely no sale of beads in our shop. The displays on the racks gather dust on the veranda. Anxiety sweeps over our faces when we sit for dinner not knowing how we can replenish the diminishing rations in kitchen containers – rice, a variety of dals, spices, wheat, and millet flour ...

A new word slips into our vocabulary – 'black market.' Haiderali and Kabir seize the opportunity that the post-war food shortages offer to make money on the black market. Haiderali tells me it has to be big profit because it's risky to smuggle products like sugar from across the border in Tanganyika and then sell it on black market in Kenya. Moreover, Haiderali does not have a licence to sell sugar in the shop. He calls that 'double risk' that deserves double profit on the black market. He leaves it to me to help hide the illegal commodity that he brings in sacks. I find ingenious ways to divide and hide the sugar under the roof and in the bedrooms – under the bed, in drawers, even under clothes in the cupboards in case of surprise police checks that were expected.

Ma and I make funnel shaped packages of a quarter pound of sugar from old newspapers - *The Colonial Times, The Standard, Africa Samachar, Chakram* and whatever newspaper or magazine we can get from the Punjabi paper vendor of Nairowua. Sometimes, *Women's Own, Drum, Filmfare* and *Life* magazines also come our way. When I see a look of surprise on the face of the Punjabi vendor because we are suddenly buying so many magazines, I tell him we need the paper for the jamat khana to put a teaspoonful of su-kreet on for each one participating in the prayer. He nods and seems happy for his business. We tie the packages tightly with sisal strings or brown gummy tape, and sell the sugar at night at the back door to those we trust and have secretly arranged at the shop during the day. They pay twice as much and in advance. The government calls our trade black-market but what do they know? Do they know how difficult it is to get sugar in these times? We too pay high prize for the sugar.

While waiting for Haiderali and Kabir to arrive from their chup chap secret trips over the Tanganyika border, I make paper flowers. They sell for five and ten cents depending on the number of flowers in the vase, an evaporated milk can that is packed with earth and pebbles and wrapped around with coloured tracing paper. The profit is marginal. With a month's profit, I can purchase just two days' vegetables in the market. I learn to make curry without tomatoes and ghee. I have to make one onion last a week. We drink weak black or almost black tea. However, I cannot sell many paper flowers because people keep money for food, and the rich who have money to decorate their homes, prefer to buy plastic Chinese flowers from Nairobi's bazaars.

Then one day Haiderali says he has ordered a Singer Sewing Machine for me from Nairobi through Rhemu Bai. My heart soars with joy when the sewing machine arrives with Rhemu Bai's bicycles on top of Merali Bus. I had not felt such elation since arriving in Nairowua.

I now machine embroider bridal saris and long frocks for the rich men's family. That helps to feed the family and keep me sane. The family depends on my embroidery and Ma pretends she does not know that my earnings feed the family. The whirr of the pedal-run Singer Sewing Machine fills the house as I trace lines - straight lines, cross lines, parallel lines, lines making boxes on a new slippery cloth called nylon and neon nylon. There are also zigzag lines that Ma calls jig-jag, the new fashion word. Then there are circular lines and random dots; lines in entangled mesh of strings like re-done balls of wool. All that's the new style of embroidery called 'modern design'. Modern design emerges out of playing with the Singer Sewing Machine - doodling, pecking and tap droning. But inside, I miss the poke-in-pull-out treading in zari work with my eyes quietly telling the fingers where to go. The taak taak machine is impatient and it talks like Ma. It leads me. I have to follow. Quick, quick. I miss my thinking quietness and the rhythm of my art that had a voice that called me to rass. I was the master of my art then. The monotonous machine mutter brings neither joy to my eyes nor any feelings to my fingertips. Nevertheless, I must work all day to sustain the home, bending over the black gibbering widow, my nose at her piston, pumping the needle that dictates the stitches that run in haste like the Ford. I let my doubts that come with unhappy thoughts drain out of me into the mechanical drone. It too can absorb the unhappy inside sounds and has its own machine rhythm in the hit hit noise. After some months of machine work, my right leg feels pinching pain that travels up from my swollen ankle and sometimes my right shoulder freezes while I work. I work hard yet there are times I have no money to buy milk for tea and when my rich clients ask me if I need their charity, I say to them, "Haiderali is doing well in the bead business." I lie because of family shame called sharam. And because they ask, "Do you need milk? Do let us know in the quiet, hengh?" I am too proud to say we have not had milk in tea for a week. You don't ask a woman in need if she needs your charity. You don't ask a woman if she needs milk for the family. You don't ask a married woman her obvious want at times like this. You don't reduce a woman to have to ask. I writhe in the anger that comes from humiliation but keep face to show I am not a mothaj. I shall never be a mothaj on you. I shall never be a mothaj on the community's Social Welfare Board.

I embroider for the wives and daughters of men who are wealthy leaders of the Satpanth Ismaili jamat of Nairowua. They want modern machine embroidery now and look down on hand embroidery as old fashioned if not backward. They even call it 'too desi', meaning rural India, peasant India, folk India, poor India as in pictures and movies, and the old country fashion. Some Khoja men grow prosperous because of the European war and some because of the depression after the war. There are men like Mamdu Bhai who became wealthy buying hides and skins of animals killed by rinderpest and selling them to Nairobi's tanning workshops. There are others like Rhemu Bhai who started a scrap metal business when the war erupted. He saw an opportunity in the scarcity of broken metal things that people throw away. From his profit saved over months, he bought a Raleigh bicycle on hire purchase from Nairobi and sold it for a small profit to a local teacher on his payday. Then he bought two more Raleigh bicycles from Nairobi and sold them both to local teachers on paydays. Then three, and later, more bicycles began arriving on Merali Bus and Rhemu Bhai sold them at the end of the month to clerks on their salary days. First, he sold only for cash and now he runs a hire purchase bicycle business. Now they call him Bwana Bisekeli and in his bicycle shop, he hangs a picture of a laughing man on a bicycle out speeding a lion in hot pursuit to eat him up. People say the man on the bicycle is Rhemu Bhai himself speeding on with business. There are also itinerant pawnbrokers and moneylenders who profit from poverty of the bead store families in remote parts of the savannah stricken by the cattle disease.

When I am tired of both the frustrations of the machine's taak taak and Ma's taak taak, I sit under the mango tree in the courtyard. There is a bench there where Haiderali and Kabir smoke at night after dinner. Nowadays, they can only afford to smoke 10 Cents sigara kali, meaning strong cigarette in Swahili. They would smoke and scrap out a khokharo to clear their throats of kali bitterness, spitting sputum at the side. In the afternoons, a breeze flows over from the endless savannahs and slaps my face. I stay still in solitude thinking nothing. That does not mean I am not doing anything. When I am thinking nothing I am regaining my strength and bringing my mind to myself.

"Moti! Eh Moti Bai!" Ma calls from I don't know where. Instead of rushing towards her voice as I usually do, I go to the kitchen. I don't want to be in her face. She angers me. Irritating taak taak. My mouth salivates. I am gripped by a sudden urge to lick tamarind chutney, sweet and sour with a pinch of red-hot pili-pili chilies in it. I cannot find it! Instead, I lick the crusted slime crystallized inside the tops of Ma's cough syrup bottle, then the Eno bottle top, lime pickle, Peptang tomato sauce, whatever I can find on the kitchen shelf. I lick the vinegar bottle cork. Nothing diminishes my urge. I rush to the bedroom and lock myself up. Opening the clothes cupboard, I remove the brown paper bag. Ah! I find Haiderali's bottle of whiskey with a label of a round fat bellied Englishman with a walking stick lifting his tall hat, bowing foreword and smiling broadly. I take a sip. My throat is on fire. Something blazes down my gullet. My belly flares into an inferno. I am seized by fright. Will my baby be charred?

55

Filling my Lap

A group of Bais in long frocks and pachedis over their heads gather in the jamat khana on the morning of my first pregnancy rite. Every woman at the sacrament of 'Filling of the Lap' is a mother and has been selectively invited by Ma so no barren woman's jealous eye would cause bad luck kisirani to the Devji child in my womb. We sit in a circle with a prayer food plate placed before me that has a mango, a coconut, a handful of mung lentils and a jug of milk. Ma and Khanu Bai sit beside me on either side. This time my pregnancy has developed to the sixth month. I am serene and contented, my green pachedi over my forehead to the eyes in decorous laaj. Ma is euphoric but tries not to show it lest an evil eye envious of her joy strike the baby. I am a woman with a prayer in my heart for a boy child. My motherhood is celebrated today.

Khanu Bai starts a song. It's about 'Khoro Bharave' meaning 'Filling the Lap'. Others join in, singing and humming with their heads moving lightly with the rhythm. I am full of expectation for a male heir.

Aaje Moti Bai no khoro bharave che
Moti Bai ne vathavo reh

Today Moti Bai's 'Lap is filling'
Let's celebrate Moti Bai

The woman elder sitting with folded legs across the low table says a brief prayer followed by a silent collective telling of beads by the others. In the chalet of their communal tasbih are told the names of the avatars and guru-pirs. I feel as though each bead is from God's own embellishment, for in it are the mountains, rivers, and trees. Our heads are bowed, our eyes closed. The ceremony takes me to Ma Gor Bai's satsang gatherings at our home in Jugu Bazaar in Nairobi. How I wish, Ma Gor Bai was by my side to share this sacred time when I am receiving the sacrament of my first pregnancy! How I wish Meethi Bai were here. Then the women escort me ceremoniously in a group to Saheb's picture that stands on his square divan takht at the back of the prayer hall. I pull back my pachedi so his darshan look would cover the baby in my womb. I ask for forgiveness, and then blessings for wholesome completion of my term. I say shukhar for the baraka of mamta motherhood. Ma Jena Bai prays aloud, pausing after every line to hear a chorus of stretched out aameen from the women:

Ya Mowla Naklank!
Ya Sarkar!
Bless us with peace
Keep us in good health
Protect the child in the womb
And the family name

Before we leave the jamat khana, I put the money that the women had circled over my head to ward off the evil eye at the base of Saheb's photograph among fresh white, red and pink roses from home gardens. The photo is framed in a slender line of red and green lights that blink alternately - first red, then green, red–green, green-red, on-off, off-on, pulsating on-off-red-green-green-red, persistently in running circles. I see an aura over his white face.

Later that night, after dinner, I eat the blessed mango from the ceremony that the woman elder took from my fruit-offering platter and gave back to me. I cut a slice for Haiderali to eat too. The next day Ma makes it known in the jamat that I am expecting her first grandchild. Two days later, I ask Haiderali to place a silver piece in the offering tray before Ambe Ma at the Krishna Temple on Temple Road. She is Nairowua's Mamta Ma, the Goddess of Motherhood. I pray for a boy.

56

Luchi Bai

A few days after my 'Filling of the Lap Ceremony', I begin to bleed as it had happened in the past during my previous pregnancies. I would not go back to the Singer Sewing Machine. I would not leave my bed keeping my legs pressed together. I would not eat and take only a sip of sugared water, a spoonful at a time, to avoid going to the washroom. I would hold on to my tasbih and plead to Saheb's picture sitting on my abdomen not to take away my child again. Everyone shows concern. They bring their cures to my bed.

Thus before the day is over, Haiderali comes home with the white doctor from the Catholic Mission Hospital on the hill. Fatha Dakitari, as he is called, advises Haiderali I should not do any housework if he wants to see his baby. He tells Haiderali I should sleep with my feet raised, and that he should put bricks under the two front legs of our bed. Then Fatha Dakitari tells Haiderali I should not travel to Nairobi to my parents' home for the delivery so I could be hospitalized if the bleeding continues. He knows it's our custom to have the first delivery at the mother's maiden home. "Rest, rest, rest. If the bleeding continues bring her to the hospital," he says. Now there was no question of home birth as it has been the Devji family tradition and as it was Ma's expectation. "No ispital," she would say, "whether you go to Nairobi or remain in Nairowua, the women in my family give birth at home."

However, Ma already suspects the one in the community who she knows has cast an ill-intended kisirani on my baby. It is Nooru Bai, the wife of the crockery store man. She suspects her to be in love with Haiderali and calls her an avatar of black Kali. I have heard women call her Luchi Bai for she is a shrewd business woman, who would not let a debtor sleep in peace. They say one can see wickedness in her eyes though she is not barren. When her eyes narrow, they would say, there is a spark that shoots out. "I have seen her making filmi eyes at Haidu," Ma tells me. "I will fix her." That day Ma pokes a pin through four limes and tucks them under my mattress at each of the four corners of the bed. She, Nooru Bai will writhe in pain and leave the baby alone. Then during the same week, Ma consults a Kikuyu spirit medium just in case the limes failed. Soon after, it so happened, that one morning we see crows fighting over remnants of a cockerel where Nairobi Road and Temple Road cross. There was no doubt that a night sacrifice had taken place there. The cockerel's glossy feathers spluttered in red globules on dirt before they were carried away by cheerful crows and pasted onto the road by trucks. No one said anything about the night ritual, though we all suspected that it was to avert the gaze of Luchi Bai that boded misfortune of kisirani.

Every day I chew roots from the herbalist at the homestead of Ole Lenana. Ole Lekakeny had them delivered to me secretly through Zarina. Then I sent him some money through Zarina to buy a sacrificial goat and offer prayers at Ol Donyo Lengai for my baby's well-being. Now under my bed, I have a branch of the Ol-orien tree, the wild olive of Africa that Ole Lekakeny sent me when the sacrifice was done, and the leaves of the sacred tree on which lay the sacrificial animal, were distributed. I feel relieved because the ancestors of the savannah will have peace with me. Our house and store stand on their land.

Though Ole Lekakeny does not visit me, I know he is with me every afternoon when he sits alone on the veranda of the shop working through heaps of beads. I wonder if the ancestors take eye pleasure from bead patterns the way Kini and Ntinti do. The way I do. I wonder if they too sing the song of emankeeki and dance below the ground where they live.

I miss the afternoons on the veranda - the muted breeze from the acacia tree, the earth's body smell on the nomads, their engrossed murmur, their ochre plastered heads touching, and their hands on each other's shoulders as they discuss the beads on display. And the sudden bursts of laughter throwing back their red locks. Most of all, I miss the colours of the beads in my eyes and their feel slipping through my fingers. I dream of rangoli of beads that I create each day on my table by the armchair. I wonder if the bead colours were alive what they would say. I wonder if bead colours have memories. I wonder if the bead colours know how beautiful they look on a woman's body. I wonder if the bead colours know how beautiful they look on a man's body in Maasailand. I close my eyes so I can dream of colours.

I do not bleed again yet I feel anxious all the time. I still keep Saheb's picture on my abdomen and tasbih tied to my wrist if I am not using it. "Please invite Ma Gor Bai to Nairowua to be with me at this time. I feel unwell," I beg Haiderali. But Ma does not agree, "It is not necessary. I am here," she would interrupt with a look that would blaze through me. I know superstitious Ma believes that absakan women like my Ma Gor Bai cast shadows of kisirani, and she would lose her grandchild again.

Then one day, to my relief, Ma Jena Bai receives a letter from Ma Gor Bai. She gives it to Haiderali to read for her because her eyesight is fading. As Haiderali reads aloud, I watch how Ma Jena Bai lips contort:

The first child needs to know the mother's family at birth. It's our way. The mother's family nurtured her and her womb nurtured him. Her childhood, her youth, her parents, her home; brothers and sisters; her aunts and uncles, her neighbours – that's the infant's birth community. The infant first needs to hear his mother's family sounds, their voices, their feel, their touch, and know their odours and the kitchen smells. That's the breath of the mother's home and her street. He has to know her jamat khana. Hear how her people sing the sacred song. Its sound echoing from the walls and ceiling to his ears. He will sleep under my pachedi so no flies will worry him during the day or mosquitoes at night. His grandmother's pachedi will be his comfort cloth when he wants to sleep. That's how the child enters the world from the womb through to the mother's childhood. I cannot offer the baby all this, but let me come so I may sing to the baby and put him under my pachedi and tell him stories about his mother when she was a baby.

418

It takes much coaxing from Haiderali before Ma reluctantly gives her consent to invite Ma Gor Bai. More days pass by before Ma Gor Bai arrives by the Merali Bus churning dust along the hardened murrum road. The top soil was washed away in the torrential rains and the road was recently re-carpeted to fill in the cracks made by the dry spell.

Seeing Ma Gor Bai again, I breathe in a deep sigh of relief. I am exhilarated and my body feels better. I especially want Ma Gor Bai to see the colours of the Maasai landscape. How they sing in ragas over the Maasai sky. I want her to see the beadwork on their bodies through my eyes. How the pattern of the zebra gallops across the grassland, and how that is mirrored in the clouds and how that reflects in their beads on their slender necks and hanging ear straps. I want to show her my own emankeeki in my English suitcase, my dowry suitcase that she had bought from European bazaar of Nairobi and packed for me when I was a bride. That always stays under my bed.

57

Mama Dakitari

At the Catholic Hospital on the hill, Naaras Nasira, a Maasai, once a traditional midwife herself, now trained in modern midwifery, attends to my delivery. As I lie down on my back with just a clean white sheet covering me, I hear the clinking sounds of instruments among padding feet in tennis shoes and then slip sounds of plastic aprons. Fatha Dakitari comes in briefly, looks at some papers, talks with Naaras Nasira, smiles at me, and leaves.

I feel the baby is stuck inside me. He will never come out. Perhaps he is dead. Could it be the whisky I drank? Or could it be someone's kisirani? Feelings of panic begin to surge in me when I feel a sudden move. Shukhar! Then he is still again as if he were dead, or was he pretending to be dead? Teasing me. Boys do that to their mothers. In mischief. Then he kicks again. Before I can breathe a long sigh of shukhar, a long sharp cramp seizes me descending from the belly to the legs. "Help me!" I scream out in Swahili, "Saidia! My legs are breaking!" Naaras Nasira is smiling at me, telling me to take in deeper breaths. "Never again!" I tell her clutching the sleeves of her white coat, "If I get through this one, I will never come back here!" She puts her hand on my forehead. The cramping pain just comes and it goes, tormenting me. I feel the come-go pain would never end. I want to tell the nurse to do something because I have no more strength. But I have no strength for words either. She keeps on repeating, "Breathe in deep and long. Relax, mama." I am sweating, trying to relax but the cramps push me up off my back and I find myself sitting. The nurse keeps pressing me down and talking garble. I see her white teeth. She has no face. I have lost my hearing. My body is pounding. Gr...gr...gr... rotations of the stone mill grinding echoes in my ears. One more thrust and I fall into a fathomless pit. I float in a vacuum of a silence such as the one that rebounds at the split moment following a blast and numbs the body. I am seized by emptiness and then a great relief comes over me. My baby from the other world slips into the hands of Naaras Nasira. I feel I have broken loose from the grip of vice pressing into my abdomen from two sides, compressing my ribs, breaking my legs, mangling my body.

"You have a boy, mama!" exclaims Naaras Nasira. I breathe in deep and exhale santosh. Shukhar.

Naaras Nasira who is also known as Mama Dakitari in town, takes the scissors up and down the umbilical cord two times. Each time she resists cutting the cord saying, "Shall I sever this natural relationship of mother and child that is osotua?"

Finally, after what seemed like a lifetime, she clamps and ties the cord with a string. Only then, with the third attempt, does she cut the umbilical cord. But my baby does not cry!

Picking up the boy by his ankles, Naaras Nasira pats him several times on the back. I see he is turning blue holding his breath. Panic seizes me. Grief of my lost babies seizes me. A sharp cry tears through my head.

When at last, when he does cry, I am not sure if what I hear is in my head or is it my baby crying. I see Naaras Nasira smiling but I feel numb, exhausted from intense though short-lived tension. My son's screams now sail over the room. The nurse mumbles blessings in Maasai into his baby red ears and puts him by my side. The boy sucks at my breast with long awaited eagerness. I feel the woman in me as I have never felt before. My womanhood grows deeper now awakening my delayed motherhood. His eyes are closed sticky wet. I cannot see the colour of his eyes. He has entered the world with closed eyes, angry and hungry. Like all Indian mothers, I examine his flannel hands and feet and count if he has all ten toes and ten fingers. I say santosh and I will send a silver piece to Ambe Ma's shrine on Temple Road. She is the giver of contentment of mamta motherhood. My lap is filled at last. My mamta, the sacrificial love of motherhood, is fulfilled. Now I know contentment. Do you hear like how my body hears? How it feels to have your child at the breast? What contentment means? He is my Dadabapa come to land on the African coast. If Dadabapa were first, my son is fourth generation in my African family. He is the root of the baobab anchoring into the ancient loam.

Through the tears in my eyes I see a blurred image of Naaras Nasira sitting by my bed smiling with a question in her eye as if she is researching to see how I feel, my heart, my joy. Half-awake, half-asleep, I listen as she speaks in Swahili between her smiles. She talks to my son, not me, explaining about life he has just entered. I can tell she is a storyteller.

"The Maasai call the umbilical cord osotua," says Naaras Nasira. "It also means a gift of connection for it stands for the first human connection that's made by God." Naaras Nasira pauses to cover me now with a blanket before she continues to say, "The relationship between the mother and her baby is the first sign of the social human and with that men's dependence on each other. I am a Maasai midwife and a mother who is always reluctant to cut the cord and break the first relationship. We tie ol-peresi grass not a cotton string to be the mediator when there is a conflict in your home. Ol-peresi is the grass that masquerades in the wild as ordinary until it blossoms when the rains come and then you know it's the sacred ol-peresi. Its sweet smell fills your home with joy. The grass like the nourishment in the womb gives life, and that which gives life is sacred. Grass is born of the womb of the earth." Naaras Nasira now stands up and takes the boy laying him at her shoulder and patting his back. He burps, softly in his sleep. "Grass is food of the cow," she says. "Your mother will drink cow's milk and nurse you. Then you will drink cow's milk and you will grow strong. May all your relationships be of peace and beauty like the umbilical cord, osotua. Grass nourishes relationships, grows in abundance and is shared. When the Maasai greet each other saying, "Osotua!" we remember that the first human relationship is made in the womb. Now go in peace, walk in beauty, and make relationships that make your people. Osotua! Osotua! Osotua! Peace is beauty."

Then Naaras Nasira puts the boy by my side, fixes the blanket over the white sheet covering both of us, and is gone. Two attendants in white coats put us in another bed that has wheels and roll us out of the room. I hear excited voices of Haiderali and Ma Jena Bai asking many questions about my

423

boy – Is he healthy? Did he cry? His weight? When can we see him? Does he look well? I strain to hear my stepmother's voice. She would ask about me. I want her to touch jaggery water on my baby's lips with a prayer so he may have *Sweetness of Life* not Ma Jena Bai. I want to see Ma Gor Bai at this moment when I feel transformed as if I have suddenly grown up with a responsibility thrust on me. The smell of floor disinfectant lives on in the still overnight air of the hospital. I hear the first cries of babies just born in the morning as I walk in fulfilment. Half asleep, half awake. I am beautiful in my dream walk in-between wanting to run away and wanting to stay and be a mother. Will I be a good mother? Can I be a good mother? Shame and guilt torment me. Suddenly I am asking myself, "Why did I have a baby?" like it's not my own voice.

58

Circumcision

It is a week since I have been home from the hospital. We are sitting around a matching set of Chinese teacups on the dining table in the courtyard veranda. I stare at the English biscuit tin. Ma is overjoyed because a bablo boy is born to her son. Zarina gives a name to my baby, Diamond. It is a custom that the father's sister names the baby.

"Diamond is English," says Ma looking at my son. "But Saheb gives his special blessings to Diamond." It's also a custom to name our children with names that please Saheb.

"The name marks his Diamond Jubilee," adds Kabir out of nowhere.

"I wish him to be circumcised this week," I whisper. Ma widens her eyes. I spoke partly to spite Ma, partly because I do not want Diamond to go through the pain when he is older. I cannot see him bleed the way they bled my brother, Shamshu.

Ma Gor Bai tries to hush me diverting the talk towards Diamond as if he were a king needing all attention.

"What shall we cook for you today, mee-tho raja? You are a brave young man now. Kheer or sheero, hengh mee-tho raja? Your mother's sweet raja, hengh?"

But Ma interrupts not wanting to let go, "We will wait until he is six years or seven, and strong for the barber's blade."

"While he sits on the patlo, legs held apart and a Lala Prashad's ladoo stuffed in his mouth like the way I was circumcised," says Kabir while rubbing my bablo boy lightly below the lip to tickle a smile out of him. "O yes! I remember the Punjabi barber. Kasim Khan, no? Who can ever forget him? He will probably use the same blade on Diamond he used on me. That blade has history. It has shaven a thousand beards and done a hundred circumcisions after me." Kabir disguises his disapproval in jest. I hear Zarina's muffled giggles coming from the kitchen.

My brother, Shamshu, was circumcised at age seven in the Jugu Bazaar. He had run away on the day of his circumcision and hidden under the staircase of the jamat khana. The ritual cut had to be postponed to the next day when my father held his arms and Kaka Noordin uncle held his feet. He screamed when they sat him on the patlo stool. Then they stuffed Lala Prashad's ladoo in his mouth. I cannot imagine Diamond going through that.

"Diamond has to be circumcised in the hospital," I speak again feeling bolder. I had given birth to a boy. Now, I know, I have some privileges in the family though I feel my mind breaking down.

Having changed into his pyjamas after bathing, Haiderali walks into the veranda and sits at the table. "The traditional way," says Ma loud enough for Haiderali to hear her "is the proper way to initiate the first born male in the family. Like how his father and uncle were circumcised. That's proper, barabar. It is custom."

"We must listen to Ma. She is the elder," says Haiderali.

"I prefer the hospital, Haidu. There is less pain and it is quick and clean," I repeat.

"We must have the circumcision rite and host guests to share a meal. That is auspicious. A hospital is no place to shed the blood of the new born. Diamond's blood shedding must be done at his family home, witnessed by all our neighbours and blood relatives, and it cannot be so soon after the naming ceremony. Every ceremony has its time in life," says Ma. I can see that she is irritated by my insistence. Or is she envious now that I have given a boy to the family? That now I am a mother too? That I am nearly her equal now?

"Ispital-circumcised boy is half a man. We should wait until he is strong and understands what is happening. He must feel the pain when he goes from childhood to becoming a young responsible man," says Ma.

"We must do as Ma wishes," says Haiderali. I leave the table and go to the bedroom.

All the time we argued, I heard Ma Gor Bai whispering, "Pirshah, pirshah, pirshah ..." hoping her prayers would bring peace to our hearts.

I cannot control myself. I have worked hard for this family without any appreciation. Suddenly, as if told by a feeling inside, I scream. I have no control over my words anymore.

427

"Even during my pregnancies, I milled lentil and rice on that broken stone mill, I pounded hot spices and churned ghee," I shriek out. The family had never heard me speak like this before. They all come into the bedroom and stand there before my bed looking at me in shock. Ma Gor Bai puts her hand on my forehead and tries to calm me, but I would not listen. "And when I made a mistake, Ma hit me with whatever was in her hand, ladle mwiko, a rolling pin, or her bare hands. My body ached but I did not complain. Now, I will not bear it any longer." I get up from the bed and go to the kitchen sobbing, and shouting, "You stole my grandmother's bangle … You stole my grandmother's bangle … You stole my grandmother's bangle." Ma Gor Bai and Zarina come to me. I begin pulling my hair. Zarina holds my hands. I push her away. Ma Gor Bai hugs me and sobs. I push her away.

The two of them show me back to the dining table, tell me to sit and give me water from the clay pot to drink. Ma Gor Bai fills the white enamel basin with cold water and submerges my feet into it. I do not scream again but continue to sob ceaselessly, while tears blur my vision. Everyone is silent. A gloom falls on the house. Ma stands frozen over me as if struck by the power of my eyes, wide open, staring and smudged. Spirit eyes.

"Do not touch my baby! He is my body too!" I shout pointing a finger at my sass, Haiderali's mother not mine. She takes a step back almost falling over Haiderali. Then almost instantly, almost concurrently, all eyes shift - from me to Ma, from Ma to me. Finally, they fix on me with a look - as if there was a beast in me that spoke. Stillness such as the one that waits for nothing to happen pervades. No one speaks. No one wants anyone to speak fearing another outburst from me. No one wants to listen anyway. There is quietness without expectation. Like a quietness for the sake of quietness. The house feels empty in spite of the birth of a boy.

That evening, from the bedroom door left half open, I gaze wide eyed at Haiderali sitting at the table like I had not seen him before. Is this the man I married? He looks different now, or am I not the one who married him? Am I looking at him or is it some other woman in me? Doubts bewilder me. He is not my eighteen-year-old bridegroom. He is not the one with the English sports jacket in the photograph I adored in my heart. Haiderali is not eating. He merely looks down at his empty plate. Kabir eats quickly, silently and goes into his room. Zarina and Ma Gor Bai do not even come near the table. They would be eating in the kitchen, I assume. I see Ma taking slow steps towards the table and sitting down on Kabir's chair. I see her clearly. She wears a noticeable sulk. That's not unusual. Then inclining towards Haiderali, she starts to talk under her breath, "Her steps are unlucky. Wherever she goes, she brings bad luck. She aborted your children. Her own mother died in childhood. Now you bring her stepmother into my house! I told you not to invite an absakan woman here." Haiderali looks at his mother, narrowing his eyes like he would want to strike her. Ma, aghast, throws her head back hit by the fire in her Haidu's look. But in no time she composes herself, leans forward once again, even closer than before showing defiance as she speaks, "You have been spoiling her ... You deserve an arrogant wife ... You ..." All of a sudden, smacked by Ma's half spoken sentences, Haiderali throws his head down as if to knock it on the hardwood top, but stops an inch away. Then just as abruptly, he stands up deliberately throwing his chair down with such vehemence that the crash reverberates through the silence of the house like an echo in a cave.

"Pirshah!" exclaims Ma Gor Bai.

In the wake of the resonance, the house falls into a cold stillness quietened by the crack on the polished cement floor as if it were a scream, "Shut up!" Haiderali leaves, walking into the darkness without a word. Ma clumps her forehead on the table. She knows he would be walking towards Majengo, the migrant workers' mud-walled township where ethnic women, ostracized from their villages because of unwed pregnancies or widowed with children in towns, entertain lonely if not frustrated brown shopkeepers and white plantation settlers. This was Haiderali's habit from his teenage days, which Ma could not stop in spite of their frequent mother-son quarrels over morals, or her old and his new ways.

My husband had never before behaved in this manner with his mother. A smile comes to my lips. Is it really me or *her* in me smiling?

59

Fatha Dakitari

Fatha Dakitari, the Christian priest, circumcises Diamond at the Catholic Mission Hospital. There is no ceremony at home but Ma does send ladoos to relatives, neighbours and friends. Hospital circumcision does not calm me down. Nothing can. I sob silently whenever there is an argument, no matter how small. I remain in bed even during the day and give my breast to my bablo when he asks for it sucking in his lips in air. I cry. I have no sleep. I have no appetite. I have no hopes of tomorrow. I hold my bablo tight to my heart. I want to be lost in the endless pleasures of the eye in the maze of colours of the beads. They are the spirit beads like the ones that appear on the river acacia at dawn. But I cannot see them. All the time I feel I am on the verge of a convulsion or death. What will happen to my son, my bablo? Will Haiderali marry again? What will *she* be like? These are my recurrent thoughts that come to me in questions. Sometimes I walk out of the house at night thinking someone is calling me. "What is the meaning of your life?" she asks standing by my bed. She has an emankeeki on her shoulders. She is an ancestor native of the land. Then she asks again, "Do you think there is really a God? Do you think there is really Saheb's Light? Do you think there are guru-pirs? Do you think there was ever a guru-pir?" She tells me Ma Jena Bai is a demon in Ravana avatar. I must punish her. Kill her. Then panic grips me and I want to run as far away from home as I can.

Once, Haiderali finds me at midnight sitting with my knees pressed to my chest by the brook at the acacia grove. "You were talking to someone but I saw no one," he says half-chastising, half worried, half annoyed. "Who are you talking to? I see nobody. Why are you sleeping in this damp litter fall?"

"Stand up my Moti Bai. Let's go home. You will catch cold." Haiderali calms down and coaxes me. I hold on to a stolon with tapered roots creeping though the river rocks into the silt at the meander. I would not move. The spirit holds me back. It's her arms, not mine that wrap around the stolon.

"You will catch cold. There are hyenas in the forest." But the spirit does not let go of the root. "Come home. Diamond is waiting for you. Come! He is hungry. He cries for you." Haiderali tugs under my arms heaving me up, but the iron arms clamp harder onto the stolon.

Then Haiderali sings the lullaby that I sing to Diamond when he presses his cotton lips to my nipple. I feel the warmth between his palpitating tongue and fleshy palette.

Diamond maro nano
Rakhi aank waro maro dhinglo
mmm…mmm…mmm
Patle besi naayo
Lala, lala, lala

My little Diamond
My boy doll with grey eyes
mmm…mmm…mmm
Sitting on stool to bath
Sleep sleep sleep

We walk home. I keep pushing away Haiderali's arm when he tries to support me at the waist. A forest hare emerges from the bush and stands upright ahead of us, shocked and nervous in the riverweeds, wanting to dart yet waiting to overcome his suspicion.

"Keep away from my body!" I shout. "Because of you, I cannot let anyone hold me anymore. Not anyone, because of you! Because of you!"

Haiderali reels back. He walks behind me.

The medicine from Fatha Dakitari makes me sleep deeply. He comes home to see me and has become a family friend. In gratitude, Haiderali gives him a donation for his maternity ward at the Catholic Mission Hospital and Fatha makes him an honourable patron of the hospital and a member of the board. "You are not like other Asians," Fatha says to Haiderali. "You are different. You are generous." Haiderali blushes like a little girl.

My husband is thrilled with the honour bestowed on him, an ordinary Indian dukawala on the hospital board! At once, he invites Fatha for a chicken curry and rice meal. Real Indian curry, he tells him. Ma too wants to celebrate her son's rise in social status. Being a hospital board member lifts Haiderali's image in the jamat khana, and Ma's image as well. Perhaps she will get a promotion and become the captain of the Naandi Committee when Khanu Bai leaves town for Nairobi. Haiderali's name will be spoken of in casual conversations at the English golf club where unfortunately, he being brown, cannot be a member. That would be second best to the privilege of sitting by the fireplace in the club's drawing room with other notable citizens like the DC, the Chief Tax Collector and the Commissioner of Police. Nevertheless, he sits with them on the Board Table and that is a beginning. Haidu especially wants to be noticed by the district administration staff and the white settlers – the English, the Greek and the Boers. He hopes he can regularly visit the Wagon Wheel, as the clubhouse is called, and befriend the white patrons. He hopes they would come to the bead shop to purchase farm tools that he has just introduced as his new line of business. He is also thinking of stocking wines and spirits for this exclusive community of coffee growers and dairy cattle farmers that is now beginning to bloom and find bigger markets after almost half a century of trying. Both Kabir and he think that would be a profitable venture in the changing post-war East African economy. However, in apartheid Kenya where can he socialize with the white community? Unless, of course, he calls them home one at a time? Fatha's visit was the beginning.

"See how the Englishman licked his fingers," Ma tells Kabir the next day referring to Fatha at the chicken curry and rice meal. She was overcome by the white priest doctor's compliment. Everyone saw how he licked his fingers before he had a second helping from the curry bowl. This act Ma took as a compliment to her cooking and her victorious nudging to have a little more in the manner of taan-maan courtesy shown to the guest.

434

"Nah! Nah! Ma, Fatha Dakitari was just cleaning his fingers!" Kabir tells Ma. "The English eat with steel tools and use tooowals that they keep in their laps while eating. Did you not see how Fatha had messed up his hands?"

"Fatha does not know how to eat with fingers, Ma. Haiderali should wait before inviting him again. I will bring some English eating tools from Nairobi. Remind me. And next time, keep a small toowal on his plate."

"What, wipe his hands on the toowal without washing them?"

"Yes, Ma! That's the English way."

"I was also wondering if he uses the same right hand to eat that he uses to clean his dheko arse. I hear the English use paper to clean their dheko arse! Is that true, Kabir? Do they really use the right hand? The same right hand with which they also eat?"

"I hear so, Ma. I have not had the opportunity to witness."

"Aar...r...r."

60

Ole Lekakeny

Sometimes I feel I am falling into an endless water hole by the dry riverbed. The heat of drought sun scorches my body as it does the land killing its green. I feel Haiderali's viced hands tighten over my breasts, hips, all over, killing my girl dreams. I hate hands. I hate the touch of all but my bablo because he is me too. My own body from my womb. Sometimes I feel I am a vulture soaring high into the sky, running away from hands, merging into the beam of Light, becoming Light while my body on the bed lies by my baby. Sometimes, I dream I am walking on the savannah with Kini and Ntinti. Kilimanjaro smiles down to me and the sunrise sparkles hues of changing red on my emankeeki. I am intimate with the first light when the dawn is dark and my bare feet soak in the first dew over green lushness. Then at midday the abode of the ancestors of the savannah, the powdery dust from the volcanoes a thousand years old will cushion my bare soles. I would hear blessings oozing from below as I walk to the pendulum swing of my single braid tracing an arc over my

436

back. I must put these feelings out of my body at once into beads and zari thread. If not, I will keep falling deeper into the black void hole. But how can I be free? I am shackled in this house and him.

One day I dream of Ole Lekakeny standing by my bed. He is carrying healing herbs wrapped in a banana leaf. Behind him, he pulls a spotless black goat that he wants me to touch at the forehead and bless. He says it is the sacrificial goat for my healing. He will be taking it to Ol Donyo Lengai, which is the Mountain of God. God of Colours. God of Beads. God of Dawn. God of Healing. I remove the hot brick that Ma Jena Bai had positioned on my abdomen, vacant of child and loosened up like an old elastic band. I place Ole Lekakeny's leaf wrap there.

The next morning, as I am just waking up, half asleep and half wake, I hear Ma complaining, "This house stinks like a kraal!" Trailing over her angry aura were strands of milky smoke as she rambles around the rooms shuffling in her long dress, carrying sandalwood sticks. Taak taak. Her anger comes from fear that breathes exasperation in her. She pokes the incense sticks in the corner of Saheb's framed posters of the Golden Jubilee and Diamond Jubilee, two sticks on either side of each picture. Finally, she thrusts out a sigh and stops complaining. No sooner does Ma stop her taak taak taak, than Zarina begins her morning murmurs, her memorizing multiplication tables, her muffled singsong Gujarati in rhythmic cycles of garba music: 1 times 6 equals 6; 2 times 6 equals 12; 3 times 6 equals 18; 4 times 6 equals 24. The hissing alliteration in her curt phrase rhymes when she says 6 times 6 equals 36, and then 7 times 6 equals 42 and 8 times 6 equals 48.

"Practise the tables in dadra beat like how you dance the garba, and know the rhyming couplets," I hear Dadabapa teaching me in my half-awake mind. He is pattering his fingers on his palm to show how the math rhythm flows in garba claps, 1 2 3 - 1 2 3. "It's the rhythm, the alliteration and the rhyme which plant math memory in your little mind. They make the loam that holds the root. When your memory fails, the music remains. Once the Gujarati math music sets in you, you will be able to add, subtract, and multiply infinite numbers in sound patterns. Run your thumb up the indices, adding and subtracting, and let your little fingers speak the rhythm of math music to your ears like zari stitches to your little eyes. Math, like music, like zariwork, is in patterns. So know the sounds of multiplications and you will not forget it even when you remember nothing else." Zarina's voice in dadra music cycle - dha dhi na, dha tu na, floats over the filmi songs from All India Radio. But Zarina annoys Kabir. The annoyance would be on his face if I could see it. However, he says nothing, and goes on with his morning routine at the mirror over the tin basin at the courtyard veranda - grooming his hair, brushing his teeth and humming into songs from All India Radio over Zarina's monotonous mathematical renditions 1 2 3 - 1 2 3, 1 2 3 - 1 2 3 . . .

Haiderali comes to take Diamond to play with as he does every morning after Diamond has had enough of my breast milk, when he has burped, feels contended and readily smiles at the slightest hiss from his father's lips. Alone they play father son games. I listen to them for a while. Then I listen to my breath and thoughts of disappearing from this house to somewhere where I am alone and happy.

Later that day, I tell Ma Gor Bai about my dream. "A voice in me, I don't know who, speaks to me," I tell her apprehensively.

"Do not tell anyone about it, not even Haiderali," says Ma Gor Bai opening her English biscuit tin. "It is the voice you have ignored. It's calling you. See here, I brought katlo for you." Katlo is diamond shaped crusty-crackled wheat biscuits bonded in yellow eating gum. In it are nuts cooked in ghee and jaggery. "Here take a bite. I made it myself. It will help your body to strength, seal the lacerations, nourish the baby with creamy milk from you and calm the mind." Ma Gor Bai brings a piece to my mouth. I crunch into katlo's richness and let its nutty sweetness disintegrate and melt in my mouth descending the gullet to the vacated part of my abdomen. "Stories spread in a small town like Nairowua. They will say your mind has shifted. They will call you a mad woman, Mama Wazimu. The name will stay with you like an ugly birthmark on your forehead." I have not spoken about the spirit visitation until now.

Ma Gor Bai then winds my mother's Satpanth tasbih around my wrist over the red and green sacred thread from the mukhi of the jamat khana. I look at the chipped wooden beads and then the two-faced silver medallion where the string is knotted into three miniature silver gunguru bells. I do not take my eyes off the tasbih on my waist wandering over its darshan glimpses.

"When the voice speaks to you again, put your eyes on Saheb's picture and your fingers on your mother's tasbih," she says pointing to the photo on the wall with her chin and taking my hand into hers over the tasbih on my wrist.

439

61

Setting sun over the Ngong Hills

That day, Ma Gor Bai talks to Ma Jena Bai. "It's time for me to return to Nairobi. But Moti Bai is not well. She needs to rest and learn to nurse the child. I want to take her and bablo with me. She will heal in Nairobi. She needs to drink the sweet water of the Kikuyu springs again where she was born. I know what else she needs to heal. I have that too."

"You can take her with you. After all, of what use is she here? She who speaks to the spirits?" says Ma. Ma would be happy to get rid of the spirit that accompanies me. She has no control over spirits and that terrifies her.

Next day, I hear Haiderali and Ma arguing behind closed door. I have never before heard such a sharp argument between the two or anyone else in the house. Then I hear a hard knock, a gasp, a throaty rasp, and silence. Ma Gor Bai and I look at each other, our eyes questioning.

In the afternoon, Haiderali goes to book two tickets at the Merali Bus office near Rhemu Bhai's bicycle shop. I don't see him again until the next morning when Ma Gor Bai and I have packed our bags and are ready to leave Nairowua. Before giving the tickets to Ma Gor Bai, Haiderali looks at them in his hands as if he were in doubt and reluctant to hand them over. Then he looks at Diamond for a long time awake in my arms smiling slightly at him and also looking up into my face. Haiderali does not play his usual father's game - sh-sh hissing from his stretched lips, his head nodding like a guinea fowl, the play that never fails to bring gummy smiles to Diamond's lips. When he takes his eyes away, Haiderali lets them fall to the ground as if to avoid meeting mine as we always did, as I was expecting today. That's how we always said goodbye with eyes, not in arms' embrace, whenever he went on safari to buy beads. We would part only after our eyes had said goodbye. It was then that I noticed a bluish red bulge on his forehead at the corner where the bone rises. It was then that I saw his hair like his clothes was dishevelled. He had slept the night in the mud town Majengo.

The bus passes by the mission hospital. I hear the church bell toll on the hill calling the new converts to come to pray. I imagine Mariam, mother of Prophet miracle maker, standing still, white, lonesome and patient with her tasbih falling through her fingers pressed tenderly together holding on to silent hope. I turn my head towards Kilimanjaro and look out to the far distant sea of grass. I wonder if Kini and Ntinti would be milking cows at their new homestead like all Maasai mothers at this time in the morning looking East into Blue of En-Kai, the Supreme One of the Sky. Already I see the clouds busy beading patterns on her. Will Kini and Ntinti be thinking of me when they sprinkle the first drops of the milk in the air,

441

an offering for peace to the East, West, North and South —
the whole wide world they know? The bus jumps, jerking into
and out of a pothole bringing my eyes to fall on Diamond. He
is asleep on Ma Gor Bai's folded legs over the seat. He
slumbers into the drone of the Merali Bus bouncing over the
dry murrum road absorbing the fading ring of the church bell
into its belly. Suddenly, Diamond opens his eyes. I look into
the shine of his bright grey eyes and smile. He stares back
expecting more of me. I take him into my arms and press him
to my heart. Outside, the savannah rolls on endlessly ahead of
the whirring machine of the bus obtrusive on its geography.

When it's evening, I shall watch the orange halo of the
setting sun over the distant shadow of the Ngong Hills of
Nairobi. I shall watch the five blue humps descend like a
passing camel caravan into the womb of the night where a
new day will be conceived. Some will call the sunrise Akyni,
the beauty of dawn. Others will say it's Njoki, because the day
is born again. They would say Njoki was the daughter of Mary
Muthoni Nyanjiru who hurled a rock at the mighty Empire
and Akyni, a new dawn, broke over Kenya when I was born.

Glossary of Key Words and their Cultural Contexts

Absakan: Literally means unlucky. Opposite of sakan or good luck. Mostly referred to women or girls who became widows or were divorced or even when their engagement was broken. Socially they were stigmatized and avoided, lest their misfortune affect other women and girls.

Chandraat: The evening of the new moon that's also the beginning of the new month in the Islamic calendar. It's the evening when Satpanth Ismailis offer confessions and when many prefer to pay the tithe.

Dadra: The rhythmic cycle of six beats in two equal divisions of three that make the garba and dandia dance pattern for footwork and handclap or stick sounds. The beat goes in this rhythm: *dha dhi na - dha tu na* or 1 2 3 - 4 5 6. There is a higher emphasis laid on the *dha* than the following *dhi* and *na*. In dandia rass two strikes of *dhi* and *na* are on the sticks held by the player, and the third *dha* falls on the partner's stick. Singing aloud of math tables in Gujarati is put to *dadra* beat for easier memorization. The emphasis on *dha*, however, changes due to rhyming of numbers.

Dapandayo: Referred to one who says or does what's not necessary or not suited to his age or status. Sometimes used to refer to an interfering person.

Darshan: Darshan is auspicious vision. It is the propitious *act of seeing* or *being seen* by an imam, guru, pir or a deity. It is so powerful a look that a glimpse is believed to bless and even cleanse the believer of his/her misdeeds. Darshan is also used by humbler folk to refer to meeting their superiors like a king or queen, or even their benefactors.

Deedar: As in darshan above. Nowadays, Satpanth Ismailis use deedar more often than darshan. However, in their ginans or religious songs, the word darshan is more common.

Desh: Indians refer to India as Desh or motherland. Adj. Desi.

E'sikar: E'sikar in Maasai can mean joy, freedom, or splendour. It can also mean adornment. All meanings imply delight as from beauty.

Ginan: Satpanth devotional literature in form of lyrics and hymns that is recited daily in the jamat khana.

Haraakh: Inside joy that is not expressed openly, like being bashful and quietly pleased.

Kafir: Unbeliever as in Arabic.

Jamat: In the Satpanth Ismaili vocabulary, the jamat can refer to the community or an assembly of Satpanth Ismailis at a gathering.

Jamat khana: Jamat khana means an assembly house. The central area of the jamat khana is the prayer hall. Some jamat khanas have a second prayer hall or chamber that is reserved for meditation. Many jamat khanas have a social hall for communal meals, talks and other events. Often there is a library and an adjacent garden. Jamat khana is like a church, synagogue, mosque or temple.

Jitherka: Scruffy, unkempt hair or dress.

Kisirani: Misfortune, evil or mishap. This could be brought about by, or refer to a thing, time, an event or a person.

Merikani: Coarse white cotton cloth that came from America.

Mukhi: Head in charge of all jamat khana religious functions such as marriages, births and funerals. He also manages all the volunteers, committees and secular functions in the jamat khana.

Mothaj: Mothaj refers to dependency especially on relatives and the community. Mothaj is a highly emotional word that has connotations of loss of dignity, shame and humiliation. The dependent feels (or is made to feel) obligation in a way that carries family or public disgrace and embarrassment. All this is combined with personal guilt. Mothaj is a sort of dependency that's unwanted, reprehensible and a burden yet unavoidable because of circumstances such as poverty, illness, old age, disability or being orphaned. The family or the community is obliged to bear the responsibility of supporting the deprived because of custom and social pressure. So painful is mothaj that one would hear Satpanth Ismailis say: *Death is better than mothaj.* At funerals, it is not uncommon to hear Ismailis say: *He/she has been freed of mothaj* or *Shukhar for he/she died without being a mothaj on anyone.* This means he/she died with dignity. So dreaded a condition is mothaj that in the daily collective jamat khana prayer, one line pleads God *'not to make us mothaj on anyone.'*

Murid: Someone who takes an oath of allegiance to the imam. Satpanth Ismailis consider themselves murids of Hazar (Living) Imam known as the Aga Khan in the non-Ismaili world.

Naakhra: Coyish behaviour

Naandi: A collective word for various types of food offerings taken to the jamat khana for daily, monthly, and annual thanksgivings and prayers of peace for the departed.

Nisasa: Sigh of emotional pain often breathed out in desperation by the aged, disabled, poor or one who feels wronged. Can also be as a relief venting out the depth of the suffering. The belief associated with such a sigh was that it would affect the one who caused the pain. Nisasa is like a curse even if not intended as such. Opposite of blessings.

Pir: Sufi master of a specific path. He is often a guide to his followers. Formerly, the imam was also called pir. Satpanth Ismaili ginan ends with a pir's name reputed to have written it.

Prayo-pavesa: Ancient practice of Saurashtra that denotes voluntary fasting to death of elderly or terminally ill who feel they have lived long enough and have no more responsibilities. Often those who commit themselves to prayo-pavesa are at a stage when they cannot take care of their daily needs such as body hygiene or eating with their own hands due to failing health. They ask to be free of *mothaj* (see above) from their close relatives and start prayo-pavesa with full knowledge of the community and blessings of the priests.

Rass: Rass is the essence of temperament, mood or disposition of aesthetic bliss in a performance such as dance, song, music, ritual, drama or visual art. Rass is the pitch of artistic mood and pleasure. It is considered to be an emotive internal expression be it love, beauty or devotional pitch. Rass is also said to be the experience of "the mood as a tenor of the heart."

Roji: Important word among the Satpanth Ismailis to show reverence to food that provides not only nourishment but is also medium of offering prayers especially for the dead. Roji vaguely relates to destiny in that one's nourishment, no matter how small, is fated. Thus, Satpanth Ismailis would say *One eats* *what's in one's roji* which suggests one's meals are written in one's kismet that is destiny.

Saheb: Title showing respect and honour.

Sarkar: Title showing authority as in government.

Shukhar: Among Satpanth Ismailis, the word 'shukhar' (from Arabic 'shukhran' meaning thank you) has come to mean more than thank you. Shukhar conveys a sense of self-humility as well as gratitude. When shukhar is said to another person it is meant to address God not the person spoken to. Shukhar may also be said to oneself like a one word prayer. Shukhar may be said to show gratitude for anything like good fortune of having daily meals, health, opportunities or work. It is said as an expression of gratitude for safe return from a journey, recovery from illness and even for a happy marriage and happiness of oneself or of loved ones. It is also expressed when an unhappy experience has passed away like an escape from an accident or a bad day. Shukhar is often said as a one-word prayer of thanksgiving after a meal. It could also be a prayer for peace. Or it may be simply for blessings of contentment and gratitude that one often hears Satpanth Ismailis whisper. At funerals, Satpanth Ismailis pass on consolations to the bereaved in repetitions of shukhar expressing gratitude to God for the life of the deceased who has closed the journey on earth as well for the bereaved to bear the loss while thanking God for whatever he wills for us. The reply to shukhar is also shukhar.

Sumph: Bond

Acknowledgements

There are so many friends, neighbours, relatives and community people who have contributed in different ways to the making of this book. There are also artists, storytellers and writers I have not met face to face, but from whom I have learned much.

From among the friends, I would first like to thank Janet Ansell, for being the very first reader. For her gentle comments on the first few chapters, "It's very rich," she said, and I knew I had to work on the pages to make them simpler –'less rich'. Deborah Foster for a big push forward with her first words after reading several chapters still raw. "I am convinced this book will be published." She put confidence in a writer trying to wean out of making ethnographies yet wanting to be nourished by ethnographies. Zulficar Mawani for being a collector of community books and magazines, always a critical thinker, my reader of the first complete draft and an astute commentator on our shared memories. Kutub Kassam for his very early comments, "Reading your book, I felt like I was celebrating my history." Jody Wright for suggestions to make the beginning 'more personal' – she meant more of my own and less academic. Jatinder Chana for a slow, careful read of the first proof, pointing out typos and unclear sentences and for teaching me how to listen to tabla beats. Kulwant Grewal for useful observations from 'the reader's point of view' and some historical notes. Gwynnette Johnson for arduously counting how many stories make each chapter that I wrote as words flowed without actually counting the number of stories in stories. Fatima Mohamed for looking over the Gujarati alphabets in the book. Christian Stickler helped me overcome my dilemma when he told me to keep the language the way it was for a natural narrator's voice, and the rhythm over grammar. Thank you Christian for this, and much more. Jackie Weinstein for material and conversations on Aboriginal and African tales. Made me think more deeply about how invisible was the line between legends, the inside stories and reality, the outside stories. How important it was to evoke the Aboriginal in oneself because we all have it, and often, we suppress it. Guli Bai Sachedina for the loan of the bandhani shawl, visits to Seniors' Homes, and conversations about her early immigrant experiences. Mohamed Alibhai for comments from his life's experiences and 'objective academic' views. And his father, the most loved Satpanth Ismaili scholar, Missionary Abu Ali, for confirming the information that I was using to build on, and for his carefully documented books on early Satpanth beliefs and rituals in East Africa. A valuable undoctored heritage of Satpanth Ismailism that now resides in a special collection at Simon Fraser University in British Columbia. And a special thank you to Taj Bibi Alibhai for her memories still pulsating with vitality as she approaches her 90th birthday.

Akbar Bapa and Gulzar Bai Kassam for their memories, for singing of Om Ali, the Das Avatar and narratives from their spiritual lives. And their daughter Shainul Kassam the singer of sacred songs, for her smiles of acknowledgement and enthusiasm to listen to more stories than I could cope. I acknowledge with gratitude the East African Satpanth Ismaili community in Canada for sharing their photo albums and stories with me. Thank you Sherally Janmohmed and Shamim Manji for telling me about your photographer fathers and showing me photos taken by them. Many thanks to all who told me their family stories while I was curating the Asian African Heritage Exhibition (National Museums of Kenya, Nairobi 2000 – 2005) and for showing me their photographs and artefacts from their treasured boxes. Thank you to the open heart of Akbar Husein, the photo archivist of Nairobi, who embraces all writers who walk into his studio on Mama Ngina Street and like his heart, he opens up his well-documented collection for them to use as they please.

Also to the many volunteers of the Ismaili Community Counselling and Seniors Welfare programmes, the chairperson Gushan Bai Fazal, when we jointly staged 'Ma Aging Gracefully', an exhibition on the 'Coming of the Satpanth Khoja to Africa' (Nairobi 1994). To the seniors who have long passed away, I want to say that I listened to your songs and memories, and also to your hearts working through your precious material culture that you wanted me so much to see. I hope this book will bring your pioneering days and memorable lives in East Africa to your descendants in the Diaspora.

Thank you Africana-Orientalia and the East Africa Circle, the two vibrant online information and discussion groups of Asian Africans that connect the Diaspora to the old homeland that refuses to recede from our memories. Here I found snippets of your reminiscences that bloom into discussions, carrying feelings of growing up in East Africa and how we experienced history. Your personal accounts are valuable as oral traditions of Asian Africans of East Africa that, thank God, are now preserved in the cyberspace because of your collective efforts. Thank you Ismailiweb, Simerg, Ismailinet and Mumtaz Ali Tajddin for archiving community heritage, past and present, especially works of artists and writers. A prime civil society effort.

450

My gratitude to the storytellers of my childhood. Mariam Bai Somjee, my mother who lived in Jugu Bazaar of Indian Nairobi. Her neighbour was Rajan Bhai Lalji, who started the beads store in Nairobi in 1905. The store supplied the commodity to the bead merchants settled in the most isolated areas of ethnic lands radiating from the railroad stations completed in 1902. More than half a century ago, travelling from Nairobi to Arusha, my uncles, the bead merchants around Kilimanjaro, would collect their bead stock from the Rajan Bhai Lalji beads store in the Indian Bazaar and I would collect some samples and images to keep in my mind. I still have the samples with me and I used them to make sentences to write this book. Thank you Ramzan Bapa Rajan Bhai Lalji for your vivid mental pictures of Indian Nairobi, the Bead Bazaar also called the Khoja Bazaar, and for pioneering the bead trade on a large scale in early 20th century.

I remember Ratan Bai, my grandmother, mostly because of her stories of the Ramayana and Mahabharata and for making dry chapattis and eggplant bharto. Somjee Bapa, my grandfather, the harmonium singer of Mombasa, for his singing of the Das Avatar, worship rituals at home, readings from Khojki scripts and the Satpanth chants in the jamat khanas of Mombasa and Nairobi. I sat by his side, and felt the tremble in his throat shake his body, my hand over him. I did not realize how instilling were the sermons of the post war Satpanth Ismaili preachers (we used to call them 'meeshnari' as M G Vassanji said) until I started to write this book. How their vocabularies weaved Vedic texts with Sufi metaphors and their folklore in songs into stories of virtues and faults of the yoogs, the karmic cycles and the ten avatars. You know, I have used your oration to structure this book. It's closer to the learned pundits' orations in Indian temples than to imams' sermons in mosques.

Guli Bai Haiderali Karim also known as Guli Bai Kanji Mohamed Jivan of the Beads Store in Arusha, Tanzania. She is the granddaughter of Ma Jethi Bai, the Bead Bai at whose feet, literally, I sat and first learned to make simple Maasai bead patterns. Dr Shivji, the dentist and storyteller at a senior's care home in Vancouver, for sharing anecdotes about my family story and other community stories. Ada Glustein for telling her story, a Jewish story, reading mine and for weeding through my large manuscript. Thank you. Zarina Bai Lalji for your stories and the emotional touch you still keep with the stone mill, and your fabulous Satpanth bandhani shawl that was stolen at a wedding in Vancouver. Not an unusual story.

I have built some of my chapters on sighs between expressions of shukhar and emotions of loss that flowed with your stories and songs as is often the case listening to migrants.

My special thank you to the Canadian Broadcasting Corporation (CBC) for widening my imagination and bringing me home to writing in Canada. Right through 2003 to 2012, you kept me connected to Canadian and international writing and writers. You introduced me so understandingly to Canada, her life, her geography, her people, and most importantly, her stories. I would recommend all new immigrants to listen to CBC in their formative years when making new identities, values and worldviews as Canadians, and how you too can work for a pluralist civil society when you let your own story grow. Keep CBC as independent as it is, please. Thank you also TV Channel 4 for the same and also to the Vancouver

Storytelling Society and Burnaby Public Library. There is not a book, no matter how old and rare that you did not find for me.

Thank you Robert Fulford for the use of the quote from *The Triumph of Narrative: Storytelling in the Age of Mass Culture*, the book that I feel is important for storytellers. I also remember with gratitude the following persons, some of whom died a long time ago, whose words, observations and thoughts I have used: John O'Donohue, Thomas King, Rabbi Chaim Gruber, Anna Watson (the co-organizer of the exhibition *Indian Royal Splendour on Display* at the Victoria and Albert Museum, London 2009). I thank Khal Torabully for founding *Coolitude*, a genre of literature that studies creative writings about journeys and lives of Indian indentured labourers during the colonial age. Carl Gustav Jung needs to be remembered for his observations in East Africa and Oscar Wilde for his thoughts on art. I acknowledge with gratitude Dominique Sila-Khan for the quote that I use in the Introduction. Also Shri Amritlal Raishi, pioneer merchant of East Africa; S.D.Pradhan, the methodical recorder of Indian military history in East Africa; Sudhanshu Bhandari for the enlightening work on *Prostitution in Colonial India* and Louis Werner on Mughal embroidery. Thank you also to Wikipedia, Neera Kent Kapila and Neera Kapur Dromson. Najma Dhanani for writing books on the indigenous trees of East Africa. Her book on the acacias helped me to identify trees told in local stories.

Maqueritte Pequin for sharing your knowledge of the ancient Mayan art and writing time, and for your suggestions on putting more to the personal dimensions, a valued neighbour-writer-friend. Thank you Frankie Sutton for your reading assistance and email conversations. Writer Tariq Malik for walking together, your advice on the Indian crows, generous sharing of your best movies, podcasts, books and research on the Ghadar activities on the Pacific coast and East Africa. Thank you to the McGill professors, Boyd White, John Galaty, Thomas Eisemon and Marie Maguire for steering my research and writings in art, ethnographies and education. And thank you Professor Corie for many things I cannot even begin to count.

Finally, I acknowledge my family support. I thank my sister, Leily, and her husband, Salim, for providing a writing space without which I would not have completed this book. Sadiq, my younger brother, for being a reader and a copious visualiser who builds images out of keyboard clicks. Farida Somjee for her practical hints and Nizar, my elder brother for searching out old books for me. Rifaat, my younger sister and her husband David, for looking over the recipes, glossaries, reading the first draft and opening roads into vocabularies on spiritualities. Zera, my wife, for her trust in the book as in all my other time-consuming projects, for readings of drafts and comments on sensitivities of communities, families, women and individuals who may be touched by the story of the Bead Bai. And for being the true patron of this work. To all the women readers on educating me on 'how the women feel', and what I may have ignored about women's feelings. Jasiriat, Ummat, Ardhiat for the understanding and for your patience, and impatience, living with a 'weird' Baba.

My profound admiration and gratitude to the Maasai bead artists, all women with whom I spoke collectively at different times between 1968 and 1988. They lived in homesteads across Kajiado, Loitokitok, and Narok districts of Kenya. They showed me their beadwork and how they bead, and we discussed what was beautiful and not so beautiful comparing bead patterns with nature, looking at the sky, rocks, trees, and animals. It was from your visual language and metaphors that you call 'eye knowledge' that I learned more than from any books. How very much was Father Frans Mol of the Ngong Diocese in Kenya like you in his thinking that added to my understanding of ethnic art vocabulary. My profound admiration and gratitude also to Bais of the Satpanth Ismaili community who have passed on to another day since we last met. I need to elaborate here a little on the Bais in order to write a fuller appreciation, because this story is theirs.

The three Bead Bais who influenced me in different ways to begin research on this book, were Jethi Bai Mohamed Jivan of Arusha (Tanzania), Santok Bai Javer of Ngong Town (Kenya), and Shiri Bai Mapara of old Nairobi. The latter two lived in Canada in their senior years. Today, the children and many grandchildren of the three Bais live across Canada and the Western Diaspora. My profound appreciation to them and other Bead Bais who have left an art heritage to East Africa that they probably never realized during their time. I was moved also by the story of Ma Khati Bai Sachedina's bandhani. She was from Masaka in Uganda. The bandhani is the most significant surviving cultural object of the East African Satpanth Khoja community. When Ma Khati Bai died at the age of one hundred in Canada, her zari-bright bandhani covered her on the day in 2006 as it did in Nairobi in 1917 on the day of her marriage. Placing the cloth with a 'shine' or 'light' on a woman at her wedding and funeral, are two feminine rites of passage signifying not only becoming a bride and leaving home, but also beginning a journey. This was a Satpanth tradition that she maintained, shukhar.

Note on the book cover

The Gujarati writing on the book cover appeared on Bead Shops in East Africa: ખોટા મોતી ના સાચા વેપારી meaning *Of imitation pearls we are genuine merchants.* It may be that the storekeepers in East Africa had taken this phrase, that never fails to amuse Gujarati speakers, from the bead shops in Gujarat. Beads from German glass manufacturing families in Bohemia (that later became a part of Czechoslovakia) were popular in Gujarat. Gujarati bead merchants in East Africa imported a large variety of beads from Czechoslovakia for the ethnic people when they came to know them and trade.

My first discussions on the cover picture were with Maqs Jivan, a West Coast artist from Delta, British Columbia. Maqs was born in Arusha, in the heart of Maasailand in Tanzania where his family ran a beads store in the same building where he lived. His grandmother, Ma Jethi Bai was the Bead Bai at the store.

http://maqsart.blogspot.com

Subsequent discussions were with Zia Somjee, a graphic design student, who then produced the final book cover.

http://ziasomjee.wordpress.com

Print, eBook publication and eMarketing assistance by Sadiq Somjee.

www.SadiqSomjee.com

About the Author

Photo by Jasiriat

Working as an ethnographer in Kenya, Sultan Somjee collected material culture, staged exhibitions, and trained young Kenyans. He also listened to stories that emerged from the artefacts of both Africans and Asian Africans*, the citizenry that today comprise descendants of inland and oceanic migrations to Eastern Africa. In 2001, the United Nations listed Somjee as one of the twelve 'Unsung Heroes of Dialogue among Civilizations'.

Somjee has published several articles and two guide books, *Material Culture of Kenya* and *Stories from Things*. Based partly on his PhD research, and partly on the stories he heard, *Bead Bai* is his first novel.

He now writes from British Columbia, Canada, where he lives with his wife, Zera, and three children.

*South Asians in East Africa, as in Central and South Africa, were collectively referred to as 'Asiatics' in the three racially tiered societies of the British Empire. The other two were called 'Europeans' and 'Natives'. After several generations, many 'Asiatics' prefer to be known as Asian Africans honouring their two heritages – Asian and African that shape their history, identity and lives in the 21st Century.

Made in the USA
Charleston, SC
27 November 2014